Dear Target Reader,

So you have found me. Now take my hand, and let me transport you to a place that I have dreamed about since I was a child. A land of astonishing beauty, where lion and wildebeest roam the sun-drenched plains. We will pitch our tent on the bank of a river, while below us hippo blow water into the inky darkness, and in the morning we will saddle our horses and ride along the rutted stone track to Kisima—a farm perched on the edge of the Great Rift Valley. The house has a troubled past, but don't let that scare you. We are looking for adventure.

I was twelve when my father took me to Kenya for the first time. We put our lives into the hands of a hardened army officer who was famous for his horse safaris. We rode across the Maasai Mara, camping out at night under a sky glittering with stars, listening in the dark to the low grunts of lion carry far across the plains. We galloped alongside herds of zebra, clouds blackening into storm, the grasslands lit up beneath to an iridescent gold, and I remember thinking—as the horse pounded under me—that there could never be anywhere in the world as beautiful as this. We chased ostrich, and—on a hot day—stripped the saddles off our sweat-soaked horses and pushed them deep into a lake, where hippo slept just a stone's throw away, until our horses' hooves left the ground and it felt as though we were flying. I fell madly in love with the raw simplicity of the life, with all its danger and isolation. When I came home, I read Blixen's *Out of Africa*, and Hemingway, and they fueled my hunger.

Over the years I wondered how I might write this passion for Kenya into a novel. I knew I wanted to evoke the beauty of the landscape, and the romance of the settlers who first braved the wild to farm in remote corners of the Rift Valley, but I didn't want to be sucked into another Happy Valley romp about white farmers living like aristocrats on land which was not their own. I read more widely, and learned that there was a darker side to the European experience in Kenya which didn't appear in the tourist brochures; something hidden and degenerate which Blixen and Hemingway—with their white hunters and big game safaris—had omitted. The colonial story was rotten at its core—Africa was not a place about which one could spin fantasies. If I was going to write something, it would have to be something real; a story which would explode the myths.

Then—out of the blue—a story fell into my lap, in the form of a small, battered, red canvas suitcase. It was handed to me in an unassuming office in Piccadilly by a man who had read and admired *The Fever Tree*, my first novel. *Perhaps you can do something with it*, he said, tapping the dusty lid of the suitcase. *It belonged to my grandmother.* I took it from him somewhat reluctantly—the contents were clearly important to him, and I was hesitant to be their keeper. Sitting on the train on my way home, I inspected the suitcase. It was small enough to sit on my lap. There was a handwritten label on the front which read simply "- *after my death.*" I slid open the rusted iron buckles. Inside, the suitcase smelled musty, and faintly intimate in the way that old people sometimes smell, and the floral fabric lining was shredding at the edges. At the top of a pile of papers was a jumble of photographs, each one giving a picture book tour of Kenya: his grandmother's house in the Rift Valley on the edge of Lake Nakuru; palm trees blowing in the breeze on the shores of the Indian Ocean; a lion—oozing a casual sexual ease—rubbing necks with a lioness; *come away with me, and be my bride* she had written on the back.

I picked up another photograph, and came to an abrupt halt. It showed a very young child, naked, sliced open by a knife so that her guts—swollen in the heat—bulged out of her waist. I let it fall, shocked, but there were more. Men, women, children, and cattle killed by careless strokes of the blade. I turned one over. On the back was written *victims of the Mau Mau*. And there were other photographs which showed Europeans who were killed by Mau Mau, taken before their deaths; a boy of four sitting on the grass with his brother; a young couple posing on their verandah. Below the photographs was a policeman's handbook, dated 1953, and below that a manuscript—the author's history of the Mau Mau uprising.

I knew almost nothing about Mau Mau—it was only later that I learnt it was a political movement fuelled by the Kikuyu who wanted land back from the whites in Kenya—but as I began to read, a subtle chill crept down my spine. Here was this suitcase, and like Pandora's box, it held treasures and horrors, encapsulating that complicated mix of feelings—part longing, part foreboding—which defined the way I felt about Kenya.

Over the next few weeks I felt a story stir itself into life. It was a story which would peel back the myths—the glamour and the gin slings—so that I could write about the real Kenya. It was a story which would contravene every unspoken rule of Colonial society, and bring together two people from profoundly different backgrounds—a Kikuyu man and the daughter of a white farmer. And it was a story which—though it had come about quite by chance—would embody my own uneasy response to a country which had stolen my heart.

It is an honor to have *Leopard at the Door* chosen as a Target Book Club Pick. I hope you enjoy the journey, and feel transported—as I was—to Kenya in the 1950s.

Stay in touch. Let me know what you think. If you are a member of a book club feel free to ask me questions—I would love to join your discussion.

With warm wishes,

Jennifer McVeigh

TITLES BY JENNIFER MCVEIGH

Leopard at the Door
The Fever Tree

LEOPARD

AT THE

DOOR

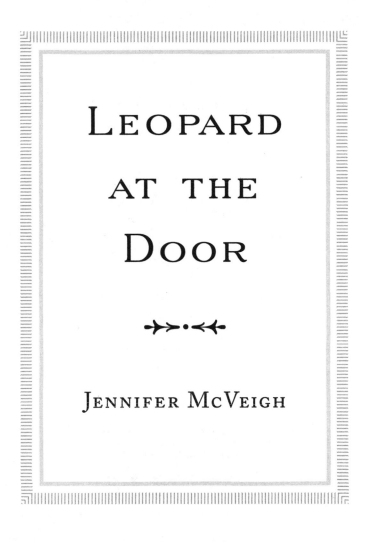

JENNIFER McVEIGH

G. P. PUTNAM'S SONS
New York

G. P. Putnam's Sons
Publishers Since 1838
An imprint of Penguin Random House LLC
375 Hudson Street
New York, New York 10014

Copyright © 2017 by Jenny McVeigh Ltd.
Excerpt from *The Fever Tree* copyright © 2013 by Jenny McVeigh Ltd.
Penguin supports copyright. Copyright fuels creativity, encourages diverse voices,
promotes free speech, and creates a vibrant culture. Thank you for buying an authorized
edition of this book and for complying with copyright laws by not reproducing, scanning,
or distributing any part of it in any form without permission. You are supporting writers
and allowing Penguin to continue to publish books for every reader.

The Library of Congress has catalogued the G. P. Putnam's Sons hardcover edition as follows:

Names: McVeigh, Jennifer, author.
Title: Leopard at the door / Jennifer McVeigh.
Description: New York : G. P. Putnam's Sons, [2017]
Identifiers: LCCN 2016030856 | ISBN 9780399158254 (hardback)
Subjects: | BISAC: FICTION / Historical. | FICTION / Literary. | FICTION / Coming
of Age. Classification: LCC PR6113.C835 L46 2017 | DDC 823/.92—dc23
LC record available at https://lccn.loc.gov/2016030856
p.   cm.

First G. P. Putnam's Sons hardcover edition / January 2017
First G. P. Putnam's Sons trade paperback edition / October 2017
First Target Book Club Edition / October 2017
Target Book Club Edition ISBN: 9780735218802

Printed in the United States of America
1   3   5   7   9   10   8   6   4   2

Book design by Gretchen Achilles

Leopard at the Door

I

✦➤•◀✦

1952. Mombasa, Kenya.

The steward has said we will dock at 9:00 o'clock, but I am too excited to sleep, and I walk onto deck in the dark, long before the sun comes up, watching for the first sight of land. I pull a packet of cigarettes from my coat pocket, light one and inhale, smoke curling up into the warm night sky. My heart beats out a rhythm born of long anticipation. After six years I am finally coming home.

The lamp casts a small pool of light onto a black metal bench. Someone has left a book behind. *The Settler's Guide to Up-Country Swahili: Exercises for the Soldier, Settler, Miner, Merchant and Their Wives.* I open it and cast my eye over the introduction: "This book aims at teaching, in a simple way, just that degree of Swahili that is understood and talked by the average intelligent up-country native." A curious use of adjectives, not something you would find in England. It is a long time since I have used my Swahili and I wonder how much will come back to me. The book starts with greetings, and I turn the phrases over silently on my tongue, enjoying the familiar rhythm of the words: *Jambo, Bwana. Jambo, Memsaab. Habari gani hapa? Habari mzuri tu, Bwana.* What's the news here?

Only good news, master. I slip the book into my pocket, unconsciously reciting the phrases as I stare out into the dark, waiting for our arrival.

An hour later the sun rises huge and heavy from the horizon. Through a screen of mist I make out the shadow of Mombasa Island. A couple wander onto deck, clutching cups of coffee and bread rolls, whispering excitedly. My eyes are fixed on what lies ahead. Green coconut palms and a scattering of white buildings emerge out of water so blue that I realize I have forgotten the meaning of color. The sky is clear and limitless. In England—a country in the grip of rationing, where the sun struggles to illuminate even the clearest winter day—no one has understood my descriptions of the sky in Kenya. My skin burns in the early-morning sun, my neck damp beneath the weight of my hair. The white sails of the Arab dhows soar like the wings of huge, prehistoric birds, their decks crammed so full of men, grinning and shouting, clinging to every mast, that sinking seems an inevitability.

They shout up their greetings in Swahili. *"Karibu."* Welcome. And I grin down at them, waving.

We dock, and I step giddily down the gangplank into a city that smells of fish, of salt, of acrid wood smoke and sewage—the smell of a city whose people live life outdoors under a hot sun—down into the sweltering heat of the customs sheds where I am left waiting, sweating for a few hours before being released onto the small, crowded streets of Mombasa's port.

Bougainvillea tumble over white walls, purple, orange, crimson red, amidst the trumpets of white datura flowers and clusters of pink hibiscus. Dhow captains spread their intricately woven carpets on the street for sale, beating out the dust in thick clouds. Porters in bare feet and white lunghis pad across the hot cobbles between piles of old newspaper and fish bones, past the Arab men dressed in white robes, who sit on low wooden stools drinking tea. I can smell roasting fish rising from a charcoal fire tended by two sailors in brightly colored *kikoys*, who stand prodding the coals, spitting out jets of red betel nut into the street, while others unload their cargo— boxes of fish, dates, henna, great piles of copper wire. Indian women in saris gossip in close groups. I stand and watch, dazzled by so much noise and color, happiness soaring inside me. I have escaped England. I am back in Africa. But I am not home yet. There are still over four hundred miles to travel, up-country, before I see the farm, before I see my father.

"Aleela," a voice says behind me, and a hand touches me on the shoulder. *Aleela*—"she cries" in Swahili. It was the name the Africans had given me as a baby, when I was born healthy, after my mother had given birth to a child who never breathed.

I turn and see Kahiki, our headman, standing there, his stick in one hand.

"*Jambo*," I say, smiling as hard as I have ever smiled in my life.

"*Jambo sana*," he answers, his eyes smiling back at me, grasping my outstretched hand in his sinewy one. And—just like that—I have come home.

II

→→•←←

We come out onto the main road, into a cacophony of beep-
ing and shouting. There has been an accident. A truck carrying pigs has turned over in the middle of the road and the traffic
is at a standstill. A crowd of Africans gather round, watching.
Tight rolls of pig flesh squeeze out of the slatted sides, their squeals
sharpening the gloopy midday heat. *Downers*, my uncle used to call
them; pigs which were all cut up. He owns Uplands—the bacon
factory which supplies Kenya's Europeans and safari outfits with
the sausages, hams and pork pies that remind them of home.

We nudge our way past, the pigs grunting as they struggle to
find a footing on the small slither of space which forms the side
panel of the truck. Those who do find a foothold on the floor are
being crushed under the weight of those on top. The truck emits a
dark, dense heat, palpable with the wet stench of their panic and
the dry chafing of their bristles.

They must have been on their way to the train which would take
them to the factory. They'll be loaded anyway, once they get the
truck back on the road; and finished off when they get there. I look

away, struggling to suppress the memories which are threatening to take shape inside me. I have forgotten this other side of Kenya: a raw physicality that has no shame in the inevitability of pain.

The jeep is parked just beyond the truck. Kahiki throws my luggage into the back and I see a man of about my father's age, with a closely cut blond beard and a dark, suntanned face, making his way through the crowd toward us. He is wearing tattered khaki shorts and desert boots, and he holds a black camera in one hand. He is broad and tall, and moves easily, though his face is creased with sun and age.

"You're Rachel?" He holds out a large hand and grasps mine in his. "Nathaniel Logan."

"Hi," I say, unsure why he is here. His voice has the mellow, slow drawl of an American. He is a curious mix of down at heel and well kitted out.

He gets into the driver's seat, and I realize, with a swallow of disappointment, what I hadn't trusted myself to ask Kahiki—that my father has not come to meet me.

Nathaniel Logan leans over and opens the passenger door with one hand. "Your father asked me to pick you up. He's stuck at the farm. They've had some trouble with the harvest."

He stows his camera in a box, then glances up at me, still standing in the street. "Hey, kiddo, it's not so bad. I won't bite."

I swing myself up into the passenger seat. Kahiki is in the back. The American starts the engine and hands me a bunch of bananas, toy size and sunflower yellow. I tear one off the bunch, peel it and bite into an almost impossible sweetness—after three weeks of tinned food on the ship, the sensation of something so sun soaked and sweet makes me catch my breath.

"The truck turned over an hour ago." Nathaniel pulls the jeep out into the road, his hand on the horn, the crowd parting to let us through.

"Why don't they let the pigs out?"

"They don't want even more of a mess."

Once we have maneuvered onto the clear road, he looks at me and smiles. "First time back in a long while?"

"Six years."

"I'll bet you missed it like hell."

I smile back at him. He has just about summed it up.

The white houses of Mombasa give way to lush vegetation, banana palms and fruit trees. He must sense the question in my silence, because he says, "I was coming as far as Nairobi anyway. I needed to buy some gear." He gestures at the back of the jeep and I see a tarpaulin strapped over the boot. "Trying to keep the dust out. Damn stuff corrodes the kit."

"How do you know my father?"

"I've been staying at Matabele for the last couple of months."

"With the Markhams?" Matabele bordered our farm, though it was more than an hour's drive from Kisima. Lillian Markham had been my mother's closest friend, and we had written to each other over the last six years. "What are you doing up there?" Our corner of Kenya was out of the way, and we rarely had visitors who weren't farmers.

"I'm working for the American Museum of Natural History. Trying to track white rhino. I've found some good specimens up in Laikipia, near the Markhams' farm."

"To hunt?"

"To photograph. This man"—he turns in his seat and grins

at Kahiki—"found them for me. One of the best trackers I've ever met."

Kahiki nods at Nathaniel, which is as close as he comes to smiling. He is Dorobo. He is small and strong, and made of muscle. He has quick eyes and clever hands. He carved wooden toys for me as a child, his knife shaping the wood into a lioness or baboon so real it was as though his hands had coaxed it into life. He knew the land better than anyone else on the farm—he could track any bird or animal. He could find the claw marks of a leopard on a yellow-barked acacia, and tell you how long before he had climbed down, and when he had last made a kill. He hunted with a bow and arrow, and I used to love watching the flick of the thin arrow floating high up into the air, its soft flight belying the deadly accuracy of its aim. It was Kahiki who set the trap for a lioness who was raiding my father's cattle; who found an elephant tusk buried deep in the earth which weighed nearly ninety pounds, the largest ever recorded on our land.

"You used to take me into the forest, and call for the honey guide bird—do you remember?" I ask Kahiki in Swahili.

"Yes, Aleela. And you would not eat the honey in the forest for fear that the bees would come back for you."

I laugh—remembering. "The bird would lead us to a hive nesting in the branches of a tree and Kahiki would rub sticks into fire, and smoke out the bees. When we had collected what we wanted we used to leave the comb for the honey guide—" I smile at Kahiki. "You always said that the bird would next time lead us to a mamba if we did not."

"And it is true," he replies, his yellowing brown eyes soft on mine.

"Kahiki used to walk with my mother," I say, feeling a sliver of

8 *Jennifer McVeigh*

pain in remembering, but pleasure too in sharing this, like the turning of a tooth. I can see the sitting room where she worked at Kisima,
the shelves crammed full of strange objects gathered from the land.
And the early-morning walks along the narrow tracks which spun
like spider's webs through the dense bush, Kahiki in front, his bow
in one hand, my mother's footsteps just behind my own. "She used
to collect things."

"What kind of things?"

"Fossils, bones, bits of stone. Anything that hadn't moved in a
thousand years. That's what my father used to say."

"She was interested in paleontology?"

"I don't know," I say, realizing as I say it that there is very little
that I do know. I knew her only as my mother; the feel of her hands,
rough and warm against my skin, the dry smell of the sun on her
hair, the quick laugh that transformed her face. "She used to say
that the first humans came from Africa." I have not remembered it
until now, and I realize that this is what Kenya will do for me. It
will unlock those hidden places, and bring them out tight and full
of pain.

"It's not impossible. Darwin thought it might be true." He
glances at me as he drives. "Are you interested in natural history?"

I shake my head. "I was a child when I left Kenya. I didn't know
anything about natural history." And as I say it I hear the bitter
edge to my voice: that my mother eludes me; that I did not know
her better.

I turn in my seat, asking Kahiki about the farm, his children,
my father, eager for any news he can give me, and happy to find
that my Swahili is coming back to me.

"They are good," Kahiki says, nodding his head. "All good,

Aleela," but he is not a man who likes to talk, and I will have to wait until I am home to see how things are at the farm.

We drive through the outskirts of Mombasa, past the corrugated shacks and roadside stalls that make up the straggling edges of the city. Nathaniel overtakes two police jeeps, the officers dressed in soft khaki shirts tucked into holsters, rifles pointing in the air. One of the soldiers takes off his red beret and puckers his mouth in a silent whistle as we drive past. I look away, embarrassed in front of Kahiki and the American.

"What kind of trouble with the harvest?" I ask, remembering what Nathaniel had said.

"A couple of nights ago someone broke into the barns at Kisima. Your father had just brought in the grain. They didn't take much— a few bags. The police are making inquiries."

"Was anyone hurt?" The newspapers on the ship were littered with stories of Mau Mau—the secret society which had sprung up in Kenya. It was said that they wanted to unite the Kikuyu and overthrow the whites.

"No." He glances at me. "It was more than likely a simple case of theft."

But nothing more than a bag of sugar had ever gone missing at the farm. Who would risk breaking into my father's barns?

When sleep washes over me I am standing by the dam at Kisima. My mother is kneeling on the bank with her back to me, slacks hitched, her fingers feeling for something buried in the earth. Her blond hair is plaited—the same plait she used to work into my own hair, my scalp tingling with the tug of her fingers. The sun glows through the fine hairs that have worked loose, and she draws one arm across her face to wipe the sweat from her eyes.

I run toward her—*Mama!* With a flood of relief I see that she has heard me, but as she turns the dream dissolves and I have not seen her face. I jolt awake. The car rattles over the road. Nathaniel Logan is driving, one elbow resting on the open window.

I must have slept for longer than I thought. We are in open country. The plains of the central highlands stretch into the hazy distance like the shimmering, tawny back of a lion. Herds of wildebeest and zebra mingle in the long grass, and far off I can see elephant moving, their bodies silhouetted against the afternoon sky like dark storm clouds. The smell of the dry road, the rolling grasslands, the warmth of the sun against my skin make the last six years seem almost as though they were a dream.

I draw a finger across my forearm, through the yellow dust that has settled on the blond hairs. My first night in England, I crept down the carpeted stairs of my grandparents' house, unable to sleep, unused to the sound of the rain spitting cold and damp against the window.

"And you honestly believe she will be happy here?" My father was asking, unaware of me crouched on the stairs, listening.

"Of course she will. This is the right place for her. Think of her education. The friends she will make." My grandmother, a woman I had met only a few hours before, paused. "You can't be selfish about this, Robert. She has lost her mother. She needs rest and the chance to recover. The stability of an English school, it's what she should have been given years ago. We can provide all of those things." I could hear her voice deftly untying the elaborate knot that links a parent to his child.

"Papa," I had said carefully the next day, when I had him to myself, trying to articulate my concern. "Are you going back home?"

"Don't let's think about it, Rachel," he said.

"But if you do—you'll take me with you. You won't leave me here?"

He leaned down, held my head in his hands and kissed my forehead. I had taken it as an agreement but a week later he was gone and my grandparents had enrolled me at a boarding school.

You need to finish school, my father's letters had insisted, *then you can come home,* but I was twelve years old, bewildered and sick for home in an institution that smelled of bleach and wet plimsolls, where we undressed for strip washes once a week in the early-morning dark, and our letters written home were strictly censored. The years looming ahead of me seemed unconquerable. It was as though I had been buried alive. There was always the promise that he would come and visit me, but one year rolled into another and he never came—a new shipment of cattle from England; a fire in one of the barns; the long drought of '51. Managing Kisima—trying to break in its acres of rough country and extract a profit from them— took up all his time.

The farm became the repository for all my dreams. The failures at school, the rigid discipline, the pining for my mother, the friends I made but was prepared too easily to lose were resolved in my imagining of a homecoming. Finally the time came, my exams were over, but his letter, when it arrived, was completely unexpected.

Don't think of coming back, Rachel. Your life is in England, with your mother's family. You talk of home, but you have not been here since you were a child. Have you forgotten how isolated we are? Kisima has little to offer a girl of your age—no shops, no movie theaters, no opportunities, nothing but miles of

*uncut country. This is no place to build a life. It is too far from
the people you are familiar with and the world you have grown
up in.*

The world you have grown up in. He thought of my childhood as
England, but England meant nothing to me. Did he know that
each of his letters had been filed away in a box which I kept under
my bed at school? That I would wait until Sunday afternoon when
all the other children were outside playing games, and lift the lid,
inhaling the faint smell of incense and wood fires that carried me
home, extracting—in the quiet of the dormitory—every last ounce
of sharp pleasure that his letters could give me?

I scarcely knew my grandparents. I had seen them for a brief few
weeks every year—at Christmas and Easter—when I went to stay in
the dark, stone house on the outskirts of Hull, where the hours of the
day ticked by mercilessly slowly. My grandmother asked me not to
walk in the fields beyond the house, forbade me from going into
town on my own, and—either out of grief or disapproval—disliked
me talking about Kenya. Their lives were quiet and fiercely conser-
vative, dominated by the weekly church meetings and charity teas
that my grandmother insisted I attend, dressed in long wool skirts
and buttoned blouses. There was no life for me in Hull. Kisima was
the only home I had known and its land was my inheritance. I wanted
to go back to the place where I was born; see its colors, its people; I
wanted to help my father on the farm as my mother had done.

The day his letter arrived, I bought a ticket on a ship from
Southampton to Mombasa, using the entirety of the money that
my father had sent me on my eighteenth birthday. I wrote him a

note and posted it from Southampton, telling him that I was coming home.

Now I wonder what we will say to each other after so long. I am caught between an awkwardness that I have come back when he explicitly told me not to, and something else. He chose to leave me behind, decided not to take me home with him. When my mother died I lost two parents, and this betrayal sits sorely within me. A bullet with no exit wound.

"We'll stay the night in Nairobi," Nathaniel says, when he sees I am awake. I nod in agreement; Kisima is too far from Mombasa to make the drive in one day.

We are at higher altitude here, and the air settles cool against my skin. We drive through the outskirts of town, past a white post-and-rail fence marking off the long gallops of Nairobi's racetrack. A man is walking in the road in front of us, behind a herd of sheep, a stick resting across his shoulders. Nathaniel slows the car behind them. The sheep stand bleating in the road, their wool filthy and matted, until the man beats the earth around them and they are stirred into scattered motion. We pass a sagging wire fence, children kicking a ball on a dusty patch of earth. Flat-topped acacias cast their latticed shade over huts nestled into the landscape, metal roves winking in the sun. We drive past Kikuyu women with babies tied to their backs, wrapped in scarves, walking into town. A donkey grazes on the side of the road, black barrels strapped to his sides, and beside him, under a lone tree, a man is resting. Clusters of green leaves emerge from the tangle of white thorns above him. His clothes are worn and tattered, and a panga is strung from his belt.

"Where are we staying?" I ask, when he turns off the main road.

The car rattles past the green lawns of a golf course. I don't remember this part of town.

"The Muthaiga Club."

"My father isn't a member." I am worried that he has got the wrong idea. The Muthaiga Country Club is for private members, the wealthier settlers of Kenya Colony; the second sons of English gentry who have been here for generations, not the farmers like my father who came out after the first war and bought their fifty thousand acres with loans from the government.

"It's all right. I've told them to expect you," he says. "I'm meeting clients there in the morning. We'll head off after that."

The road takes us past a row of squat, single-story buildings set back behind freshly painted blue railings. There is something about the institutional neatness of the place, a coldness—like a premonition—which makes the hairs on my arms stand on end.

"Is it a prison?" I ask, trying to get a better look.

"Mathari Mental Hospital," Nathaniel says, "for Kenya Colony's insane."

"People who are mad?"

"Mad, epileptic, and more than likely a handful who simply don't toe the line." He runs a hand over his beard and shakes his head in mocking respect. "The codes of conduct in Kenya are unspoken but not to be transgressed."

"What codes of conduct?" I ask, hearing the irony in his voice, but not quite understanding.

He looks at me, as if assessing my age, as if he might have overestimated me. Then says, "It doesn't do to let the side down in Kenya. Europeans have to keep up appearances, set a good example to the Africans—no seedy living, no fraternizing with the labor.

And those who don't—well, the colony gets rid of them as best they can."

Then it is behind us, and we are driving up to the Muthaiga Club—a deep pink building with white colonnades and a red-tiled roof, bordered with immaculate lawns. It sits comfortably under the shade of acacias.

Kahiki jumps out and hands our luggage down to the porter.

"Eleven o'clock tomorrow?" Nathaniel asks in Swahili, shaking his hand.

"*Sawa sawa*," Kahiki replies, nodding his good night and walking around the back of the building to the African quarters.

I follow Nathaniel Logan through the doors of the club. Inside, the walls are paneled with dark wood and lined with English hunting prints. The air is thick with cigar smoke and the low murmur of voices.

We eat dinner at the hotel bar and I feel, for a moment, very alone. As if reading my thoughts, Nathaniel Logan asks, "When did you last see each other?"

"My father and I?"

He nods.

"Not for six years."

He pushes his plate away and offers me a small, thin cigar from a silver case. I take one, and he leans forward to light it, then lights his own, drawing deeply, looking at me over clouds of dark smoke. "He never came to England?"

I shake my head, giving in to the strength of the smoke, its grip on my lungs, the looseness it brings to my thoughts. It is strange to hear it articulated, my father's absence. Boarding school was full of girls who had been left behind. Our lot was unremarkable.

"He sent you back to go to school?"

"Partly," I say, breathing out smoke. "I went back when my mother died. He left me with my grandparents." He looks right at me. His gaze is too direct. I swallow down the sudden urge to cry. "He couldn't come. It was too difficult for him to get away from the farm."

"Well, I'm sure that's true," he says, looking away and drawing on his cigar, but his words hold no reassurance.

A man with a long, black mustache passes our table. He clasps a hand on Nathaniel Logan's shoulder. "Are you back in the land of the living?"

"Not yet," Nathaniel says, shaking his head.

"Damn it, Logan—why bury yourself in Laikipia with your cameras, when you could be on safari with me?"

"Who is he?" I ask when the man has gone.

"Just another English aristocrat, cast adrift in Africa. He's been trying to persuade me to track elephant for him. He wants a record set of tusks."

"Do you hunt?"

"I used to."

"Why don't you go?"

"Because I'm driving you up to your farm," Nathaniel says, smiling at me, and taking a long pull on his beer. "Besides, I don't go in for killing anymore." He grinds his cigar out in the silver ashtray. "I've had my fun. I'll leave it to the rest of them."

I realize that I like Nathaniel Logan. Years of boarding school have taught me to be wary of people who mold themselves too easily to the common cause, but he seems to keep himself just enough apart from people to make his own judgment.

At eight o'clock a hush falls over the dining room. The men put down their cards, and the women stop their chatting. Across the room comes the sound of Big Ben chiming in London. It is the news broadcast from England, and the men and women strain forward in their seats to hear the voice, brittle with distance, emanating from the radio. The BBC Overseas Service, the sound of home, exercises its power over all of us. There is news from England: a crash at an aviation display and the death of the first British pilot to exceed the speed of sound; the Ministry of Food announces the end of thirteen years of tea rationing. At the end of the broadcast there is a local report from East Africa. *Fifty-eight unexplained grass fires broke out today on farms around Nyeri, destroying thousands of acres of prime grazing. Local farmers are attributing the fires to the secret society Mau Mau. It follows reports of mass oathing ceremonies across the region, and the murder last week of several Kikuyu who refused to take the Mau Mau oath. A curfew has been imposed. Meanwhile the Roman Catholic Bishop at Nyeri declares that he will excommunicate any Catholic who supports the Mau Mau secret society or takes its oath. He confirmed that there had been desecration of pictures of Christ in the Nyeri area.*

On the ship the news of a secret society whose members have taken oaths to kill white men and throw them off their farms had seemed alarmist and unreal; there have been no reports of violence against Europeans, only against the Kikuyu who resist the movement. And yet hearing it here—in this small room clouded with the breath and smoke of the men and women whose lives like mine are intertwined with it—is like seeing a dark shape stir itself and shake off sleep. Nyeri is over a hundred miles from Kisima, but in Kenya a hundred miles is not such a great distance.

Nathaniel Logan has his camera out of his case. He is standing against the wall of the room taking photographs. I see the scene through his lens—the women in their evening dresses, looking at each other with glittering eyes, the men leaning back in their chairs, cheeks reddened by whiskey, the waiters hovering in their red fezzes, their black faces carved into that familiar, unmoving attitude of subservience.

"I thought you photographed animals," I say, when he comes back to the table.

"Technically people are animals," he says, smiling and putting down his camera. "But I don't just work for the museum. I write for newspapers."

"About what?"

"Archaeology, natural history, anything newsworthy."

"And what will you write about this?"

"That these good people feel under threat. That they will put whatever pressure is necessary on their government to protect them."

"And will it?"

"Protect them?" He puts the lens cap back on his camera. "We're seeing collective punishments, suppression of the Kikuyu press, closure of independent African schools. I'd say they were certainly trying."

"Which is a good thing," I say, hearing the reticence in his voice.

"I try to stay out of politics in this country." He rubs a hand over his beard and smiles ruefully at me. "Gets me into trouble."

The man at the table next to us drains his glass of whiskey, pushes back his chair and says, to no one in particular, "This country is going to the fucking dogs." He limps out of the room.

Later, in the small single room on the ground floor of the Muthaiga Club, the story of Briar Rose catches at the edges of my waking mind. She sleeps for a hundred years, but that isn't the magic. The magic is that the castle sleeps with her so that when she wakes the world is just as she left it—her mother, her father, even the animals are there just as they had been when tragedy struck. I want the farm to be that way, and the thought that it might not be is eating me alive. After all—my mother is dead. How can anything be the same again?

III

→⇒•⇐←

I wake in the middle of the night, my heart pounding. I am in the grip of a memory so strong that it bleeds its panic out of the dream into my waking. As a child, I learned not to think about it, to control it, but Africa is unraveling the past, and now it has come back, hot and alive, to haunt me. I go to the bathroom, draw water from the tap and splash my face until my skin is hard and cold as stone, but when I climb back into bed the memory still sticks to me. The squealing of the pigs in the truck has awakened it. I squeeze my eyes shut but it follows me into the darkness; there is no holding it back.

IT IS 6 SEPTEMBER 1946. I know the date because I have been counting the days on the calendar until my parents come home. I am twelve years old, staying with my uncle Eliot—my father's brother—in his house at the meat factory near Limuru. There is a strike on and my uncle—instead of sitting down to lunch with me in the quiet of the dining room—is up at the factory. I am sprawled on the newly cut floorboards, sharply aromatic, reading an encyclo-pedia, with Juno, my puppy, snapping at flies and making small charges at my hair. My parents are in England—this is their first trip away from Kisima. My uncle is not married, and he is awkward with children—I am unsure how to behave in his company. The days are long and quiet, but I am happy to be left alone.

The managers' cottages are built at the back of the factory, far enough away that you can almost, but not quite, forget it is there. The slaughterhouse is open every day but Sunday, and it processes nearly twenty-six thousand pigs a year. I take a pencil and a bit of paper and do the calculation. Close to a hundred pigs a day. From Monday to Saturday the metal machinery grinds on, and it is dif-ficult not to think about the steady stream of animals being butch-ered just a few hundred yards away.

When I arrived at the factory, my uncle took me onto the kill-ing floor. I stood transfixed, the smell of warm blood, of wet metal in my mouth, the clanging of machinery roaring in my ears. I couldn't tear my eyes away—the long line of pigs toiling up the chute, heads down in protest; pressed inexorably forward by the steel paddle; the turning of the great metal wheel; the pig jerked off its feet, so that it hung upside down, screeching, until it was carried within reach of the African with the knife; the silence that came with a long gush of blood. I wanted to leave, but he kept me there, talking. "Much more efficient than a man with a knife at the back of his shop," but all I could hear was the squealing.

My uncle has mechanized the process as far as he is able—within minutes the pigs are boiled, scraped, burned to remove hair, gutted, beheaded and cut into two halves—but they can't be silenced. Death is still death.

Nothing is wasted—the livers, hearts and glands are sold, intestines are cleaned and salted and used as sausage skins. The backbones and pig heads—still with some fresh meat on them—are sold to the Africans for food. "We use everything but the squeals," my uncle says with pride. When the wind blows in the wrong direction the stench from the rendering house lines the back of your throat and makes you choke. That is where they tank the scraps—huge vats of blood, gristle and bones, boiled down and the fat pumped off to make soap, glue and fertilizer. I have never been in—no visitors are allowed—but when the fires are burning the smell of rot hangs like a pall over the cottages.

Today the strike has shut down the machines—the Africans have put down their knives and aprons—and everything is as quiet as a Sunday. My uncle left breakfast in a hurry, expressly forbidding me to go up to the factory, and I am on my own as I am most days, listening to the hornbill rapping at the window and the rhythmic slice of the gardener's blades as he shears the grass outside.

Juno pricks up her ears, listening for something, letting out a low, purring growl, and I laugh at her earnestness, ruffling her coat with my hand. I found her on the farm two months ago and took her in, and I was happy when my uncle agreed to let me bring her to the factory. She is a squirming ball of warm fur with needle-sharp teeth and sleek oversized ears; all gold, with three black paws, and a ripple of fur down her back like my parents' lion dogs.

Now she growls and scrambles, slipping across the floorboards to the door before I even hear the car pull up. Then I hear the crunch of tires and the engine cuts. Through the open door I can see a man stepping out of the car.

"Miss Fullsmith?" he asks as I pad out onto the porch, unsticking my dress from my legs and blinking in the hot sun. He licks his lips, dry in the heat, and looks up at me.

"Rachel Fullsmith?"

I nod.

Juno is teasing his trousers, and he kicks her off irritably so that she slides across the floorboards, yelping. I scoop her off the steps, her back legs windmilling beneath her, her teeth gnawing at my hand.

"My uncle's at the factory," I say, tilting my head back down the road, in the direction he has come. The engine of the car is ticking over in the heat, the air settling thick and dusty around us. I am standing in a patch of sunlight, the boards hot beneath the soles of my feet so that I have to keep shifting my weight, lifting one bare foot then the other. He gives a slight nod, which is disconcerting. Visitors usually mean news, and news is something reserved for adults, but he doesn't look about to leave.

"I've come from Nairobi," he says, not really talking to me, but looking at me curiously, and suddenly—in a gulping moment of unease—I know that whatever he is here for is something to do with me. "Your father," he says, stepping onto the porch, pulling a small yellow envelope from the pocket of his trousers. It is stuck to a packet of cigarettes and he unpeels it. "A telegram. I was hoping to find your uncle. You'll give it to him? Best to wait until he's home." His gaze slips up my bare legs, and I smell his warm breath, faintly mentholated, as he hands it over. Then he walks back to his car and drives off in a rattle of dust.

I slip the telegram into my pocket, slide on my plimsolls, shut the door on Juno who is scrambling at my feet and run up to the factory to find my uncle.

I remember the strike again when I come up to the pigpens. I can see—looking under the barn roves—that the pens are full to bursting. Usually the pigs are content and placid for the time they are kept here, nosing and rolling in the dusty earth, strangely resigned to the sudden change in their circumstances, and I would lean over the rail, the metal bar hot against the thin cotton waist of my dress, and lay a hand on the coarse bristled skin of the nearest, soaking up the feel of the warm, rolling firmness of its back beneath my hand. But today they are jammed in so tight that heads are lifted onto the buttocks of the ones in front, pink, brown and black packed in so close you can't tell one pig from another.

There is a noise coming from the yard beyond the walls, an undercurrent of voices which rises up above the grunting of the pigs; a group of men protesting, their shouts lifting on a tide of anger. I think of the knives each man carries at the factory, the long blades used for cutting through muscle, fat and bone. What if they haven't put them down after all?

The whole place feels out of kilter, as if anything might happen. I stand beside the pigpens, under the hot sun, pushing my sweating palms against the cotton of my dress, wondering what to do. I know I shouldn't be at the factory, but I don't want to leave just yet—I need to see what is happening in the yard.

I run through the barn, between the pens—hot with the smell of pigs, until I reach the factory wall. I am careful not to be seen— my uncle will be angry with me if he finds out. There is a door— usually left open for the managers in the engine room, along the corridor, to get a breath of air. It is heavy on its hinges, and swings open silently when I pull on it. I step inside a cool, dark corridor. It is quiet inside, and there are no lights on. At the end there is a square of sunlight on the cement floor: the stairwell.

I pad up the concrete steps into the light, crouching down as I come out onto a balcony on the first floor, emerging into a swell of noise. I slide forward on my belly so that I can see through one of the round drain holes in the wall. It gives me a circular view of what is going on below, without the risk of being seen.

I am overlooking the courtyard of the main factory. The workers aren't carrying their knives—a relief—but some carry large stones in their hands. They sweat and shout in the heat, hemmed in like the pigs outside. They look stronger and less knowable without their brown tunics and white aprons. My heart thuds with a sudden fear. I have never seen so many men, so many Africans, brought together by anger. Their faces are taut, and a few of them cry out in defiance.

An idea—absurd but compelling—grips me. What if the Africans rise up and in their anger herd us through the killing line, to be stunned, strung up and butchered? They far outnumber the group of European managers and their *askari* who stand in a cluster by the far wall. My uncle is standing with them, his posture rigid. I turn, hearing a noise behind me. Voices in the stairwell and the flat tread of feet coming up the stairs. A heart-racing terror—I don't want to be found up here, on my own. There is an open door a few yards away. An office—empty. I dart inside and pull the door shut. All I can hear for a long moment is the milling of voices from the factory yard, but then—with a freezing of my spine—the door handle turns. I look round the room in desperation, my eyes still adjusting to the dark. Should I stand up and declare myself? There is a cupboard in the corner. I open the slatted door and before I know what I am doing I am folding myself inside, next to a bucket and a box of files, and I am pulling the door closed. The telegram folds stiffly in my pocket.

A European officer walks in, dressed in a khaki shirt, followed by two *askari* in uniform, with rifles over their backs and revolvers in their belts. I can see them through the slats. They push an African into the room in front of them, so hard that he falls forward onto the metal desk. Its feet screech across the floor and I flinch. He is a slight man, wearing leather shoes, a ripped collared shirt and trousers; he looks like an African from Nairobi. The officer barks a command and the door swings shut. My heart thuds in my chest. It is too late to do anything other than stay quiet.

The European officer isn't tall but he is bulky, not quite fat but fleshy as a fruit might be when overripe, and his thin blond hair is combed down into a side parting. He is looking at the African in dismay, shaking his head from side to side in a demonstration of disappointment.

"So, you're the leader of this circus?" he asks in Swahili, sitting with half his weight on the desk. He speaks with a casualness that borders on disinterest.

"*Ndiyo*," the man says, *yes*, pushing himself upright and brushing his hands slowly on his trousers.

The officer lights a cigarette, inhales, and says as he blows out, "And what the fuck are you kaffirs hoping to achieve here?"

The African has a piece of paper crushed in his palm, and he straightens it and hands it to the officer. The officer doesn't move, doesn't take it, just keeps on staring at the striker and smoking his cigarette. I have the impression of certain teachers at school, who accelerated the will of my rebellion with their implacable refusal to acknowledge my point of view.

The African steps forward, folds the piece of paper into a square and pushes it into the officer's shirt pocket. Then he leans forward—

so close that I imagine the wash of his warm breath on the officer's mouth—and says, in perfect English, "Kenya is a black man's country. You should go back to where you belong."

The officer doesn't flinch. He takes one last, slow drag on his cigarette, gives the African a slight smile, drops the cigarette to the floor and grinds it out with the toe of his heavy black boot. Then he pulls the revolver out of his belt, walks around behind the man and slams him on the back of the neck with the gun so that he collapses onto the floor.

When the striker tries to stand up the officer lifts his gun and smashes him in the face. Blood explodes. I shut my eyes. When I open them again the man is on the floor, curled up, sweeping his feet along the cement in an attempt to slide away. The officer pauses for a moment, takes a few dancing steps on the floor to line himself up, then swings his boot at the man's head, under his chin, so that his neck snaps back. After that the man doesn't move.

I swallow heavily. A trickle of sweat runs down between my eyebrows. I have to make a conscious effort not to scream. The officer hands the gun to his *askari*, pulls a handkerchief from his pocket and carefully wipes down his hands, his face and his shirt. "Fucking kaffirs," he says as he walks out, slipping his gun back into his belt. Then—in Swahili—"Leave him here—we'll go deal with the others. There won't be any *shauri* now."

And they walk out of the room, closing the door behind them with a click.

IV

⟶⟶•⟵⟵

A s we are driving out of Nairobi, through the Kikuyu reserves, we hear a rattle of gunfire and three African *askari* dart across the road in front of us.

"What is it?" I ask Nathaniel, who is pulling over on the side of the road. I can hear a woman screaming.

"A sweep maybe," he says, bringing the jeep to a juddering halt. "The police have started making random searches."

He switches off the ignition and we sit, listening. My heart is racing. "The reserves are a hotbed of discontent. They'll be hoping to pick up any Mau Mau hiding here."

The gunfire stops, and after a moment he opens his door, and I do the same.

"Aleela," Kahiki says, putting out a hand to stop me.

"She'll be OK," Nathaniel says, slipping down onto the parched grass which grows on the side of the road. He has his camera in one hand. "We won't go far."

We walk toward the shouts, squinting into the glare of the sun. There is a market square up ahead, baskets overturned, vegetables rolling in the dust, and someone screaming, hysterical. Police jeeps are gathered on the verge. Five or six *askari* in khaki uniforms, with rifles, are herding men, women and children together. Nathaniel takes a few photographs, then walks over to a European officer and asks him some questions. My eyes fix on the girl who is shouting. She must be about my age, in a headscarf which has slipped back off her hair. Two African officers are blocking her from going forward and she is begging, screaming, trying to break through. "Give him to me!"

And then I see the baby sitting in the dust twenty feet from me, crying softly. He is small and brown, the same color as the earth, and too young to walk. It would take nothing for one of the *askari* to go back and pick him up, but they keep pushing the group back, and she is crying for the boy. I can see from the posture of the two Africans, from the way they let her bounce off them—between the butts of their rifles—that they find this a kind of spectacle. That they are enjoying the drama of it. Perhaps they are just baiting her, and will go back in a minute and pick up the boy. There is no reason to think that they won't. Except I cannot watch what they are doing to her. There is something so awful, and so ugly, in their proving to this girl that she is unable to protect her child.

I walk into the square. The officer talking to Nathaniel is distracted—he hasn't seen me. I pick up the baby—a bundle of warm, dry skin against mine—and for a moment he stops crying. I have barely walked two paces when the European officer shouts at me.

"Hey!" he calls out. "Put it down."

"It's her child," I say, turning to face him. Nathaniel is standing next to him, watching.

"Put it down," the officer says, swinging his gun at me, "or I'll arrest you like the rest of them."

"Lower your gun," Nathaniel says in a sharp voice. I realize the officer is not much older than me, but he ignores Nathaniel and lifts his gun level with my stomach, and says very slowly, "Put—it—down." And so I obey—just like that my courage fails me and I begin to place the child, crying, back on the ground.

Nathaniel closes a hand on the officer's rifle, lifting the barrel so that it points to the sky. The officer shouts at him, backing up, but Nathaniel has his hand on the gun and the officer isn't strong enough to wrest it away from him.

"Go on—" Nathaniel says to me, and I carry the child across the market square, under the eyes of the *askari*, my legs shaking underneath me. The boy sees his mother and begins crying for her, and she reaches out her hands for him, grabbing at his arms. *"Asante,"* she says, clutching the child to her, holding him away from the *askari. "Asante."*

Nathaniel lets go of the rifle and says to the officer, "The world is ugly enough without you pissing all over it."

"You've got nerve—" Nathaniel says, when we are back in the jeep and pulling out into the road, but I'm not sure it's true. I would have put the child down if he hadn't been there. I feel no satisfaction, only shame. I think we both feel it. Kahiki says nothing as we drive past, and I wonder what he is thinking. He is one of the few laborers on the farm who isn't Kikuyu. He and his family aren't directly affected by what we have witnessed here, but this surely touches him as well. I crane my head to see whether I can spot the woman with her child, but there are too many *askari* in the way.

"A goddamn circus," Nathaniel says, almost to himself. He pulls a small silver flask from the side of the door, puts it between his legs and unscrews the lid. Then he tilts it to his lips and drinks.

"Do you think it will blow over?" I ask.

He laughs, softly. "I heard a Kikuyu once say that when a man steals your ox and kills it, you can forget. But when he steals your land—you never forget."

"But the Europeans didn't steal their land. There was no one at Kisima when my father came."

He looks at me. That assessing glance again, that holds no blame, only a measuring of what I am. And caution—he does not want to say too much. "I said you shouldn't get into politics with me."

"I want to know what you think."

"Your father might not want you to know what I think." He takes another sip from the flask, sucking whiskey over his teeth. "Nor might Sara."

"Who is Sara?" I ask.

He looks at me for a long moment, then turns his gaze back to the road and doesn't say anything. I do not want to ask again. I do not want to seem more naive, more vulnerable than he already thinks I am. But the name stirs an unease inside me. It is the way he said it; the connection with my father.

We drive through the afternoon, through the small town of Nakuru, until the tarmac runs out and we are juddering along the rutted washboard of the track which will take us deep into the bush, to the very edge of the Rift Valley, though there is no indication yet of the plunging gorges on which the farm is precariously balanced.

Lush mountains rise up, punctured by flat plains where giraffe bend their patchwork heads to the tops of yellow-barked acacias. I spot a bull elephant, his body hidden in the undergrowth, his trunk looping up to pull down the branches of a tree, and a little later a troop of baboons fling themselves over the road in front of us, one huge male watching his troop go past before following behind them. We drive until the parched grasses turn green and the earth becomes soft. My heart soars. I begin to recognize the contours of the land, my mind feeling its way over an old blueprint. This is as familiar to me as breathing.

"The rains came two weeks ago," Nathaniel says, swinging the steering wheel to avoid the ruts in the road, as we slip and slide over the track, splashing into deep puddles which spray our arms with brown spots.

The track deteriorates until, in the end, we get stuck in a slick of mud so implacable that we have to climb out. It sucks at my feet and I lose my plimsoll almost immediately and have to plunge my hand into the wet stickiness to retrieve it. Kahiki pulls two shovels from the boot of the jeep and he and Nathaniel begin to work at digging us out.

I climb up the track to higher ground. All around us is bush—as far as the eye can see. Thorny scrub, grass clearings and the occasional acacia tree casting its umbrella of shade. It would be hard for a stranger to distinguish this place from any other that we have driven through, but I have grown up here. I used to ride my pony down this track. It took the better half of the morning, and I know we are over an hour's drive from the farm.

Everything is a luminescent green. In all the years I have been away, I have never seen anything as beautiful as the land that lies before me now. The sun beats down and I feel the mud shrink and dry against the skin on my calves until I can rub it off in flakes. There is not a sound, except for the liquid, dropping call of the doves. Between the trees I see the flickering white bob of a tail—a gazelle, and I breathe more easily: there are no lion lying here panting in the shade. Stillness settles over everything; the fears which have haunted me since leaving England—that my father might not want to see me, that home will be altered—slip away. I belong here; and this place is too wild, too remote for change.

I help Nathaniel and Kahiki roll stones under the wheels of the jeep, stamping them in close to the tires, then pull myself into the driver's seat. They brace themselves to push but when I press the accelerator the engine roars, and I can feel the wheels spinning helplessly beneath me. We repeat the process over the next hour, but succeed only in digging the car deeper into the mud.

I climb down. Nathaniel leans against the back of the jeep, groaning, and lights a cigarette, holding out the pack to me. As we stand and smoke, a group of Kikuyu appear in the distance. Their bodies are slick and muscular, skin shining in the sun. "*Jambo*," we call out, and they shout back, friendly and open. I do not know them—they are not from Kisima, but they push us rolling into motion, one of them running alongside as we speed away, to grab a packet of cigarettes from Nathaniel's outstretched hand. We shout our thanks behind us and drive on, the can of soda pop I brought with me from Nairobi boiling in the heat, sticky against my legs.

We dip down a rutted track into a sea of green, lurching over stones. The jeep slips and slides until we are deep in the bush, branches scratching against the metal doors, releasing the sweet, dry fragrance of *leleshwa*. Antelope dart down the track in front of us. The road climbs, the ground falling away behind us to a view so vast and wide that the land appears endless. In the hazy distance I can see animals moving, the switch of a tail. Our windows are wound down, the road rattles on, and the soil, the damp taste of the earth, is in my mouth.

Then—just as the sun is sinking behind the trees in a pool of deep red light—I see the peeling white post that marks out my parents' farm, shimmering in the dusk. The memories thicken, and my throat catches. Here is the track that I ran down so often to greet my father. The years drop away. It is just as it was in my dreams. Only the potholes in the track have taken on a different pattern. I lean out of the rolled-down window, the metal hot against my arm, and feel the warmth rising from the earth. Here is the old African olive tree I climbed as a child, its gnarled trunk thick and dark against the luminescent sky. I can see light glinting off water—the dam. Then—all of a sudden—we are here. The house—so long imagined—stands just as it did, the purple creeper is a little thicker perhaps, but otherwise the same. The two acacias which grow behind the house cast their long shadows over the ground, the evening light turning their branches to a deep yellow. How can something I have dreamed of for so long be so suddenly upon me? I realize I haven't allowed myself to believe that I might ever come back, and only now am I giving in to the joy of it.

I step down from the jeep, the dusty, sun-baked earth warm beneath the soles of my feet. A jackal barks in the clear, cool evening light. I haven't stood here since the moment I climbed into my parents' car, onto my mother's lap, so many years before. My throat is choked with emotion. She is so close to me now that I can almost hear her voice. I know from the hours spent staring at the handful of photographs my father sent me that the first few moments are when I will feel her presence the most; the house will soon lose its power to conjure the ghost of memory.

I see a tawny dog with black paws trotting toward us, head low, barking a warning.

"Juno?" I call, softly.

She stops for a moment, head cocked, then bounds forward, coiling herself between my legs, whining in excitement. She remembers me and I realize how much I have been hoping that she would. The door bursts open, and my father is walking toward me. "Look how tall you are," he shouts, and I run to him and press my face—wet with tears—against his chest. I cannot meet his eye or look him in the face. There is too much emotion. But I am home, and he is here, beneath my hands, and all the absent bitterness of the last six years will be rolled away. And then—blinking through tears—I see a woman standing in the door behind him.

V

❖

"Rachel, this is Sara," my father says, disentangling himself from my embrace. "She lives here—" He boldly speaks the words as though there is no shame in them, as though his tone might remove any awkwardness that the revelation holds.

The woman walks toward us with a neat step and a smile that never quite reaches her eyes. I can tell by the formality of the introduction that she is more than a recent acquaintance; she has been here for some time. I dry my eyes with my hands and we kiss—Sara barely leaning forward so that I end up just grazing her cheek. The saturating, sweet smell of lilies envelops me.

"You haven't been here since you were a little girl, is that right?" she asks.

"I haven't," I say, leaning down to sink my face in Juno's fur, breathing in the animal smell of her, trying to hide the tears which are coming now for a different reason, or for the same reason all muddled into one. I don't want this woman to be here to witness my homecoming. Every second is a chance to bring my mother alive, to feel her presence as it was when we left, me scrambling onto her lap in the car, her soft whisper in my ear.

"Nate Logan," Sara says, turning her gaze away from me.

Nathaniel is shaking my father's hand.

"Can we persuade you to stay the night with us?" my father asks.

"No—thank you. I've picked up a new camera. I want to be out first thing tomorrow." He takes a small package from the front seat of his jeep and gives it to Sara. "Extra film for Harold."

"He's out on the farm," she says, giving him a tight smile, "taking photographs." I sense a friction between them.

"Well—send him my regards," Nathaniel says.

He turns to look at me and I stand up, pressing the heels of my hands into my eyes to stop the tears. I swallow down the choking that is catching at my chest. I scarcely know him, but for a reason I cannot explain I would rather he stayed.

"Thank you," I say, smiling.

"That's all right, kiddo," he says, laying a hand on my head. "You look after yourself."

A moment later he is gone, the rattle of his engine receding into the dusk.

Sara links arms with my father, one arm wrapped around his, and smiles, and I notice the coolness of her gaze as she looks at me.

"I hope you won't mind," she says, "but we've moved you into a different room. There's Harold, you see, my son. It seemed silly to let that big room go to waste." She pauses for a moment, then says into the awkward silence, "If I had known you were coming back—" as though she had thought I might never come home.

I smile brightly at them both. "That's fine," I say, but all I can think is that she is not a guest. She is talking about our house as though it is her own. Who is she exactly? How could my father not have told me?

My father clasps my shoulder, bridging the distance between us, and the familiar weight of his hand sends a current of emotion through me. "Come on in, Rachel." I am aware of a thread of tension. It seems to me that their backs are all to the house, on guard, but perhaps I have imagined it. Evening has come, the sun has gone down, and the air is chill—we are at over six thousand five hundred feet here in the highlands, and on the equator nightfall is swift.

They turn toward the house, and I glance involuntarily behind me—the wind is rustling the long papyrus grass in front of the house, and the silver spires move as though someone is walking through them.

"It's all right," my father says, quietly. "There's no one there."

Kahiki has left my bags by the front door, and I thank him. He calls to Juno as he leaves, but she puts her tail between her legs and drops her head, unwilling to follow.

"She's not coming in?" I ask.

"Not in the house," Sara says, standing in the doorway.

"Why?" I ask, looking at my father in surprise.

"She's riddled with ticks," Sara says, but we have always deticked our dogs, and they have always slept in the house. I can't imagine this evening without Juno stretched out in front of the fire.

"She sleeps in the stables," my father says. "It's comfortable enough."

"I'm afraid I haven't adopted your family's love of animals," Sara says, with a small, brittle laugh.

"What about leopard?" I'm shocked. "Don't they try to get at her?"

"They haven't managed it yet," she says, drily, but I am sure my father can't approve. Even if they bolt the stable doors so that a leopard can't get in, it would terrify her with its circling. Leopard like dog almost as much as baboon.

"Can she stay now that I am here?" I don't want to go in without her. I will sleep better with her by my bed.

My father looks at Sara for approval, and I can see the struggle in her face, a flare of irritation that this is out of her control. "Of course," she says with an indulgent smile that is just a little tight around the edges, and—as if she can sense the outcome—Juno trots past her into the hall.

My father shuts the door behind us. Standing here, I feel as though I have slipped through time. The house is just the same, with its thick plaster walls stained dark over the years by wood smoke and the rub of shoulders. The grandfather clock—brought by my parents from England on the wagon which drove them to the farm—ticks out the time, achingly slow. In the sitting room a fire spits and crackles in the stone hearth, and the air is sweet with the smell of burning *leleshwa*. Arched over our heads is the pitched timber ceiling beneath the thatch whose patterns I had endlessly tried to memorize as a child. The mahogany dresser—which used to hold my mother's collection of fossils and stones—now shows off rows of matching pink and yellow floral plates and china teacups, but little else has changed. Here are the armchairs gathered round the fire, draped with zebra skins; the rugs my mother and I bought on a trip to Zanzibar, and the floorboards she had laid by hand with my father—the line of the equator—which crosses right through this room—picked out in red cedar. The dark, waxed table where we ate supper every evening is just the same, set in front of the three windows that look out onto the lawn beyond.

"Where is Jim? And Joseph?" I ask, looking around. Jim was the cook—overweight, sweating and full of laughter—he had been with us for as long as I could remember. Joseph was the houseboy. His long face, his wrinkled hands and his soft, padding feet had been an intimate part of my childhood.

"Jim is in the kitchen," Sara says.

"And Joseph?" I ask my father.

"We had to let him go—"

"He was half blind—always knocking things over," Sara says. "Mungai, the new boy, will get you anything you need." A slightly built, young Kikuyu boy is hovering in the doorway.

But I don't need anything. I only want to see Jim. A homecoming isn't a homecoming without him bursting out of the kitchen to greet me, clasping me to his huge belly, his arms smelling of onions and treacle.

"I'll go find him in the kitchen."

"Don't you think you'd better have a bath first?" I follow Sara's gaze to my shoeless feet, and my calves, spattered red-brown with mud. I pause for a moment. There is something in her voice—a challenge—that stops me from going.

It is Sara, not my father, who shows me to the guest room, on the other side of the sitting room. I step inside, with Juno at my heels, and Sara hovers at the open door watching me.

"I expect you're wondering what I'm doing here," she says, her gaze settling unflinching on mine, her forefinger winding round the thin gold chain at her neck. I look at her then—taking her in. She must be in her midforties—a little younger than my mother

would be now. Her dark hair is cut short around her ears, accentu-
ating the white curve of her neck, and she wears a sleeveless silk
shirt that tightens over her breasts. Her mouth is a glossy lipstick
red. The skin on her arms is pale and smooth, and as she drops
her hand to her waist, thin ivory bangles slip down her wrist,
clinking against each other like bones. She is so pale she might be
in England, and I wonder if she ever goes outside. My eyes slide
away from hers. She seems the very opposite of my mother, who
wore only the simplest things, who smelled, not of lilies, but of the
warm sun mingled with antiseptic, and of the sharp, green lettuces
that she cut from her garden.

"I said he should write and tell you but he never did," Sara says.

"Why not?"

"Men don't like change. They choose the path of least resistance,
and generally don't step off it unless pushed." I struggle to match
this assertion with what I know of my father, the way he was with
my mother when I was growing up. But then—with a hot rush of
blood—I remember how easily he gave me up to my grandparents.

"Are you married?" I ask. I know it's a risk and I feel my blood
beat a little faster.

"Not yet," she says, holding my gaze, letting me understand
there is no shame for her in their arrangement. I feel a tiny chink
of relief that she is not yet family. That my father hasn't given all
of himself away.

She calls Juno to her as she leaves, but the dog drops to her
haunches on the floor beside me, her head low in apology for not
following.

Sara clicks her tongue in irritation. "She's filthy."

"I'll give her a bath," I say, wanting to hold on to this one thing.

"As long as I'm not the one who has to do it."

Just as she is about to leave, she turns in the door. "Why did you come?"

I stare at her. The question is so direct, so lacking in grace, that I do not know how to answer.

"Why would anyone come back to this place—" She says in a low voice. I do not think she wants me to answer. After a moment she glances at me. "If you need anything in the night, you know where your father and I are sleeping."

In my mother's bed.

When she is gone I sit down on the floor, stroking the smooth, whiskered fur around Juno's muzzle. A sudden, panicked sense of unbelonging wells up inside me. I am a complete stranger in the one place where I expected to feel at home. Even this room isn't familiar to me. The walls are covered in a blue-flocked wallpaper, which has dark patches where the damp has crept in over the years. It is on the north side of the house, and it feels chill and unused. The three rooms on this side were reserved for guests—the family bedrooms are on the other side of the house, off the main hall. I have always been, ever since I was a child, afraid of the dark. I know I will be scared here, on my own, so far from the others, but I am determined not to show it.

Juno is all skin and bones, and her coat is matted stiff with blackjacks—burrs that cling tight to her fur. And Sara is right. There are ticks—fat, leathery sacks—nestling behind her ears and in the corners of her legs. I'll get rid of them later, but for now I am eager for a bath.

One of the boys has lit the boiler that sits at the back of the house. When I test the water it runs hot. I undress, peeling off my shirt, my trousers, the layers of my dusty journey from Nairobi. The baths at Kisima are twice the length of my grandmother's in England. I am no longer a child, but they are still long enough to swallow me whole. I shake out the thick, matted coil of my hair, letting it fall to my chest, and step into the mineral brown water. My hands and feet are darker than my legs and arms, and I rub at the rings of dust until they dissolve in clouds in the water. The lamp flickers its orange light over the walls, and I lie back as I did as a child so that I am submerged, my hair weightless. Except my body is not the same as it was. My thighs are longer, heavier, and my breasts emerge like pale rocks from the water. Along the soft curve of my belly, there beneath the surface, are the dense, dark curls between my legs. I shut my eyes. There is this—a woman's body. I am not the same at all.

Once I have risen dripping from the water, I get changed in a hurry, squeezing the moisture from my wet hair, twisting it into a bun and pulling on a sweater over my shirt. I have forgotten how cold the nights are here.

There is someone standing in the corridor when I step out of my room. I get a fright when I see him because it looks as though he has been waiting for me. There is a camera in his left hand. His cheeks flush a hot red, clear even by the kerosene lamp that hangs from his hand, illuminating him from beneath. I feel a moment of unaccountable fear which I banish by speaking.

"You're Harold?"

"Yes," he says, stepping forward, breaking the spell. He is a fraction taller than me, but he must be a few years younger. He puts the lamp on the floor and holds out his hand. It is hot and dry in mine. He gives me a quick, shifting glance, a small intense look that is over in a second, before he looks away, embarrassed. I see the door is open to the small room at the end of the corridor, and realize he has come from there. He must have heard me running my bath, perhaps he even heard the conversation with his mother.

"Any trouble on the way up?"

"Not really," I say, thinking of the raid on the market, the woman with her baby. I'm not ready to share these things with a stranger.

"Sara won't like her being in the house," he says, nodding his head at Juno, who stands at my heels. I find it strange that he should call his mother by her first name. "She doesn't like dogs."

"I'll keep her out of the way."

We stand in silence for a few seconds, then he looks up. "Your room. I'm sorry—"

"I don't mind," I say, although it is not quite the truth.

There is a whooping, leering call outside and I start. It is the first time I have heard a hyena since I have been back and it catches me unawares. I had forgotten its awful, mocking sound, the undulating wail of a lunatic.

"Are you scared?" he asks.

"Should I be?"

"They mimic the call of wild animals."

"Who?"

He looks at me strangely and all of a sudden I know who he means—Mau Mau. In that moment his fear is contagious, and I am acutely conscious of how unprotected we are against whatever might be outside. I glance down the corridor to the dark panes of the uncurtained window. It is a long time since I have been in the bush, so far from other people, other houses. My father has cleared a few thousand acres for his crops and grazing, for the native *shambas*, but most of the fifty thousand acres on the farm are still forested, thick heavy scrub with gorges and valleys full of caves—perfect hiding places.

"There aren't any Mau Mau here," I say, banishing the fear by naming it. He must have been wound up by the stories in the newspapers and the reports on the radio of men living in the forests, stockpiling weapons.

He shakes his head slightly, then beckons with his hand—the hand with the camera—and walks down the corridor to the spare room, taking the lamp with him. I find myself following, unsure what he wants of me or what to make of him. He is all angles, narrow hunched shoulders, slender hands, a rash of fuzz on his cheeks. His hair is muddy blond, but I can see his mother in the delicacy of his cheekbones, in the curving slope of his lips.

He has taken ownership of the room, turning it into a workplace of sorts. The single bed, with its metal frame, has been pushed against the wall, and there is a wide plank of wood resting on crates which serves as a desk. One section is covered in little bottles with screw tops, a stack of trays, Kodak boxes, clips, something that looks like a thermometer. The curtains are open but a piece of felt has been tacked neatly to the window frame. He has made a darkroom. He lifts his lamp to place it on the desk, and I see a pile of photographs strewn across the worktop. They are all of the same image, in varying exposures, showing the lower half of a man, upside down, protruding from the earth, his body held up by the depth of the hole.

"Did you take this?" I ask, my voice dropping to a whisper.

"Mau Mau buried him alive," he says, behind me. "Facedown in an ant hole. An informer in Nyeri."

"But why were you there?" I'm shocked. He seems too young to be witnessing something like this. To be allowed to pause over it and make a record.

"The District Officer took me on a field trip for a few days. He is a friend of our parents," he says, tipping more photos from a pile onto the desk in front of me.

Our parents. There it is. My father and his mother; the two of us linked now, whether we like it or not.

"Where did you learn to take photographs?"

"An American taught me. He stayed with us for a few weeks—gave me a camera, showed me what to do—" I remember the extra film that Nathaniel brought for Harold. Sara's words, like an accusation—*he's out on the farm, taking photographs.*

"Nathaniel Logan?" I ask.

"Do you know him?" His eyes lift to mine.

"He drove me up here."

"Nate Logan? Is he still here?" His voice is tight with anticipation.

"He left about an hour ago—" I say. "He gave your mother some film for you."

His face drops, raw with disappointment.

I glance down at the photographs on the table: a bull elephant lifting his head from the muddy shores of the dam, water dripping like rain from his tusks; a lioness crouched low over the carcass of a zebra, its body held tightly beneath her own; an impala, ears erect, staring. More striking than these are the photographs of the Kikuyu: young workers, bare chested, leaning against heavy, wooden-handled tools; the slick, muscular backs of a group of boys dancing; a laborer on a stool, hands pulling the long, white teats of one of my father's cows. And there are other images, which must have been taken at Nyeri. A man lying on the floor, his arms strung behind his back, a woman kneeling, barbed wire, a pile of guns. I don't look carefully. I don't want to see. They are all too intimate, wrested from the people they are capturing.

But there is one I glimpse among the others which I cannot turn away from. I slide it from the pile. My father embracing Sara, his hand making an impression on her skirt, grasping it so tightly that it is hitched up to her thigh. She is looking over his shoulder, oddly detached from the embrace, her eye steadily catching the camera, aware of her son's glance. I swallow, uncertain, and look away.

"They've been oathing on the farm. In the *shambas*," Harold says, though all I can see is the photograph of my father and his mother and I know he must be conscious of it too.

"I think what you have seen in Nyeri has scared you," I say softly.

He shakes his head. "Your father says it isn't true, but I know. I've seen their faces change." He gives me a quick look. "Do you know about their oathing ceremonies?"

"Only what I have read in the papers."

"They drink goat's blood. And they make a vow. *When the war-horn is blown, if I leave the European farm without killing the owner, may this oath kill me.*"

"Even if you are right—even if some of them have taken an oath—I don't believe they can mean it," I say. "Perhaps in Nairobi, in Nyeri, but not out here."

He looks down at his hands, the pale, fine-boned fingers, and does not speak. There is something disconcertingly adult about him, as though he has spent a great deal of time on his own, learning to map out his fears, and how to handle them.

I leave him standing there with his photographs, and make my way back along the corridor, through the sitting room, and out of the back door into the night. The air is cool and fragrant, and I stand for a moment—my hair damp against my neck—breathing deeply, letting the conversation with Harold dissolve into the dark. Down the flagged path is the kitchen; a low brick building, separate from the main house, and shielded from view by a dense honeysuckle hedge. Juno trots across the patch of light that spills out of the open door and disappears into the night. I stand in the doorway and look in. Smoke curls up from the old stove oven. Onions frying. The familiar smell of food being cooked outdoors.

Two kerosene lamps hang from the low corrugated roof, throwing out flickering pools of light, swimming with the shadows of moths and long-legged insects which pop against the glass. A long table stretches down the center of the room. I used to sit here as a child on hot afternoons and peel the crayfish I had caught in the dam. And when my mother was working late on the farm, Jim fed me here in the darkened kitchen, *posho* and cooked beans scooped up with my hands, legs dangling from the chair, eyes itching with tiredness, the throbbing of the cicadas in my ears, my fingers sticky and warm. And I would watch Jim standing in the open doorway, smoking, listening to the noises of the night.

He has his back to me now, stirring a huge black pot. He has not heard me. The familiar broad shoulders force a catching in the back of my throat. A gecko croaks and flickers across the wall.

"How are you, Jim?" I say.

He swings around and stares at me for a moment. Then laughs, and I see his gold tooth gleaming in the light. "Aleela!" He comes toward me, pulling me into him, and like a child I give myself up to his embrace.

He draws back, wiping his hands on his white smock. "I heard your car—"

"But you were too busy to come and say hello?"

His gaze shifts away from mine, and I remember the way Sara had said, *Jim is in the kitchen.* I should have known. She does not like him in the house.

"I've brought you something—" I hand him the two English reading books I bought in England.

He takes them from me, his dark hands falling across the cover of the one on top—an English girl and boy in a green garden, behind a white picket fence. "*Asante,*" he says softly.

"You don't want them?"

He doesn't reply.

"Where is your primer?" He always kept the grease-spattered English grammar book that my mother had given him tucked into the pocket of his tunic. If witches cast spells while they stirred their cauldrons, Jim cast his magic with conjugations.

"The new *memsaab*—" he says, handing the two books back to me. "She doesn't like me reading," and I flinch at the title which had always been reserved for my mother.

"I'll have a word with her," I say. "She can't mind you improving your English. It's absurd."

He shifts his weight, but says nothing, and I realize he knows better than I do that my authority is less than hers. "Well, I'm sure she won't mind you reading these," I say, giving him the three women's magazines I have brought with me from England, their back pages full of recipes.

He turns the thin pages over with his large fingers. My mother had spent days with Jim in the kitchen, unraveling recipes from an old cookbook of my grandmother's, and he had supplemented this knowledge from the back pages of her *Women's Monthly*, teaching himself rudimentary English and showing an extraordinary talent for concocting strange dishes from the far-off country that my parents called home—soufflés, trifles and pastry cases—that he had never tasted. Now he places the magazines carefully on a shelf, shakes flour out onto the table, picks up a mound of dough and begins flattening it with a hand-fashioned rolling pin.

"What are you making?" I ask in Swahili.

"Beef and onion pie. Raspberry sponge."

"My father told you I was coming home," I say, smiling. These were the dishes I asked for as a child, when my mother let me choose.

"It has taken you a long time," he says.

I watch him work, the rolling pin heavy in his hands, the pastry turning deftly in his fingers, and wonder what never occurred to me as a child: how he produces such things in the near darkness.

"Is your family well?" I ask in Swahili.

"*Mzuri,*" he says. "*Mzuri sana.*"

"And Ngina? Mukami?" I ask after his two wives.

"Both well. And I have a new wife now."

"A new wife? Your third?"

"Yes, Aleela," he says, still turning out the pastry. "I call her Waceke."

"Waceke—the slim one?" The Kikuyu word comes back to me.

"Not anymore," he laughs, a deep, rocking sound, not looking up from his work. "She is with child."

MY FATHER IS ALONE in the sitting room when I come through. The fire is lit and the flames throw a shifting yellow light over the room. Incense—burning sandalwood—fills the air with its heady, aromatic smoke.

"You've been to see Jim?"

"Yes," I say, sitting down in the old armchair opposite him. My father is a tall man, and broad, with a physical presence that can dominate a room. He nurses a glass in a large, knuckled hand, his fingers round and flattened from years of clearing the land. He is wearing a felt waistcoat and brown leather shoes with laces, instead of the old slippers which he used to wear around the house, and he has shaved off the thick beard that used to cover his heavy jaw. He looks naked without it. His hair—cut shorter than it used to be and combed into a parting—is graying at the temples. The whole impression is more refined than the one I am familiar with— smarter, more ordinary. I realize with a small shock that when I look at him I don't see my father. He is a man, a stranger, and this detachment makes me feel as though I am losing my grip on reality, spiraling away from what I know to be real. The same panic I felt when I was alone in my room rises in my throat and I swallow it down.

"He has been looking forward to you coming back. We all have—" he says, and I wonder who he means by *we*. For the last six years my father has been out of reach. I thought I only needed to come home for things to go back to the way they were, and yet— now that I am here—he feels farther away than ever.

"I brought him some books—Dick and Jane—but he wouldn't take them."

"He doesn't read anymore—not like he used to," my father says, without blinking.

"Oh—" I lean forward. "But he didn't say that. He said he wasn't allowed to read. That you had forbidden it."

His eyes flicker away from mine. "I don't think we said anything as strong as that. Sara felt he was spending too much time with his books and not enough time working. She had a few words with him, and that was the end of it."

"What about the primer?"

But my father's attention has shifted. I follow his glance. Sara is standing in the doorway, dressed for dinner—a white collared shirt tucked into long, tailored khaki trousers. She looks both too sophisticated for this unpolished room, and strangely compelling—there is no one else here to impress—it is all for my father, and as he stands up and puts a hand to her waist, she lifts her chin to kiss him on the mouth, her lips slightly parted. The gesture is intimate and I find myself looking down at my hands.

"You're talking about Jim?" she asks. "I'm afraid I felt compelled to throw that book away."

"But why?" I ask, unsure of the tone in her voice.

"Because it was filthy—" She goes over to the bureau and pours herself a drink. "I saw mold growing between its pages. And it was distracting him from his work."

"It was given to him as a gift."

She sips her gin. "What possible use could it be to him?"

"He was learning English."

"And why does he need to speak English?" she asks, with a

small, tight smile. "It was only putting ideas into his head. Sooner or later he would have been spoiled, and then he wouldn't have been any good to anyone."

"Why should he be spoiled by learning English?" I am not sure I completely understand.

"Darling, he's a good man," my father says in soft admonishment, calling on her for respect, if only—I see—for my sake, trying to put an end to the conversation. "He has been with us for years."

"I reserve judgment," she says, sitting down at the other end of the sofa, cradling her glass in her lap, "on a man who has married three times."

"It is their custom—" my father says, and I realize they have had this conversation before.

"His last wife is not a day older than you, Rachel"—she says my name for the first time, slowly—"and he laid his sweating, greedy body over hers, and now she is with child."

Despite myself I feel my face reddening. And then—cutting across my awkwardness—come the crisp tones of an English voice. It is the news broadcast. I look up. Harold has come into the room without me noticing and has turned on the radio. *This is London.* We fall still, listening. The notes of "Lillibullero" fill the room, and for a moment I think I can smell the rain, the wet concrete, the streets of England four thousand miles away. There is news of the Queen's Coronation—an official proclamation has been made in London, with the date set for the second of June next year. A British expedition is being put together to make the first ascent of Everest. And then local news. My father leans forward in his chair, listening more keenly. More Mau Mau crimes in Nyeri and the Kikuyu reserves; the bodies of several Kikuyu police informers have been found beheaded, floating in the Kirichwa River. The government has responded with a wave of arrests and an extension of the curfew across the region.

When I ask my father afterward what he thinks, he says that he is confident the government will do what is necessary to control the rebellion, that the violence is unlikely to come to as remote a place as Kisima.

The new houseboy, Mungai, serves us dinner, dressed in a uniform I haven't seen before—white, with a burgundy sash, and a matching burgundy fez—something Sara must have introduced.

"You didn't tell me Nate Logan was coming," Harold says to his mother when Mungai has left the room.

"Should I have done?" Sara asks, her fork hovering in midair, her voice lifting in surprise.

"You know I should like to have seen him," Harold says.

"I'm sorry, darling—I forgot you two were such close friends." There is just the hint of sarcasm at the edge of her voice.

Harold does not say anything more, but the color has rushed to his cheeks, mottling his pale skin red, and I sense that by asking about Nathaniel he has given her the upper hand, a clear target on an old battleground.

Jim's cooking is as good as I remember it. The pastry on the pie is soft and buttery, and the sponge—with its hot, sticky layer of raspberry jam—welds itself to the spoon so that I have to peel it off with my teeth as I did when I was a child.

After supper Sara goes to bed and Harold disappears to read. At last my father and I are alone together. He pours himself a drink, throws a log on the fire and stirs it with an iron. I sit down on the huge hearth, with my back to the mantelpiece. Juno turns a circle in front of the flames and lies down, the tips of her coat glowing red in the fire's light. My father stretches out his legs, kicking off his shoes, rubbing the arch of one giant, socked foot against the other. "He's a decent boy, Harold. A little quiet, but decent all the same."

"Yes," I say, looking up, waiting for him—now that we are alone—to say something about my mother's death, to bridge the years that we have spent apart, to ask about the long journey from England. But instead he says something that completely throws me. "I hope you'll make a particular effort with Sara, now that you are here."

"Of course—" I say, swallowing uncertainly, trying to hold back the emotion that is rising inside me. After all the years that have passed, he has chosen only this to say to me.

"It's not easy for her living up-country." His mouth twists, and I see both anger in his face and embarrassment. "Not everyone has been welcoming. She has had to give up an awful lot, and she isn't used to it yet—the distance from Nairobi, the lack of friends."

"Nathaniel Logan stayed for a while?"

He takes a long sip of his whiskey. "Yes—for a few months. I rather liked him, but in the end there was a row; he made some comment about white settlers in Kenya clinging on to their status as self-made aristocrats, lording it over the African. I can laugh at that sort of thing, but she took it too much to heart. And she didn't like the way he and Harold used to disappear into the bush for days on end with their cameras. Now even the Markhams rarely come." He looks up. "She'll enjoy having you here as company."

"I hope we will get along—"

"I know she does too." He smiles at me, pleased that I have acquiesced, that I have put to bed the niggling worries of this domestic drama. But I am left with a bewildering sense of isolation. And something else that sits heavily on me. A foreboding that I will not be able to protect him. That he has irrevocably attached himself to someone who is dragging him into unhappiness.

After a moment I say, in an unsteady voice, "When did you meet?"

"Two years ago. You remember the Norfolk?"

"Yes." The Norfolk was a hotel in Nairobi, popular among English safarigoers. "She was in Kenya on holiday?"

"No—she was working there. Her husband was an engineer—got a job in Nairobi before the war. She followed him over with Harold, and six months later he left her—no money, no house, nothing. She worked for twelve years to support them both. A hell of a life." It explained why she seemed different—not entirely at ease out here in the bush, the smart clothes, the lipstick. She wasn't from a farming family.

"She's done as good a job with Harold as she was able, but it wasn't easy, all on her own. I've tried to get him interested in the farm, but his heart isn't in it. His mother would like to see him out hunting with me, but it's obvious he would much rather have a book or a camera in his hand than a gun. He spends all day on the labor line, at the plantations, down at the *shambas*, taking photos of Africans. Drives his mother crazy—" He swills the rest of the whiskey; the yellow liquid clings to the sides of the glass. "I thought Nate Logan was a good influence on him. Before he came Harold barely said a word, but—" He shrugs his shoulders.

"But Sara didn't approve?"

"His mother wants him to be what all mothers want their children to be."

"Which is what?"

"Oh, I don't know." He knocks back the last of the whiskey. "He's all she has. I suppose she just wants him to be a regular boy. Equipped for a good shot at happiness. Someone she can be proud to call her son."

Silence falls between us.

"When were you going to tell me—about Sara?" I ask eventually.

He looks up. "There was no time—you were on a ship to Mombasa before I could reach you."

"But before that. Why didn't you tell me before?"

"I would have done if I had thought you needed to know. But what difference did it make when you were in England? It might only have upset you."

"I had a right to know," I say, hearing my voice shake with the courage of saying it. "The truth is still the truth even if I wasn't here to witness it."

My father looks at me, his eyes lit with a weary impatience. "I warned you not to come, Rachel. Don't blame me for what you see now that you are here."

I RISE AND GO into the hall, where I stand with my head against the tall mahogany bureau, listening to the ticking of the grandfather clock, breathing to steady myself. When I think there is no longer any danger of my crying, I open the bureau drawers and find what I am looking for—a pair of steel scissors, a cloth and a tin, and a screw-top bottle of paraffin. I go back into the sitting room. My father isn't there. I crouch down next to Juno and begin cutting the burrs from her fur, as my mother used to. It takes time, and her coat is rough and uneven when I have finished. Then I pour the paraffin into the tin and dip the cloth into the cool liquid, rubbing it onto the ticks to loosen their grip.

"I didn't want to upset you, Rachel." He is standing in the doorway.

I don't trust myself to speak.

"I'm happy to see you. Of course I am. But I am worried too. You asked earlier about the violence in Nyeri. The truth is I cannot pretend that I'm not concerned. Men from Nairobi have stirred the Kikuyu's imagination with talk of land restitution. There is a discontent in Kenya that I have not seen before. Perhaps it will all blow over—but I don't want you getting caught up in any trouble."

"I have nowhere else to go, Papa," I say, looking up at him. "This is my home."

"I know," he says, hovering above me. "I know." I catch the note of something desperate in his voice. I think he might drop his hand onto my shoulder—I anticipate the weight of it, the breadth of his palm, the strength of his fingers gripping me, but it doesn't come, and I feel its absence just as strongly as if it were there. After a while he moves across the room, and I hear him checking the latches on the windows, bolting the door.

I work on removing the ticks, tight and fat, nestled in Juno's coat. Her skin twitches, and she lifts her head to watch me, but the stillness of her body speaks her gratitude. I pull out the last one, grasping it between my thumb and forefinger, watching it for a moment—its legs crawling on air, before flicking it into the fire. Then I gather up the handful of matted hair that I have snipped from her coat, and throw it onto the flames. The hairs curl and singe—a thousand red filaments dissolving into a sharp acrid smoke that coats the back of my throat and makes me cough.

MY FATHER WALKS ME to my room. I am aware of the house very quiet around us, and the knowledge that soon I will be left on my own at the end of this corridor.

"Are you all right down here?" he asks as we reach my door, the floorboards creaking under our feet. "Sara thought you might be happy to have a bit of privacy."

"Yes, of course."

"You're not still scared at night?"

"A little," I say, smiling in the dark and he reaches out and squeezes my hand, an acknowledgment of my old terrors, the nights when I crawled into their bed, scared of the moon's shadow on the wall. The sudden intimacy of the gesture—the rough graze of his hand closing over mine in ownership and protection—shocks me. I want to turn to him, but I do not dare; he might not pull me into him as I need him to.

When he drops my hand, I reach for the door handle, but do not turn it. I want to hear him speak my mother's name. I want—just for one moment—to resurrect the past. For things to be the way they were before. But I find I can't articulate any of this—I am worried he will not understand. So I say instead, "Where are Mama's things?"

"We saved the bits and pieces that we thought you might want."

I have an image of her wardrobe full of cotton trousers, hats, jodhpurs and dresses where I used to sit and read under the window as a child; her books; her collection of fossils and stones. "We?"

"Sara and I. They're in boxes down at the stables, in the barn."

"But what about you? What did you keep?" I ask, wanting to believe that he held on to something for his own sake. That he hasn't so completely renounced the past. I want to know that it was difficult for him living here after my mother died. That he struggled to cope without us. I need to know that it meant something, the life we had here. That it cannot be so easily forgotten.

"Oh, I don't know, darling." He draws a hand over his face and breathes out. "It was all a long time ago. I don't like to think about it." He leans down to kiss me on the cheek, and says, "Good night, my love." But I am not sure, as I close the door of my room, that the word has any meaning.

Juno sniffs the corners of the room, then—satisfied—flops down on the floor beside the bed. I change into my nightdress, check that the two curtained windows are closed and latched, then slip between the cool sheets.

I hear Harold walk past my door, from his room along the corridor, see the glimmer of his lamp, leaving behind him darkness and silence.

In the end—despite the dark, and my unease—I fall into a deep sleep, and when I wake it is morning. I lie in bed watching the light filtering through the edges of the thatching. Outside I can hear the rhythmic sound of a broom being swept over the dry earth. The cattle bellow as they are led down to the dairy, and—far off—I can hear women singing as they collect water from the dam. Juno sniffs wetly at my face and I slide a hand through her warm fur. It is hard to imagine that anything could be wrong on the farm.

VI

✦

Mungai is laying the breakfast table when I come out onto the veranda.

My father will be at the dairy checking the milk yields. He won't come back for his eggs for another hour or so. I slip round the back of the house to the kitchen. Juno follows me, waiting at the open door—she knows not to step over the threshold.

I gulp down a cup of tea, and Jim gives me a bread roll spread thickly with butter, a wedge of cheese in the middle. I take it gratefully, heading off down the track.

"Where are you going?" a voice behind me asks. I turn and see Harold watching me from the back door. His face is pale and there are dark rings around his eyes.

"I'll be back in time for breakfast—" I call out, leaving him standing there. It is my first morning home and I don't want company.

I take the route I have always taken. The earth is soft and damp, and dust rises in heavy plumes from the soles of my shoes. The sun has only just risen, and a jackal barks somewhere in the bush. A moment later something moves ahead of me in the thorny scrub, and I stop—my heart in my throat. All I can hear is the chattering of the weaver birds making their nest in the tree overhead. A buffalo charge is dangerous. My father calls them the "black death"—they have gored more white hunters than any other animal. A sudden explosion of sound, and a flock of guinea fowl burst out of the bushes, running down the track in front of me, cackling at each other. I laugh softly, my heart rapping against my chest. Where the large old olive tree stands, casting its black seeds onto the earth, the track splits. I head left down to the stables.

If the house was where I spent my evenings—the place I came back to at dusk, my legs scratched, and my hair stuck full of thorns—then this was where I spent my days, in the stables with the horses.

In a clearing are three outhouses built around a courtyard. On the left side is a mechanic's garage, and on the other—facing it—four loose boxes. The center section is a storage barn, with large sliding doors, where my father keeps the tractors he imports from England. The stable doors are closed, top and bottom, and I feel a pang of disappointment. My pony was sold years ago—my father had written to tell me—but he hadn't mentioned the horses: the black, long-legged thoroughbred that had belonged to my mother, and the neat, sure-footed Abyssinian horse with his soft, velvet nose who—though his withers were taller than my shoulders—let me slide onto his back in the stable, and slip my arms around his neck. There is still a scattering of old straw on the stable floor and the faint smell of sweat and leather. Without a horse I will have less freedom. I won't be able to roam so far from the house, and I will be more reliant on my father.

Everything is quiet in the garage, and I wonder if anyone still works here. A jacaranda tree drops its soft violet flowers like blossom over the dusty earth. Then I hear the clink of metal, and see an African pull himself out from underneath one of my father's jeeps. He is lean and tall, and moves with a supple strength that is familiar.

"Michael?" My voice is tentative. I had not expected to ever see him again. His sleeves are rolled high on his long forearms, and he cleans his hands on his overalls as he walks across the yard toward me.

"*Memsaab*—" His wide eyes settle on mine and I feel a gladness rising inside me, as it did when I was a child and he came to take my lessons. He represents something of my old life here, the way it was when my mother was alive.

He crouches down, giving a short whistle through his teeth, and Juno pads over to him, ears back in pleasure, pushing her nose into his dark, slender hands. He was a farm boy whose family had managed to raise enough money to send him to school. He had done well. So well that he had been accepted into high school, and when he returned from the war, my mother, defying convention and unable to find a governess who would live in so remote a place, had taken him on as a teacher. For a year he had given me classes on geography, English history and mathematics.

"She knows you," I say.

"She comes down here sometimes, when I'm working."

"She's grown."

"So have you," he says, standing up, his gaze holding mine, unembarrassed by the truth of it though I find myself reddening at this unexpected turn of attention onto me. "I was sorry to hear that your mother had died."

He is the only person to have said it, and I realize how much I have wanted someone to talk about her. Grief turns in my chest like an animal shifting in its nest; stretches its needle limbs into the corners of my body, into the backs of my eyes. I want to tell him what it was like—losing my mother, leaving Kenya so suddenly, about how strange it is to be back, and how much has changed, but six years is a long time. I am no longer a child. Instead I say—only now remembering—"I saw you the day she died. At the factory—"

"Yes—" he says, and I catch the flicker of something in his eyes. "I was staying with a cousin who worked there."

I would like to ask him about the man who was killed in that upstairs room; for him to say something to soften the horror of what took place, but he has closed down the conversation, and I do not know how to open it again.

"Why did you come back to Kisima?"

"There was too much violence in Nairobi, too much unrest. When I wrote to your father a year ago he offered me work."

"As a mechanic?" I ask, surprised. He is wearing the same overalls and sandals issued to all the farm workers. In 1945—just back from the war—he had worn his khaki uniform and army cap; it had set him apart from the rest of the Kikuyu labor; now he looks less like himself, more African; and I am aware of a different man—a stranger—who lies outside the grasp of my knowledge.

"Yes—" He turns over his black, oil-stained hands. "I trained in the war."

I have the uneasy sensation, standing here in front of him, that I want something from him—an acknowledgment of the past perhaps—that is as meaningless to him as it is to my father.

The sun beats down on us, and I feel myself slowing, unused to the way it crushes, layer upon layer of heat. I look over at the shuttered stables. "The horses have gone?"

"Your father sold them." His tongue flickers over his lips. "*Memsaab*, I have work to do—"

"Of course—" I say, letting him go, his words working on me as a kind of dismissal. He used to call me *memsaab* in gentle irony—I was only a child—but the title carries a different meaning now, though it isn't as simple as my being a European woman. It reinforces the inevitable distance that time has put between us. He is no longer my teacher, and as a laborer on my father's farm, there is little now to connect us.

I leave the yard and walk down to the dam. It is a shock seeing Michael again. I knew almost no one of my own age as a child, and when Michael returned from the war, I came to rely on the lessons he gave me; the world he opened up beyond the farm, beyond my parents. I had forgotten that I had seen him the day of the strike, at the factory; the memory lost in the events that came before, and the news that followed after. But time is unraveling, like ripples on the surface of the dam. In my mind's eye I can see the upstairs room at the factory.

IT IS EERILY QUIET. I am crouched in the cupboard, too afraid to move. Eventually I let out a moan, and push open the cupboard door. The African lies a few feet in front of me. The angle of his head—so still now—articulating the outrage of his death. After a moment I run, tripping over the dead weight of his legs, wresting open the door, out into the searing light of the balcony.

I stumble down the stairs, desperate to get out of the factory, back to my uncle's house. The blood is pumping in my head. I no longer dread the factory workers—but the officer's men—walking up the stairs and finding me here. The white plastered walls of the building fill me with horror; the dead man, the anger of the crowd, the factory's subtle stench of blood and death.

I turn and run, sliding down the concrete steps, into a tunnel of darkness. The voices of the crowd are a dull throb, almost as though the machinery of the factory is still turning. I swing round the corner into the corridor and run smack into a man who is coming the other way. I slam into him so hard that I slide off my feet and come down on my back, winded. He grips my arm and for a moment I struggle, not realizing that he is helping me up. We both see—in the murky light—the color of his hand against the white of my dress. I look up. *Michael.* He stares back at me, caught in the beam of recognition. I am catching at my breath, my chest tight and pounding.

He holds a handful of metal tools in one hand and a fold of papers.

"Who else is up there?" His voice is urgent. I am aware that we are both scared of being seen. His gaze flickers down the corridor. "*Memsaab*—tell me—did you see another man up there? An African?"

"He's dead," I say, my chest heaving with the horror of what I have witnessed, and the relief of saying it. "They killed him."

He swears. Slams his fist against the wall.

"What are you doing here?" I ask, rooted to the spot, my breathing short. I can see the engine room door open along the corridor, and a light on inside. Michael is supposed to be in Nairobi—he left the farm a month ago to become a clerk in an office in the city. What is he doing at Uplands?

There is gunfire in the yard and we look at each other, caught—

the two of us—in this strange middle world, outside of reality, where neither should be.

"Go." He nods at the door.

"You don't work for the factory." I am staring at him. His hair is no longer shaved. My eyes slip to the wad of papers he holds in one hand. They are yellow, the same color as the one the lead striker folded into the officer's pocket. His eyes settle on mine for a moment: the teacher caught out by his pupil, a conflict of interest, dislike for me or for the situation, something inexplicable. It all flickers across his face.

"Are you going to tell your uncle that you saw me?" He glances down the corridor behind him. "I need to know—are you going to say something?"

I swallow, shaking my head.

"It's all right if you do. But I need to know. Now. Whether you will lie or not? Maybe you do not want to lie?"

I shake my head again, sure that it is true. "I won't say anything."

There are voices outside, coming closer. "Go on—" he says again. His voice has that familiar American twang, picked up in the army. I slowly back up, then run down the corridor, conscious of him watching me the whole way, kicking open the steel door to reach the bright day outside.

I HAVE REACHED the dam, a shimmering, silver slip of water that stretches almost as far as the eye can see. White egrets float like flags over the banks, dipping their long bills into the mud. I shake off memory and walk down to the water's edge. The women have already drawn their water and left, leaving behind them footprints on the muddied shore. I see a hamerkop sitting on a branch which emerges from the water like the mast of a sunken ship. The bird's deep brown plumage and strange prehistoric head seem to come from a world long forgotten.

As I stand and watch, a herd of elephant emerge from the bush on the far side to drink, crowding round the water's edge. A hippo bursts air from his nose and it sounds like a greeting.

VII

-+>-•-<+-

I leave the dam, cutting across the valley through the cool acacia forest to the *shambas*. There is someone I want to find. Colobus monkeys chatter in the yellow branches of the trees overhead, and from somewhere in the forest comes the warning cough of a bush-buck. I hear the *shambas* before I come to the clearing. A lifting of voices filtering through the trees, a baby crying, the thump of a blade brought down on wood. Then a handful of children are at my legs, running in their bare feet, laughing and shouting, their shaved heads soft and warm beneath my palm.

Small, hard fingers search for the sweets which I dig out of my pocket, prying them from my closed hand, their mouths momentarily silenced by the sucking of sugar. I do not recognize these children. Most of them were not even born when I left.

In a clearing in the forest two dozen huts with thatched roofs are scattered across the hard ground. Smoke drifts into the pale sky. A scrawny cockerel struts across the dirt, crowing, and a dog trots up to us, sniffing Juno with easy familiarity.

Outside the entrance of a hut, two women stand beating out colored mats. One of them—stocky and strong—stops when she sees me.

"Aleela!" She raises a hand. It is Mukami—Jim's second wife. My mother enlisted her help in the house, sewing, mending and making clothes for the children. She has a child on her back, folded into the bright colors of a cloth. She smiles at me, speaking in Kikuyu—too fast, and when I shake my head she switches into Swahili and I begin to understand. She wants to know if I am happy to be back, if I am going to stay at Kisima. "Yes," I say, smiling, "yes." A drove of children weave in and out of where we stand. "Which ones are yours?"

"This one and this one," she says, placing a hand on their backs, but the children move so quickly among each other that I cannot tell them apart. Their clothes are stained and torn, the toddlers drowning in old shorts that have been hitched up around their waists with string; I have never seen them look so ragged.

Beyond Mukami waits another woman. "Njeri—" I say, breaking into a wide smile. I have found her. She smiles back, her wide, tapering eyes, edged with thick black lashes, glistening as she looks at me. Her head is shaved close to her skin as it had been when she was a child, throwing the smooth contours of her face into relief; brightly colored beads on her forehead shift against each other, a thousand drops of color. We were born in the same year, but I no longer see the girl I used to play with. She has a grace in the way she holds herself—none of my physical awkwardness.

She raises a long, smooth forearm, reddened with ochre, and touches her hand to my cheek. "Aleela," she says. I do not notice—

right away—what I should have noticed at first. That her belly—beneath the cloth that is knotted over one shoulder—is swollen. She laughs softly when she sees that I have seen and takes my hand, placing it where the cloth parts beneath her breasts, on the hard warmth of her stomach. I feel her womb tighten and stretch beneath my hand as the baby moves.

"When will it come?" I ask in Kikuyu.

"Soon," she says. In the strength of her hand holding mine to her belly is an understanding. Her mother was my *ayah*—she helped to look after me from the hour that I came crying into the world. My mother—immersed in her work—did not always have time for a small child. Njeri had shared her mother with me, without ever resenting it. We were brought up side by side when we were young, eating, playing and sleeping together. When her mother died two years ago, my father had written to tell me, and in the feel of this new life kicking beneath our hands, our shared sadness is transformed into joy.

"Who is your husband?" I ask, curious to know what it is like to be married.

She says a Kikuyu name, but I do not know it. "Jim"—she says, lifting her eyes to mine, shy suddenly, the word sounding awkward in her mouth, giving his English name. I feel a moment of surprise, of aversion, and struggle not to let it show in my face. Jim used to play with us in the kitchen at the farm; tossing us up in the air until we shouted for mercy; feeding us toffee on spoons, still warm from the pan. He had been like a father to Njeri. Sara's words ring in my ears: *his sweating, greedy body over hers, and now she is with child.* But Njeri does not have a father or a mother. As the cook of a European family Jim is considered a good proposition for a girl in Njeri's position; she needs a family who will care for her.

"He called you Waceke—" I say, puzzled.

She smiles again. "It is his name for me." And I wonder if Jim deliberately kept her real name from me, knowing it would be difficult.

There are two hundred Kikuyu men, women and children living in the *shambas* scattered across clearings in the forest. Most of them are out in the fields, or in the dairy, working for my father. I do not see in the faces of these women any sign that they have changed, that unrest has come to Kisima. Two girls I do not know pound maize with long poles, taking it in turns, and the rhythmic, knocking sound measures out time. A woman sits outside her hut, bent over on a stool, scraping and beating a hide to soften it. She stands up when she sees me, straightening out her back, grasping my hand in both of her gnarled ones. It is Wangari; she used to work in my mother's garden.

Then I see Joseph walking in from the field where the women grow sugarcane, beans and yams. He has a woolen blanket over his shoulders, and he nods his head, giving me a near-toothless smile. As he comes closer I see his eyes are milky in the sunlight. He has become an old man.

"Aleela," he says simply, smiling at me as he has always done, and I feel tears prick at the back of my eyes. He lived in the house with us. He witnessed every triumph, every knee scrape, every burst of tears. He was as much a part of my childhood as my parents, as the farm itself.

One of the very small children keeps losing his trousers—they are too big for his waist, and he has to collect them from the dust every few steps and hang on to them as he trots to keep up with the others. I feel Joseph's eyes, like mine, are watching him.

"Your mother brought fabric," he says, in Swahili, "and clothes. But now—" He gestures at the boy.

"And my father?"

He shakes his head slightly.

The children have gathered round us, and they are tugging at my shirt. A few of them hold on to slates that they have dug out from inside their huts. "They want you to sing them a song—" Joseph says in Swahili.

"Does anyone teach them English?"

"Not anymore," he says.

I let them pull me to a bare patch of earth, where they sit quietly, waiting. I feel awkward now that they are watching me so intently. I try to remember the lessons my mother used to give here, when I sat side by side with Njeri, on the benches she provided. For a long moment I think nothing will come to me.

Then I put both hands on my chest, and—feeling foolish— sing, "Aleela is here today, Aleela is here today, hi-ho the merry-ho, Aleela is here today." Njeri is laughing, one hand on her belly, remembering my mother. I turn to the child nearest me, the one who was holding on to his ragged trousers. He is startled, his eyes as round as bronze pennies. The other children laugh at his embarrassment. Then one of them shouts out his name—Mumbi. And I crouch down, hold on to both of his tiny hands, and looking into his huge brown eyes I sing softly, "Mumbi is here today, Mumbi is here today, hi-ho the merry-ho, Mumbi is here today . . ." He giggles shyly, pleased at being picked out.

I WALK BACK from the *shambas* to the house, past the kitchen garden. It used to grow an immensity of fruit and vegetables, but now it is overrun with weeds, waist-high, smothering the vegetable beds and competing with the fruit trees. The chicken coop, which produced fine eggs for my mother, is empty; the wire has been torn out and lies straggling in the soil. In Kenya, work for Europeans needs an overseeing eye, and in my mother's absence her garden has been left to go to seed.

My father is not yet back from the dairy when I come in for breakfast. Sara is the only one at the table. I stand at the door and watch her for a moment, not wanting to interrupt. Sparrows flit across the table, picking up crumbs. She has on a silk dressing gown, and she is reading a magazine from England.

Breakfast. Cheeks of mango and thick wet slices of red pawpaw, their middles scooped out, their flesh granular and streaked with yellow. Bowls of sugar, a jar of sweet peas, a jug of orange juice covered with a beaded muslin to keep off flies. Fig jam, plum jam, peach jam. Tea from a neighboring farm. An apple turnover that Jim has made, and which she is eating delicately, sucking the sugar granules off her fingers one by one.

Hull, with its miasma of concrete, its freezing winters, fuel shortages, and docked electricity seems like another world I dreamed up. There is no rationing here, no portioning out of sachets of sugar and our meager two ounces of butter and bacon, no limit on sweets and cakes, but a glut of all things. My grandmother—who struggled to scrape enough lard from her rations to cook Sunday dinner—would not have believed it. The farm is like an idyll of a perpetual

English summer, before the war, and I feel a stab of guilt that this fantasy of home is being lived out here, in Kenya, when back in England it is nothing but a distant memory.

"Rachel—" she says, without looking up, and I blush, realizing she knew I was standing there all along. "You've been out already?" She glances up at me, and I see a faint disapproval in her eyes as she takes in my dusty clothes.

"Yes—" I say, sitting at the table. "I've been down to the *shambas*."

"Well, we'll have to make sure there's plenty for you to do, now that you're back. Keep you occupied as a girl of your age should be."

"I was thinking I could give lessons to the children—" I pour out a glass of orange juice. "There isn't anyone teaching them."

"Ah—" she says, sitting back and looking at me in amused appraisal. "I suspected as much."

"What do you mean?"

"You're a sentimentalist. By all accounts your mother was the same—always wanting to make things better for the African."

"Shouldn't we?"

"Yes—as long as it doesn't set up unreasonable expectations."

"Why would they be unreasonable?"

She looks at me. "Show me a native who has ever benefited from an education."

"What about Michael?" His name sounds both familiar and strange; and I feel a moment of regret as I say it, as though by bringing him into this discussion I am somehow putting him at risk.

"Michael—" she says ponderingly, tapping her fingernails against the tablecloth. "Oh yes—the mechanic. Well now, that's a case in point. When he first started working here he was strutting about the farm like a peacock."

"What's this?" my father asks, walking into breakfast. Mungai steps forward pulling out his chair and pouring his coffee.

"Rachel was just saying that your mechanic was a fine example of an educated native." She turns to me. "In the end I had to tell your father to ask him not to wear his uniform. We couldn't have him distinguishing himself from the rest of the labor. Making it look as though all the Africans have a bad lot. Putting ideas into their heads."

"Sara," my father chides softly, "he fought in the war—"

"And what? That makes him entitled to the privileges of a European?"

I expect my father to defend him but instead it is Sara who says, "He'll only resent us, Robert, and then where will you be?"

A small silence falls over the table. Sara breaks it by saying, "Rachel wants to start up a school."

"Not a school—" I say, hurriedly, embarrassed by how formal she has made it sound. "I thought I could teach the children for a few hours in the morning."

"Well—why not?" my father says, absently. Perhaps I want his approval. I am disappointed when he takes a sip of his coffee and opens his copy of *The East African Standard*.

"Papa, have you been to the *shambas* recently?" I ask him when Sara has left the table.

He looks up from his eggs. "Why?"

"The children's clothes—they're dirty and tattered."

"Well—I can't do much about the dirt."

I think of the *shambas*, the children's ragged clothes, the washing strung up on the *boma* fence to dry. The Kikuyu who worked on the farm had made their way up from their lands around Nairobi many years ago, looking for work. Squatters, we called them, and my father had let them live on the land, grow their crops and graze their cattle, in return for work. They have almost no income and little access to outside help. "It's not a case of washing. They're ragged from being overworn. Most of them are half falling apart."

"What do you want me to do about it?" he asks, looking up, his voice hardening. He has a way, my father, of shutting down a conversation. An edge to his tone that is a warning. The conversation angers him, and I am not sure why. He was not, when I was growing up, unsympathetic to the Kikuyu who worked for him.

"Mama used to hand out fabric, make clothes for the children."

"I'll ask Sara to look into it—" His eyes hold mine, a challenge, and my heart beats a little faster.

I swallow and say, "I could organize it. If it would be easier for her?"

He gives me a fixed half smile. His eyes are cold. I can see he resents my involvement, the light it casts on the way things have changed. "I'm sure Sara would be more than capable, but if it's what you want to do, then by all means go ahead."

MY FATHER DRIVES into Nakuru the following day to pick up parts for his tractor. He gives me two hundred shillings and leaves me outside one of the large emporiums—huge, temporary structures smelling of incense, run by the Indians who came to Kenya to build the railway. Inside, the shelves are crammed with goods: rolls of printed fabric, boxes of lanterns, whitening powders, packets of insecticide, cake tins, ironing boards, mops and brooms and rows of cedar dining chairs—anything a settler might need to live. There are other women sifting through the aisles—women wearing trousers, men's shirts and straw hats—and when I see them out of the corner of my eye, I can imagine for a moment that they are my mother, but as they come close I look away, realizing with a lurch of disappointment that I do not know them.

I buy yards of colored fabric for the women, and two rolls of plain cotton for the children's clothes, needles, pins and thread. At least I can do this for them. The Indian man at the till wraps it all in brown paper and twine, and holds it for collection.

Afterward, I walk down to the Rift Valley Club where I have agreed to meet my father. In the street, men are unpacking a delivery for the fishmonger; baskets spill out ice and sawdust—lake fish from the Great Victoria Nyanza, delivered by the Uganda Railway, the lifeline for the Highlands.

From the windows of the club I can see the green mountains rising up above Lake Nakuru, the waters of the lake flushed pink with the flamingos who stand with one foot sunk deep in soda mud. A woman drops into the chair opposite; a wrinkled face, thin gray hair hanging greasily to her shoulders, her head shaking slightly as she looks at me. "Caught three Micks last night," she says, pointing with an arthritic finger to her folded copy of *The East African Standard.* I glance down and see a picture of three Africans—dreadlocks, wild eyes and white smiles, their chests naked under old army overcoats and animal skins. "Says the Africans will rise up and murder us all in our beds. A night of the long knives."

"Mother—" a man says admonishingly, hovering over her. "Sorry—" he says to me, grimacing in apology and taking her by the arm. She stands up and lets him lead her away, frail and suddenly obliging, leaving her newspaper behind.

When they have gone, I reach over and turn the paper around. The article says:

> The Mau Mau kill for pleasure, coming down from the forests with guns and pangas to cut open men, women and children; there are gangs of them living like animals beyond the reach of the law, and they take their vengeance on their own people for supporting the white man. They learned their guerrilla tactics during the war—and it is thought to be only a matter of time before they muster up the courage to start killing the Europeans whom they claim inhabit their lands, against whom their fury is really directed.

The article is almost certainly fearmongering. There has been no violence against Europeans—only against the Kikuyu who refuse the oath, collaborators and police informers. But my heart is beating a little faster. Try as I might, I can't put the picture of those men out of my head.

"*MEMSAAB*—" It is Mungai, stepping close to where I sit by the fire. "Mukami is waiting for you. Outside."

"What does she want?"

He does not answer.

The light outside is fading. I see Mukami and another woman standing like ghosts in the half light. Mukami gestures, and the woman unwraps the child on her back and places her feet down on the earth. The girl is scarcely two years old, and she squirms away when she sees me, unused to Europeans perhaps. I crouch down. She is naked below the waist, and I see immediately the wound which wraps around one thigh and across her buttocks, white and suppurating, the infection eating away at her flesh.

"What is it?" I ask.

"She fell into the fire—a few days ago. It is getting worse."

I place a hand on the girl's forehead. She has a fever.

"I am not a doctor," I say, standing up.

"Your mother helped many times," Mukami says, not moving.

Kisima is too far from Nakuru for the Kikuyu to make the journey when they are sick. I open my hands. "My mother was—" What is it I want to say? My mother was an adult? She was experienced? Neither of these things feels true of me; I have no idea how to help the child. "I will fetch my father—"

"We brought her to your father, when she fell into the fire. He asked *memsaab* to help—but she sent her away—"

Someone puts a record on the gramophone inside, and the voice of an American singer drifts—incongruously jolly—into the immensity of the landscape.

"I am sorry—" I say, shaking my head.

"Your mother had medicines—" Mukami says, ignoring my refusal, and miming the shape of a large box with her hands.

My mother's medicine chest. I find it in the bureau in the hall. It looks smaller than I remember it. There is a brass lock, with the key inside. I was forbidden to open it as a child, and I feel my mother looking over me as I turn the key; I do not have her approval yet. In the early mornings, before breakfast, she treated the Kikuyu who waited for her at the foot of the veranda. I would sit on the step in the shade, listening to her quiet voice, watching her skilled hands bandage, mend and heal. Inside are gauzes, rolls of bandages, a tin of iodoform, a large bottle of castor oil—its lid gummed up—Epsom salts, Dettol soap, cough stuff, aspirin and other bottles of pills whose names I do not recognize.

The smooth steel handles of the chest are cold against the palm of my hand. I carry it outside and place it on the veranda. Mukami squats down and waits for me to open it. Mungai is hovering on the veranda behind us, watching, and she barks at him to fetch water.

"Warm water," I say, understanding that Mukami wants to clean the wound. She is right. The first thing is to stop the infection.

When Mungai sets down a bowl beside me, I take the Dettol and pour out a capful into the water. I am reminded all at once—as the clouded liquid spills into the warm water—of her, of the moment when she had finished treating the Kikuyu and she would take me onto her lap and I would smell the same sharp odor on her skin.

I bring the lamp closer to the child and begin to wash the pus from the wound with pieces of cloth, dipped in the water. Mukami helps me peel away the dead skin around the burn. The girl stands very still, crying quietly. I find the iodoform—the same tin she used on my own cuts and grazes—and shake out the powder onto the wound. Then I take out an assortment of gauze, cotton wool and bandages and look at them, unsure. Mukami's hands take them from me, and deftly she does what I could not—bandages the child's leg and buttocks, the bandage winding around the child's waist. I should not be surprised. She used to help my mother in the house; I am not the only one who remembers her. I go inside and fetch two clean hand towels for the child to lie on at night, to keep the dirt from the bandage.

"Come back the day after tomorrow," I say, "and we will change the bandage."

"*Asante*," the child's mother says, and Mukami takes my hand briefly in hers. They turn and walk away, silently into the dark, their children soft, heavy bundles on their backs.

VIII

⇥ • ⇤

I rummage through my clothes and pull on a pair of clean, loose-fitting cotton trousers, bending down to roll up the bottoms. There is a crunch of tires outside my window and the swing of headlights across the wall; the District Officer arriving for supper. I slip on a blouse, fiddle with the buttons and pull over it a long, woolen cardigan. In the mirror on the dressing table, I can feel my grandmother's disapproving glance—she disliked me wearing trousers. I worry that I should change into something smarter, but I don't like showing my legs, and I feel comfortable in these boy's clothes which hide the curves of my body. I brush out my hair in the mirror, roll it into a tight knot at the back of my neck and look back at my reflection, bracing myself for dinner.

Sara is sitting in a corner of the sofa wearing a blue wool skirt and a silk shirt, the first few buttons undone so that I can see the top of a lace camisole underneath. Her shoes have slipped off and one calf is stretched along the length of the sofa, her foot resting in my father's lap. He has a glass of whiskey in one hand, and his other hand is kneading her foot. He stops when he sees me and slides her foot off his lap. Harold is sitting in one of the armchairs by the fire, reading, and his eyes flicker up from his book, in greeting.

It takes me a moment to notice the other man. He is standing by the bar pouring out a drink. I recognize him before he has turned around—the bulk of his body, the heavy, slouched shoulders, his thin blond hair. My hand grips the side of the doorframe.

"Rachel," my father says, standing up, gesturing toward him. "This is Steven Lockhart, the District Officer. A good friend of your uncle Eliot. Used to operate down at Uplands. Now he's on our turf."

The man turns around, drink in one hand, and looks at me, and there can be no doubt now—it is the officer who killed the striker at my uncle's factory. My heart is racing in my chest and my throat has dried up.

"Ah—Rachel—" he says, smiling at me. "I have been looking forward to meeting you. I'm afraid you'll see rather more of me than you might like. I'm setting up a Home Guard post to help monitor unrest within the Kikuyu. Kisima is my nearest stop for refreshment, and I have been taking undue advantage of your parents' hospitality."

I feel my cheeks burning. Memory rushes in on me; not just what I saw him do in the upstairs room of the factory, but what happened afterward, at my uncle's house. My hands flicker in and out of my pockets. They are all looking at me.

"A drink?" Steven asks, tipping the gin bottle at me, his eyes shining, enjoying my discomfort.

"Rachel?" My father's voice is touched with concern.

"I'll be back in a minute," I say, turning to walk out of the room, down the corridor to the bathroom in the hall. When I am inside, I shut the door and lock it.

I put my forehead against the door and close my eyes, taking in a ragged breath. It isn't just what I saw him do at the factory. There is something else.

TWO MEN ARE SITTING on the veranda of my uncle's house when I come running back from the factory. One is Roger Manning—a factory manager. The other man is the officer who killed the African striker.

"Where is my uncle?" I ask, swallowing heavily.

"Up at the factory," the officer says in a slow drawl, ashing his cigarette on the floorboards and kicking a chair out toward me as though he has been waiting for me. "Why don't you sit down?"

I walk up the steps onto the veranda and sit, hesitantly, on the chair. I can feel the telegram still crushed in my pocket.

"He was worried about you, Rachel," Roger says. "Came back and you weren't here."

"Been up at the factory?" the officer asks, swilling a bottle of beer in his left hand.

I nod slowly. I am so thirsty my throat is sticking, and I don't trust myself to speak.

"Should have listened to your uncle," Roger says, running a hand over his jaw. "Said he told you not to go anywhere near the factory today."

There is something surreal about both men, their speech slow, their conversation inward. I know drunkenness—I have seen it before at the farm.

"Don't be rough on her," the officer says, leaning forward to look at me, with both elbows on his knees. He is younger than my father, but his cheeks are coarse and red. There is something corpulent and louche in his manner. Not quite the neat self-discipline of the army officers who are my parents' friends. His eyes—now that he has turned them on me—have a flashing, intuitive directness, as though he might poke about in my soul and fish out what he wants. I swallow, wishing my uncle would come home. "She might have learned a thing or two. What did you see?" His voice is slow and inviting, a deep drawl. He is seeing what he can wind in.

"The pigs. They were scared." I look him straight in the face. "They shouldn't have taken in so many of them."

"Ah—the pigs," he says with slow sarcasm, leaning back in his chair and kicking out his boots. "They do tend to be the losers in a place like this."

They both laugh.

"Have you been fixing something today?" the officer asks suddenly, his eyes settling on mine.

"What do you mean?" I ask, confused.

"The mark on your dress," he says slowly. "It looks like engine oil." I follow his gaze. There is a dark streak of grease across the white sleeve of my dress, running under the seam. The grease that covered Michael's palm, oily black against the cotton. For a moment I think it might all tumble out of me—that I was on the first floor of the factory, that I saw him kill a man, but I swallow it down. "My bicycle," I lie, "the chain came off. I tried to fix it."

His eyes slide away from me, and Roger stands up, waving us both good night, walking heavily down the steps of the veranda into the darkening evening. I stand up, wanting to shout after him,

Don't go. Don't leave me here with him, but my chest is too tight, and no words come out.

Instead I walk past the officer, into the house. My heart is rapping against my ribs. *My uncle will be home soon.* I try to breathe in the truth of it—but it doesn't stop the giddiness. I have caught his interest—I saw it in the way he looked at me.

The clink of a beer bottle, then the scrape of his chair as he stands up. I hold myself absolutely still, willing him to leave, but after a moment I hear the tread of feet on the veranda and the door pushes open. He comes a few paces into the room and stands in front of me, his face breaking into a slow smile, and I am immediately afraid. I see the blond hair on his thick forearms, his tongue licking at his lips.

At the last minute I move, but he reaches out, catching hold of my wrist, drawing me into him so that my face collides with his chest. I cry out, trying to get away, but his hands hold me fast, the skin on my wrist twisting under his fingers. Then he turns me around, so that my back is to his stomach, wraps his forearm around my waist, and sinks down into the armchair behind him, drawing me down with him, deep into his lap.

"Shhh shhh shhh," he says, pinning me effortlessly against him, laughing softly as I hit out at him with my free hand. "You're a prickly thing, aren't you?"

Like a dream in which your limbs are powerless—I feel with horror the feebleness of my own strength. After a moment I stop fighting, realizing it is only making it worse.

"That's a good girl," he says, loosening his grip, his hands cradled in my lap, his breath so close that I can feel the wetness of his mouth against my ear. "Now tell me what you saw today at the factory."

"I didn't see anything."

"Oh, but you see, I don't believe that's true. You came back looking like a rabbit that's been shot up the arse. You must have seen something."

"I heard the strikers. And the guns."

"Were you scared?"

"Yes," I whisper, praying for my uncle to come home.

"So you should have been. Have you thought about what those Africans could do? They're the ones with the knives, who know how to separate the soft parts of the body, bone from bone." He picks up my hand, unfurls two fingers and traces them down my throat. "The anatomy of a man is not so different from a pig. One slice to cut you from end to end." His hand drags my fingers over my shirt, down my chest, across my stomach, until my skin crawls and I can't bear it any longer. I leap up. He laughs and lets me run into my bedroom.

I sit on the floor with my back against the door, panic roaring in my ears. But he never comes, and eventually I hear his footsteps walking down the steps of the veranda. When my uncle comes home—in the dark, I can smell the stench of sweat on him and the thick, animal smell of blood. His eyes are hard and staring.

"Why didn't you come back sooner?" my voice breaks.

"There were four hundred of them," he says, sitting down to pull off his gumboots. "The engine was shot to pieces—we had to finish them all by hand."

His hands have been scrubbed clean but the bottoms of his trousers, where they tuck into his boots, are clotted with a thick, wet ring of blood.

I pull the telegram from my pocket and hand it to him, my heart beating darkly in my chest. He glances at my face before taking it, then sets his boots to one side and stands up. He turns on the electric light, and I blink in the sudden glare. He holds the note up to read it, and I see his fingernails edged black with blood. He has no choice then but to look at me. The crickets keep up their steady, urgent throbbing outside.

He shakes his head and passes me the bit of paper.

"What is it?" I ask in a whisper, not taking it from him, all the muscles in my body tense in anticipation as though this might make me less vulnerable.

"An accident. In the car, on the way to Southampton." He pauses for a second, dragging the words into reality. "It's your mother. She is dead."

His words fall on me like a knife—cutting through that soft part of me that I hadn't known was there until the moment it was severed. I reach out my hands to pull it back, anguish spilling out of me in a cry that comes from deep in my guts. Everything is quiet. I see my uncle lick his lips, uneasy with the responsibility the message thrusts upon him. I see Juno, oblivious, scratching at the door to be let out. And there is me standing in the middle of the room, my arms outstretched, the world falling away beneath my feet.

She died on her way to the boat that would take her home to me. My head explodes in a kaleidoscope of fractured images: the slaughtered pigs, the African on the floor of the factory, the blood in the car, on the road, and my mother, motionless, caught in time so many thousands of miles away, while I spin on into a future without her.

"WE'VE MET BEFORE, you know," Steven Lockhart says in a low voice as we make our way to the table. He has grown a mustache since I saw him last, trimmed short and not so thick that I can't see the pink skin between the white blond hairs. He licks at the tip of it, his tongue flickering in the corner of his mouth.

"I know."

"I hoped you might remember. That's good. I like to make an impression."

I don't reply and he says, "You've grown up." He brushes my hair lightly with one fat hand, an intimate gesture, and I flinch. "You were a scrawny brat when I last saw you." He doesn't say it with affection. There is something assertive and controlling in his voice. His gaze falls to my wide, turned-up trousers. "Do you enjoy dressing like a boy?"

I feel the blood rushing to my face, and I look away without answering.

"So, Steven—what's the news?" my father says at dinner, helping himself from the platter of roast beef that Mungai is serving.

"You heard they burned down a power station last night?" Steven chews at his meat and takes a slug of wine. "A farm on the foothills of Mount Kenya."

"Yes—" says my father. "And slaughtered some cattle?"

"A dozen heifers—hacked about with pangas."

"Where was the farm?" Harold asks, quickly, voicing my own concern. We can see the snowcapped peak of Mount Kenya from our terrace.

"About fifty miles from here—" Steven says, his eyes flickering to mine. "The Commissioner flew police dogs up from Nairobi this morning. They'll be out all night I expect—hunting them down."

"Honestly—" Sara says, licking wine off her teeth. "Talk about biting the hand that feeds you. You'd think they would be grateful for everything we have done for them—"

"I don't know about gratitude—" my father says. "They're caught in the middle of this—and what is the government doing to protect them?"

"Robert is right—" Steven pushes away his plate and leans back in his chair, and I find there is something unpleasant in the assumption with which he uses my father's name. "We're looking at a community which has advanced from the early Iron Age to modern times in little more than fifty years. Naturally it hasn't had time to adjust to the pressures of civilization. What we are seeing is the inevitable return to the kind of savagery from which they so recently emerged." He lights a cigarette, then turns his silver lighter end over end on the table. "The important thing is how the government tackles it from here. They need to come down on Mau Mau swift and hard."

"I believe we need a show of British justice," my father says, slowly. "They need to see that the law is both fair and firm."

"You've been here as long as I have, Robert," Steven exhales smoke, "and you know as well as I do that the African doesn't understand legislation. He only grasps what touches him on the raw; land, cattle and—ultimately—his neck. If this is a rebellion, and it obviously is, then anyone who takes part in it is guilty of treason and the proper punishment is hanging by the neck until dead."

"After a fair trial," my father says, holding Steven's gaze.

"After a fair trial," Steven agrees, his voice yielding, as if surrendering to the trivial niceties of a meddling conscience.

I glance at Harold. He has stopped eating, though he has barely touched his beef. He must feel the tensions around this table as keenly as I do. He has spent time with the Kikuyu; but he chooses to say nothing. I wonder as I look at him what he is thinking. There is a strength in him, in his quietness; he has learned to be invisible. I understand why my father—a man who likes to look something in the eye, and say it how it is—might not know what to make of his sideways, awkward reticence.

"I blame it on the whites in Nairobi," Sara says, dabbing at her mouth with her napkin, "mixing with the Africans, drinking at the same bars, sharing the same boardinghouses. If you had seen what I have seen, living in the city. The worst thing this government ever did was encourage immigration. I believe that what we're witnessing is a whole-scale loss of respect for the white man, and it jeopardizes our entire mission here in Kenya. Our prestige is being eroded by the bricklayers, electricians, hairdressers—who rub shoulders with the blacks, share their workload, and don't give a damn if this country goes to the dogs."

"Hear, hear," Steven says, jovially, raising his glass. I look at my father—he is staring across the table at the curtained window. I do not remember my parents ever talking this way before, and I wonder what is going through his mind. Why does he put up with Steven, sitting here at his table, dominating the conversation?

When Mungai comes in to clear the plates, Harold stands up from the table.

"Where are you going?" Sara asks.

"To my room to read—"

"Why don't you have another drink with Steven?" Her voice is quick with disappointment. "We don't have visitors very often."

Harold hovers over the table, unsure what is expected of him.

"That's all right—" Steven says, standing up and putting a hand on his shoulder. "You get yourself a good night's sleep. There'll be plenty more chances." When Harold has gone, he asks, "How old is he?"

"Coming up to sixteen," Sara says. "If only he would stop taking those wretched photographs of Africans and do something useful with his time. It's become an obsession!"

"Almost old enough to join the King's African Rifles," Steven says, licking his lower lip, not quite in earnest, testing the waters. "A boy of his age should be kept busy. Not left too much to his own devices."

"I don't think he would like the army," I say, surprised that he would even suggest it.

"Rachel is right," my father says. "It wouldn't suit him."

"Might do him good," Steven says. "Toughen him up a bit."

"Would they take him?" Sara asks, lighting a small, thin cigarette and inhaling deeply, her eyes squinting into the smoke.

"They might do," Steven says. "If I have a word."

"We'll think about it—" she says, sitting down on the sofa next to my father. Mungai serves coffee, black and pungent. Sara leans forward to whisper in my father's ear, her polished fingernails slipping across the inside of his thigh. His expression softens, and I look away, blundering into Steven's gaze.

He smiles at me, at what he knows I am thinking, and I stand up and leave the room, my face on fire. I wonder how much of a threat Steven Lockhart really is now that I am no longer a child.

The door in the hall is unlocked. I pull it open and stand breathing in the cold night air. From far off in the forest comes the slow cracking of huge branches. No terrorist could make a noise like that—it is elephant, moving through the acacia trees, looping up their trunks to bring down the high branches so that they can eat the leaves.

"Not scared?"

I turn and see Steven Lockhart standing behind me. I want to step away—a shiver runs from my neck to my torso—but I force myself to stand still. I am no longer a child. I will not be afraid.

"I thought," he says slowly, "that if we listened very carefully—we might be able to hear the dogs."

There is a small, charged silence. After a moment he opens the door a little wider and stands leaning into the frame. His gun is slung from his belt. He pulls a packet of cigarettes from his pocket and offers one to me. The cigarettes I brought with me from England ran out yesterday. I feel a tight yearning in my chest, but hesitate. He gives a low laugh. Unable to resist, I pull one from the packet and, holding back my hair with one hand, I dip my head to his lighter. His fingers—chunks of flesh—glow red in the flame.

I draw deeply, feeling the familiar, satisfying rush fill my lungs. He takes a cigarette between his teeth and lights it. I look at him. My father is in the next-door room. He cannot do anything to me here. When the flame goes out the night outside is black—only the shadows of trees, the whispering of the papyrus grass and the slow timeless destruction of the forest cracking in the night like thunder.

"I tracked a large bull once for a week in Uganda. The hunter said he had never seen such big tusks. He weighed seventeen thousand pounds. He was traveling with an *askari*—a young bull to protect him." He inhales, licking tobacco off his lower lip. "The hunter lined me up for the bull."

"Did you shoot it?"

"I shot the *askari*."

"Why?"

"Curiosity." He exhales slowly, looking at me. "I wanted to see what the bull would do."

"What did he do?"

He takes another short pull on his cigarette. It is the same motion I saw in the office at Uplands, before he killed the striker. I look away, but I can feel his gaze still on me. "I wanted to know if he would feel shame in running away, if it would try charging us, but in the end I felt like an idiot. All the fever that had consumed me while I tracked it was gone. It was just a damned animal running away through the bush, with shit running down its legs."

I take a last drag of my cigarette and grind it out against the wall. I am careful not to look at Steven, and I walk quickly inside.

His bedroom is at the end of my corridor, next to Harold's darkroom. A single room that shares a wall with mine. I lock my door, clean my teeth, pull a brush through my hair and climb into bed. Juno lies down against the door, and when—much later—I hear the heavy tread of his feet in the corridor, she growls low, the vibration filling the room. I hold my breath. He pauses outside my door—his weight seesawing on the creaking boards—just long enough—I think—to let me know that he is there. My heart is thumping. After a moment he walks on and I take a ragged breath, exhaling into the dark, reaching down a hand to steady Juno.

It takes a long time for sleep to pull me under. Just before it does a thought slips like a ghost into my mind. Briar Rose. A hundred years she sleeps and when she walks down from her tower the castle is unchanged. I have been hoping all this time that the farm would be the same, but no gentle fairy has built a forest of thorns around my home; or made sure that those I love would be waiting for me, unchanged, just as they were when I left them. I have come home to find the farm ransacked by a future I don't yet understand.

IX

→>·<←

Steven leaves early, his car rattling away in the milky light of dawn. There are footsteps in the corridor—Harold, going to his darkroom. He spends hours in there, behind the locked door, careful to avoid my father and Sara, only coming out for meals and to walk on the farm with his camera. In the late afternoon he returns to develop the rolls of film. I know because the smell of the chemicals he uses drifts under the door of my room.

I dress quickly in the cold and walk down to the stables to see what I can find of the things my father and Sara packed up. The yard is empty—it is too early yet for Michael to be working. My father has given me a set of keys for the padlock on the huge doors of the barn. I fiddle with the lock until the key catches, then slip off the padlock and push back one of the doors, letting the light flood in. Against the far wall, behind my father's tractors, I find three leather trunks piled on top of one another. I drag them down onto the floor and brush away the thick layers of dust.

My name has been inked onto the lid of one of the trunks in writing that is not familiar—Sara's, I expect. The other two are not

labeled and do not open when I try them—they need a key. Only
the trunk with my name on it yields when I unclasp the buckles. I
drag it close to the door of the barn, where sunlight falls on the
hard earth floor, and push back the lid. Inside are mostly old
clothes—crinkled and musty from years in storage. A pair of small,
white plimsolls, the rubber edges pulled back from the canvas, the
glue yellowing along the inside rim like the curling of old lips; a few
dresses; a handful of books; a photograph in a frame. An album full
of stamps collected from the letters which had arrived from across
the colonies—Malaya, Uganda, Somalia and from my grandparents in England. The plastic crackles as I peel it back to run my
finger over the many colored faces of the King. I look but do not see
the python skin I found on the shore of the dam; the king baboon
spider in a glass jar; the discoveries that marked out one day from
another, and sent me racing to the house to show my mother.

What remains is a small catalog of a childhood interrupted. I
look at the photograph. I must be about eleven, a year before my
mother died, with long, plaited blond hair and wide eyes, sitting on
my mother's lap in the Land Rover. I am grinning out at the camera, and she is looking down at me, smiling softly. My father must
be smiling as he takes the picture, her smile after all is for him, the
proud collusion of a mother and father, over the object of their love.

There are two cardboard boxes next to the trunk. They are too
heavy to carry, and I drag them forward into the light. Inside are
books. Some are my mother's—a few journals on fossils, the origins
of early man, a handful of novels, and two sewing manuals with
pull-out patterns.

The other holds my schoolbooks. I lift them from the box. A
geography textbook, a compendium of English history, mathe-

matical equations and a stack of leather-bound volumes—*David Copperfield*, *Robinson Crusoe*, a poetry anthology and a few Shakespeare plays. At the bottom of the box is my mother's book of fairy tales. I take it in my lap and turn the pages, the illustrations both beautiful and haunting. There were the evenings when she would slip, shoeless, between the covers of my bed, the lamp burning beside us, and read to me. And I would lean into her soft warmth, the sharp, earthy smell of whiskey on her breath, my whole being absorbed in the rhythmic sound of her voice.

When I step out of the barn Michael is in the yard. His eyes fall to the books that I am carrying. They are the same books we used to read when he gave me lessons.

"I found them in boxes at the back. I don't think they've been opened since you left Kisima—"

He comes close to where I am standing and takes one from my hands, wiping the dust off the cover with his palm.

"I thought I would teach the children—like my mother used to—"

"What are you planning on teaching them?" he asks, flicking through the thin pages.

"Letters, a little English, history perhaps."

I want to know what he thinks of the idea, but he has stopped turning pages and is absorbed in the text. I wonder if he has heard me. He looks up after a moment and smiles kindly, handing the book back to me, and I take it from him, frustrated by his reticence.

OUR FIRST LESSON. I am eleven years old. We are sitting in my father's study, the room which has been allocated for my schooling. There is a gentleness about him, a warmth despite the austerity of his face with its high cheekbones and wide-spaced eyes. His skin is very black, almost blue, and the insides of his hands where they lie half open on the table are pink like the underside of shells. We look at each other across the table. He seems relaxed, not threatened by me or the situation into which my mother has thrown us, but I am embarrassed and—as we look at each other—I fidget in my seat, wishing I was somewhere else.

"What have you been reading?" he asks.

I look in panic at the small collection of books my mother has assembled on the desk; I am not sure about any of them.

"*The Tempest*," I venture, seeing it in the pile. My governess insisted we read it aloud, twice right through. Something in the story of the man cast adrift on an island must have appealed to her sense of isolation.

He pulls out the old leather-bound book and turns it over in his hands. I wonder if he has read it. I am not sure what they teach Africans, and I don't completely trust my mother when she assures my father that Michael is capable of teaching me what I should be learning at school.

"Is there a good character in the play?" he asks.

"Prospero."

"Why?"

If he had read it, he would have known. "Prospero is the only civilized man on the island. He teaches Caliban to speak," I say.

"Caliban cannot speak?"

I shake my head. "No."

"How do you know?"

"Prospero tells us. He can only gabble."

"And you believe Prospero?"

"Why not?"

"What if Caliban spoke a language that Prospero didn't understand? Would it sound like gabbling to him?"

I look at him, still unsure whether he has read the play. "Perhaps. But why does it matter?"

"Because it means you cannot trust Prospero's version of the truth."

"But Caliban is just a slave," I say.

"And does a good man keep slaves?"

I look at him and blush, the blood rushing up my cheeks to the roots of my hair. I haven't been in the presence of someone like this before. It is as though all the people I have known up until now have been like toy soldiers with their feet set apart on a lead base, and he is real; in movement; on a course that I am compelled to follow.

"Authority is not a substitute for truth." He opens the book, finds a page and passes it to me. "Read it," he says. I look at where his finger marks the page, and read.

When thou camest first,
Thou strok'st me and made much of me—

I stop, look up. He is watching me.

—wouldst give me
Water with berries in 't, and teach me how
To name the bigger light, and how the less,
That burn by day and night. And then I loved thee
And showed thee all the qualities o' th' isle,
The fresh springs, brine pits, barren place and fertile.

Cursed be I that did so! For I am all the subjects that you have,
Which first was mine own king.

I look up at him again. His eyes settle on mine and he smiles. It is gentle, there is no animosity, just a stillness about him, a surety, that has a calming effect on me. As though he has a knowledge, a confidence that is also a kind of physical grace that cannot be corrupted by the fears of other men.

I ONLY SEE HIM ONCE when he is not at ease. My parents have guests for lunch and my mother puts her head round the door of my father's study at twelve o'clock.

"Michael? Come through," she says.

"He is a walking, talking dictionary," my mother is saying, proudly, to her guests. "He can recite all of Shakespeare's sonnets from beginning to end."

"I shan't believe it," the woman says, laughing, as we come into the room. We sit on the sofa, and Michael stands, awkward, in front of the cold fire. I know his body language better than my mother. I see from the way he holds his hands behind his back that he is uncomfortable. He licks his lips. I am sometimes asked to perform recitals in front of my parents, for their guests, so they can enjoy the novelty of seeing a child articulate something beyond her years. But Michael is not a child. He fought in the war. He was stationed in Burma. He showed it to me on the map—it is a country in Asia, thousands of miles from Kenya.

"Well, go on, son," the man says, looking up as he knocks the tobacco out of his pipe. "This is your moment to shine. Don't keep us waiting."

My mother looks at Michael, and I see doubt flicker across her face. She has set this up and now she sees that perhaps it is not right.

Michael shifts his feet. The silence stretches a moment too long to be comfortable. When he speaks his voice has a richness, a depth, as though the words, the way in which he says them, might overcome the situation in which he has been placed.

Being your slave, what should I do but tend
Upon the hours and times of your desire?
I have no precious time at all to spend,
Nor services to do, till you require.

I do not know the sonnet he has chosen. I look at my parents' friends. They sit still, listening, smiling appreciatively at the gentle irony of the verse. One sonnet follows another, seamlessly without pause, and I am drawn into the richness of his voice, which belies the awkwardness of his body.

There is a soft clapping when he has finished. "Where did you learn all this?" the man asks.

"At school, *Bwana*."

"What?" the man exclaims. "Africans teaching Africans Shakespeare?"

"Not all the teachers were African, *Bwana*."

"You had an English teacher?"

"Yes."

"At the Alliance High School," my mother says. "You must have heard of it? They are educating a new generation of Africans. The head should have been a professor of mathematics at Cambridge— he turned it down to teach here in Kenya."

"So much for the 'heart of darkness'—" the man says, chuckling wryly as he fills his pipe. "Kenya will be the very heart of civilization if this continues."

"Thank you, Michael," my mother says, nodding at him to leave. I think I can sense something of what he is feeling in the muscles ticking in his jaw.

"They'll cause trouble," my father said, when three of our Kikuyu laborers came back to the farm after the war, looking for work. "They've killed white men, and they've slept with white women. They won't have any illusions left." The same rules don't apply to Michael. My father says proudly that he is the ideal African—intelligent, hardworking, Westernized, always looking to the future. I tell Michael and he laughs. "Like a prize bull. All the qualities for the show ring." And I realize that my father's words are not necessarily a compliment though it is difficult to put my finger on why exactly they might be insulting.

I CALL JUNO over to the tap behind the house. I have a bottle of shampoo with me. I hold the skin on her neck with one hand and sluice water over her with the hose. Her coat is thick with dirt and grease, and I have to work at it with my fingers to get the water to penetrate. I squeeze a dollop of shampoo onto her back and lather it with both hands, the white foam turning brown as it mixes with the dirt. She curves her body into me, enjoying the feel of my fingers along her back. Then I soap her ears and around her nose, and she shuts her eyes and goes still.

When I run the hose over her back the soap slips away, streaming down her legs. She looks smaller under the slick, wet fur. I push my hand across her back and over her head, squeezing out the soap, until the water runs clear. Sensing that I have almost finished—she erupts into motion, escaping my grasp and racing across the lawn, water trailing out behind her, lips pulled back, urging herself on with the manic enthusiasm of a puppy. She chases her tail, then gathers her back legs under her in a sudden spurt of speed and turns wide circles on the grass. I watch her, laughing. She stops and begins on a long joyful shake. Then—nonchalantly, as though nothing has happened—she sniffs the earth and pads off into the bushes.

I sit on the grass, under the crisscrossed shade of the acacias behind the house, and take out a pair of knitting needles. I want to make a jumper for Njeri's baby, for the damp, cold evenings when the next rains come. I begin to cast on stitches following a pattern I found in one of my mother's books. After a few minutes Juno comes and stretches out on the grass in front of me. Her tan coat glistens in the heat, the fur tipped gold where the sun catches its edges. The clicking of the needles, the warm air, the shifting, flickering shade cast their languid spell over me, until the past has slipped its shackles and is spilling over into the present, like a waking dream.

MY MOTHER AND FATHER import ridgebacks from South Africa. *Lion dogs*, they call them in Kenya. They roam through the house, benevolently sniffing me, padding their huge paws, like lions, delicately past my stout, toddler's legs. They sleep by the fire in the sitting room, or stretched out on the leopard skin rug at the end of my parents' bed.

Eric Bowker—our nearest neighbor—has collies, the Markhams have Staffordshire terriers, and together these dogs have made their mark on our local population, breeding with the local *shenzi*, so that the mongrels that wander at the outskirts of our lives, panting in the *shambas*, suckling their litters in the shade of acacia bushes are a perverted miscegenation of pure breeding, with patchwork coats, short legs and once or twice a ripple down their backs from a lion dog forebear. Occasionally they produce a throwback that looks like the spitting image of some great-great-great-grandfather who had been brought over on a ship from South Africa or England with a document confirming the purity of his heritage.

My parents' ridgebacks disappear for days—then reappear tattered and panting, their lips stretched back from their white teeth, pink tongues flecked with dry white foam, eyes red and slanted. My mother and I spend hours picking thorns from their coats, parting the warm, dry pads of their feet to remove splinters, wondering what adventures they have got up to in the bush on their own, and where they have slept. Occasionally my mother has to administer stitches.

These dogs encapsulate the daring of adventure, and I sometimes follow them as they start out from the house, on sunbaked mornings, only to lose them in the bush as they find the scent that heads them off at a rolling gallop. Once they bait a lion and bring it right up to the house. The dogs snarl, paws deep in the dust, and the lion keeps its distance, grunting under its breath. My mother takes my father's rifle from the cupboard in the bedroom, and shoots at it from the bedroom window; the only time I see her pick up a gun.

For as long as I can remember I have wanted my own dog—but

it needs to be a good one. Lion dogs are expensive—my parents do not have a breeding bitch, and they have no plans to buy one. When my mother is in Nairobi for the weekend, an African we don't know appears at the house. Kahiki says he is *mchawi*—a witch doctor. A brass padlock hangs from one of his ears, his front teeth are missing and he is dressed in monkey skins. He uses an umbrella instead of a walking stick, and as he looks at us with his yellow eyes, I see that he carries something ragged and pliable in one hand. I stare at him from the dust of the yard, transfixed. The next day he is gone and he has left the soft bundle—a puppy—in front of the papyrus grass near the house. I can hear it mewling. The Africans are of two minds. Kahiki tells me it will die. Jim agrees with Joseph that the puppy is a bad omen—it has a *maganga* on it, the curse of witch-craft. I go to inspect it. Its ears are furless, and there are flies in its eyes that don't move when I turn the puppy over. Its fur is matted together with a brown sludge on one side, and it does not smell good. It opens its eyes and looks at me. Through its exhaustion and pain I see a gleam of humor and tenacity. Its tail lifts a fraction from the earth in a slow upward motion. And although I have no surety that this dog will grow up to be worthy of my parents' lion dogs, I know that I have decided and will not leave it to die.

"It's a *shenzi*," my father says. "It will die."

I beseech him, but he is firm. "We don't need another dog in this house, Rachel. And certainly not a *watu* dog."

"She will grow up to be strong. I know it."

"The *watu* won't like it," he says, shaking his head. It is not just Jim and Joseph. Word has spread of the *mchawi*. All the Kikuyu are saying that the puppy is cursed. "We will not take it in. End of story."

He calls Kahiki and tells him to take the puppy away, to give it food and water. I know he says it to appease me. I find the puppy on the old rubbish heap by the dairy, baking in the sun. A bowl of water has been left out for it, but it is too weak and too small to drink. I scoop it up, a dry hot bundle of ribs beneath my hands, and take it to the stables. I put it in a box in the corner of the unused stable and drip-feed it milk from my finger but it won't suck. I have heard my father say that if a lamb won't suck then it will die. My mother comes home that evening, but I don't tell her. This is my secret and I won't jeopardize it.

I don't go to my lesson that morning. A shadow falls across the open stable door. I look up in alarm. It is Michael. He crouches down and picks up the puppy in one brown hand and turns her over. Opens her mouth with his finger. She makes no sound.

"Will she die?" I ask.

"She needs worming," he says.

"You don't think she carries a *maganga?*"

"*Ajali haikingiki,*" he says, not really giving me an answer. *Fate cannot be changed.*

I steal a worming tablet from my father's office and give it to the puppy, opening her pink mouth with my finger, dropping half of the white pill into the back of her throat and massaging it down as I have seen my mother do with her dogs. I will her to live.

The next morning she is a little better. I clean her up and begin to feed her from an old baby bottle, rejoicing when she starts to suck. Michael does not tell my secret, and when I bring my mother to see her—a week later—the puppy knows me so well, following, stumbling and leaping at my footsteps, that my mother laughs and tells me I can keep her.

I call her Juno—the protector of women. She has lopsided ears. One stuck up and the other down. She is tawny gold with three black feet and she sits with such careful, exaggerated intent, holding back the energy that wants to send her careering into motion, that it is as though she is talking. I see in her the ridgebacks, and collies too, and I hope she will inherit the best of both breeds from her forebears. She is large-boned and quick-witted, and she carries the ridgebacks' dark ripple of fur down the center of her back. Only my father is not happy. He will not hold her on his lap, and I think about the *mchawi* and wonder if he believes she will bring ill luck. A few months later my mother is dead.

JUNO RAISES HER HEAD from the grass to look at me, as if she can sense me thinking about her, pants for a moment, stretches her mouth—smacking her lips—then lays her head back down, eyes open. She loves the sun, as though something in her genes—some ancestral Northern European blood—cries out to make the most of it before winter comes. I push my fingers through her coat. It is warm against my hand, a blanket of heat, and I shut my eyes, letting the knitting needles fall to my lap, giving in to the sun and the simple contentment of being home. I do not think it is possible that violence will come here and corrupt our peace.

X

⇥ • ⇤

I stay away from the house as much as possible. It is Sara's dominion, and she paces the corridors, walking restlessly from room to
room, listening to the gramophone. I feel her frustration and her
itching desire to get her hands on me and transform me into something that she can admire.

I set up my mother's sewing machine under the overhanging
shade of the stables, on a workbench—two planks of wood on a pile
of crates—and enlist Mukami's help, drawing up patterns from my
mother's books, pinning them to the fabric and cutting them out.
She works quickly, and we spend our mornings together in the
quiet of the yard.

Michael keeps to himself. Often I work for an hour, thinking
he is there, but when I look over I see that he has left the garage so
quietly that I did not hear him go.

The sewing is more difficult than I had thought, and I make
mistakes at first, and have to unpick long lines of stitches, my fingers turning red and sore. But I enjoy the feel of my mother's Singer
in my hands, the weight and simplicity of it, the turning of the wheel

beneath my palm, my arm aching, the needle flickering up and down, a tiny sword of light.

One morning, Harold walks into the yard with his camera. He lifts it in question, and I say, reluctantly, "All right."

He spends a few minutes taking photographs while we work. Later he gives me a print. It is taken from behind us; Mukami squatting down, bent over yards of fabric, Juno sprawled in the foreground, the side of my face just visible, one hand turning the blurred wheel on the glossy black machine so that the photograph has caught the whir of time, and I think it could be my mother sitting there, working.

"Thank you," I say, smiling up at him.

I WALK BACK to the house one morning to fetch a packet of needles from the bureau in the hall. Sara is standing in the sitting room at the window nearest me, gazing out onto the lawn and the track beyond. Her clothes are neat and uncreased, a leather belt gathering in the waist of her green dress. It looks as though she is waiting for someone to arrive. There are four or five farms close enough to make the two-hour drive to Kisima for lunch, to exchange farming news and recipes, and perhaps stay the night, but I haven't seen anyone in the few weeks that I have been home. Loyalty to my mother, perhaps, or a dislike for Sara, who isn't one of their kind and has made the decision to live with my father, unmarried.

In the past, our isolation at Kisima hadn't seemed so oppressive. It was broken by the university colleagues, photographers and friends who came up from Nairobi to see my mother, intending to stay a night or two and leaving after a week. And the Markhams—our closest friends—who drove over for the weekend, bringing gifts of food, settling in for long suppers under a full moon, hunting trips and fishing on the dam.

There were other farming families fifty miles or so away, who dropped in from time to time, bringing their children—and I would have the rare experience of looking at a European of my own age—face brown and hair bleached white like mine—staring as an ape does when it is shown its image in a mirror for the first time. Once or twice we drove down with other families to the coast, mattresses strapped to the roof of our car, and camped. I remember the moon glittering on a black, phosphorescent sea; a dog yelping in excitement; bodies slick and wet against mine, running through the whispering surf. I do not know where these children are now. Are they still up-country? Or have they gone to England? I did not know them well enough to write to them now and search them out.

Our only visitor has been Steven Lockhart, and I suspect my father puts up with him because we are all in need of company. Sara talks occasionally of going to Nairobi—the parties she and my father will take me to at one of the clubs, but no dates materialize. There were raised voices a few days ago when she sent out cards for a lunch party and letters came back declining the invitation. "All this tatt"—she said later, when we were having drinks, gesturing to the armchair which is molded to the shape of my father's body, the table that bears the nicks and scars of many years—"greasy and threadbare. It's not surprising no one wants to come." I saw her afterward, looking at furniture catalogs, but my father says we do not have the money for new furniture—not yet.

I do not mind the isolation. I grew up here. I spent my childhood roaming the farm on my own, and I relish the empty days; it is what I longed for in the cold, airless dormitory at school, ten girls crammed in a room. But as I watch Sara, I see that she is not happy—her posture is stiff with frustration and loneliness. I remember her saying, *Why would anyone come back to this place?* It occurs to me that she might not have wanted to come here; that circumstances in Nairobi might have driven her to Kisima.

"Are you waiting for someone?" I ask.

She speaks, without turning from the window. "Doesn't it strike you as odd that nothing which has been built on this land has ever survived? No cities or temples—no old roads, no ancient empires, no graves or burial mounds? Nothing to prove that generations of Africans have lived and died here. And when we are gone—what will there be to show that we ever existed? We shall disintegrate like everything else into an awful, blistering, sunny nothingness. I didn't expect it to be so—" She pauses, trying to find the right word. "So desolate, so barren."

"It isn't barren," I try to say. "If you would only go outside—"

She turns and gives me one of her chill smiles. "The women who come up here with their children, Rachel—what are they here for?"

"I am treating the child who was burned. She is getting better."

"Well, I don't want their lice and their diseases near the house. Before we know it they'll all be up here, asking for something or other. If you want to play doctor, you can do it down at the *shambas*."

I turn away from her, gritting my teeth in frustration. The girl's burn is healing; her fever has lessened, but I should know better than to seek approval from Sara.

MICHAEL IS STANDING in the garage. His hands are wet with grease. The various parts of an engine are laid out on a tarpaulin at his feet. He looks up when he sees me.

"Could you help me with something?" I shift my feet, conscious that this is an interruption.

He wipes his hands on his overalls and follows me into the barn. There—at the very back—are more boxes crammed full of books on farming and coffee plantations, packets of seeds and breeding manuals. Among them is a wooden case. The radio my mother bought; the one that used to be at the house, before I left, that brought news of the end of the war and the atrocities in Belsen.

I drag it out from between the boxes. "I thought you might be able to get it working." My father has set a limit on the news—he says he does not want to listen to the scaremongering of politicians, says he refuses to let Mau Mau take over our lives—so we listen only to the news at six o'clock and I am left hungry for more. The house is quiet, and the days are long. I want to listen to other broadcasts, plays and music, and I want to know exactly what is unfolding in Kenya, just as it happens.

The radio is heavy, and I struggle to move it over the earth floor. Michael squats down and grasps it in both hands, lifting it easily and carrying it outside.

The surface of his workbench is scattered with metal tools, a circular saw, a few bits of wood which have been chewed up by a blade. He clears a space and slides the radio onto it. I watch him feel the wood veneer, brushing the dust off it, touching it with care.

"You might not be able to get it working."

"It'll work fine," he says, picking up a screwdriver and opening the back.

"How do you know?"

"Your father brought it down here. I had a look at it for him."

"But you didn't fix it?"

"You don't trust me?"

"Should I?"

He glances up at me, then looks down again. He takes the back off the radio, tipping the small screws into his hand, and says, "She didn't want it fixed. She wanted a new one."

"What do you mean?"

"She asked me to tell your father that it was broken. That I couldn't fix it."

"And did you?"

He doesn't answer. It is a subtle deception of hers, but deliberate. To ask someone who works for my father to be complicit in deceiving him. There is something awful in it.

He turns the radio over and slides out the metal structure that sits inside. It is a jumble of wires and dials, but his hands move delicately over the parts, unscrewing and twisting, bending the wires to their task, malleable under his touch.

I lean against the bonnet of my father's jeep, my shins striped with sunlight.

"Where did you learn about machines?"

"I was a radio engineer in the army."

"The army trained you?"

"They picked out those of us that were literate. Turned us into signalers, medical orderlies, engineers."

"You told me once that you fought in Burma."

"Yes."

"What was it like?"

He says nothing. Goes into his workshop and comes back with a length of wire.

He looks at me when he comes out and says, "Tell me something."

"What do you mean?" I laugh nervously. He has caught me off guard. It is the first time he has spoken to me directly since I arrived. But he doesn't reply. He is cutting the piece of wire, sliding it into the machine.

When I don't speak, he looks up, his brown eyes settling on mine, and I feel my stomach contract. He is watching me, judging me, and I am self-conscious. I want to tell him something that matters; my unhappiness in England, grief for my mother, my sense of unbelonging—I might have talked about these things a week ago, but they no longer seem a part of the present.

Then I know what I want to say. That Steven Lockhart scares me—that I think he wants something from me. But I cannot talk to him about that, so instead I say, "It was Steven Lockhart—the District Officer—who killed the striker at the factory. I was in the room. I saw him do it." I can see the blood, the African's head snapping back, and—afterward—Steven holding me on his lap.

"Did he see you?" he asks carefully.

I shake my head. "The only person who saw me was you."

He looks at me for a moment longer, then back down at the radio. "But you did not tell your uncle."

"No."

"Why not?" he asks, not looking up.

"Because I should not have been there. Because you asked me not to."

The words are full and heavy in my mouth. I want him to look at me, but he reinserts the screws, the bolts, the backplate. I watch the inside curve of his arm, the smooth charcoal skin, his hands turning the screwdriver, his fingers black against the gold lettering MADE IN GREAT BRITAIN.

When the radio sputters into life with a jerk of song we both start, shocked by the strength of it. He loses it and swears, fiddles with the aerial, then it comes in again. *The British Overseas Airways Corporation has introduced its first passenger jet service.* It is the news. As always with the radio—I feel the magic of it, that it can bring the world into this far-flung place. We lose it again for what seems a long while, then it comes on again. The announcement of emergency legislation to tackle Mau Mau: greater control of the press, powers to seize and destroy unlicensed newspapers, an allowance for confessions made to police officers to be used in evidence, the right for provincial commissioners who believe a person is Mau Mau to order his removal to a restricted area.

The news report gives way to music. I watch Michael. There is a tension in the way that he holds himself—a concentration—and I do not ask him what he thinks of what we have heard.

A small airplane drones overhead. Michael raises his head to watch it inch across the sky.

"Did you ever go in a plane? During the war?" I ask.

"Only once."

"What was it like?"

"We came into Egypt, over the Red Sea. I felt like an eagle, cut loose from the world below. No family, no duty; just an immense freedom."

"And now?" The question slips out before I have considered it. "What freedom is there for you—now that you are home?"

His eyes settle on mine. "And you, *Memsaab*—" he says, watching me, a slight smile on his lips. "What freedom is there for you—now that you are home?"

WHEN MUKAMI has left for the *shambas* the following afternoon, I turn on the radio, moving the aerial from side to side to find the best reception. Michael steps out of the garage, leaning against the wall. We listen to the voice from England, cracked and fizzing with distance, reading the news; the new Governor's imminent arrival in Kenya; reports from England of flooding across the south of the country; and—in local news—the murder of two Kikuyu on a farm to the north of Nakuru, less than eighty miles from us. Despite the promises of the government, Mau Mau isn't disappearing.

When the broadcast is over, Michael drops a hand to Juno's head and says, "She's going to whelp in a couple of months."

"Is she?" I call her to me, doubtful, kneeling down beside her, running my hand under her stomach, and see that he is right. Her nipples are large and pink, and there is a firmness in her belly that I had not noticed, the skin stretching to white around her womb. She sniffs wetly at my face. "Do you know if she's had puppies before?"

"She had a litter last year."

"What happened to them?" I ask, glancing up from where I am kneeling on the earth.

"She went out into the bush to give birth and came back on her own. There were three or four of them."

"How do you know?"

He looks down at me, crouched at his feet. "I could feel them moving in her belly," he says, and there is something in the way that his eyes meet mine, an accidental closeness in the widening of his pupils—like grasping something hot—which brings the blood rushing to my face.

IT TAKES TWO WEEKS to make up enough shirts, shorts and dresses for the children, and when it is done my fingers are rough and blistered from pulling thread. I give the clothes to the children and they take them from me eagerly, examining the buttons, tugging on the shorts and slipping the shirts over their heads, laughing.

There is another theft at the farm—at the dairy. I box up the radio and ask Kahiki to drive it up to the house. I would like to keep it at the stables—I have enjoyed the closeness it brings to Michael, but I don't want to risk it being stolen. The men who come thieving in the night are supplying the fighters in the forest with their loot. A radio would give them an advantage. I unpack it in my room, string up the aerial and stow it under my bed, dragging it out in the evenings after supper, the volume turned down low so that my father and Sara do not hear.

One night there is a knock at my door. I turn off the broadcast and listen in the darkness.

"Rachel?"

Harold is standing in the corridor, a lamp in one hand. His gaze shifts past me into the room. I reluctantly draw the door open for him to come inside. When I turn the radio on he stares at me for a moment, then sits on the wooden chair opposite the bed, listening until the broadcast is over and the news gives way to a song.

"Where did you get it?" he asks.

"I found it in the barn. It was my mother's—Michael fixed it for me. You won't say anything, Harold?" I ask, quickly. "I don't want my father to know."

"Of course not," he says quietly, and I see in his face that I can trust him; that he is as hungry for this—for the escape the radio can deliver—as I am.

He comes every night, at ten o'clock, when the house is quiet and my father and Sara have gone to bed. He rarely speaks, and he comes always with a camera in one hand, which he fiddles with as he listens. When I see that he is drawn to the radio—that he does not want anything from me—I begin to relax and be content for him to sit here in my room.

I smoke one or two cigarettes at the open window, and we listen to an hour of broadcasts from England: politics, conversation and music from America. An interview with Charlie Chaplin, Churchill's speeches, India's first elections, Shostakovich's tenth symphony; the world hundreds of miles away.

On the local news a Kikuyu loyalist claims to have met Dedan Kimathi, the self-styled Field Marshal of the forest forces. He says in faltering English that Kimathi wears a leopard-skin cloak to disguise himself in the forest, that he spent a year in the British army, that he speaks good English and fights for political freedom. "Surely," the interviewer says, "we must be wary of crediting lawless terrorists with political motivation . . ."

Every broadcast brings reports on the increase of Mau Mau activities, the killing and mutilating of Kikuyu who refuse to take the oath, the burning of huts and villages, and I see in the tension that grips Harold that he is imagining the horror of this violence; we are both haunted by the idea that it might come to visit us here at Kisima. But my fears are contained by the darkness; they melt away with the sun.

I FIND THE SCHOOL BENCHES in the deserted chicken coop and with Mukami's help drag them out and scrub them clean. I set them up at the *shambas*. Occasionally I see Harold walking through with his camera, but he keeps his distance. I order more chalks and new slates for the children from Nakuru, and prop up a blackboard on a small table. I start spending a few hours each morning teaching the children. They learn how to write their name on a slate. We make up paper money, then run a shop, and they count out the paper cents to buy and sell beans. They mold clay bricks and write their names on them with their fingers, and we count the goats and chickens that wander through the *shambas*, making simple calculations.

I would like to know what Michael thinks of what I have done, but I do not see him at the *shambas* and I am rarely at the stables.

After the lesson, I sit with Njeri outside her hut. She weaves rugs and stitches clothes for her baby. The children disperse across the *shambas*, some to help their mothers, others to play—the boys making catapults, the girls collecting seeds and turning them into necklaces. I notice that it is harder for her to sit still and she shifts her weight on the low stool, stretching out her back. Mukami says the baby could come any day.

XI

-→⇒ • ⇐←-

I watch my father from the open door. He gathers up his binoculars, his rifle; slings his cartridge belt around his waist. I shiver
in the cool air of early morning. The sun hasn't yet broken above
the tops of the trees, and a web of golden shadows spreads over the
lawn in front of the house. Just when I think he has not seen me, he
turns and says, "Rachel—do you want to come?"

"Yes," I say quickly, happy that he has asked, though I am
unsure if this is an obligation or a pleasure. He used to take me on
his early-morning rounds of the farm when I was a child. Now I let
down the back of the Land Rover and Juno leaps inside.

We leave behind the clipped green lawns and honeysuckle hedges
which surround the house. The Land Rover has a canvas roof—
there are no windows, and the air is cool and damp against my skin.
I reach into the back, draw out one of the red Maasai blankets and
pull it over my shoulders. It is that strange hour after dawn—too
early still for conversation—when the land is closed and desaturated,
and we drive in silence, watching the earth seep into color under the
first rays of the sun.

The track leads us past the coffee plantation, shining dark and robust behind hedges of pale pink bignonias; past the kitchen garden, overgrown with weeds. I glimpse a flash of golden pawpaws ripening behind lush foliage; peach trees, tangled raspberry nets, mangoes and sugarcane.

We drive toward the northern boundary. My father has had a report that some Maasai herdsmen have driven their cattle onto our land to graze. Above the house the track drops down along a boulder-strewn gulley into a valley. Sun flickers through the thorny shade. An eagle pushes up from the branches of an acacia, beating its black wings into the white sky above us. We climb slowly out of the valley and emerge onto a ridge. To our left is the beginning of the long, tumbling drop down to the floor of the Rift Valley. The forest here is impenetrable by car. I have walked down into its hot humid depths; a jungle with rocks rising a hundred feet tall like totems from between thick, dark vines, water tumbling into hidden pools where snakes gather to slip their skins and copulate. The secret place of pythons, bird-eating spiders, baboon and leopard. It is no place to go now. My father thinks that there could be Mau Mau hiding there, sweating in its depths.

As we come over the top of the ridge the land ripples, golden and seemingly endless in front of us. Pockets of mist cling to the forested dells that mark the contours of the ridge. We are out of the bush now onto farmland. There are some three thousand acres of wheat and oats. In a few months they will gather in the maize—the yellow heads stored away to be ground into fodder for the cattle and *posho* for the Africans. Farther on is field upon field of white flowers—pyrethrum—which will be harvested and turned into valuable insecticide.

On the boundary we see no signs of cattle, just dust devils that rise like smoke from the track that stretches into the distance. We circle back on ourselves. Away to our left the land drops into a clearing—a quarry carved out of the earth. Men walk up the precarious path from the bottom, carrying stones on their heads, their bodies taut and creaking beneath the weight.

"The dip cracked last month," my father says, leaning over his door to see better. "We're having to build a new one from scratch. There are a hundred and fifty bags of cement that have to come up this road, one thousand five hundred running feet of cut stone and fifty tons of sand, not to mention the water."

The site of the new dip is a crater in the earth beside which men stand, breaking up rocks with huge sledgehammers. From below us—through the pounding of the stone—comes the bellowing of cattle, eager to be milked. We drop down to the dairy—not far from the house now—into a cacophony of noise; the clanking of buckets, Africans singing and shouting, the lowing of the heifers. There are eighty cows to be milked before the herd can be driven up to the grazing land, and the cream has to be separated. I watch the milking while my father checks the yields.

As we walk back to the Land Rover, his gaze lifts to the sky. Three vultures wheel and turn in a vast expanse of blue.

"What is it?" I ask.

"Looks like they're over the sheep pens," he says, taking a look through his binoculars. He starts the engine, pulling the Land Rover off the track. We drive, juddering, over the uneven grass of the plain, until I can see the wire of the pens glinting ahead of us. He slows the car. In front of us two vultures dip their long necks to the ground. It takes me a moment to spot the jackals, the same color as the grass, crouched down—eating—their eyes fixed on us.

"A Tommy?" The kill looks about the size of a gazelle.

"I'm not sure," my father says, driving the car closer.

I squint into the sun. The jackals, uneasy, trot away through the grass, looking back at us every few steps. The vultures are bolder. They shake out their wings, hopping backward. One has hold of a long piece of white wooled skin, as long as its body. It makes a gulping attempt to swallow it—but it can't get it down its throat and the skin trails out of its open beak.

My father steps out of the Land Rover and turns the carcass over with his boot. Strips of wool snag on the dry grass. Bones. The white-rimmed dome of a rib cage. A hyena must have got it.

At the sheep pens, we see that the barbed wire—twelve rows high to keep out leopard and hyena—has been cut, and one side trails uselessly on the ground. A ewe is caught up in it. Her bleats are plaintive and my father crouches down to hold her still with one hand, while I struggle to pull her fleece from the metal barbs.

Kahiki turns up on foot—he has been looking for us.

"How many have we lost?" my father asks.

"We don't know yet. Perhaps thirty."

"Where are Kiongo? Mbira?"

"They are gone, *Bwana*," Kahiki says, shaking his head. Kiongo and Mbira are the shepherds who have slept with the flock for as long as I can remember.

"Gone where?" I ask.

"Into the damned forest." My father waves his hand at the distant slopes of Mount Kenya. "It wouldn't have happened a year ago, five years ago—" He draws his hands over his face and breathes out heavily. "Bastards," he says, dragging his boot through the dirt. "They left them to any damned leopard or hyena that cared to pick them off."

We spend hours rounding up the sheep. There are more car-
casses, littered over the plains, their white fleece like patches of snow
on the short grass; black shadows sail over them, vultures wheeling
in the sky above us.

THE ROAD BACK to the farm takes us along the top of the dam.
My father pulls the car off the track. The sky reflects white and
glassy off the surface of the water.

"Walk with me," he says. I feel close to him. It was hot work
herding the sheep. My shirt sticks to my back, and the dust has
mingled with the sweat on my face. My hands are greasy with
sheep's wool and covered in fine cuts from the barbed wire, but I
feel a physical contentment, and a happiness that I have not felt in
his company since I came home.

He opens the boot for Juno and she jumps out. Then he takes a
bottle of Canada Dry from the back of the car and shakes a box of
Ritz biscuits at me. "Hungry?"

"Starving," I say, smiling. I haven't eaten a thing all morning. I
follow him down to the water's edge. He slips his rifle off his shoulder, lays it on the stones, and we sit on the bank. The water is
absolutely still. Juno laps at the surface, causing the smallest of ripples to break its edges.

He squats at the water's edge and rinses out the two tin cups. I
dip my hand into the box of biscuits. They are dense on my tongue
and salty.

"Men who haven't lived in Kenya cannot know what it asks of
you," he says, shaking out the water from the cups. "When your
mother and I first arrived here we had three thousand pounds

to our name. We worked for a cattle ranch for two years before we had a chance to buy this place. We built the house for a hundred pounds. And borrowed the money for the dip from the Settlement Board. I had to buy stock—it was fifteen pounds for a heifer in calf. I knew we weren't going to make it unless we had a dam, but we didn't have the money. We needed water for the cattle, for the dip—every success on the farm relied on it."

He takes a bottle opener out of his pocket, flips the lid off the Canada Dry and pours it out into the tin cups.

"So what did you do?" I ask. He hands me a cup. The soda fizzes cold against my tongue.

"I rented a bulldozer from a man in Nakuru who charged seventy shillings an hour. He agreed to secure the rent against the three hundred and fifty acres of wheat I had planted. It looked like it would be a good harvest, so I took the risk. I counted every minute— it took 108 hours, 28 minutes and 12 seconds from the moment the bulldozer began to the moment it finished. I didn't dare do the calculation in my head when I went to bed that night. But the harvest was good. I paid off the man, and the dam was built. It holds eighteen feet of water at the deepest point, and it covers nearly eight acres of ground. After that there were other dams, but this was the first. Your mother stocked it with bass. She loved to fish here."

"You brought me down here in the evenings—we used to watch Mama fish."

"Did we?" he asks, smiling at me, trying to remember.

"You taught me how to clean and gut a fish."

He shifts his weight—he has spotted something on the far bank. Distracted, he lifts his binoculars.

I put a hand on his arm. "You did—don't you remember?" It

matters to me that he hasn't forgotten. "You told me the story of the witch—" I say, pointing to the clump of trees that grows in the middle of the island.

He puts down his binoculars and looks where I am pointing, indulging me, but there is a blankness behind his eyes.

"You said she lived just beneath the surface of the water, guarding the island. Once we rowed out there together and you showed me the weed trailing in the water. You said it was her hair."

"Did I, darling?" I can sense his disinterest in my insisting on something he doesn't recollect. I feel panicked by it. "We used to come down here when she was fishing. We walked back in the evenings together. And at other times. We sat here and skimmed stones, and you said each stone was an offering."

I wonder if it is possible that he doesn't remember. And what it means that the things which were so important to me as a child, the memories which are seared into my mind, out of which I am assembled, might be meaningless to him. The platform on which my childhood was built has dissolved over time; like a new building built on the foundations of the old, only a shadow of the original remains.

"Was she happy?" I ask.

"Your mother?" He laughs softly. "She was happy." There is intimacy in his voice now. He hands me the binoculars. I lift them to my eyes and feel the familiar dizzying closeness. At the bank on the far side three buffalo and a calf are crowding at the water's edge. They blend so perfectly with the dark bush behind them that it is almost impossible to see them with the naked eye.

"This place would have been the end of most women," my father says. His voice is warm and soft. He is speaking unchecked—for a moment I have him all to myself. "We lived on scarcely anything.

Our first house was a toolshed—the tools were moved to one end, and we camped in the other. There was a cooker on three legs, rats, and no plaster on the walls, but she was happy. It was only the taps." He smiles. "Your mother never complained about anything— she was stoic in all things. But taps. God, how she harped on about taps. There was no running water for thirty kilometers, and everything had to be carried up to the house. In the end I took a stick and divined for it. We dug and dug and eventually—there it was, clear, bubbling water springing from the earth. That evening your mother stripped off her clothes and poured bucket after bucket of water over herself. I thought she would die of cold." He laughs. I hang on his every word. He is leaving a trail of golden thread, and later, in the quiet of my room, I will stitch it into a tapestry that will bind me to my past. But I am also bitter, that this intimacy is there after all; that he keeps so much of it hidden from me.

"A year later I bought a little pump secondhand and we piped water directly into the house."

He chooses a long, thin stone from the bank and throws it out over the water. It leaps across the surface. "It was hard in the beginning. It took years for science to catch up and help us here in Kenya—but it has come eventually. Rust-resistant wheat, Gammexane to dip the cattle, cobalt to combat deficiencies in the soil, inoculation, penicillin. We are finally at the point your mother and I dreamed about—some small measure of control over the land, so that we can work it to our profit, for all of our sakes. And now this." He gestures to the land beyond the dam. "Mau Mau."

We sit in stillness for a long moment. I put down the binoculars, and he turns to look at me. "I brought you here, Rachel, because I wanted to talk to you."

He swallows, and I realize, with a quickening of my heart, that everything he has said is just a prelude to what he wants to say now.

"I know it can't be easy for you, coming back home, to all this talk of violence. Your mother gone, and Sara here in her place. But she is sensitive, more than you might think. And it hurts her to feel you might not be getting along."

"Have we not been getting along?"

"She feels there is a tension between you—" He throws out the dregs of his cup onto the pebbles. "It isn't easy for her being here, so far from the city. She is cut off from her old life. She has had to sacrifice so much to be here."

I glance at him—is this what he wanted to say all along, when he said *walk with me*? Did he only want to use the opportunity to talk about Sara?

"Why did she come if she doesn't like the bush?"

"I think you know that life is not always so straightforward," he says. Then—in a softer voice, "We thought that it might help if we explained the situation. We are waiting for a divorce from Harold's father. She has written to him, but he hasn't responded. If and when her divorce does come through we will have a small civil ceremony. You should know that it doesn't bother me in the least that we're not married—I have never been one for the niceties of society. But it is important that you understand this arrangement between us is not something temporary. That I have made a commitment to Sara. That everything I have"—he spreads his hands out over the dam, over the land—"is also hers; that she is to all intents and purposes my wife."

"I understand," I say, swallowing.

He puts a hand on my knee and looks at me. "I would like you to make a particular effort with her. If you are going to stay."

If you are going to stay. His words slip through me like a knife. I feel the pain somewhere deep in my core. He is cutting me loose. My staying here is not something that he takes for granted, or perhaps even desires. I swallow heavily. I will not cry. We say nothing for a while. I stay quiet. I do not argue. I do not jump with pain. I want to see how far he will go—how far he will commit himself—so that I know exactly where I stand.

"Sara is very generous-spirited. She wants you to be happy, and I know there is much that you could learn from her. She has suggested that you be encouraged to spend more time in the house. She feels—and I agree with her—that your running around on the farm all day, on your own, isn't appropriate for someone of your age."

"Mama wasn't cooped up in the house all day."

"Your mother was a married woman. I am simply asking you to moderate your interests." He pauses, breathes out and looks at me. "I loved your mother, but I have come to realize that she didn't always set the best example. Perhaps she shouldn't have had you educated at home. Your childhood was too free. It brought you up to a life that isn't compatible with the Kenya we live in now. We must draw greater boundaries between ourselves and the Africans if we are going to try and make life in this colony work."

"Why must we?"

But he doesn't answer my question. Instead he retracts his hand from my knee. "You're not a child any longer," he says. "You are a woman now. You should think differently about how you conduct yourself."

I hear the disappointment in his voice. The sense that I am perhaps not what he has been told I ought to be. When he asked me to join him, in the cold, early light of morning, I had hoped it was because he wanted my company. And when he asked me to sit with him at the dam, I had thought he might want to talk about the past, about my mother, to remember her for both our sakes, but I see after all that it is Sara who asked him to speak to me, and that he had only her in his mind all along. We stand up and rinse our cups in the dam. He drops a hand affectionately to Juno's head.

I watch him, the man who is my father. I love him. There is no way for me to turn away from that, but his words have hurt me more than I can admit, even to myself.

I STAND THE PARAFFIN LAMP on the basin and stare into the mirror, looking for my mother. Light, freckled skin, large, slanting eyes, a full mouth. Perhaps this is her. And what does it mean that I carry her inside me?

The story from our book of fairy tales which frightened me the most was "Hansel and Gretel." I was gripped by the trial of the two children, led out into the woods by a wicked woman who was not their mother, and rejoiced when they found their way back to their loving father. But as I look at myself in the mirror, I see a different side to the story—it is not, after all, the woman in the story who is to blame. It is the father. He is weak. Weak enough to be convinced into abandoning his children, not once but twice. Weak enough to be talked out of his loyalties. Does he love Gretel then—and he just doesn't know it? What is love if it can change so easily, under a stranger's persuasion?

Juno has got up onto the bed before me and is stretched out on the quilt. She doesn't move—but her eyes watch me, and her tail thumps slowly against the quilt when I sit down. In the last two weeks her belly has swollen so that it pushes out to one side when she lies down. I lean my head against her warm, clean coat, feel the dry scrape of her paw against my bare arm and shut my eyes.

XII

→→•←←

Lillian Markham steps out of the car. "Damn it, Rachel. Why didn't you write and tell me you were home?"

She pulls me into her and holds me, the palm of her hand warm and firm against my neck. I slip my arms under hers and feel her chest rising against mine. After a moment she steps back, her hands on my shoulders, and looks at me, smiling through her tears.

Lillian was the woman my mother used to stay up with late into the night, drinking whiskey, when she and her husband came to stay; the one my mother went out riding with, galloping back to the farm with the dusk, smelling of cigarette smoke, sweat and horses; the one she laughed with—tears running down their faces, while my father, Gerald and I looked on in smiling puzzlement. Lillian wrote to me in England, her letters sent, every year, on the day my mother died when it seemed there was no one else but me to remember.

Her husband, Gerald Markham, is a farmer like my father and their farm—Matabele—borders ours, though it is more than an hour's drive away. They are settlers who arrived at the same time as my parents, after the First War when land was cheap and England was in the grip of a depression. They had never had children of their own. They were my parents' greatest friends, and their arrival at our farm, when I was a child, always brought a burst of happiness. My father has persuaded Sara to ask them for lunch—he says she will have to have friends if she is to live here, so far from any neighbors.

"Gerald—" Lillian says, holding me at arm's length. "Come over here and look at this. Isn't she the very spitting image?"

"Of who?" I ask.

"Don't you know?" she asks, laughing. "Of your mother of course!"

"Why—Robert—" She turns to my father. "You must have told her? The similarity is uncanny."

"It is—" my father says, agreeing, his eyes settling on me. "She is Tessa through and through," and I feel a thrill of happiness, hearing him speak her name, to these people who knew her so well.

We walk out onto the veranda. Gerald settles into a leather safari chair. He stretches out his legs and runs a calloused hand over Juno, who sinks her head deep in his lap. "How are you holding up, Robert?"

While my father and Gerald talk, Lillian asks me questions, more questions than I have had to answer since I came home, and I talk freely, telling her about the school—miles from anywhere—where I spent six long years; my grandparents' house on the outskirts of an industrial city—cold and lifeless; the shrouded windows; the pastoral evenings with my grandfather; his crushing moral exactitude; my grandmother's inability to stand up to him; the growing sense that the suburb—with its long, dreary days spent indoors, its bridge evenings and church meetings, would swallow me up and I might never get back home. I falter on the last bit and she reaches forward and squeezes my hand. "But you did come back. You escaped. Just like your mother did. Just like I did. England didn't suit us either, not a bit. Your mother used to tell me that every day she woke up at Kisima she was glad that she had left. And that didn't mean she didn't miss your grandmother. But your mother needed to be outdoors, she needed to be busy, working with her hands, in this landscape—" She spreads out her arms to encompass the wilderness, beyond the lawn, and smiles. "She would be so proud of you if she could see you here now." I smile, happy to hear her say it.

Juno wanders over and sits down next to me, leaning her weight against my legs. "She's going to have puppies?" Lillian asks, looking at her swollen belly.

"Yes."

"She's Rachel's dog," my father says, nodding at me.

"She ran away to have her puppies a year ago, and they died."

"I had a bitch who used to do that. I'd run all over the farm looking for her at God knows what hour. Keep her locked up somewhere safe, when you think it's near her time. And don't be nervous for her—" Lillian says, putting a hand on my knee. "She'll be fine."

Mungai arrives with a jug of ice water and beers.

"Take a look at my herd this afternoon, Gerald. You'll be impressed," my father says, taking a long draft of his beer.

"The Friesians?"

"I have a bull now that can produce a true black calf nine times out of ten."

"I think it's a shame," Sara says, appearing in the open doorway wearing a white dress that is pulled in tight around the waist with a wide leather belt. She looks sharp, sophisticated, too bright next to Lillian Markham whose sturdy brown legs emerge solid and firm from her safari shorts.

"They were the only thing that reminded me of home in this wretched place." She winds her way across the veranda and sits on the arm of my father's chair. "I could drive down to the dairy and look at those black and white cows and almost believe I was in Devon." She slides a hand over the inside of my father's knee and smiles at us. "Everything in this country ends up darker than when it arrived." She looks at my father. "Why do you insist on helping it along?"

"What advantage is it to breed out the white patches?" Lillian asks.

"The black skin is almost entirely resistant to the sun." My father rubs a hand across his jaw. "A completely black Friesian can graze in this climate for twice as long as its English cousin." His voice quickens with passion. "My milk yield has next to doubled, with no increase in bulk feeding. If it doesn't—"

"Robert—" Sara interrupts, with a little downward smile. "Gerald and Lillian didn't drive all this way to talk about farming."

"Sorry—" my father says, smiling sheepishly. "Sara thinks I'm a terrible bore."

"Honestly—" Sara pushes back the corners of her hair. "It's enough for him to be out on the farm, from dawn to dusk." She smiles, shrugging her shoulders.

My father pats her knee, as if to quieten her, but she won't be shushed. She wants to express something to these people.

"You know—when I first came here Robert used to eat his supper in his pajamas," she says, giving a little laugh.

"I'm afraid we're rather guilty of the same thing," Gerald says. "It's something of a tradition around here—supper in our pajamas."

"Oh, I don't believe you could have been as bad as Robert," Sara says. "He was scarcely civilized when I met him—were you, darling? All he talked about was heifers and yields and fertilizers, morning, noon and night." I think back to those evenings by the fire, as a child, my father in his slippers reading the pedigrees of bulls from England, my mother writing letters, the house quietening around us—was it possible something had been lacking?

WE EAT LUNCH on a table that has been set up on the lawn, under the shade of an acacia that drops its leaves like confetti onto the white tablecloth. Sparrows dart across the table. From the bush all around us rises the song of the cicadas, and somewhere far off is a dove, calling out its low, fluted notes.

Harold does not appear for lunch. I saw him head out this morning early, just after dawn. "He's rather preoccupied—" Sara says, apologetically, and I feel her disappointment that he is not here, making an effort with her guests.

Mungai serves poached chicken, potatoes, courgettes, peas and mint from the garden.

"It must be wonderful to have her home," Lillian says to my father, who sits on the other side of her.

"It is—" he says, but although he smiles at me, I hear the gulf between the expectation in Lillian's voice—the simple, overwhelming pleasure of a child returned—and the complicated reality of what he feels.

"Quite a responsibility for me," Sara says. "I hardly know what to do with her all day long."

"Oh, I expect Rachel is good at taking care of herself," Lillian says.

"But that's just the problem. Should a girl be left so much to her own devices, at such a formative period in her life? We're completely cut off here from the real world. I scarcely know what month of the year it is. No cinema, no shows, no shops worth talking about. We're only a hairbreadth away from living like the Africans." She pushes her potatoes around her plate, then puts her knife and fork together, and dabs at her mouth with a napkin.

"I should think it's probably rather good for a young woman—" Gerald says, smiling at me as he mops his plate with a piece of bread. "To get away from the *real world*."

"How is Nate Logan?" Sara asks, changing the subject. "It always seems rather strange to me that he casts himself adrift out here. Almost as though he is running away from something."

"Oh—I don't know about running away," Lillian says, smiling. "But it's true he is rather wild. He disappears into the bush with a Dorobo boy, and we don't see him for weeks. He comes back looking like those pictures of Neanderthals, with his beard down to his chest and his hair all matted together." She laughs.

"I heard he had been exiled from America," Sara's voice sharpens, "for being a communist."

"I'm not sure he's a communist," Lillian says, taking a sip of her water. "But he isn't afraid to express his opinions. He believes in change."

"Change for America or change for Kenya?" my father asks, and no one answers.

"Kenya is changing whether we like it or not." Gerald leans back in his chair. "They say this country will be unrecognizable in ten years. No unchartered land, no swamps and tsetse flies. There'll be tarmacked roads into the farthest corners of the country, designated game parks for tourists. Nairobi will only be an hour or two from Nakuru by car."

"God save me, I hope I never see the day," my father says.

"But surely that's what we should all be praying for," Sara says. "Just think—Kenya might begin to resemble somewhere actually *civilized*."

"And I suppose that would be a good thing?" my father asks, in a quiet voice. "If it were 'civilized'?"

"Don't take your frustration out on me, Robert," she says, her voice tipped with condescension. "It's hardly reasonable to expect me to embrace living here—" And she opens her arms at the expanse of bush which stretches out on all sides into the distance.

JIM TAKES LONGER than usual with the pudding, and Sara smiles apologetically. "I've had my hands full with the servants here. You'd never guess how badly things were being run before I came."

"Oh, I don't remember things being so bad," Lillian says, giving me a quick, kind look, and I know she wants to protect me from Sara, but there is nothing she can do to help me.

Another five minutes pass, and the pudding still hasn't arrived. Sara drops her napkin on the table and goes to the kitchen to see where it is. She comes out again a few minutes later, with her mouth turned down, carrying a tin plate. On it sits a half-eaten chicken leg. Jim hovers on the veranda behind her, holding his hat.

Sara drops the tin plate down beside my father so that it clatters on the table.

"What is it, darling?" my father asks, looking up at her, and then beyond at Jim. I hear in his voice that he wants to avoid a scene, and this seems to rile Sara.

"You know full well what it is. I caught him red-handed. Pulling it from the joint with his fingers." I look at Jim, then look away. I hate what she is doing. Dragging his humiliation onto the table in front of all of us. It has always been accepted that Jim and the kitchen boy will eat some of what we have not finished, though it has never been explicitly stated.

"It's a dirty, disgusting little habit. Who knows where his fingers have been. And it isn't his to take."

"Surely taking a little is all right?" Gerald says, looking between my father and Sara.

"A little is what got us to where we're at now. Next he'll be wanting a place at the table, then our house, then our land. We had servants who were just the same at the Norfolk and it never ended well."

I can see Gerald and Lillian out of the corner of my eye, frozen in their seats, watching the scene unfold. Sara is looking at my father, and when he doesn't speak, she says, "Robert—it is simple disrespect, can't you see? And I shan't stand for it. What kind of example does it set—if you won't discipline the boys in your own house?"

My father's eyes are hard and staring, like a jackal cornered. I want to scream at him to tell her to be quiet. The table is silent, waiting to see what he will do.

"Jim—" he says. "Come here."

Jim steps down from the veranda and walks across the lawn to the table. He looks at his feet. My father says in Swahili, in a low voice, "You're not to eat the food. It is not yours. And it angers the *memsaab*. Do you understand?"

"*Ndiyo, Bwana.*"

I think that might be the end of it, but she beckons to Jim with one finger. "Come along," she says in English, as she might to a naughty schoolboy. He walks a few paces closer.

"Show me your hands," she says, and he holds them out, palm upward, years of cooking for our family bending them into cups.

"Turn them over," she says, and he does, slowly.

Then she slaps the backs of his hands, with both of hers.

"Next time I catch you eating anything from our kitchen, you'll be gone."

"Yes, *Memsaab*," Jim says, his big head bowing in a gesture of humility. And he retreats back to the kitchen.

"I don't see why I should have to do all the dirty work around here," she says, with a deprecating smile, but no one at the table smiles with her.

Lillian holds me close in the shade of the acacias in front of the house. Gerald is waiting in the car. I shut my eyes. All around is the throbbing, grating call of the cicadas. "Christ, I miss her." Her body rocks from side to side. "And you, baby girl. She loved you."

"Don't go," I say to her, my voice breaking for the first time. I press my forehead against her shoulder. I was all right before she came, but now that she has dragged up the ghost of my mother I can see how changed my father is, how far he has fallen under Sara's influence and how cut off we are here. As I hold on to her the sobs tear through me. Lillian is not bound by the spell that grips my father, and when she goes I will feel more alone than I did before.

"There is nothing I can do, Rachel," she whispers in my ear, rocking me. "We all make choices in life. Your father has made his."

Afterward, I stand with my father and Sara, watching the Markhams' car disappear into a cloud of dust, feeling more trapped than ever.

XIII

➤➤ • ◀◀

The news is full of Mau Mau. The violence escalates. Then—at
the end of the week—there come reports of Mau Mau attacks
against Europeans. Although we have been expecting it, we are all
shocked; a line has been crossed. A settler farmer and his family are
assaulted and seriously wounded, and—a few days later—an elderly
English couple, about sixty miles from Kisima, are beaten up in their
own home. The *Times* in London describes Mau Mau as "a primitive
underground movement immured in barbaric rites, a sharp reminder
that fifty years are but a moment of time among the African peoples."

The next day a loyal Kikuyu chief—a supporter of the British
presence in Kenya—is ambushed in his car and killed on the road
in cold blood. Harold and I stay up late into the night listening to
the news. The new Governor calls the chief "a great man, a great
African and a great citizen of Kenya, who met his death in the service of his own people."

There is an expectation now that more violence against Europeans will follow, and we listen with dread to the news each night.

At the *shambas* the little girl I am helping has recovered. Her wound has dried up, and she is eating well. I am relieved, and I know my mother would be pleased if she were here.

One morning when the children are chanting letters—*A is for "apple," B is for "boy," P is for "pen," V is for "victory," Q is for "queen"*—I see Michael out of the corner of my eye, watching. The children finish and he talks to them in Kikuyu, asking them questions. I watch him, the intentness of his gaze, his loose, easy posture, both strange and familiar. I have missed his company, and I am pleased that he has come down to see what I am doing here.

"What do you think?" I ask, when he turns to look at me. His eyes settle on mine, and I see that he knows what I want him to say—and all of a sudden I wish I hadn't asked. A deep flush rises up my neck.

"You don't approve?" My voice is quick with anger. I have worked hard here, and I do not see how he could criticize what I am trying to achieve.

His dark, heavy-lidded eyes hold mine. "I think that they look like good little missionary children."

I stand there, biting the soft inside of my lip, watching him walk away.

Missionary children. Learning by rote the message of their teachers. Was all the work I have put into the *shambas* just a glorification of my own pride? Somewhere at the back of my mind is Sara's voice calling me a sentimentalist.

NJERI IS INSIDE her hut covered in a film of sweat. Her skin is wet to touch. Mukami walks with her around the small room, one arm braced around her back, taking her weight. She does not respond when I ask her what she feels, and I feel useless standing there, unable to help. The following morning I get up before the sun has risen, worried that something might be wrong. She is no older than me and does not have her mother to help with the birth. When I reach the *shambas* dawn is breaking. The grass is covered in a gauze of silver dew, and the cattle—not yet released from the *boma*—are bellowing in the cold, early-morning air.

The *shambas* look deserted; just a few hens pecking at the soil in the half-light. Outside Njeri's hut is a pile of leaves, smeared dark with blood. My heart beats a little faster. I push open the door. Mukami is squatting down, blowing at the red embers of the fire until yellow flames catch at the sticks. She scoops out grain into a large pot. The goats behind their railings sneeze, stirring from sleep.

In one of the alcoves I see Njeri. I blink in the near darkness and move closer. There is the smoke, the smell of the goats, of oiled human skin, and another smell, warm and close. She is holding the baby wrapped in a goat's skin. "*Muiretu*—" she says in Kikuyu, *a girl.* She offers her to me, and I sit on the sapling mattress and take the small, warm bundle from her. I look down. Her eyes are open, shining in the dark, staring at me. I touch her smooth, warm cheek. I do not think I have ever seen anything as beautiful. She opens her mouth and cries, a desperate sound that snatches at the core of me, and Njeri takes her in her arms, her cries growing louder, until they stop suddenly in a quiet, wet sucking.

I leave the gifts that I have brought. The jumper I have knitted, bread and milk. Outside the hut the sun is already warm. A small boy sits on the smooth ground; one of Mukami's children. He is modeling a hut out of twigs and mud, with leaves for a roof, and a strong stick for a center post. There is already a tiny thorn *boma*, with clay cattle gathered inside. It is a thing of exact precision and beauty. I watch for a moment—his fingers delicately turning the tiny saplings. He does not look up as I walk past.

I AM SITTING with Njeri and her baby outside her hut. Mukami comes close to where we sit and says to me in Swahili, "The men are complaining, Aleela. They say you should not come down here so often. That you will curse us with your white skin."

"What do you mean, 'curse'—?"

"They say you spend too much time here."

"Do you think so?" I ask, standing up, stung by her words.

She touches a hand to her cheek which is swollen, one eye closing over. "We cannot be both Kikuyu and British," she says.

Njeri says nothing. She watches me walk away. It is not that she is indifferent. She has no say in the matter.

When I get back to the house a jeep is pulled up outside. Nate Logan is on the veranda drinking coffee with my father. "Hey, kiddo," he says, smiling.

"Hi," I say, pleased to see him, putting away the hurt of Mukami's words.

"Logan wants to borrow Harold," my father says. "He's asked if you want to join them for a few days. Lillian is expecting you."

"What about Sara?"

"She's gone to Nakuru for the day." Nate rubs his jaw, a twinkle in his eye. "Your father is signing you both out."

"Go on and enjoy yourselves," my father says, smiling, looking more relaxed than I have seen him look since I came home.

I grin back at them both, excited at the thought of getting away from the farm for a few days and seeing Lillian. "Let me get my things."

I throw some clothes into a bag. When I step down from the veranda, Harold is sitting in the back of the jeep.

"Hey," I say, smiling, and he raises a hand in greeting. I have rarely seen him on the farm during the day. Only in the evenings, when he comes to my room to listen to the news, and then we talk little; sharing the strange, quiet intimacy that comes with listening to the radio.

Nate opens up the boot for Juno. She is too heavy now to jump in. She gets her front paws up and I lift her back legs until she can scramble forward onto the metal floor of the jeep and lie down.

"Harold's going to help me out for a few days—" Nate says, opening the front door from the inside. "I need an extra pair of hands."

I wonder what Sara will say when she finds out.

We drive east across the farm, through deep thickets—leaning in to avoid the acacia branches which snap against the sides of the jeep, down boulder-strewn valleys, where gazelle dart away from us into the bush, until we come out onto the bottom of a valley. The grassland stretches in front of us, iridescent green from last month's rains, zebra flicking their tails in a mirage of heat. The sun beats down, and my arm, resting on the open window, is hot against the metal.

The Markhams' house sits at the end of the valley, where it

opens out onto a long, wide plain. It is warm and homely; redbrick walls and a garden that springs up out of the earth and embraces the house with roses, hibiscus and honeysuckle. Lillian shows me to the same bedroom I stayed in as a child, a small iron bed against one wall, covered with a patchwork quilt. I watch her cross the room and stand at the window that looks out over the dam, and think as I have done before that she must have built this room for the child they never had. "God, how I have loved this place." She turns and looks at me, and I see a momentary sadness settle over her. "Gerald says he's getting too old for Africa." She smiles the thought away. "Come on—I need your help with something."

She takes me by the hand and leads me to the stables, and we tack up her horses and ride out onto the farm. I haven't ridden in the six years since I have been away, but it feels as natural to me as walking. We push our horses through herds of cattle, along the shores of the dam that sits in front of the house and up the hillside, onto the ridge. A herd of zebra scatter in front of us, and we kick our horses into a gallop, their hooves pounding on the dry earth, until we are racing side by side with the herd, the wind whipping the laughter from my mouth, so that all I can hear is the breathing of the horse beneath me, the creaking of the saddle, the thudding of my heart in my chest.

As each day passes, I decide to stay for another, helping Lillian in the dairy and the kitchen, making pickles, preserving lemons, and harvesting the vegetables in the garden. Her cheeses are sold all over Kenya, as far as Nairobi. She gives me vegetable seeds to take home and plant, and shows me how they grow, and what they need to do well. In the afternoons we ride out onto the farm, reporting back to Gerald on the cattle, the state of the dams, the herds of game that have arrived, competing with the cattle for grass. We are out of the house all day and only come home when the light is fading. The news seems far away, as though it cannot touch us here.

On my fourth evening I stand at the bedroom window. Two Africans are dragging branches across the lawn, building fires in the pits that sit beyond the veranda. From the window I can see the last of the sun's light, reflecting like flames on the surface of the dam. A line of white birds flutters over the golden waters. I lie down on the iron bed, my legs aching from the long hours in the saddle, a deep physical contentment spreading over my body. The soft sounds of the house are like whispers at the edge of my waking mind: Gerald's voice talking to their Kikuyu boy; Nate and Harold's jeep pulling in just as darkness falls; Harold's rare laugh; the chink of a bottle against a glass. Strange that I feel more at home here than I do at Kisima.

When I come down for drinks, Juno at my heels, the table is lit with hurricane lamps, glowing in the darkness. The fires are burning, and they throw out a blaze of heat into the cool night air. Beyond are the black waters of the dam. It feels as though we might be the only humans on the vast earth, our tiny place in the wilderness made more pronounced by the slow chugging of the generator behind the house and the crackling of the fires. Juno lies content at my feet. I sip at the gin and tonic that Gerald makes for me, giving in to the heat of the alcohol, firing up my stomach, making my head swim.

"You tell them—Harold." Nate is smiling, running a hand over his shirtsleeves which are ripped to tatters so that I can see the brown skin underneath.

Harold looks older and more assured than I have seen him. He is flushed with excitement, and he leans forward and tells us the story of the lioness who came padding through camp, just as they were packing up.

"I ducked into Nate's tent, fast as I could, but I couldn't do the damn zip up. And Nate—" At this point his face breaks again, into laughter, and he breathes deeply to compose himself. Nate has a wry look on his face. He brings a bottle to his lips. "Nate was in the bushes with his trousers around his ankles, and all I could see as I struggled with the zip was the lioness padding through the trees toward him. I heard a shout—and saw him leap up a thorn bush half-naked!"

"And I'll be less of a man because of it—" Nate laughs, grimacing. I catch sight of Harold—his face radiating happiness, and I see that Nate has brought something out of him that was not visible before.

"And the lioness?" Lillian asks, wiping tears from her eyes.

"Oh, she padded straight through camp. Only once she stopped to have a look at me, stuck halfway up the tree, and yawned, and I swear I saw every tooth in her pretty little jaws."

We eat hot lamb curry, dhal and rice, mangos and lime; their cook has trained with Indians in Nairobi. At eight o'clock Gerald gets up to switch on the radio. We only half-listen, talking over the news from England, but fall quiet when East Africa is mentioned. I see the tension in Gerald's face, and I am gripped by a sudden sense of foreboding—something is changing; an edifice is tumbling down, but I do not know yet exactly what it is.

The newsreader introduces the Governor of Kenya, Sir Evelyn Baring. And then comes an announcement: *A State of Emergency has been declared throughout the colony and protectorate of Kenya. This grave step was taken most unwillingly and with great reluctance by the*

*government of Kenya. There was no alternative in the face of the mount-
ing lawlessness, violence and disorder in parts of the colony, as a result of
the activities of the Mau Mau movement. The government is taking
drastic action in order to stop the spread of violence.*

There is a small silence when he has finished speaking, and the
click of the radio as Gerald turns it off.

I am stunned. A State of Emergency sounds like a declaration
of war; official recognition that the situation has slipped out of
control.

"The beginning of the end, or the end of the beginning?" Gerald asks, softly, into the quiet. The moment is charged with pathos.
The colony, with all its history, comes within the scope of his question. No one speaks for a long time.

Nate shifts in his seat. "India has gone. Surely it's just a matter
of time."

"What is a matter of time?" I ask, the wine making me brave.

"Independence," Nate says, looking at me, and I feel a prickle of
shock. As though I have known the word all my life, and yet I have
not known it at all. It has always gone unspoken, and now that it
has been said out loud, I do not think I will ever be able to put it out
of my mind.

Gerald is breathing into the knuckles on his right hand, and I
think—*What place will there be in an independent Kenya for him, for
my father, even for me?*

He says, finally, "I don't think the kind of violence we have seen
is the way forward. They need to find a peaceful way of bringing
their case."

"The Kikuyu have tried for years to peacefully address the British government. Look at Kenyatta—raised in a missionary school,

university in England, married a white woman, for Christ's sake. A Kikuyu who understands perfectly the problems of land restitution. Have they listened to him? What promises have they made? How much closer do the Kikuyu in this country really feel to independence?"

"I don't disagree," Gerald says, wearily. "But I remain hopeful that this State of Emergency might protect the Kikuyu."

"Protect them against what? Against those who believe they have the right to govern themselves?"

"Against this violence, Nate. God knows I have seen my fair share in two wars. I choose to believe that the British government is doing this for the right reasons."

Nate breathes out heavily and says in a voice touched with despair, "And when all the whitewash has been scraped off—will you still think so?" He pauses. One of the logs on the fire cracks, throwing out sparks. "The last time we saw a State of Emergency was under Hitler—and look where that ended up. Detention camps. Repression of the press. The whole damned Holocaust."

"The District Officer—" Harold says, and I see in his face the courage it takes him to speak up and ask a question. "He said that Kikuyu society has developed too fast. That Mau Mau is a backlash against civilization."

"Of course he did," Nate says, laughing. "It wouldn't suit him for a minute to admit that it might be a political movement, the inevitable economic hangover of British rule in Kenya, land hunger, a rootless proletariat, and a government built on discrimination. We have seen these things the world over and there are still men who look at the fight against injustice and call it savagery.

"Ah—" he says, catching my eye and smiling. "Are you shocked,

Rachel?" He knocks back the last of his glass of whiskey. "And I promised you I wouldn't talk about politics."

"Did you indeed, Nate Logan? Well, that was awfully dishonest of you," Lillian says, smiling. "I have never known a man more compelled to talk about politics."

We fall into silence again; each of us drawn close by the warmth of the fire at our backs, the astonishing beauty of the night, the words that have bound us together. The moon—heavy and golden— rises overhead, casting its trembling silver light over the black waters of the dam. There is a splash in the water—something swimming in the depths. Far off—a leopard makes his hoarse, sawing bark. My head swims with everything Nate has said, the State of Emergency, Gerald's words: *This country will be unrecognizable in ten years.* I was wrong to think that the unrest would be easily put down—whatever is happening in Kenya is only just beginning.

Harold drives out with Nate the following morning, fifty miles north into the bush. They will walk the last stretch, with their tents on their backs. It is Samburu country, and Nate says they will not be in any danger from the Kikuyu. Nate is tracking rhino, and they will have a chance to photograph the Samburu. Harold writes a note to Sara and gives it to me, saying, "I'll be back in a couple of weeks—I might not get this chance again." His eyes are shining, and I feel his excitement, and the guilt that taints it. We wave them off. After lunch, Lillian takes me home. "Your father will want you back now," she says. "He'll be worried, with everything that has happened."

We are quiet for most of the journey, after the excitement of the night before. I doze in and out of sleep, my head rattling on the rough roads, until at last we are driving up the track to the house.

I hug Lillian in the car and climb down. She raises a hand to Sara, declining the offer to stay for tea, saying she has to get back to Gerald, that he will worry if she stays away too long. When I am nearly out of reach, she grasps my hand and squeezes it. "Everything will be all right, Rachel. You'll see." I do not trust myself to turn around.

"And Harold?" Sara says, when we are standing alone below the steps of the veranda.

I gaze at her, feeling the weight of her emptiness, and hand her the note that he has written.

EARLY EVENING. Sara's voice carrying from the other side of the house, strident in accusation. *You should not have let him go.* The house feels empty without Harold. He was a deflection, and now it is just the three of us. It must have been like this for him, before I came.

I run a bath, change and go through to the sitting room. My father is sitting alone with a rifle across his lap. Sara is not there. I have only been away for five days but it feels as though everything has changed.

"Are you happy to use a gun?" He is cradling a small revolver in one hand, and he holds it up when he sees me.

"Do you need me to?" I ask, sitting down.

"There's Sara and I—but it would be helpful," he says, frankly, "to have another person in the house. Just in case."

He puts the revolver on the table in front of me, along with a small cardboard box of cartridges, and says, "You might find you feel safer if you have it with you."

I pick it up. It is black, the metal cold and heavy in my hand. I used my father's old .22 rifle as a child—shooting spring hares at night—but this is different. This gun speaks violence. It makes my hand shake and my head whirl. "Do you think there might be an attack? Here at Kisima?"

He runs a hand over his jaw, where his beard might have been, and looks at me. "I think we have to be careful. This is only the beginning."

I open the box and slide the heavy brass-cased bullets onto the table. "It takes six cartridges," he says. They clink against each other as they come to rest. He watches me, then comes round the table and shows me how to load the cylinder and rotate it. How to lift the gun and fire. "It has a good firing range—about forty-five meters, though you're best waiting until you're closer than that. It's easier than you might think to miss."

"What does it feel like?" I ask. "To pull the trigger. Does it hurt?"

My father looks up. Sara is standing in the doorway.

"Oh good," she says, walking into the room. "Your father thought you might be too young to handle a gun, but I said that was non-sense. You were brought up here after all. You know better than anyone what kind of violence these people are capable of."

"I haven't decided whether I'm going to take it," I say.

"Why ever not?" she asks, stopping to look at me, genuinely surprised. "When I was your age I would have been thrilled if my father had given me that kind of responsibility."

I don't know how to reply. I'm not sure she will understand my reticence, and I'm not sure I completely understand it myself. Something is taking shape in my mind. "I'm not sure I believe in violence," I say.

"How perfectly adorable," she says, giving a small, shrill laugh as she pours herself a gin from the bar. "Try telling that to the terrorists who slip into your bedroom in the middle of the night."

"Sara—" my father says.

I slide the gun back onto the table, unsure what to do with it.

"Your uncle Eliot—" My father sits down on the sofa and picks up a letter from the table, waving it in my direction; a change of subject. "They're having trouble again at Uplands."

"What kind of trouble?" I ask.

"Oh, a few of the men distributing political pamphlets, workers walking out on their shift, that sort of thing."

"Will they strike?"

"No—they couldn't do that. Not in the current climate." He looks at me more closely. "Of course—you were there during the strike in '46—"

"What strike?" Sara asks.

He glances at her. "The whole factory went on strike. Not a single African turned up to work for three days. But the thing that bothered my brother was the engine room. Someone had gone completely to town on it."

I stare at him. I have an image, suddenly, of Michael standing outside the engine room at Uplands with grease on his palm. "What do you mean—'gone to town on it'?"

"Dismantled the whole engine. Took some parts that had to be ordered in from Europe. Must have known what he was doing." He takes a sip of his whiskey. "They never did find the man who did it."

I think of the promise Michael exacted from me—*Are you going to tell your uncle that you saw me?* The light on in the engine room, the tools in his hand. I had seen the sweat beading on his forehead;

his fist slamming the wall in anger. It was Michael. He had sabotaged the engine. I look at my father and think that I should tell
him, but before I can speak someone knocks on the door, three
times. "Twice if there's danger," my father says, as Mungai comes
in carrying a tureen of soup, and the moment for me to speak has
passed. I will tell him later, when we are alone.

"GOING TO PUT HER OUT?" my father says after dinner, nodding
his head at Juno who is stretched out by the fire.

We stand at the open door, a pool of light at our feet, and watch
Juno disappear across the dark stretch of lawn. My father has his
revolver in his hand. I am about to tell him what I saw at the strike,
when something holds me back. I remember the taste of fear in my
mouth that day. The anger and frustration written into Michael's
face. In the clarity of the moment in which we had looked at each
other, he and I, it had felt as though we were on the same side. How
can I betray him all these years later, without talking to him first?

"You won't be able to wander off on your own," my father says.
"Not anymore. I'll want to know where you are."

"All right," I say, seeing Juno reappear, tail wagging. My father
bolts the door after her and kisses me good night. "If you hear anything strange, or you think there might be something wrong, ring
the bell in your room. I don't think it'll happen tonight, or anytime
soon. We'll have some warning before an attack. But still—we
should all be careful."

My room is cold, and the night outside is quiet and seemingly
empty, except for the wild animals and the men who are bedded
down in the forest, stockpiling weapons and hatred. A small steel

bell sits on my bedside table. How could so much have changed? Or had it always been like this, but I was a child, oblivious to the lines of political tension that connected the adults who protected me? I remember the morning after the strike, walking down the steps of my uncle's house at Uplands and seeing the ball of paper Steven Lockhart had thrown across the veranda. The same paper the lead striker had tucked into his shirt pocket, the same papers I had seen in Michael's hand. I opened it up. The words come back to me now in pieces, words that made no sense at the time. *African Workers' Union . . . Complaints . . . Indifference toward paying Africans equally . . . Partiality and disrespect shown to African workers . . . Deliberate devices to keep the African poor that he may keep at his work . . .* Had Michael believed in all of this? Did he believe in it now?

I turn on the radio at ten o'clock and wish that Harold was here. This side of the house feels too quiet and empty, and the voice from England accentuates the silence that lies beyond its reach. The news brings reports of mass oathing ceremonies among the Kikuyu; there doesn't seem to be a corner of the Highlands that hasn't been infiltrated by Mau Mau.

I reach over to turn down the lamp and lie there in the dark, listening to the small noises of the house; the flicker of a gecko through the thatch, the dripping of the bathroom tap. After a moment I put out my hand and feel for the gun on the table, but it is cold under my fingertips and offers little comfort.

AT BREAKFAST the following morning, Sara is not yet dressed, but she has made up her face, and the light catches the film of powder on her cheeks. She smiles at me and pats the chair beside her. "Come sit down, Rachel. Your father was up all night worrying about the Emergency. He's had such a lot to think about and now this hoo-ha with the labor."

My father gulps back his coffee. He doesn't look at me, and I realize he isn't going to tell me what she means. I have the uneasy sense that Sara is orchestrating this conversation, but curiosity gets the better of me. "What's happened?"

"Five of the men are missing from the labor line this morning," my father says. "They must have been oathing last night." He breathes out heavily. "The police picked two of them up on the road to Nakuru this morning, but the rest will be in the damn forest somewhere. They were all good men, good workers."

"All the more reason to get this over with," Sara says.

"Get what over with?" I ask.

My father looks at me then, and there is desolation in his glance, as though he has come to the end of something and—cornered— he has lost his courage.

Sara answers for him, "Steven Lockhart is coming this evening. Tomorrow he and your father will oversee moving the Kikuyu out of the *shambas*."

"What does that mean?" I ask my father, hearing the shrill note in my voice. "Where are they going?"

"Mostly back to the reserves," my father says, running a hand over his jaw.

"We are repatriating them." Sara is filling in for him. Efficiently explaining what he is finding so difficult to articulate. "We can't have so many Kikuyu here. It's too risky."

"Repatriating? But they live here. Most of them were born here." I look at my father. "What have they got to go back to?"

My father breathes into the back of his hand. "Steven Lockhart spent some time here on our labor line. He didn't feel it was safe having such large *shambas* so far from the house. They're too vulnerable to infiltration; to militants who might come down from the forest and force them to take the oath. We're setting up a *shamba* closer to the house for the Kikuyu who will stay. It will be safer for them, safer for us."

"How many are leaving?"

"About a hundred and twenty."

"Over half!" A missionary priest on the ship had talked about conditions in the reserves. Overcrowded, he said, and the land had turned to dust from too much grazing. That they were teeming with men who were back from the war with new ambition, new skills, and no means to make a living.

"Rachel—it was decided weeks ago. There's nothing that can be done about it now, so you might as well accept your father's decision with some grace."

"But how could you not have told me? After all the time I have spent there? How long have they known?"

"We told them a few days ago."

"Are there jobs for them in the reserves?" I ask my father. "How will they survive?"

"The Kikuyu have spent years living like Lords on your father's land," Sara says, "with as many goat and cattle as they like, not to mention wives, and God only knows how many children. It's time they understood that this land doesn't belong to them."

I don't say anything, conscious that I am on dangerous territory, but my silence isn't enough. She takes it as insolence. She wants me to concur.

"Rachel, your father fought tooth and nail to clear the land here."

"Well. If it's a question of sweat, blood and tears, I'd say they paid their share." My father worked hard here, I have no doubt, but so did the Kikuyu men and women who traveled here to work for him.

My father doesn't look at me, and neither of them say anything, so that my statement sits awkwardly between us, as some kind of demonstration of adolescent insolence perhaps.

Mungai comes out to serve me coffee. He asks me how I would like my eggs, and I am conscious of him listening to our conversation.

"What about Michael? And Jim?" I ask, when he is gone.

"Michael is staying," my father says. "And Jim of course."

"And his family?" I ask—thinking suddenly of Njeri.

"They will have to leave. All except his first wife and her children."

I stare at him, shocked. The world I am familiar with is crumbling down around me. "But Njeri has a baby only a few weeks old."

"I cannot make exceptions. I have spoken to Jim. I gave him the choice to stay with us, or to leave with two months' pay, and he has decided to stay. Njeri will be traveling with Mukami. There are his cousins who will be traveling with them, and he will of course send money home."

"It is better—" Sara says, "to have labor on the farm who are unattached."

"How could you agree to this?" I look at him, openmouthed.

"Goddamn it, Rachel. What would you have me do?" my father

stands up, thrusting the chair out behind him. "With Sara here? And now you? It isn't safe. Something has to change."

Sara says placidly, over the top of her cup of tea, "Your father isn't running a pension house, Rachel. The labor can't simply exist here as a picturesque backdrop to your childhood memories."

What she says stings. There is a hint of truth in it—enough to silence me.

She runs her tongue over her top teeth and says contemplatively, "You know what Steven said the other day? We should have a game license to shoot a certain number of—"

"Please, Sara," my father interrupts, through gritted teeth, looking at Mungai who has reappeared, and then at me. "It's no good for anyone talking like that."

I stare at her, unsure whether she has said it to rile me or because she genuinely believes it.

"I don't care who hears, darling. I have nothing to be ashamed about. This is your land, not theirs. We're only in this position because men like you have been too damned soft. Giving in to Whitehall, starting on the whole conversation of Africans' rights." She stands up from the table, puts down her napkin and walks around behind him. Leaning forward, she drapes her arms over his shoulders, so that her cheek rests next to his. I see one finger turning a circle on the center point of his chest. His eyes draw shut for a second, and he breathes out in a shuddering breath. She says, in a softer voice, that is for him and not me, "This is your land, Robert. And you mustn't let the cowardice of others make you feel as though you shouldn't have what is rightfully yours."

I can't believe her complacent self-conviction, and I wonder what my father sees in this woman. Something—I realize—that I cannot offer him. Some female concoction of softness and control that he craves.

"I don't understand," I say, desperately, looking away from them both. "They've been here as long as you have."

"Rachel—it's not as simple as that," he says, taking hold of Sara's hand in his and holding it still against his chest, as if he might not be able to talk while she is tracing a circle against his skin. And I feel there are two conversations going on at the table. The one between him and me, and the silent conversation between him and Sara. "In the early days so little land had been cleared. It was easy to set aside a few thousand acres for them to put up their *shambas* and graze their herds. But now we want to plant more coffee, tea, pyrethrum. There's a chance we could really make something of ourselves here in Kenya, instead of just scraping a living. It doesn't make sense to have tenant farmers. We need laborers."

"So is it a question of economy or security?"

"Both," my father says simply.

"Or perhaps the two just neatly coincide."

"What does that mean?" His voice is very cold.

"Only that it's rather convenient pushing through reforms on the farm under the cover of protecting yourself."

"Protecting all of us," he corrects.

"What would Mama say?"

He does not meet my eye. His face is tight with anger. "Your mother is not here."

"And Jim?" I ask—mustering up the courage to look at Sara. "I suppose you're keeping him on because you couldn't do without his cooking?" I stand up, and before I know what I am doing I have walked out of breakfast and I am boiling with anger. As I walk into the house I hear her say in the same soft, cajoling voice, "She's terribly spoiled, Robert. I shouldn't allow her to run all over you the way you do."

I run through the house and out of the front door. I have to get to the *shambas* and find Njeri, though I do not know what I will say to her when I am there.

THE TRACK TAKES ME past the stables, and it is only then that I remember Michael. He is working in the garage, and he looks up as I come in. We stand staring at each other. Worse than the idea that he sabotaged the engine at my uncle's factory is the sense that he might have loyalties that would make him hostile to the farm, to my father, even perhaps to me. I remember the last time we spoke, my embarrassment, *they look like good little missionary children.*

"Why were you at Uplands?" I ask him.

For the first time since I have known him he seems unsettled. He glances past the yard, down the path, and I follow his gaze but there is no one there, no one listening in. We both know how dangerous this could be for him.

"I knew Jomo Kimoi, the leader of the strike."

"The man who died?"

"Yes. The man who died." There is a tension exploding between us: a gulf of unsaid truth.

"You told me before that you were staying with a cousin."

"I was."

"Did you help to organize the strike?"

"I was involved."

"But you weren't arrested?"

He lifts his eyes to mine—and for a moment I see right into his soul, the purity of him. "No, *Memsaab*. I wasn't arrested."

"Why are you here?" I ask, desperately, thinking of the sabotage in the engine room, the political pamphlets in his hand, the promise I gave him as we stood opposite each other in that dark corridor, the gunshots ringing in our ears. I will have no choice but to tell my father.

"I told you before. Nairobi is no longer safe."

"But you knew I would be coming home—"

"They said you were never coming back," he says, softly. His words cut right through me. *They.* The Kikuyu. Whose gossip was always intuitive and never wrong. Was it my father who had said it first? Had he never believed I would come home, after all those years he had kept me in England?

"Are you still involved in politics?" The word sounds strange in my mouth. I do not know what I am really asking. I only know that it is dangerous for Africans to try to change the order of things in Kenya.

"No," he says, giving me a quick, direct look. "I have political beliefs, but I am not an activist. Not anymore."

"Why not?" I want to believe him, but I know I cannot. I want him to be real, but like everything at Kisima he has changed.

"The movement became too militant. I want to live in peace."

"Mau Mau are here, and they are not peaceful."

"Mau Mau are nothing to do with me." He says it with absolute conviction, looking me straight in the eye, wanting me to understand what he is saying, and—in that moment—I think I believe him.

As I DRAW CLOSE to the *shambas* I see men and women walking up the track toward me: whole families with their possessions—babies, pots and baskets—piled on their backs, on their heads, the women bowed beneath the weight of them. They aren't waiting for tomorrow, they are already leaving.

I step off the track and watch. Juno settles at my feet. Herds of goat and sheep are being driven before them, the men carrying switches, calling to them in soft, undulating voices. The reserves are hundreds of miles away, and they will have to walk every step of the way. I see Wangari—the woman who used to help in my mother's garden—toiling under the weight of an old suitcase balanced on her head; Joseph walking with a stick; Mukami, her youngest child on her back, and her older boy—who I watched building a miniature *shamba* out of twigs—clutching at her skirt.

"Njeri!" I see her, at last, walking on the other side of Mukami. She steps out of line. Her baby is swaddled across her front, tiny and hidden. I want to tell her to stop, to go back to the *shambas*—but who am I to promise her anything? I want to tell her to write to me, so I will know how I can find her, but she cannot write. My Swahili is not good enough to express what I want to say, and even if it was what words would I choose?

"*Kwa heri.*" *Good-bye.* I push my hands into my pockets and pull out what little money I have and press it into her hand, biting back frustration; this is all I can offer her. "*Kuwa na safari salama.*" *Have a safe journey.* She puts a hand to my cheek, as she did when I first saw her, then she turns and walks away.

I walk up to the *shambas*, staying clear of the track so that I won't be seen, tears blurring my eyes. Juno pads ahead of me, looking back from time to time to check I am following. I have to scramble over rocks and over streams, picking my way carefully in case of snakes, until I come through the trees onto the level plain. They have torn down most of the round, thatched mud houses. The *boma* fence has been stripped back, so that the acacia wall—which protected the livestock from lion and hyena—now trails across the dusty earth in a long, ragged line. Only five days ago the *shamba* stood as it had done my whole life, and now it is almost gone. A few dogs nose around, uncomfortable with the sudden destruction of the simple boundaries that defined their existence. There is no smell of smoke, no washing hanging on the *boma* to dry, no singing. They have gone and there is nothing I can do to bring them back.

I think about Michael; his admission that he was involved in the strike. It will be harder for me to tell my father, now that he has confided in me. I cannot live on the farm without saying something, and yet it feels like a betrayal. My father values Michael, but only if he can trust him. He would turn him over to the police in a second if he knew that he had been involved in the strike at Uplands.

I stay there, at the edge of the acacia forest, until I notice the air has become chill. The sun no longer filters through the tops of the trees, and it is later than I thought. There is an eerie quality to the deserted village. I stand up, stretching my legs. The forest is behind me, breathing its tapestry of sound. And then—like a radio being switched off—it falls silent. A chill flickers down my spine. Juno stiffens beside me and I put a hand on her neck to keep her quiet. In all the years I have been away, I have not forgotten the language of the bush—the chatter of birds when an eagle is near, the slow cracking of branches which heralds the approach of elephant, the low snort of a buffalo. But this sudden silence means one thing—a predator.

A jackal barks a warning. I look around me, but can see nothing through the tumbling layers of rock and trees. The gun that my father gave me is by my bed. I step out onto the track and begin to walk in the direction of the farm. Juno walks at my heels, ears back and head low. I know it is there before I see it—the whole landscape holds its breath—then the lion crosses the path in front of us—a huge male with a black mane which shimmers in the still air as he shakes off flies. He stops in the middle of the track and turns his head to look at us. My heart stops. Juno crouches, her body trembling in a low growl. I feel the distance between us, how easily he could cross it. Then he is gone, padding into the trees on the other side. My heart thuds back into motion and I take a juddering breath. I wait a few moments, then continue along the track. I know he will not be back—lion generally keep their distance—but his presence has unsettled me. For a moment I had forgotten that the forest is full of menace.

As I APPROACH the stables I breathe more easily. I am nearly home. The air is full of a soft dust that seems to catch and hold the last particles of the sinking sun, so that the earth is drenched in a haze of golden light.

A man in blue overalls is walking down the track toward me. It is Michael—his sandals slapping gently against the dry earth. I feel no fear when I see him—only relief; he has not left with the rest of the Kikuyu.

"*Memsaab*," he says, acknowledging me, "your father is looking for you." He is going to walk past me, but stops when he sees that I have stopped. It would be disrespectful for him to walk on. The sun is behind him, and his face, his body, are difficult to read.

I look down at the red earth. His sandals are the same black leather that all the Africans wear, the soles curved to the shape of his foot, from so many days of friction, his toenails smooth and pale like slivers of bone, and I feel a flicker of revulsion that takes me by surprise.

"Is he angry?"

Michael does not reply. He glances beyond me, down the path, and I sense his impatience. It is an effort to keep himself here. He would rather be on his way back home, to the hut behind the stables. To gather his things, perhaps, and slip away into the night. He will not say good-bye. I cannot expect him to. I feel betrayed, although the betrayal is all mine.

"Michael—" I notice for the first time the feel of his name in my mouth, the strange breach of respect that comes with using his first name—the same assumed intimacy you adopt with a child. "I've been down to the *shambas*. I did not know. I am sorry—" The apology carries a note of triteness that I wasn't expecting, and this distorts what I am trying to say.

Still he does not look at me.

"What about your family? Have they gone?"

"Yes."

"But you will stay?" I say it because I do not think he should have to leave, but I realize that I am a coward. It is not enough. Without thinking I articulate the thing that has been forming inside me. "I want you to know that I won't say anything." I look up the path, toward the house, checking we are alone, only at this moment making up my mind. "About the strike. I won't tell my father, or anyone else. You should stay at Kisima if you want to."

He doesn't reply. He is standing with his back to the house, to the sun which has slipped beneath the horizon. It has grown too dark for me to read the expression on his face. Almost before I realize he has moved, I see the dark shape of him walking away from me down the path. It is late. The air is very still. I walk quickly toward the house, aware of the gathering dark at my back, bracing myself for my father's anger.

MY FATHER IS SITTING on the veranda when I come up to the house.

"Where have you been?" he asks quietly.

"To the *shambas*," I say, my heart knocking against my chest. I can hear the anger in his voice, but I do not want to apologize.

"Sit down." He motions to a chair beside him.

"They have left already," I tell him, sitting. "You should have been there to watch them go."

"And you should not," he says, his voice cold. "I told you not to go anywhere without telling me. What were you thinking?"

"The *shambas* are deserted." I am sure that if he only hears what I have to say, then he will understand. "Even the small children had to walk. Joseph was there, with his family. They were carrying everything they own on their backs."

"I am disappointed in you, Rachel," my father says, ignoring what I have said. "Your behavior since you arrived has not been what I might have expected. There are others in this household besides yourself, and we all have to live together."

I was sure that he would want to hear what I have seen, but now I feel mortified, as though I have behaved like a child.

"Sara was shocked by the way you spoke at breakfast. I told her that it was not really you; that you are struggling to adjust to life here."

"I am sorry, Papa," I say, and the tears come despite my trying to stop them. And I am sorry—that I have angered him, though I cannot be sorry for everything that I have said.

He stands up and motions to the land beyond the house, falling into darkness. I notice now the revolver in his hand. "It isn't easy for any of us. And we cannot be too careful. They are getting bolder and stronger every day."

"I need to have some freedom," I say, wiping the tears away and standing up with him. "I cannot be in the house all day. You said yourself it was safe as long as it was light."

"You can go as far as the stables."

"And the dam?"

He pauses for a moment. "As long as you tell us when you are going."

"Thank you," I say, and he puts a hand on the back of my neck, in an old, familiar gesture of affection, as though the issue has been resolved. But I am uneasy—he has forced an apology from me, and it was not given entirely in truth. I feel as though a part of me has been driven outside the realm of his authority, and it does not seem so difficult now for me to keep my promise to Michael.

"Rachel—we were worried about you—" Sara says, when I come through to the sitting room. My father smiles at me warmly, an acknowledgment that the conversation on the veranda is behind us. "You remember Steven?" I see him then, standing at the bar. "He's here to organize the move from the *shambas*."

"They have already moved," I say, quietly.

"So I gather," Steven says, smiling at me, his eyes settling on mine. There is an assessment that flickers from my face down to my chest and back to my face. A kind of unashamed evaluation, as though he knows exactly what I am and why he is interested in me, and what I think and how much I know it is irrelevant to the outcome. "A drink?" he asks, raising his eyebrows.

"Water," I say, sitting down in one of the armchairs by the fire.

"We were just talking about Michael—" my father says to me. He takes a long sip of his whiskey and puts a hand to the shotgun resting against the sofa beside him.

I focus on his face, feeling my heart swallow itself, then thud into motion. What about Michael? "I saw him on the track this evening."

"Yes—Steven and I met with him. His brother Samuel was one of the boys missing from the labor line."

Steven Lockhart walks across the room to hand me a glass and I smell the soap he has used, sour and strong, and feel his fingers cold against my hand as I take it from him.

"What did he say?" I ask, thinking it explained Michael's terseness. They must have tried to tease information out of him, and he must have wondered if I had already said something to my father.

"That he didn't have anything to do with it. Went to their *shamba* this morning and his brother was gone. He's probably not lying—the other three left to be repatriated today."

"Didn't he used to teach you?" Sara asks, and I feel Steven's eyes settling on me.

"He taught Rachel for a year," my father says. "When he got back from the war."

"How old were you?" Steven asks.

"I was eleven."

"It seems very young, to be left alone with one of them," Sara says. Then—to my father—"What on earth drove you to that decision?"

"Rachel's mother insisted," my father says.

"And you agreed," she says, as though it is proof of his weakness.

"I rather respected her decision at the time. She didn't want Rachel sent off to school so young. He was a good, hardworking Kikuyu boy."

"The only good Kikuyu . . ." Steven says, picking his teeth with his fingernail. *Is a dead Kikuyu.*

"But schooling is so incredibly important. Particularly in Africa," Sara says to my father. "You can't have a child growing up like a native."

"Did he ever talk about politics with you?" Steven asks me.

I hesitate for just a second. "No," I say, thinking that it is—after all—not quite a lie.

He looks at me for a moment, a slight question on his face, as though I might reveal myself to him. As if he has caught my hesitation, and he can take it in his mind and mold it into something.

"Did you ever feel threatened by him?"

"In what way?"

"Physically?" He pauses. "Sexually?"

I shake my head, cheeks coloring.

"Steven—honestly. Everyone has a brother or a cousin who is Mau Mau." My father draws a hand over his face. "He's been through the war, for God's sake. He was an engineer in Burma.

He has a better grasp of English history than half the Europeans living out here. I can't see he's going to embrace a return to some kind of tribal idyll."

"Still—" Steven says, running a hand over the top of his revolver, "you must be careful thinking that because he's *civilized* he's on our side. Those are the ones you have to watch out for. They've fought in the war, shared a mess tent with a bunch of English boys, pulled the trigger on Europeans who look like you or me. They've probably slept with a few white whores, and it makes them feel all of a sudden like they could have our job."

"I trust Michael implicitly. We've got to draw the line of suspicion somewhere," my father says, putting an end to the conversation, but it sounds weak, the plea of a man who is asserting himself in the face of defeat.

XIV

-≻•≺-

I am kneeling down in the large barn behind the two tractors with their jutting metal arms. The yard outside is empty. Michael has been working up at the dairy for a week, helping my father install new equipment. It is cool and dark in here at the back, under the tall, pitched roof. A few shards of light, escaping through seams in the corrugation, illuminate the spiraling dust. Everything is quiet except for the scratching of crows' feet on the metal roof above me.

The two locked trunks are at my feet. I have a penknife and I am trying to flick open the lock on the one nearest me. My father has mislaid the keys. I swear again as my knife pops uselessly out.

A scraping noise behind me. I turn around. One of the wide doors pushes open and a shaft of light slides across the floor. Michael walks a few paces into the barn, blinking in the darkness. For a moment I can see him before he can see me. He runs a hand over his cropped hair and breathes out. His overalls are peeled down to his waist, and his vest is illuminated white in the dark.

Then his eyes pick me out, crouched on the floor.

"Michael—" I swallow, standing up, feeling caught out. I see him watching me, waiting. "I can't get the locks open—" To my surprise tears prick at the back of my eyes and I bite them back.

For a moment I think he might walk away, then he steps forward and pulls a bit of wire from his pocket. He crouches down in front of the trunk. I look down at his brown, curled hair, the dust-soaked white vest, the bunched muscles of his shoulders. A rivulet of sweat runs down the dark indentation of his neck.

It only takes him a moment—a few seconds with the piece of wire, and he has sprung open the lock. He does the same for the second.

"Thank you," I say, unnerved by how quickly he has achieved what I have spent the last hour trying to do. He stands up, moving away from me toward the doors.

"Michael—"

He stops, but does not turn around.

"I heard about your brother—they were talking about it at the house."

He says nothing.

"You should know—my father trusts you."

Still he is silent. All I can see is the curve of his vest in the shadows. I feel I have nothing to lose. Somehow it is easier to speak the truth, here where there is scarcely any light. "Why don't you say anything? Why do you ignore me?"

"I am not ignoring you, *Memsaab*."

"You don't trust me," I say, standing up. "You think that I will say something about the strike to my father."

There is a long silence. Then he shifts his weight in the liquid dark of the barn. I hear him breathe out heavily. His voice is different when he speaks. It is softer, more natural. "It would be difficult for you not to, Rachel." He has called me by my name, and the sound of his voice articulating it, the sense of closeness it brings, sends a current right through me and I realize with a shock that this is what I have wanted. "If things get difficult on the farm. If there is an attack, why should you not tell your father?"

"Because I trust you. I don't believe you would do anything to put us in danger."

"That is easy for you to say now."

"How can I convince you?"

He walks a little way toward me, close enough that I can feel the heat rising from his body. "Why are you so determined to convince me? It would be much easier for you if I left."

The question throws me. I am not sure myself. Why do I care so much? Am I still trying to patch together the broken bits of my childhood? Is it because my mother had faith in him? But there is more to it than that, more than I can articulate, so instead I say, "I want you to stay. We're virtually under siege here. Who else am I going to talk to?"

I say the last bit with desperation, and he laughs, softly, in the dark, looking down at me, and I notice his height, the closeness of his body, the slow softness with which he moves. He has shed his other self and has become, all of sudden, real. It is what I wanted from him, what I have wanted since I first came back to the farm and saw him in the yard, but it is more frightening than I imagined. I have opened up something that he wanted to keep hidden. Now that it is open there will be no closing it again. The light catches the side of his face, shining in the dark.

"You know that I would be arrested if you said anything?" His voice drops to a hoarse whisper. "Even an allusion to what happened at Uplands would be enough to have me transported to a camp. They are lawless places. Men are tortured and executed."

"I know."

"I don't say this for my own sake—though I won't pretend it doesn't scare me—but because all of this becomes your responsibility if you find you cannot stay silent."

"I understand."

We both start at a noise in the yard. Footsteps and my father's voice calling Michael's name.

He wipes his hands on his overalls and walks out, leaving me sitting in the near dark. I don't follow him. I don't want to see my father just at the moment.

I listen to their voices talking about the replacement parts they need to pick up for one of our Land Rovers in Nakuru, a new digger that should be arriving next week to dig up the forest that stands in front of the old *shambas* so they can cultivate it for coffee.

As my father says good-bye, he asks in a quieter voice, "Is Rachel there?" And I think for a moment he might come in and see me, to apologize perhaps for the way things have been and help me sort through the trunks. But I hear his footsteps walk out of the yard and I wonder if it even crossed his mind to come inside, and whether I am glad after all that he didn't.

I hover over the trunks full of my mother's things. Now that they have been unlocked, I cannot bring myself to lift the lids and see what is inside. I am not ready. I want to keep them as they are— full of possibility. I cannot have this moment twice. Instead I pick up my mother's old, split-cane fishing rod, lying on the floor against the back wall, and sift through the cardboard boxes until I find some rusted lures which I can polish.

When I emerge from the barn, Michael is squatting with his back against the wall, stroking Juno. I jump—not seeing him at first—and then stand a little awkward now in the bright sunlight, after the things I said in the barn.

"What news is there of the Emergency?" he asks, softly, and I glance down at him. He meets my look, unflinching, and I realize that he can ask something of me that he wouldn't have asked before, and it scares me a little.

"You haven't read the papers?"

"The Kikuyu papers have been banned. Your father used to pass on his copy of the *Standard*, but he stopped a few weeks ago." I remember Michael listening to the radio in the yard, the concentration on his face, and realize that this is what drew him to me—he was thirsty for the news. I had not seen that it was so important to him, and how cut off he must feel without it.

"There have been more sweeps in Nairobi. Arrests."

"Kenyatta?" His eyes sharpen on mine.

"Yes," I say, quietly. It was on the radio last night. Jomo Kenyatta—the political leader who had so far managed to keep himself free of association with the violence of Mau Mau. Nate had said he was the great hope for *uhuru*—independence—in Kenya.

His jaw clenches, the muscle ripples in his cheek. If I was closer I think I might hear his teeth grind. "On what charges?"

"Leading the extremist wing of the Mau Mau. Inciting hatred and violence against Europeans. The creation of the Mau Mau oaths."

He looks away, down the track. I can feel the anger in his silence, in his absolute stillness. I asked Nate about Kenyatta, the morning after the State of Emergency was declared. Well-educated, articulate and seemingly moderate in his politics, Kenyatta had spent sixteen years in England, had written for the *Times*, even published books. He represented hope—if the British were going to consider independence, they would start by talking to Kenyatta. By arresting him they had made their position absolutely clear.

Michael doesn't look up at me again, and I leave him sitting in the yard. As I walk back to the house I feel uneasy. Have I done the right thing, promising that I will not tell my father? If Michael's loyalties are pushed, which side will he choose? But there is something in him that I trust, and it feels stronger and more truthful than the politics put forward by Steven Lockhart.

My father may have warned me away from the new *shamba*, but I cannot spend all day indoors. I take my mother's spinning rod, with its cork handle, and walk down to the dam. The reel glides easily under my hand. She stocked the long dam with black bass. My father used to bring me down at the end of the day, when the sun was losing its intensity, and we would find her on the bank, wading knee-deep in the water, reeling in her catch. He never fished himself—said he didn't have the patience—but he would show me how to gut the fish that she had caught, sliding a knife into the smooth belly, scooping out the guts, then rinsing the blood-flecked body in the water. We would walk back together in the cool evening air, me trailing behind them, running a stick through the dust, their voices lifting softly into the fading light.

The dam is vast. It stretches as far as I can see, and the forest borders the far eastern bank in the distance. I push through the scrub and long grass along the bank to get to the casting platform. It has rotted a little and isn't as steady as it used to be, but it will

hold my weight. I pull my gun from my belt and lay it on the platform behind me, then take the lure from my pocket, spit on it and
polish it against my shirt. I throw out my line. The spinner makes
a small splash, sinking deep into the water. I reel it in slowly.

The bank of trees is dark and heavy, and I feel isolated here, but
I am not unhappy because of it. A herd of buffalo come down to the
shore on the far side to drink. In the distance I can hear the dull
ringing of cattle bells. The birds calling across the water are soothing, and I soon grow to believe that this is my territory and that
beyond in the trees belongs to elephant, buffalo, leopard and lion;
and to the men who share the forest with them. That I am safe in
this small clearing on the bank, at the edge of the platform.

I catch three bass, gut and clean them, and carry them back to
the house. I will offer them to Jim. I have not talked to him about
his family leaving; about the *shambas* being dismantled. I do not
know what to say, and my shame keeps me silent.

"RACHEL—" Sara says at dinner one evening, "I gather your dog
is going to have puppies soon?"

"Yes."

"I hope you're not expecting her to have them in the house."

I look at her in surprise. "Where else would she have them?"
She doesn't reply. "What if something goes wrong? I want to be
with her when she gives birth."

"She's not a pedigree. I'm sure she'll manage just like all the *shenzi*
manage. God knows they don't seem to have any trouble breeding."

"Can I not keep her in my bedroom, when she whelps?"

"I really don't think so. There'll be such a mess."

"Rachel—" my father says, looking at me across the table, "Sara was very accommodating when you asked her if Juno could sleep in the house, but I think you can understand how she feels about this." I do not see in him the same man who sat on the veranda with Nate two weeks ago, and said—smiling—that we could go to the Markhams. I wonder if this careful support of Sara's wishes is the price he has had to pay for letting Harold go.

"From tomorrow," Sara says, slipping her fingers over my father's hand, "she can sleep at the stables."

"Of course," I say, remembering my father's words at the dam: *I would like you to make a particular effort with her. If you are going to stay.*

THE NEXT MORNING, I open up one of the stable doors and sweep out the dust. The yard is empty. Juno watches me from the open door—she is walking more slowly now, moving between patches of shade to keep out of the sun.

This is the stable I brought her to, when I found her on the rubbish heap at the dairy and I thought she might die. I shake down straw to cover the concrete floor and—as if showing her satisfaction—she sniffs it appreciatively, turns a circle and lies down heavily. She will be comfortable here, but if the puppies come at night I won't be able to help her.

I lay my hand on her belly; the smooth, hairless skin, split now by a dark line down the center, and her nipples, swollen and pink, the milk already gathering. As my hand rests there I feel a movement underneath it. A turning like the rotation of a ball beneath her skin. I remember Michael saying, *I could feel them moving.* My pulse quickens. She will have her puppies soon.

I AM WOKEN in the night by the grating call of a leopard, guttural and low, like a saw being drawn roughly through wood. I shiver, turning over in bed, listening. It is some way off—the stables, perhaps, attracted by the smell of Juno. Of all the predators, I fear leopard the most. They are silent and full of cunning, hunting under the cover of darkness, stalking their prey until they can pounce, deathly and quick.

It calls again, a rough coughing, splintering the quiet. It is unusual to hear one so close to the house. A leopard took one of my parents' lion dogs. I was six years old. We could see its paw prints deep in the dust the following morning, just a few meters from the front door. For a week afterward it circled the house, grunting, until one evening my father hobbled the legs of a goat and tethered it to one of the trees on the lawn. He sat at the sitting room window with his shotgun. All night I could hear the goat's desperate bleating. My father waited for hours. When he put down his gun to relieve himself in the bucket at his feet, the leopard struck—almost, he said, as though it had been watching him. By the time he had his gun in his hand a few seconds later, the leopard was nothing more than a shadow slipping through the long grass. The goat had been ripped from the tree. The leopard did not come back, though my father waited for it night after night, and for months afterward the goat's terrified bleating haunted my sleep.

THE NEXT MORNING, before I let Juno out, I look for the leopard's tracks in the yard, but I can't see anything. I sink my head into Juno's soft coat, wondering if it has been here, and whether it will come back.

XV

➤➤•◄◄

Sara suggests a trip to Nakuru. "It's time you saw a little civilization," she says. "We don't want you turning native."

I am happy to go with her—it has been a month since I was last in town.

I leave Juno locked in the stable—she is large now and moves more slowly, and I do not want her running away to have her puppies. When I step down from the veranda, Sara is slipping on her sandals and sliding into the Land Rover. She is wearing a yellow dress, which rides up above her knees when she sits, and she has a white canvas holster around her waist to hold her revolver.

"Do you like it?" she asks, laughing, running a hand over the canvas. "I ordered it from Nairobi."

The short rains haven't come and the land is dry as tinder—I can hear it in the grass snapping under my feet and the trees rasping their thorns along the side of the car.

As we drive down onto the road to Nakuru we pass a large white sign, newly painted in capitals. WARNING: IT IS MOST DANGEROUS TO PICNIC IN THIS AREA BECAUSE OF TERRORIST GANGS.

A convoy of army jeeps crawls along the road ahead of us, loaded with troops wearing red berets and khaki shirts—British troops erupting from hiding, like termites from a ransacked mound.

"Lancashire Fusiliers—shipped in straight from England," Sara says, as she maneuvers past them. Two of the soldiers tip their berets and whistle at us as we drive past, and Sara smiles knowingly at me, as though we have colluded.

On the outskirts of town, we are forced to stop at a roadblock. Military jeeps are parked up on the side of the road, and crowds of Africans are being corralled into groups by Europeans and *askari* in uniform, carrying guns.

"A raid?" I lean forward to see better. A canvas tent has been erected, and a few *askari* are milling round a European officer.

"I expect so," Sara says. "Steven said they would be making arrests."

A soldier in khaki waves us on, but Sara pulls in behind one of the army vehicles.

She takes a pocket mirror from her bag and touches up her lipstick, her lips pulled back against her teeth. "Let's have a little look around," she says, giving me a crimson smile, and pushing her hair behind her ears. She is excited by the army jeeps, the soldiers, the shouts coming from the market.

"Are you sure?"

"Where's your sense of adventure?" she asks, rebelliously. "Come on. You must be a little curious?"

I climb out of the Land Rover and follow her over to the small tent. An officer is sitting on a safari chair in the shade of a canvas tarpaulin, with a small camp table in front of him, writing notes on a piece of paper. It is Steven Lockhart. My stomach gives a lurch. I want to turn back. I am about to step away, when—"Hey!" a soldier shouts, stepping abruptly in front of us. "Where do you think you're going?"

Sara smiles at him sweetly, and the English boy—who is about my age—is caught between duty and admiration. Steven looks up, his pale eyebrows raised in a flare of irritation, but when he sees it's us, his face breaks into a wide smile, his pink lips spreading to show a row of neat square teeth. It is too late for me to back away.

"You girls here to see a bit of British justice in action?" he asks, jovially.

"If you don't mind," Sara says, ducking under the shade of the tent and bending down to kiss him on the cheek.

"By all means," he says, waving his hand, "stay. Watch the charade. They're wily buggers, but we have our ways."

From where we are standing, in the shade of the canvas, I can see past the vehicles to the Africans. More—on their way to town, a long walk on a hot day—are being forced to squat down in lines, their hands behind their necks, while policemen prod guns at their backs and shout at them for talking. It is almost midday and the sun is directly overhead. There are over a hundred men waiting to be interrogated. I am hot just standing under the canvas, but they will be squatting here in the dirt for hours before they will all be seen. A soldier jabs a boy forward with the tip of his gun, so that he walks right past the table where we are standing. It's then that I notice the figure in a white pointed hood with holes for his eyes, standing in the shadows at the back of the canvas. As the boy walks past him, the hooded figure says, "No."

"The *gakunia*," Steven says. "He's from town. Pretty reliable at pointing them out."

We watch six more men go past, then—just as Sara begins to shift her feet and look restless—a man is prodded forward, next in line. As he walks past us the *gakunia* gives a little nod. The man standing before us is in his forties, unshaven. His hair is long enough to form small dreadlocks. I realize—with a jolt—that I know him. It is one of Michael's brothers—Samuel—the one who had been missing from the labor line. His eye catches mine, and he looks away. Michael was the lucky one, the bright one, picked out by his parents to go to school. Samuel has not eaten on both sides of the table.

Steven talks to the *gakunia* in Swahili, then turns back to us. "He says he does not recognize the man. He is new to town. Which means he is either on the run or he has been drafted in to cause trouble; to oath in other men."

"This will be interesting," Sara says to me in a hot whisper, excited by what we're watching, and I realize she doesn't recognize him.

Samuel steps forward in front of the table.

"Your *kipande*?" Steven holds out his hand for Samuel's registration card, which is hanging around his neck. Samuel pulls it over his head and hands it to him.

"Do you understand English?" Steven asks, looking at the *kipande*.

Samuel runs his tongue over his lips as if preparing himself, then says, "Yes."

"Yes, *Effendi*," Steven corrects him. "Where have you been?"

"The market."

"Say *Effendi*," Steven says.

Samuel pauses, just for a second. I feel his humiliation. A man, reduced to a child, so that Steven Lockhart can flex his muscles and assure himself of his own strength. "*Effendi.*"

"Where do you work?" His identity card must be forged.

"I have no work."

"*Effendi!*" Steven snaps, spittle flying from his mouth.

"*Effendi,*" Samuel repeats, licking at his lips, glancing at the guard, his gun and us, then back at the District Officer as though unsure where the threat is going to come from next.

"Do you have brothers?" Steven asks.

"Yes," Samuel says, then—too late—adds, "*Effendi.*"

"Bugger you." Steven pushes back his chair. His face is hot and red. "Say it again," he says, giving him a slow, hard slap across the cheek.

"*Effendi,*" Samuel says, not flinching.

"And again," Steven says, slapping him on the other cheek.

"*Effendi,*" he says, his eyes watering, dripping out hate.

"Where are your brothers?" the District Officer asks, sitting down.

"One is in Nairobi, *Effendi*, working for the government. The others are in Lari," his eyes never venture to mine.

"And you—what are you doing in Nakuru?"

"I came to Nakuru to find work, *Effendi.*" The emotion has drained from his face.

"Do you recognize him?" Steven asks, pushing back his chair and looking up at us both, turning his pen end on end with a slow tap on his desk. I feel the muscles in my neck stiffen.

Sara shakes her head. "I can't say that I do—but all of Robert's laborers look the same to me. Rachel—you used to go down to the *shambas*—"

Steven turns his gaze on me. His cold, blue eyes settle on mine, and I feel for a moment as though I am the one being interrogated.

"I don't know him," I say simply, looking away, my heart thudding in my chest so that I can barely swallow. It is the second time that I have lied to Steven Lockhart, and I know him well enough by now to know that he is more perceptive than he seems. And I know also that I am not sure lying is the right thing to do. This man could be dangerous, to me, to my family and perhaps even to his brother.

"Are you sure?" Steven asks, and there is something in the suspicion that hovers at the corners of his mouth, in the hollow emptiness of his eyes, that makes my blood turn cold, but it is too late to change course.

"Yes," I say, my voice very quiet.

"Take him away," Steven says suddenly, wearily, with a wave of his hand, and the man is muscled down the line, the policeman holding a gun to his lower back, nudging him forward, tripping into a cordon of Africans who are crouched under the glare of the sun with no shade.

"Where will he go?" Sara asks, dusting down her yellow dress.

"To a detention camp. I don't trust him. A few weeks at Yatta and the truth will sweat right out of him." He makes a note in a book. A bead of moisture drips from his forehead into his mustache and his hair is pressed mousy and wet across his forehead. Yatta was a detention camp run by an officer with a reputation for being outside the restraint of the law. "We can't afford to take any chances."

"He's rather impressive, don't you think?" Sara says, as we get back into the Land Rover.

I don't reply. I feel sick to my stomach. From Steven Lockhart's bullying, from the ease with which I lied to him, from the sense that I might not have done the right thing.

THE DUSTY STREETS leading into Nakuru are a riot of color and noise: rolls of cotton fabric are laid out on the grassy verge, a donkey stumbles under the weight of a cart piled high with tires, cars beep their horns as they wait for the road to clear. The main street is more sedate: Europeans shopping for Christmas, calling to each other from their open-topped jeeps to exchange news and gossip. A newcomer might not guess that we are under a State of Emergency, but looking closely you see the revolvers at every hip, the *askari* on the street corner, the anxious faces.

Sunlight glints off the corrugated roofs of roadside shacks, dotted amongst newer, faceless buildings made of concrete and brick; shops, banks, dress shops, agricultural warehouses and hardware stores. Sara pulls up outside the hair salon and disappears inside. I make my way to the grocer. The tarmac is sticky under my plimsolls, melting in the heat. Outside, wooden crates are stacked with mangos, figs, runner beans and huge, gnarled squash. Green and yellow bananas hang in bunches from hooks. I duck my head and step inside. A fan turns on the ceiling. Canvas bags full of spices are packed waist-high on the concrete floor: cinnamon, cloves, nutmeg, paprika. I stand breathing in the potent, heady smell of India as I did as a child. A Sikh boy serves me, filling brown paper bags full of the raisins, almonds and sugar I promised Jim I would buy for the stollen my mother used to make at Christmas.

Outside the Rift Valley Club—where we have agreed to meet for lunch—Sara smooths a hand self-consciously over her newly cropped hair and touches up her lipstick. She smiles at several people as we walk in, and the women smile politely back at her, but they do not rise from their tables, or ask us to join them, and I feel a pang of sympathy for Sara, who cannot fit in here, and dislike for these settler wives I do not know, who make no secret of their disdain.

A waiter comes to our table. I order a soda, and she asks for a martini. "Don't tell your father," she says, winking at me.

"Now—I don't want you being a sourpuss about Steven," she says, when our drinks arrive.

"He enjoyed us watching. He was harder on the man."

"Honestly, Rachel—you'd think we were the ones hacking people to death in their beds as they slept. You can't tell me you sleep easily at night, knowing they're out there?" She takes a sip of her martini. "You have to remember these officers are the ones out fighting the Micks. It's their friends—just like ours—being picked off."

And I know there is some truth to what she is saying. I don't sleep easy. In fact, I barely sleep at all. The nights sift out slower than an hourglass, and they are full of noises which bring me— startled—upright in bed, reaching a hand out to the gun that lies by my bedside. But I know what it is to be teased by Steven Lockhart's claws. I have seen his injustice, and I feel sympathy for those who fall across the threshold of his power. But something else haunts the edges of my waking mind. What if Steven Lockhart finds out that I have lied to him? What power would that give him over me?

XVI

→>•<←

Harold returns from his expedition in the bush. He looks stronger—more robust—and older. His skin glows from the sun, and his eyes shine with happiness. He shows us photographs of the Samburu village where he and Nate stayed for a week, sleeping in a hut, recording the customs of the tribe. And the camp in the bush where their Samburu tracker found rhino. In the cold early mornings they heated coffee over a small stove, and at night they roasted antelope over the fire. He exudes a contentment which I have not seen in him before, a confidence that radiates, like the newfound words which tumble out of him.

He tells us stories of the bush—the two bull elephants who ambled through camp, delicately stepping over the guy ropes of their tent, the lionesses who fought over a kill under the silver light of the moon, just a few yards from where they were sleeping. He has transformed, but Sara hovers at the edge of the room, withholding her approval. She won't sit down to look at his photographs, and he glances at her every few minutes, and I can see he is hoping for a word of interest or praise. Slowly his enthusiasm flattens under her silence, until he puts his photographs away and his eyes lose their quick spark.

"You'll have to get down to some proper work," Sara says eventually, when she sees that her disapproval has had the desired effect, "now that you're back. You've spent enough time roaming around in the bush with Nate Logan."

I glance up at her, trying to read in her face what her voice will not tell me—the threat she feels from Nate Logan. Is it simply his liberal politics; or is it that when Harold is with Nate, he slips beyond her grasp?

I GO DOWN to the stables in the late afternoon to put Juno inside for the night. Michael is in the garage looking at the engine on one of my father's jeeps.

"How long do you think she has?" I ask him.

He crouches down, and Juno pads over to him. Her belly is heavy, and she walks awkwardly. He lets her push her head into his hands, then he runs them down her neck and she shudders. She stands with her head low. He puts a hand under her belly and pulls at one of her teats, and a few drops of milk fall into the dust.

I lead her into the stable, and she turns circles in the straw, but she is too restless to stay lying down for long. I sit with her for an hour. When dusk falls, she is standing in a corner facing the wall, shuddering. She vomits a little on the straw. It is late, and I have to go back to the house. When I step out into the yard I see that Michael has already left.

I go to my room after supper, but do not undress. I stand at the window. Outside there is no moon, and the land is completely dark. They say Mau Mau never come down from the mountains unless there is a moon. I hear my father checking the windows in the sitting room, turning out the lamps, the tread of his feet moving away from my bedroom toward his own. After a long moment, I open my door carefully, walk into the hall and take my father's torch from the bureau near the door. I go back to my bedroom and pull a chair close to the window. I rest the torch and my gun on the window ledge, open the latch and scramble out. My feet drop onto the earth outside.

The torch casts a small pool of yellow light onto the ground. I swing it over the bushes, looking for eyes reflected in its beam, but all I see are the tiny white pupils of a dik-dik. I pick up the gun. A bird calls out into the blackness—*wheep wheep wheep*. I am afraid out here on my own, and I stand caught between the house and the path for a long moment, the blood pounding so loudly in my head that I can scarcely hear my own breathing. Could the same leopard I heard a few nights ago be out again tonight?

I push myself into motion, walking down the path toward the stables, the bush close and dark around me. The light from the torch makes a tiny imprint on the vast blackness of the night. My plimsolls grind too loud on the dry earth. At last I see—with relief—the edge of the garage wall. I am here. Within the walls of the yard I feel safer. I feel for the top of the stable door. My hand slips forward into dark, empty space. With a lurching sensation I pull it back. Someone has opened the top door. I can hear a panting inside. Juno. I grip the gun—cold and damp in my palm—and force myself to lean over the top of the door and scan the torch over the stable. Blades of straw, Juno lying down on her side, and then—the legs of a man, crouched in the corner. Just as I find his face with the beam, he says, "Rachel—" and I breathe out a ragged breath.

"Michael?"

"Come inside."

I hesitate for only a moment, then I lift the latch and slip beyond the door. He is Kikuyu and I should not be alone with him like this—I cannot forget it, but I do not feel afraid.

Juno's ribs are heaving up and down. Her tail wags a little when she sees me and I remember the same look on her face when she was a small puppy. The goodwill, in the midst of her pain.

"Turn off the torch," he says, softly.

I sit down against the wall, a little way from him, my feet deep in the straw, and switch off the beam of light. The darkness closes in around me, thick and tangible. I blink to clear it—to see something in its depths, but there is nothing.

I feel the graze of his skin, dry against mine, as he pushes his hands toward me, then something warm and soft between them. I take it from him and hold it to my face. It smells of blood and milk and I can feel its short, damp breath against my cheek.

After a moment, he reaches out a hand for the torch, turns it on and rests it on the straw. I see a wet sac, newly born, and Juno licking at it until the sac splits and comes away and there is a puppy. She licks it, over and over, coaxing it into life, her tongue rasping on its wet fur, but it lies motionless, wet and black and not moving.

"Is it all right?"

Michael turns the puppy over with one hand so that it lies on its back. Juno is still licking with her tongue and I can see its pale, hairless belly, then—just when I am sure that it must be dead—it stretches out its tiny paws and opens its pink mouth, showing a set of sharp white teeth.

"It's alive," I say, breathing out.

"Yes," he laughs softly. "She has done well."

He takes the other puppy from me and places it close to Juno—where a third puppy is already suckling—and she lies with her head in the straw and then the three puppies are at her nipples and I can hear the mewling, the gentle sucking. I can see the fur of the two older puppies already drying to a golden color, the same color as their mother, the same color as the straw.

He turns off the torch and we sit with the darkness settling thick and impenetrable around us.

"I saw your brother in Nakuru," I say.

He says nothing.

"He has been sent to Yatta."

"Yes."

"You know?"

"A man said that there were two white women from Kisima. That you told Lockhart that you did not know him."

So he knows that I lied. "Yes."

"Why did you lie?"

"Would you rather that I had not?"

"It is not a question of what I want."

"I would not have lied to another officer." I breathe out. "In the end it didn't help—Steven Lockhart sent him anyway."

We are silent in the darkness. There is just the puppies stirring in the straw. The small sound of their sucking.

"What news is there of Kenyatta?" he asks.

"Have you heard anything?"

"Nothing—" There is hunger in his voice. "Just men talking. I want to know what the newspapers are saying."

"They have a British Magistrate overseeing the trial."

"What do you know about him?"

"He has served the Supreme Court of Kenya since the 1930s. An old settler, living in Nairobi."

"One of their own. Who is defending him?"

"An English Queen's Counsel, with a team of Indian lawyers. The newspapers are calling the QC a communist. Kenyatta has pleaded not guilty, but they have witnesses standing against him. They are saying that he orchestrated Mau Mau. That he is a drunk."

"They will say what they can."

We sit in silence for a long while. When he turns on the torch I see that only the last puppy has not turned golden. Its fur has dried to black, and it has a patch over one eye like a pirate.

"You should go back," he says. "There won't be any more now."

"I am scared."

"You don't need to be afraid," he says. "It is too late for Mau Mau."

"And leopard?"

"There are no leopard so close to the house."

"I heard one—a few nights ago."

"I do not think it was a leopard."

"What else could it have been?"

He does not reply, and I shiver, thinking of the men who come down from the forest at night.

"Does my father know?"

"Why do you think he moved the *shambas*?" The straw rustles as he gets to his feet. "I will walk with you," he says.

I put a hand to Juno before I go. "What a clever girl," I whisper, kissing the soft fur beneath her ear. "What a good, clever girl." The puppies are nestled in close to her. I will come back in the morning.

We walk up the path to the house in darkness. Neither of us want to be seen. I feel safe walking beside him—under the mantle of his fearlessness. We stop at the pale papyrus grass, whispering silver in the blackness. I reach out to touch his arm, a gesture of good-bye, but my hand touches nothing but air—he has already gone.

When I turn on the torch and shine it at my window, the white gleam of a face looks out at me. I jump, taking in breath.

"Rachel?"

It is Harold.

"What are you doing?" I hiss at him.

"Where have you been?"

"Juno had her puppies." I pass him the torch, and my gun, and he takes them from me. "Help me up."

He reaches down a hand and I grasp hold of it, and he pulls me up so that I can slide myself over the windowsill.

"Who was the other man? The African?" he asks, turning the torch on me in the room.

"It was Michael." I swallow, looking for his reaction. "He was helping Juno when I got there. He walked me back." I put my hand out and touch the edges of his pajamas. "You won't say anything to our parents? They might not understand."

"I won't say anything," he says, shaking his head. "But you should be careful. You do not know who could be dangerous."

XVII

✦➤•◀✦

Reports on the radio each evening bring bad news. The violence escalates. There are a cluster of murders in the White Highlands; thefts and arson attacks. Troops are flown in from the Middle East, a cruiser arrives with more troops in Mombasa, and the Kenyan Police Reserve and Home Guard are mobilized in greater force to tackle the threat. They say thousands of Kikuyu have fled arrest and are living in the forests of the Highlands. Naivasha police station is raided in the middle of the night; three policemen are killed and a cache of weapons are stolen, including thirty rifles and eighteen Lanchester submachine guns. There are rumors that Mau Mau have told houseboys to put razor blades under our mosquito nets, and release poisonous snakes into our bedrooms to kill us while we sleep. And the brutal murder of loyal Kikuyu who refuse to take the oath continues.

So far at Kisima we have seen no violence, but the sense of being under siege grows every day.

Steven drops in for lunch, full of news of arrests, violence in the forest, an attack on the Home Guard post that was forced back.

When Harold walks into the room, he clasps a hand on his shoulder—"Harold, my boy, you're in for an adventure!"

Harold gives him a quick smile, but his face drains of blood.

"What do you mean?" I ask.

"Hasn't he told you? He has volunteered to a police post near Gilgil. He'll be patrolling with the big boys. Right where all the action is."

"Is he old enough?"

"He's old enough to hold a gun—aren't you, my boy?"

Harold nods, his cheeks breaking out in a rash of color. I wonder why he has agreed. Unaccountably—I feel my heart break.

"We're all so proud of you, darling," Sara says, leaning over to kiss his cheek, and I realize that she has orchestrated this.

There is talk at lunch of my father volunteering for the KAR. They need men who know the land, and they can't train up the troops from Britain fast enough. I cannot imagine how we would cope without him.

"WHAT I CAN'T BEAR," Steven says at the end of lunch, spooning sauce over his crème caramel, "is these young, jumped-up kids from England, who haven't a clue about natives, whining on about the exploitation of the African. There was a boy shipped in with the troops a month ago—a correspondent. Kept harping on about land rights for the Kikuyu." He slides his forefinger and thumb into his mouth and sucks off the caramel. "Taking all the wrong sorts of pictures."

"What sort of pictures?" Harold asks, and I glance at him.

"Oh, you know—Micks with their hands cut off, village raids."

He spoons the white custard into his mouth, dripping dark with caramel. "Things that don't look good in a British newspaper."

I think about Harold's photographs—the brutality implicit in some of the shots he took at Nyeri. Has he shown them to Steven? Is this a warning? I have the sense that there is a silent struggle being waged between Nate Logan and Steven Lockhart, over Harold's soul. Harold eats slowly, his face closed.

"What did you do?" Sara asks, taking the dish and serving my father.

"The boys called him a negrophile. Took him out on patrol. Spooked him up a bit. Kid got stuck in an ambush with a gang of Micks. He was given a gun—had to shoot his way out." Steven laughs, turning over his spoon and cleaning it with his mouth. "In the end he notched up a greater head count than the rest of our boys put together. That was the last we heard of him saving the African."

"Do you think the boy was entirely wrong?" my father asks, glancing at his plate. I can see he has no appetite.

"Is that a serious question?" Steven asks, looking at him closely.

"Yes. It's a serious question," my father says, meeting his gaze.

"Without us the Africans would still be eating *posho* in their huts, performing clitoridectomies on their women and gazing at the sun and moon as if they were gods." Steven wipes a drop of dark caramel off his mustache with the corner of a white napkin. "Of course he was wrong."

Harold sits with his eyes to the table, saying nothing. He is under Steven's jurisdiction now, and the less he shows of himself, the safer he will be.

"I wish it were that straightforward," my father says.

Sara looks at my father. "Robert—eat up. You sound terribly maudlin today. Almost as though you feel guilty."

My father turns his spoon end over end on the table. "Not guilt, exactly. Perhaps it's just a sense of futility. That what is good for me may no longer coincide with what is good for the Africans."

"Well, that's absurd," Sara says, giving a stiff laugh.

"Is it?" my father asks.

"Look—" Steven says, casually helping himself to another spoonful of white custard. "If the African—either through ineptitude or laziness—has failed to cultivate the land that surrounds us— then what right have they to say it is theirs? If they have proved themselves incapable of lifting themselves from barbarity, then what is it but a gift if we teach them the principles of Christianity?"

"And what are the principles of Christianity?" The words come out before I can stop them. It is the hypocrisy in his voice. I do not believe that anything Steven Lockhart teaches could be Christian.

They all look in my direction. The blood beats thickly in my head.

"Why, Rachel," Steven says, smiling at me, licking at his spoon. "I would have thought they taught them to you at school. Why don't you tell them to us?"

"Love. Charity. Humility," I say, staring at him, the dislike open in my face.

"Very good," he says, putting down his spoon and pushing away his plate. "Anything else?"

"Whoever says he is in the light and does not love his brother is still in darkness."

A silence descends on the table. Steven looks at me, a half smile on his face, unabashed, almost as though he is pleased, and I wish I had said nothing. I had forgotten that he enjoys resistance.

"But what of the future?" my father asks Steven, and I feel his gaze shift away from mine.

"We should aim for a dual society in Kenya, founded on the principles of Western Christian civilization." He lights a cigarette and draws deeply on it. "One in which the educated African is allowed to participate and profit alongside Europeans, whilst acknowledging that the Europeans are the backbone of this country—economically and spiritually. Of course this Mau Mau debacle has set the Africans back a hundred years. They have proved that they are unable to stand up to the pressures of modern civilization . . ."

I have no sense of Steven's words; all I know is that if he is the spokesman for empire, then empire is an ugly, dissolute thing. His voice is like the whisper of the devil. Sugarcoated words, designed to make what is evil palatable so that more evil can be committed. Listening to him is like listening to the clean, efficient turning of the wheel at my uncle's bacon factory.

"Come, Robert. That's enough of politics," Sara says, and she eases herself over the table, picks up his spoon and pushes it deep into the pure, soft white custard, golden caramel sliding off the top.

"You need to think less and eat more." She raises the spoon to my father's mouth and I see his eyes steady as they lock onto hers. He opens his mouth like a child and she slides the spoon in, and I see my father swallow the sweetness, all thought of the farm, of politics, draining from him.

IN THE NIGHT I hear crying from the room at the end of the corridor. I light the lamp, walk down the hall and push open the door.

Harold is sitting on a corner of the bed by the wall. He looks up when I come in, then presses the palms of his hands against his eyes to stop the tears. He takes a ragged breath. "I did not mean to wake you."

I put down the lamp and sit on the edge of the narrow bed, the metal frame cold through my nightdress.

"What is it?" I ask, but he does not answer me.

"Are you scared of going?"

Still he says nothing.

"Harold, tell me, why did you agree?"

"My mother—she needs me. I have to try. For her sake—" His voice breaks off.

"Try to do what?"

He doesn't reply. Eventually I lean forward and put my arms around him and he rests his head against my shoulder, his chest rising and falling silently against me. I feel his tears wet against my shoulder and smell the boyish warmth that rises up from his body. I want to protect him, but I cannot.

JUNO'S PUPPIES BEGIN to sprout ears, and their eyes open. She is a good mother, and she cleans them, and suckles them often. They are all golden, except for Pirate who is gleaming black with a golden patch over one eye. He is the longest at the nipple, until she nips him away, and I see that he is growing stronger every day. I love to sit in the dim light of the stable, warm and drowsy with the smell of milk, and watch them nestle in under the solid warmth of their mother.

My father is short of labor now that so many of our Kikuyu have left, and Michael is away from the garage, supervising work at the dairy and the cattle dip. I am alone in the yard except for Juno and her puppies. When my father passes his copy of the *Standard* to me, I read it, then bring it down to the stables and leave it there for Michael, thinking that he will see it when he passes through the yard on his way to his hut. A small betrayal, but he has a right to know what is happening in his country. The next day it is always where I left it, folded neatly on a milking stool, just outside the stable door, and I cannot be sure if he has read it.

STEVEN LOCKHART ARRIVES in the evening to collect Harold. He will spend the night and take Harold away with him the following morning. When I come through to the sitting room they are all there, having drinks.

Steven is telling a story, but he stops when he sees me.

"Carry on," Sara says to him.

Steven glances questioningly at me.

"Oh, she can hear it." Sara waves her hand to dismiss his concern. "We all need to hear it."

"It's Eric Bowker," my father says. "He has been murdered."

I feel a coldness seep like water into my veins. Eric Bowker was our closest neighbor—a solitary man who used to help on my parents' farm from time to time. His farm borders ours.

"Who did it?"

"The Micks got him," Steven says, rubbing the short edges of his mustache with his fingers.

"He started a local store a few years ago, selling supplies, clothes, tinned goods to the Africans who worked on farms nearby," my father says to me. "He wasn't exactly friendly with the natives, but he wasn't *kali* either."

"They came for him at sunset yesterday," Steven says, taking a sip of his gin and sitting back in his chair. His eyes flicker over mine—it is just a second—but I feel my throat constrict. "He was in the bath."

I look away, unwilling to hear this story, but irresistibly compelled.

"They got his two houseboys first. He didn't even have time to get out of the bath. He was stark naked and they just went to work on him with their pangas." He takes a long sip of his gin. "I spoke to the policemen who found him. Said he looked as though he had fallen in front of a combine harvester. They'd disemboweled him, and his entrails were floating like jelly in the bathwater."

And I find I can picture it with complete clarity—the blood pooling in the water, the gray hairs on his chest, the body sliced to pieces.

"It's a bloody atrocity," my father says.

"Savagery," Sara says, "pure savagery. They ought to hang them all."

"Oh, I don't know that hanging isn't too respectable," Steven Lockhart says, in his slow drawl. "What they need is a bit of rough justice. We ought to tie them to stakes and put them out next to hyena holes, like the old chiefs used to do."

He is smiling as he says it, his lips shiny with gin, and I feel a lurching sensation in my body and a pounding in my chest, as though I might be sick. Eric Bowker slaughtered, my father under the spell of another woman and Steven Lockhart thickening this nightmare. I breathe deeply and press my hands to my eyes. I have fallen down a rabbit hole—home has been turned inside out, inhabited by ghouls and strangers who sit where my mother once sat, and the African protectors of my childhood have become killers. And somewhere at the bottom of it is a sense of forewarning, and displacement. *Kenya is a black man's country.*

That night I push a chair against my door, jamming it under the door handle. Later, I hear him walk down the corridor, his feet pressing against the floorboards, hovering outside my room. I wish Juno was here to growl a warning. A low laugh reverberates on the other side of the door. "Good night, Rachel," he says, and to my relief he carries on down the corridor to the spare room.

STEVEN AND HAROLD are leaving just after dawn. The house is quiet when I wake, and I dress and step into the corridor. I can see Steven's door is closed. Harold is outside, eating breakfast on the veranda with Sara and my father. I walk into the sitting room and pour myself a glass of tomato juice.

"Sleep well?"

The hairs prick up on the back of my neck. I turn around slowly. Steven Lockhart is standing against the doorframe, watching me, a half smile on his face. He must have been waiting in his bedroom. His eyes are cold and blank like the eyes of a fish. "Do you know how the Kikuyu make their promises?"

He walks a little way toward me, slipping his gun holster around his waist and doing up the buckle, and I feel a mixture of fear and revulsion.

"What do you mean?"

"The Kikuyu," he says casually. "Do you know what they force each other to drink, during their oathing ceremonies, to ensure that they keep their promises?"

"Blood," I say.

"Y-e-s," he says, as if I am only half right. "But can you guess what kind of blood?"

"Goat's blood," I say, my voice very quiet.

He laughs and walks a little closer to where I am standing.

"No. Not goat's blood, Rachel. They drink menstrual blood. Taken from their women. And semen." His voice drops to a whisper. "Do you know what semen is, Rachel?"

I feel my face flush red. I know what semen is—my father's heifers are impregnated with semen from England—but these are dark, secret things that I am not able to talk about. Steven stands close to me, his hands deep in his pockets, his frame very still, watching me, feeling out my awkwardness as a measure of his success.

"I don't see why he should go," I say, forcing myself to speak, refusing to be intimidated by him, but my voice is shrill despite myself.

"That is Harold's decision," he says, stepping forward and taking the glass of tomato juice from my hand. "Besides, his mother is quite set on it." He brings the glass to his lips and drinks, and when he has finished the red juice clings to the edges of his mustache. He wipes at it with the back of his hand.

———

THERE ARE NO TEARS when Harold leaves, only a paleness in his cheeks, and a darting, uneasy look in his eyes. Sara does not embrace him—she puts a hand to his cheek and says, "You'll do a fine job, Harold." And I have the disturbing feeling that he is being asked to make amends for something. He has his camera in one hand. I wonder what Nate Logan would say if he saw him now, on his way to join the Home Guard. I do not want him to go. I will miss his quiet company in my room at night; the radio spinning its news into the darkness around us. But I accept that if Bowker was murdered in his bath, not fifteen miles away, then it may be no more dangerous at the Home Guard post than it is at Kisima.

MY FATHER HAS PROMISED Steven that he will go over to Eric Bowker's place, after he and Harold have left, to help pack up the house and deal with the livestock that remain. I ask if I can go with him.

"You won't be squeamish?" he asks.

I shake my head, pulling myself up into the Land Rover beside him.

We drive down the track to the old olive tree, then cut across the valley following a dried-up riverbed. This is the quick route— the route we took when riding horses. It is fifteen miles pretty much as the crow flies, and down here there isn't another soul. It's impassable in the rainy season, but the ground has dried out in the last few weeks, and we plunge deep into the bush, through the dense thickets of the gorge. My father stops occasionally to check on a concrete dam or to clear from the track a branch felled by an elephant. And in the quiet of these moments I can hear all around us the forest throbbing with the songs of birds and insects.

The track cuts away from the riverbed, up the side of a hill, and comes over the brow. My father turns off the engine. In front of us is a wide, smooth rock overlooking a hidden valley, a small river dividing the grassy floor below. We are not too high up, and the valley floor is not wide. My mother called it *Kidogo Mara*—Little Mara—because it looks like the great plains of Southern Kenya in miniature. She loved it here. We took turns with the baboons to sit on the rock and picnic. They always moved off when we arrived— but when we left, our horses picking their way down the hillside, they would stand on the rock and scold us, in loud, jabbering voices.

We climb out, my father sliding his rifle into his hand, crouching down, looking into the valley. The engine ticks over in the heat. The rock is warm beneath my rolled-up trousers, hot against my bare ankles. The world below is caught in a hazy, languorous heat. It is hard to believe that there might be anything dangerous here and I feel no fear. A herd of zebra are drifting down the hillside to the pools at the bottom, their gait short, their heads swaying as they walk. I can hear the soft clopping of their hooves on the dry earth. Two giraffes—a mother and a baby—are already on the valley floor. The baby splays its legs to drink from the river.

The zebra smell something and they stop, heads raised, listening, then trot out of the valley, their flanks, wet with sweat, making a hollow chafing sound; the same sound my pony made when I pushed him into a long uphill trot. The giraffes remain but they are spooked, and the mother has her neck poised, listening. I spot it before my father does and lift a hand. A loping figure that stops periodically and raises its head like a man might, cutting across the valley. A hyena. A few minutes, and it has crossed out of sight.

"Cattle," my father says, and I stay very still, listening, until I hear the low, hollow clunking of their bells. It is this that scared the zebra and the hyena, driving them through the valley. A car engine will not frighten game, but man on foot, and cattle, will.

There is a cave behind the rock. Kahiki showed us the paintings deep in its interior, holding up a torch to its walls, and my mother found old stone tools buried in the earth. At the mouth of the cave are the scattered ashes of a fire. My father feels them—they are cold. Nothing to suggest that someone has been here recently. That anyone is hiding out.

"The cattle," my father says, when we are driving away, raising his voice to be heard over the noise of the engine, "they must be Bowker's. Mau Mau drove his herd into the forest and they scattered. I'll have to try and pick them up later."

Erik Bowker's house sits on a flat plateau a few miles above *Kidogo Mara*. It is a strange place, surrounded by bush, with no view beyond the clearing that was made with his own hands. Eric Bowker built this place himself, as any European did who arrived more than thirty years ago. Unlike many others, he had never enlarged it, modified it, adjusted it for the increased sociability that usually came with a wife and children. He lived alone. I remember him as an older man, tall, wiry gray hair, always with a hat on his head. Eccentric, and tough.

I see smoke above the scrub, before I see the house, and then we pull onto the main track and come into a clearing. The house is a simple bungalow. A trail of belongings is strung along the path that leads up into the bush—a shirt has snagged on an acacia tree and hangs like a puppet stuck full of thorns. Two young policemen sit smoking, their rifles propped up against the wall of the house. They stand up as we approach, stubbing out their cigarettes.

The barns have been burned to the ground, the walls are black and the corrugated roof has fallen in. I can feel the heat from the fire, still smoldering, as I approach.

"Does he have any family?" my father asks the soldiers.

"We haven't been able to reach anyone."

There is a dark patch on the earth by the door. Flies gather over it, buzzing. "Dog had water?" my father asks, looking at an old collie standing by the house, head low, panting. The soldiers look embarrassed—it hasn't occurred to them—and one of them goes inside to fetch a bowl.

We walk around the barn. There is nothing left of any value. The Land Rover has been stripped down. "They use the metal to make guns," my father says. When we step back out into the sun the dog limps toward the bowl and laps softly at the water.

Inside the house is dark, the ceilings low. No one takes off their boots. I step behind my father into a small hall—to the right is a sitting room, with a fireplace, a small sofa and a single chair. The room has been ransacked: cushions slashed and pulled onto the floor; shelves emptied; three plates broken where they fell; books spread open facedown, spines trodden in. I can feel the size of the men in this small room, I can feel the adrenaline, the speed with which they rifled through what was here. And I can smell the thick sweet smell of their bodies, unwashed, high and strong. Or is it Bowker's body soaking in the bath?

"I don't want you going into the bathroom," my father says. "Just in here and in the bedroom. Two piles. One for anything his family

might want—a few things, keep it small. Who knows whether anyone will ever turn up. The other—anything we might find useful
on the farm."

"Can we just take his things?"

"No use leaving anything here. The Micks will be back to strip
the place. Better we have it than them."

I hear him walk into the bathroom. Try to picture what he sees.
Hear his silence. The creak of his boots on the wood floor. In the
bedroom the chest gapes open, drawers pulled out onto the rug. I
make a small pile of personal belongings, choosing quickly, trying
to imagine what I might want to remember this man by. The
book—open—on the armrest. A photograph of him as a boy, with
a man who must be his father. A pen on the floor that has pooled
its ink into the rug. And a handkerchief initialed *EJB*, which lies
trodden on the boards.

My father comes to help me pack. I want to ask him what is
next door, in the bathroom—is Bowker's body still there? But I
don't dare. We sort through religious books, farming manuals,
packets of seeds, breeding pedigrees, letters from England, an old
diary, addresses.

"Back in a minute," my father says, stepping into the hall. I wait
inside, the air settling around me, my breathing loud in the small
bedroom. It is unearthly in here and I shiver. I have the odd feeling
that now my father has gone the walls might start talking to me.
Telling me their secrets; what they have seen. I step into the hallway. Here is the bathroom door. My father has pulled it to—but it
has swung open a little. I can't see inside. My father's voice is far
off—he is talking to the soldiers. I push the door with my hand
and it swings open silently. A white tub smeared with blood.

Handprints black against the side. The floor dark and wet. Something sticky and solid inside the bath. And a buzzing, filling my ears. Like a pig at the factory, the blood washing over the floor. A fly settles on my hand, another on my face. I wave my hand and more rise and fall, the sound of their wings roaring in my ears. There is no body. Only this—the butcher's bath. My jaw is clenched. My stomach rises in my throat.

I think I might be sick—when a gunshot shatters the air. I freeze in terror, this world of horror suddenly become real. Have Mau Mau come back? There is silence for a long moment, then I hear my father's voice. Ordinary, relaxed, talking to the soldiers. I run from the room, from the smell, tainted, contaminated by what is inside.

My father sees me. He is hitching his gun into his belt.

"What was it?" I ask.

He doesn't say anything. Walks past me inside the house. And I know from his posture what he has done. I stumble around the back of the house and see the collie on the ground. Blood pooling from her head. Thick drops sitting in the dust. Lips pulled back on yellow teeth. The crickets call grating and urgent. I turn away, crouch down and vomit on the earth, and watch as the flies settle in the liquid at my feet, before I have even had time to stand up.

"He would have done it himself in a month or two," my father says, when I come back round to the front of the house. He is carrying a pile of linen to the car. I lean against the bonnet, waiting for my head to stop spinning, the metal hot against my forehead.

The soldiers have taken it upon themselves to retrieve the belongings which are scattered along the track. After a moment I lift my head and watch—one of them holds up a pair of graying white underpants and he gyrates his hips, miming a dance. The other smiles at him. He has a pipe in one hand and he polishes it on his trousers, sucks it between his teeth, then slips it into his pocket. Two vultures wheel in the sky overhead, and I wonder if they can smell the blood inside the house.

"They've taken the pots and pans, the cups, the kerosene, any fuel that was here. His coats, his rifle, his revolver—all gone." My father looks up into the bush, to the mountains that rise green and heavy against the sky. "Every time they do this they get stronger—more supplies, more fuel, more weapons, more confidence. The cattle will keep them going for months."

"Why haven't they cleaned it up inside?" I ask.

He looks at me, his eyes reading in mine that I have seen it.

"These boys will do it once we're gone."

I glance at the soldiers, and they smile, walking back down the path to help my father load things into the car. The smell of blood is in my mouth, the taste of vomit in my throat. I am numb.

WHEN WE GET HOME my father hammers wire grills to the windows to stop anyone getting in. The danger feels much closer than it did before. Erik Bowker's house is only fifteen miles away—Mau Mau are close by. When he is finished, we feel more like prisoners than we did before. I have heard stories of Mau Mau throwing flaming torches onto the tinder-dry roofs of settlers' houses, and I imagine the crackling of the fire, the windows barred, the doors guarded by men with guns. My father sleeps in the sitting room, his rifle pointed at the door, and I feel safer with him closer to my bedroom. I keep my gun loaded by the bed.

XVIII

✦➤•◆✦

The newspapers are full of descriptions of Kikuyu oathing ceremonies. The oaths the men take, to burn European crops and cattle, to steal firearms, to kill no matter who is the victim—all this is nothing new to me. But there is one oath that sticks in my throat and I wish I hadn't seen it. They are said to vow—when killing—to cut off the heads of their enemies, to extract the eyeballs and drink the liquid from them. I keep telling myself that it is the Kikuyu who are being killed, that only a handful of whites have been murdered—but each night the news seeps like fear into the quiet of my bedroom.

   . . . *This is the third attack on the same Catholic Mission School. One of the fathers was injured whilst raising the alarm. He is now seriously ill in the Nairobi Hospital.*

   . . . *The girl escaped by climbing onto the roof. Her mother was killed as she was attempting to scramble up after her. Her father, who went onto the veranda, had disappeared. It is believed that the terrorists carried him away.*

   . . . *The disappearance of a man who had lived all his life since coming to Kenya among the Kikuyu. He was loved by everyone in the nearby location and some years ago was "blooded" as a member of their tribe and was one of the few white men so honored. Two sporting guns and ammunition were stolen. The funeral . . .*

. . . The Mau Mau society is demanding immediate self-government . . . Members are called on to steal firearms from Europeans and to kill Europeans when asked to by the leadership.

. . . has still not been found. The police fear that, since he has been missing for six days, he is dead. The search for his body is still going on. Tracker dogs, police and troops are . . .

. . . Reports that a captured terrorist said that a young girl, operating with one of the gangs, claims to be a seer. She dreamed that things would go well for Mau Mau if a white man were taken and . . .

. . . feared that he may have been buried alive. The search still continues.

. . . The terrorists got away with two rifles and two hundred rounds of .303 ammunition.

. . . The funeral will take place at 3:00 p.m. at the European Cemetery.

. . . Up to two-thirds of the Kikuyu population are thought to have taken the oath.

. . . a precision rifle and a revolver were stolen.

. . . at 11:00 a.m. at the European Cemetery.

The *Standard* lists the names of the Europeans who have been killed; eight in total, and as many again seriously wounded. This doesn't include the Seychellois farm manager and his six children who were brutally attacked and murdered, or the two elderly European women—Dorothy and Kitty—who managed to fight off their attackers in their living room, killing three of the assailants.

Meanwhile, the article says, hundreds of loyal Kikuyu have been murdered.

A letter is released from an official Mau Mau source. It says there will be a spate of Christmas killings. *We want a dozen heads this month.* My father admits he has taken to having a bath with a revolver in the soap dish.

A WEEK BEFORE CHRISTMAS, I am sitting against the barn wall reading the *Standard*, when a jeep pulls into the yard. It is Nate Logan. I jump up, happy to see him.

"How are you holding up?" he asks, putting a hand on my head.

"All right," I say, and it is the truth. Despite everything, I am glad to be at Kisima.

"Are these your puppies?" he asks.

"Yes," I say, smiling proudly. They are a month old, and they have found their legs, tumbling over to greet him and chew at the laces on his boots.

"Who's this fellow?" He scoops one up with a large hand.

"That's Pirate," I say, laughing as Pirate snaps at his fingers.

"He's feisty, isn't he?" he says, rubbing a hand over him. Then— "I couldn't find anyone up at the house. Have you seen Harold?"

"Haven't you heard?" I ask, surprised. "He volunteered. He went off with Steven Lockhart to the Home Guard post. A couple of weeks ago."

"Did he really?" he asks, looking at me, his jaw squaring off in anger. "Why in hell's name did she let him do that?"

He isn't looking for an answer and I don't say anything.

"The boy can't have been barely sixteen!" He swears under his breath, placing the puppy on the ground. "I was hoping to take him back with me to the Markhams' farm as an assistant. Damn it, I should have come sooner—" He kicks the toe of his boot through the soil, and I feel as though he isn't sorry so much for himself as for Harold. As though perhaps he had come to save him and now it is too late.

"I tried to tell him he didn't have to go—"

"But of course we both know that's not true—"

"Isn't it?"

"You don't know about Harold?" he asks, slowly.

"What is there to know?"

"There was a scandal in Nairobi—" He breathes out and his eyes flicker to mine. "Harold got too close to a regular guest at the Norfolk—a boy."

"Too close?"

"He was found in Harold's room one morning—"

And I understand suddenly what he is implying. I remember Harold struggling to explain—"I have to try"; the photographs on his desk; the unambiguous masculinity of the Kikuyu boys which had made them so striking; his mother's refusal to look at his photographs. He liked men. I don't know why I hadn't seen it before. It explained why Sara kept such a close eye on him—why she didn't want him spending so much time with Nate, who was too liberal for her tastes and most likely wouldn't discourage him. And it explained her power over him—he lived in fear of her shame, of his own shame perhaps.

"Sara had to get him out of Nairobi. They couldn't afford to go back to England—"

"So she came here," I say, finishing what he does not wish to make explicit: that Sara aligned herself with my father to escape a city which would ostracize them both.

"I have something for you—" Nate says, dropping the subject and turning to rummage in the front seat of his jeep. When he turns around, he has a package in his hand—something wrapped in a bit of newsprint. He hands it to me and I pull open the paper. Inside is a triangular black stone, its edges ridged and sharp.

"What is it?" I ask, lifting it from the paper. It is cool and smooth against my fingers, and it is so black that it seems to swallow the light.

"An arrowhead. Obsidian. Did your mother ever find one here?"

I shake my head, feeling my finger down the blade. Where the blade thins to transparency, it is sharp enough to cut through skin.

"Someone made it—hundreds of thousands, possibly millions of years ago. It suggests that early man was here in East Africa long before most paleontologists have suggested. So perhaps your mother wasn't wrong after all—"

"Do you not need to take it back with you?" I ask, looking up at him, feeling the weight of this object in my hand, the history that it carries and my own sense of gratitude that he has remembered.

"We found several. This one is for you."

"Thank you," I say, smiling.

"I am glad you will have it," he says, laying a hand on my shoulder and smiling down at me.

When he is gone I wrap it back in the paper and slide it into my pocket. Perhaps it will bring me good luck.

—————

It is only when I am back in my room, and I unwrap the paper, turning the obsidian over in my hand, that my eyes fall to the crumpled bit of newsprint in which it was wrapped. A headline leaps out at me:

AN APPEAL TO THE TOILING, OPPRESSED
AND EXHAUSTED PEOPLES OF THE WORLD

I smooth the paper out and lift it to the light to read it better. It is a political speech of some sort, printed on cheap paper. Phrases leap out at me. Words that burn.

> We must put a stop to a condition in which the strong can by force of arms compel the weak to assume what conditions of life the strong may desire; every people, be it great or small, must be the master of its own fate.

I feel as though I can hear the speaker shouting over the crowd. Hear his passion. See the sweat running off his brow as his voice lifts, as his message gathers potency. I have never heard language like this. *Every people, be it great or small.*

> Workers! Exploited, disfranchised, scorned, they called you brothers and comrades at the outbreak of the war when you were to be led to the slaughter, to death. And now that militarism has crippled you, mutilated you, degraded and annihilated you, the rulers demand

that you surrender your interests, your aims, your ideals—in a word,
servile subordination to civil peace.

I turn over the paper—what country is he talking about? Russia, I think. The name of the speaker is Russian. This is the language of Communism that my father and Sara say is so dangerous; the red devil. But this man could almost be talking to the Africans in Kenya. And what conviction in the words—

They rob you of the possibility of expressing your views, your feelings, your pains. The press gagged, political rights and liberties trod upon—this is the way the military dictatorship rules today with an iron hand.

I think about the Kikuyu newspapers; the African schools shut down in Kenya; the sweep outside of Nakuru; Kenyatta arrested. Was this pamphlet accidental? Had Nate Logan meant for me to read it? The paper feels like a message, there for me to make something of it if I am willing.

ON CHRISTMAS EVE, my father cuts a coconut palm for the sitting room, and I find some of our old Christmas decorations and hang them up. Harold comes home for two days. He has not shaved, and where the thin, blond stubble does not spread, his skin is a thick dark color, and his hands are black. His eyes show up very white, as though he is staring at us from behind a mask. His mother sends him to wash, but when he comes back there is still black in his hairline and around the edges of his fingernails.

"What is it?" she asks, turning his hands over.

"Boot polish," he says.

"Why?"

My father answers for him. "Makes it harder for the Micks to spot them when they're in the forest."

I wait for him that night—the radio on—but he does not come.

THE QUEEN MAKES her first Christmas broadcast and says of the forthcoming Coronation, "You will be keeping it as a holiday; but I want to ask you all, whatever your religion may be, to pray for me on that day." Sara orders two dozen souvenir spoons in hallmarked silver, showing the Queen's profile.

Harold disappears on Christmas morning and is not back for lunch. Jim has cooked a feast—turkey, roast potatoes, swede, carrots, Christmas pudding and stollen, but we are all brittle with tension, and we take little pleasure in the meal.

After lunch I go to Harold's room, at the end of my corridor, to see if perhaps he is hiding there, but it is empty. From the light in the corridor I can see a pile of photographs on the desk. He must have developed them in the night. I lift a corner of the curtain to see better. The photograph shows a Kikuyu child of about four, naked, sliced open by a machete so that her guts—swollen in the heat—bulge out of her waist. A Mau Mau killing. I look away, sickened, but there are more spread out over the table. Men and women, some naked, some clothed, all black. Careless strokes of the machete slicing open buttocks and lopping off ankles. Not strokes designed to kill with any kind of speed. There is one photograph of a line of dead men—Mau Mau—on the ground tied to stakes by their hands and feet, like pigs that have been hunted. I recognize the officer standing over them. It is Steven Lockhart. And there is another that shows Steven Lockhart crouching next to a man who is being pinned by an *askari*. He is holding a pair of long steel pliers in one hand.

I jump when I hear a noise behind me. It is Harold. He walks over to where I am standing, drops the corner of the curtain and pulls a cloth over the photographs.

"I'm sorry," I say, backing away from the table. "I should not have looked."

He doesn't say anything.

"Why have you taken so many?" I ask, unable to help myself, revolted by the photographs, as if each one is a murder he has committed, though I know it is not his fault.

When he does not reply, I say what I have been wanting to tell him since he came back. "Nate Logan came to find you. He is looking for an assistant. He wanted to know if you could help him with his work. Perhaps it would not be too late for you to go." Harold grips the table with both hands, his shoulders hunched, and I do not dare to say anything more.

I remember, later, the photograph Harold had taken of my father and Sara—my father's barely contained desire, her indifference, the shame that suffused it; the other photographs, raw and physical, of the Kikuyu boys working on the farm—and I understand that for Harold these images are the articulate outpouring of all his desire, his anger, his shame and his fear.

IN THE AFTERNOON, I walk over to the new *shamba* with stollen to give to the children who remain. Kahiki comes with me, carrying his bow and arrow, and a young boy, who carries the yards of cloth I have brought for the women. We walk across open grassland, zebra and kudu cropping at the short, dry grass, jerking up their heads to look at us.

The new *shamba* rises out of the earth in front of us. A scattering of small, round thatched huts with low doorways, smoke seeping up into the still blue sky. Three girls I do not recognize come to the boundary and sing as we approach. The sound lifts beautiful and arresting into the clear light.

An old woman with gray hair hangs washing on the thorn fence of the *boma*. The cattle will be driven in here later, and the thorn enclosure closed to keep off lion. The grass around the huts has already worn away to earth, under the tread of so many feet. I hand out slices of stollen and yards of cut fabric as my mother used to do. It will make clothes for the year ahead.

The woman finishes hanging clothes and beckons to me with a stiff, brown hand. I hesitate for just a moment. What possible danger can she pose? I stoop inside the low door. The fire burns in a pit in the floor. There is no chimney, just a small hole for light, and the hot sweet smoke, the thick mud walls and the darkness create a hypnotic fug. This is where she will sleep tonight, in the small alcove, with her grandchildren next to her, one warm body pressed to another. We sit on the packed-earth floor of her hut. She sways as she sits, whittling a piece of wood, not looking at me. Time unravels. The world outside seems very distant. She presses the wood into my hands. I turn it over—trying to see what it is in the near darkness. Then I make it out—it is the crude carving of a baby. I do not know what it means.

The light is fading when I emerge. The sheep and goats are scattered across the plain, walking back to the *bomas*, bringing the night air with them. They are a ragged bunch of matted hair and bleats which seem to want to hold back the dusk which is rapidly falling. Some crop the short, yellow grass that still remains in patches here and there, and are moved roughly on. A man shouts as he pushes them along. Two identical black-and-white lambs jump instead of walk, leaping into the air, their joy setting them free. A dog scratches its fleas in the dirt and gets up to sniff around, the heat receding, his night beginning.

As we leave I see Michael talking to a man outside his hut. His eyes glide over me, then back to the man he is talking to. He has seen me, but he will not stop. This is his world, not mine, and he does not wait on me. I bite back disappointment. I have not spoken to him since the night Juno had her puppies, and I miss his company at the stables.

When Christmas is over three more Europeans have been recorded dead. Not as many as Mau Mau promised, but their deaths take their toll on all of us.

XIX

➤➤•◄◄

It isn't until the New Year that I pluck up the courage to go through the trunks that belonged to my mother. I walk down to the stables and drag them out into the yard, under the overhang of the barn. Michael is still overseeing work at the dip, and I am alone here except for Juno and her puppies. I lift the lid of the first trunk, releasing into the dry air the almost tangible smell of my mother, aromatic and soft, like cedar wood. I have the sudden sensation that she is standing over me, but when I look up there is nobody there, just the clapboard wall of the barn, dark and worn against the clear blue sky. A lizard darts up the wall, stops, flicks its tail. Everything is quiet except for the grating of the cicadas.

Inside the trunk are things I haven't seen in years: my mother's dresses, letters, photographs and books. There is a folder with my name written on the front. Inside is my birth certificate, a photograph of me as a baby, a few of my drawings. Long ago I had written *For Mama* across one of them.

I am choked with longing. I want to be a child again. I want to have back all those years with her that I missed. Everything that has passed since seems empty and meaningless. I was whole then, and I feel as though I might never be whole again. I am crying, for her, for myself, for everything that cannot be undone.

A MONTH INTO the New Year comes news of a massacre. The first we hear of it is on the wireless.

Last night, a band of terrorists thought to be some two hundred strong, attacked a location of professed loyal Kikuyu at Lari. It is believed that over one hundred and fifty peaceful Kikuyu were murdered. Women and children were sadistically disemboweled and whole families, who refused to open their doors, were burned to death. One man, who escaped into the bush, said that the terrorists . . .

Lari instantly becomes a byword for the savage bestiality of the Mau Mau. The following day the *Standard* says that Mau Mau tied ropes around the huts, to stop those inside escaping; that babies were chopped into pieces in front of their mothers.

I walk down to the stables, the newspaper folded in my right hand. Michael is in the garage working. I give him the paper. It is an accusation. I am shocked by the brutality of what has happened at Lari. There is no room any longer for political sympathies. I can tell from the way he takes it from me that he already knows about the massacre.

"How could they do such a thing?" I ask, my voice full of the horror of it.

He glances at me, then unfolds the paper.

"It's utterly senseless."

"Not completely senseless," he says, reading the article. "You won't read it in this paper, but the attack was targeted. They wanted to kill the families of those who supported the giving up of Kikuyu land to the British."

"By killing women and children?"

He looks up from the paper. "The British gave these families land as a reward for their support. By killing the inheritors, they prevent them benefiting from the corruption of their fathers."

"You cannot excuse such brutality!"

"No. But you should remember that these are men who have nothing. They have no home, no livelihood and no land on which to raise crops and farm. They are driven by desperation."

"But it is not human—to hack people to death with pangas."

"Would it be more humane if they had killed with guns?"

"You sound almost as though you disagree with me."

"I disagree with this paper's refusal to present the political narrative that explains what took place; I disagree with your assumption that what you read here is the whole truth." He points to the newspaper. "What it doesn't say is that the government retaliated that night, killing twice as many in the reserves; women and children, with equal brutality."

"How do you know?"

"Men have legitimate voices, even if they are not sanctioned by your press."

I remember our first lesson. Prospero's tyrannical hold over the reins of civility. *Authority is not a substitute for truth.*

"I do not believe you," I say, putting out my hand to take the paper back. He holds my gaze, a slight smile on his face, absorbing all my anger, so that I find I want to hit out at him. How has he managed to gain such power over me? To say these things to me without concern that I will repeat them to my father? His trust feels almost like a form of control. He is taunting me with it, and it frightens me. This closeness between us. As though it will close round me like a trap. I feel as if I have raised a Frankenstein and now I cannot put it back to sleep, and soon my father will see what I have done.

"I do not believe you," I say again, trying to hold on to a truth that is not his. "The newspaper would have reported it if it was true."

He folds the newspaper and gives it back to me, his long fingers brown against the paper. I take it from him and feel his gaze still on me. I meet his eyes—dark and white together—full of a soft strength, a surety in himself, as though I am only a child refusing to see the scope of the world we inhabit. He is not threatened by me, and I do not see why he should not be.

I DREAM THAT I am standing with my back against the garage wall. Michael is walking toward me. There is a knife in his hand and I am afraid. But when his other hand touches me—the hand without the knife—it is dry and warm. He pushes back my hair, his hand circling my neck, pulling my head into his chest, and I hold myself against him, sobs choking in my throat. "It's all right," he says, and it is his voice, and I realize in my dream that I have wanted to hear his voice speaking just for me. And I am crying for one thing but wanting another. His hand slips down my spine, touches my lower back, and I lose my weight against him. With a shock of pain I feel the knife enter me—his hand, driving it in. I feel the sharpness of the blade, the release of blood, and his body now hard and implacable against me as he pushes the blade deeper.

I wake up, my heart racing, my head tangled in another place in which Michael has cut me open. I lie there for a moment—trying to calm my mind. Nothing helps. My nightdress is wet and sticks to my back. I push myself upright and sit with my legs hanging over the bed, in the dark, my heart still pounding. The secret— what I know about Michael's past—weighs heavily on me. Perhaps I have been naive. Perhaps I shouldn't have trusted him at all. I feel an urgency, compelling me. I want to see my father. It is as though in this moment I might lose him—and I have a chance to stop it happening. Tears wet against my lips, my breath heaving, my mouth open in a silent cry. There is an ache inside me, a pain—like grief—that burrows through me, sickening and full of anguish. I know there is purity in this feeling, which comes with the midnight hour—I should not wait until morning. It needs to happen now.

I pad across the floorboards. If I can wake my father—tell him what happened when I was staying with my uncle at Uplands, what I saw Steven Lockhart do, how he scares me; if I can tell him about Michael—perhaps I will cut through the barrier that separates us. He might put his arms around me as he did when I was a child. I walk through to the sitting room. The sofa gapes emptily at me, the blankets thrown back. On through the short hall, the door bolted, the silence buzzing in my ears. Here is the door to my parents' room, ajar. I haven't been inside since—when? Since I played checkers with my mother on the floor, the day before we left for Uplands.

He is just across the threshold. Everything that has divided us seems meaningless in the dark dead of night. I put my hand out to push open the door and freeze. I can hear it now—a breathing, a stirring. I hesitate. Her breath lifts into a short high panting, a seesawing, that alternates with the rhythmic chafing of the bed against the floor. I can hear her nakedness. His nakedness. The photograph that Harold took—his hand was grasping her buttocks, his head turned into her shoulder, hiding his hunger. It is what I hear as I stand outside the bedroom. In his silence, in the grinding of the bed, is all his need, his wanting, his vulnerability. And I know there is no place in it for me.

"RACHEL—" Sara's voice calls to me from her room, as I walk down the hall.

The door is slightly ajar, and I hover outside, as I had the night before.

"Come in," she says, and I push the door open. She is sitting at my mother's dressing table, rubbing a thick white cream into her face. She is undressed. Her bra—the color of skin—is barely visible across her narrow back. The cool line of her leg strikes out from the small blue pattern of the chair.

"Sit down," she says, picking up a bone-handled brush and running it over her short hair in brisk strokes. It was my mother's. She would sit cross-legged on the bed, and I would brush out her hair. The sun streams through the window. I sit now on the edge of the bed, feeling hot and awkward in my pullover and trousers. The bed has been made, but I can smell my father in the room. The same bed I used to crawl into as a child, in the dark, hiding in the thick warmth of my parents' arms.

"Your father wanted me to talk to you." She turns the brush over and picks the dark hairs from the bristles, then drops them into the bin, and I see them fall weightlessly through the air like a spider.

"Did he?" I am reluctant. Any conversation that my father cannot bring himself to have with me himself is bound to be unpleasant. And I am uneasy with the intimacy of her near nakedness. I feel as though she might use it against me.

"I think he felt there are things you might tell me that you wouldn't want to tell him."

She uncrosses her white legs and stands up, and I see the edge of her briefs against the tops of her thighs, also the color of skin.

Had they heard me outside their door, listening? I can feel myself reddening, and she says, "You mustn't be embarrassed, Rachel."

She comes over to the bed, and I am caught between watching her—wondering what she is going to do—and not wanting to look at her body. She puts a hand to my head. I feel her fingernails against my scalp. She is unwrapping the elastic that holds up my hair.

I move my head away slightly, but her hand doesn't leave off its work—untying the knot with her fingers. It is a long time since someone has touched me. I feel the close warmth and elasticity of her body. Remember the warmth of my mother that was softer than this. I think about my grandmother. A woman with her books, her newspapers, her pens and paper. She had no tangible physical presence. England desaturated; my grandmother desaturated. No bodily smell. No warmth. No inhalation.

She unwinds my hair, slowly. "How old were you when your mother died?"

"Twelve," I say in a quiet, choked voice.

"Did your grandmother tell you anything about men? About what they want? What they like?"

My face floods with fire, and my neck prickles with heat.

She lifts the winding coil of my hair, working her fingers into it, then shakes it out against my shoulders.

"There—" she says, stepping back and looking at me. "I was worried you might be a boy, but there is a girl under there after all."

I cannot meet her eye. If I do—I might begin to cry.

"There must have been boys in England," she says. "Someone you were particularly fond of?"

I shake my head.

"I rather feel you're my responsibility now. I want you to know that if there's anything you want to talk about, then I'm here." She lays the back of a cool hand against my cheek. "He wants us to get along." And I know what she says is true, but I don't like her any more than I did before, and when I am out of the room I wind up my hair into a coil and twist the elastic around it so tightly that I can feel it drawing back the skin on my face.

XX

-➤-•-◄-

Sara is alone at the breakfast table when I step out onto the
veranda.

"Now—no running off—" she says, patting the chair beside
her. "I want to talk to you about an idea I've had. Something the
two of us could do together." She smiles at me. "What do you say
to us organizing a party?"

"What sort of party?" I ask, sitting down, surprised.

"For the Coronation. A show of support," Sara says, pointing to
the *Standard*, folded in front of her. There is a picture of Princess
Elizabeth and Prince Philip on the front page, holding hands, with
the little Prince in the background.

"Do you really think the Queen cares about Kenya?" I ask.

"Why on earth wouldn't she?"

"Another troublesome colony airing its dirty linen in public?"

"Oh, don't be absurd! Of course she cares. She was in Kenya
when she found out that she would be Queen."

"When she found out that her father had died," I say.

Sara looks at me queerly, as though it hasn't occurred to her.

"She'll have put that aside now. He was sick for a long time before, don't forget. And she has a special place in her heart for Kenya."

My father walks into breakfast, looking tired, his face unshaven, his head hanging. "The dip is a bloody mess—I can't get the labor I need to finish it, and the cattle are riddled with ticks."

He sits down, pouring out coffee.

"We're plotting," Sara says, smiling at him, "Rachel and I." She runs a hand over my hair and I involuntarily shiver.

"What's this?" my father asks in mock concern, looking pleased that we are getting along, and I wonder at how easily people believe the things they want to believe.

"A party!"

"A party?" my father asks, looking a bit thrown.

"The Coronation. Rachel and I are going to organize the whole thing. She's my accomplice, aren't you, darling?"

I smile at her weakly.

"She'll be Queen of Kenya after all," Sara says, peeling an apple with a small knife, so that the skin separates in one long curl.

My father stirs sugar into his coffee. I cannot tell if he is listening.

"Who will come?" I ask, wondering about the Emergency.

"Oh, I think people will pull together when they see what a fuss we're making. There'll be your father and I. Robert—you can invite some of your old friends?"

My father nods, but I see the tension in his face; that she might be setting herself up for disappointment.

"Harold should be able to get a few days off. And Steven can bring a couple of the boys from the Home Guard post. We'll ask the Markhams and a few of my friends from Nairobi. And Eliot will come up from the factory . . ." I haven't seen my uncle since I have been home.

"It'll be a good chance to get the new setup at the *shamba* off on the right foot. We'll put on a tea for the *mtotos*," she says, thinking about the Kikuyu children.

She is gathering momentum, talking the idea into reality. "We'll all dress up, of course. Your father, Steven—they'll be in uniform." She looks at my father. "Well, Robert—what do you think?"

"About what?" my father says, looking up slightly startled from his coffee.

"The Coronation party—" Her voice is clipped. "What do you think I've been talking about all this time?"

He looks at her blankly for a second, and I wonder if she is going to slap him. Then his eyes focus, and I can see he has dragged himself back from his morning on the farm.

"Are you sure it's a good idea?" he asks. "You don't think in the circumstances it might be a little inappropriate? A rifle in one hand and a piece of cake in the other?"

"But that's just the attitude we need to guard against. If we give in to their savagery and forget ourselves and what we stand for, then they'll have won. This is the perfect opportunity to show the natives a little of the old spirit. Remind them what we're about." She smiles at us, and I can see she is excited. She is still working the little knife. There is something unlikable in her determination to peel the whole apple without breaking the curling strip of shiny green skin. "Harold will take some photographs for us. I might even be able to get my friend Linda, in Nairobi, to have a go at approaching *The Times*. She writes all their features, you know.

Maybe they'll run a few pictures. 'Africa Remembers Her Queen' and 'The Spirit Lives on in the Colonies'—that sort of thing."

My father's face relaxes, as he gives in to the idea. "Well, why not?" he says. "We'll be giving the labor a day off to mark the occasion." It seems to me that he has given in not so much because he believes it is a good idea—with everything that is going on across the farm, a Coronation party will be an unwanted distraction—but because he feels responsible for Sara's discontent and he wants to make amends for her unhappiness.

Sara looks up suddenly, struck with some new idea. "Robert— do you think we can get them to dance for us?" My father glances up from his eggs.

"Oh, don't look at me like that. There's no harm in a bit of dancing. They love to dance, don't they? If you handpicked just a few?"

"Is that really necessary?" my father asks.

"Well, I should think so. It wouldn't be Africa if we didn't involve the natives. The photographs would look a little drab if it was just us lot standing around drinking tea. There'll be the children, of course, but we need some of the boys. An old-fashioned *ngoma* with those drums of theirs and dancing. We want it to feel like their day. It needs to be a collaboration. The new face of Kenya."

And I see my father isn't going to fight the idea—although in the circumstances asking the Kikuyu to hold an *ngoma* feels anything but appropriate.

"Rachel—you can help me with Jim—we'll get him to organize a grand tea. Constance Spry has a recipe for chicken in curry sauce which they'll be serving at the Queen's lunch. I have a copy of it in one of my magazines. We'll see if he can have a go at making it. And we'll have sandwiches, cakes, jellies."

I nod my assent—supporting her because my father has asked me to—but the truth is I don't want anything to do with this party. The event itself doesn't mean much to me, and she seems to be using it as an excuse to rewrite the lines of the community here on the farm. It seems not just simpleminded but possibly dangerous—inciting the very hatred that we are trying to protect ourselves against.

"COME IN, COME IN," my father says, waving Michael in through the door out of old habit. "I'll be just a second." He goes out of the room to retrieve some papers—drawings of the dip—and Michael is left standing in the entrance to the sitting room.

My father is struggling on the farm. He has got rid of so many of his laborers and now—to make matters worse—a herd of zebra, two thousand strong, have descended on the grazing fields, bringing with them a plague of ticks.

It is cold and overcast today—the long rains have come. I am sitting in the corner of the sofa reading a book. Sara has called me from my bedroom where I have been hiding since Steven's jeep pulled up after breakfast.

Steven and Sara do not lift their eyes to Michael—perhaps they do not know he is there, or perhaps they simply do not care. He stands in the doorway, taking in the room. I wonder what he sees— in Sara, in Steven, in me; if he can sense the tensions that bind us. His eyes settle on mine—he has seen me watching him—and I look away, embarrassed, remembering our last conversation; the sudden closeness of it; the control he held over me.

Steven is sitting in my father's wicker chair, legs sprawled out on the floorboards in front of him, drinking a beer. He has a newspaper folded in one hand, and he is doing the crossword.

"*Millions read this novel,*" he mutters. He has been working on it for nearly an hour.

"Don't ask me—" Sara says, flicking through her magazine. There is a picture of the Princess Elizabeth on the front cover. "I'm no good at that sort of thing."

"*Millions read this novel*—" Steven exclaims. "Is it a bestseller?"

"What's so terrible about the zebra, anyway?" Sara asks. "I think it's rather charming to see so many of them so close to the farm."

"Ticks. They carry diseases," Steven says, not looking up. "Rift Valley fever makes a cow run a temperature, and miscarry if she's in calf. Then there's Black Leg and Red Water—flesh decay, urinating blood. It's a disaster for Robert if he can't get the dip finished."

It begins to rain outside, and I can smell the wet earth through the open door.

"I do feel a little safer now that most of them have gone back to the reserves," Sara says, after a moment. "They say collective punishment is going to make a difference."

"At least they have a license now to hang—ought to intimidate." Steven is only half-focusing on the conversation.

"Is it true they're leaving the bodies of Mau Mau out in the villages at night? That all sounds terribly medieval." Sara shudders.

"I swear they're getting more damned difficult every week." Steven crosses and uncrosses his legs, cursing at the crossword. "*Millions read this novel.* What in hell's name can it be?"

"I'm rather excited about our party," Sara says, still flicking through the pages of her magazine. "Only six weeks to go. You will come, Steven—won't you?"

"Of course," he says, turning his pencil end over end.

"I want a real Coronation Cake like they're making in England, and we'll have to order in some new china. You know, Rachel—" She puts down her magazine suddenly and looks at me. "I don't like the idea of you spending so much time on your own."

"I'm not always on my own," I say, reddening, conscious that Michael is standing in the doorway, listening to our conversation. He has not seen the way Sara is with me, and I would rather have kept it hidden from him.

"Well, those puppies are hardly civilized company. You're idle most of the day—I feel you should be busy with something."

"We're eating your catch for lunch, I gather?" Steven says, looking up and smiling at me. "A bona fide fisherwoman." His voice is teasing, flushed through with sarcasm, and I look away.

"I'm not sure that's any good either," Sara says. "Being down at the dam in the current circumstances. It's hardly safe. No—I mean a job of sorts. Something that isn't entirely for your own pleasure." She smooths down her skirt. "What about contributing something to the party? Bunting perhaps. We'll need a good deal of it to decorate the trees over the lawn. You're good with a sewing machine—you could sew it for us."

She looks at me with her head slightly cocked, as though I might refuse. "I'll have a word with your father. It would be good for you to have a project."

"*Millions read this novel*," Steven says again, pronouncing each word very slowly. "Damn it, I don't know," and he throws the newspaper onto the coffee table.

"*Hard Times*," Michael says, and we all look up as though stung. His voice generates an outward ripple of silence.

"Did you say something?" Steven asks after a moment.

"*Hard Times*," Michael says again. "It's an anagram." Steven looks at him blankly. "Charles Dickens," Michael says.

"I know it's bloody Dickens," Steven says, irritably. He picks up the paper and casts his eye over the crossword. I watch him, my heart knocking in my chest. I have seen what Michael has not—I know what it is to draw his attention.

"So it is," Steven says, after a second or two. He looks up at Michael. "Well—aren't you a bright button?"

Sara stands up. "What are you doing in here anyway, Michael?" she says. "Why don't you go on and wait outside?"

She is shooing him out of the door, and he turns and leaves.

A SHOUT FROM the kitchen. My father and I leave our breakfast and run to see what is the matter. Sara is standing by the table—her face red. Jim is backed up in the corner sweating. I see the silver Coronation spoons spread out on the table. The round heads that decorate the top of each spoon—printed with the face of the Queen, have been snapped off. A series of small decapitations.

"What were they doing in here?" my father asks.

"I gave them to him to polish." Sara points at Jim.

"*Bwana*, it was not me," Jim says, his feet shuffling. "I left them here last night to finish in the morning. I didn't think. Someone must have been here—" He casts his eye around the kitchen.

We look at the bare earth walls, the blackened pots on the open range, the tins of food behind their wire enclosures.

"Is anything missing?"

"No, *Bwana*," Jim says, shaking his head.

"What kind of a country is this?" Sara screams, sweeping the spoons off the table with her hand. They fall soundlessly onto the earth floor. "I won't be made fun of, Robert. Not in my own house." She brushes past me, out of the kitchen.

Jim stoops down and begins to pick the spoons up off the floor. My father watches him for a moment, then turns and walks after Sara.

"I'm sorry, Jim," I say quietly, bending down to help him gather up the broken spoons. He does not answer.

My father questions the houseboys but comes up with no answers. There is talk of Jim being dismissed, but it comes to nothing.

THERE ARE NO FISH this afternoon, and I put down my rod and pick my way through the bush toward the back of the dam, which tucks behind the trees, out of sight. The expanse of the water is a basin for the sun, holding it gleaming on its surface, reflecting it back up at me. There is a hide up above here—the eagle's nest—which looks out over the dam, and a small clearing in the forest where my mother put a salt lick for the elephant. We used to camp there on a full moon and watch leopard come down to the bank to drink. I am about to head up the track, when ahead I see a black body at the water's edge. I stop and watch. The body is tall, graceful, male. He is naked. I see the firm buttocks, the long, curved legs, his feet arched against the ground. It is Michael. His overalls, shirt, sandals, lie in a small heap. Without them he is transformed into something timeless.

I see the skin on his back, across one side from the shoulder blade to his hip, is mottled with scarring. The skin doesn't move, doesn't ripple with the rest of his body as he walks. It looks as if it has melted. There is flesh missing.

He is—naked—like a warrior sculpted in bronze, an archetype of masculinity, and I am both compelled and repulsed by his strangeness. He wades into the water, then dives in and stays underneath for a long moment. I can see his shape gliding under the sun's reflection like a fish. I watch enviously. The water ripples outward, cool and liquid against his body, and I want to be swimming too, submerged beneath its surface.

My mother's fishing rod is in my hand, when I hear the District Officer's car pull up. He steps out and walks toward the veranda where I am standing.

"Going out?" he asks, looking up at me. He is dressed in khaki shorts and a short-sleeved, khaki bush shirt, the buttons undone at the top. His blond hair—greased back—makes his face appear overly large, and there is something chilling in the heavy tread of his boots as he walks up the wooden steps.

I am conscious suddenly of the house silent around us. And I find—now that I am alone with him—that he makes me afraid. I might be twelve years old again.

"To the dam," I say, my voice not quite steady.

"Is your father in?"

I shake my head.

"Sara?"

"She's resting."

"That suits me fine. It's been a long day." He sits down on one of the chairs on the veranda and stretches out his legs, the floorboards creaking under his weight. "Can I trouble you for a glass of water?"

"Of course." I lean the fishing rod against the wall of the house, noticing as I do so that my hands are sweating. I pad down the steps past him, across the narrow strip of grass, under the burning sun, to the kitchen hut, conscious of him watching me the whole way. It is the middle of the day and Jim has gone back to the *shamba*. The heat is saturating. It scalds my face, and my back runs with sweat. It smells of earth in here, and food. Flies circle and alight in a lazy dance. One side of the kitchen is open to the air; it is cooler here at the back and I pour water from the jug into a glass, then stand for a moment, wondering if I have to go back, or whether I can slip off without him noticing. I hear a noise behind me and glance round. Steven is standing in the open doorway, watching me. Anxiety slides like acid through my stomach, and I swallow heavily.

"Did I interrupt?" he asks, looking at me, but not going away.

"I was just coming out."

He walks a little way into the kitchen, and I have to force myself not to step backward. There is not much room in here for both of us. I remember his hands, when I was twelve, pinning me in his lap. He is more my father's age than mine and—although I want to run past him—I struggle under a sense of his authority.

"The water?" he asks, smiling.

When I hand him the glass he doesn't take it, just looks at me with pleasure, as though I have been naive, and I am embarrassed. I put the glass down behind me and go to step past him, but he sidesteps in front of me at the last moment and laughs when I flinch.

I move the other way, and he sidesteps with me, copying my

movement exactly as though we are dancing, and my heart is thumping in my chest.

Then he steps forward into me, so that his stomach nudges against my shirt. I back up against the sink. He smiles slowly, putting a hand to the waist of my trousers, watching for my reaction. My skin crawls under the pressure of his fingers, and I try to move out of his grasp, but clumsily, not wanting him to think he has me trapped. He gives a low laugh, putting his other hand lightly on my hip, so that he is pinning me, and there is something both intimate and assertive in the gesture. I remember what it was like before— the struggle—and try not to move, not to make this worse by encouraging him to use any kind of force.

"It can't be easy for you, being home after so long."

"It's fine," I say, willing him to let go of me.

"And your father too busy to notice you, eyes only for Sara."

"That's not true." I muster the courage to look him in the eye, but when my gaze meets his I wish I hadn't. It is too knowing, too intimate, and I look away.

"Oh, you can't tell me it doesn't hurt. I've seen the way you watch them, him looking at her with those big eyes. You're all on your own here and I think it scares you."

Even though I dislike him—I know he is right, and I can feel myself coloring while he watches me. With his eyes still on me, he steps a little to the side—letting me escape—and I dart past him, the skin on my back crawling, into the bright day outside.

MICHAEL LOOKS UP when I come into the yard. I stop when I see him, taking in a ragged breath. He puts down his tools and watches me. My hands are at my sides, and my head is ringing. I can still feel the pressure of Steven's fingers on my hip.

"What is it?" he asks, stepping out of the garage. I can see him trying to read in me what has happened.

"Nothing," I say, shaking my head. I had not anticipated this. I came down here for something else. We are watching each other across the yard. The light, the colors—they are too bright. I bite my lower lip, staring at him, tears frozen in my eyes.

I want something—I am molding it in my mind. It is to do with him—but I shake it off. I walk over to my mother's trunks and push back the lid of the first, bend down and pick up an armful of dresses. My hands are full of soft fabric. There are almost too many for me to carry and my mouth is buried. The smell of them is overwhelming. Musty, dry, and of my mother. It is the smell of her dead.

He moves, closer to me now.

I stumble away from him, trip and fall on my knees. The dresses are scattered on the earth—green, yellow, silver. One of my knees is bleeding.

His shadow slides over me—I see his feet—the arch of his foot pale like the inside of his lips.

"Where are you going?" he asks. I can't bring myself to look up at him. The skin on my knee has peeled back, and the flesh beneath is bleeding small pinpricks of blood. My head feels heavy. I gather up the dresses, clumsily, and carry them out of the yard.

THE SUN IS A HARD, flat glare. My arms sweat beneath the weight of the fabric. I reach the dam and throw the dresses into the boat, untie the old rope from the post, throw it in and step in after it. I take one of the oars and push against the bank, and the boat dips out into the dam. I drift right into the middle, close to the swell of earth where my father said a witch lived. The water laps at the sides of the hull, all around me its depth falling away, the light turning it a murky yellow, full of particles that sift down through its many layers.

I take one of the dresses and hold it over the surface. Water laps at the bottom of it, turning the bright yellow cotton a dull green, limp and wet as though my mother has walked out here herself. It grasps at the dress. I let it go and the dress floats, with the substance of air, for a long moment, then the water—like fire to paper—slowly takes hold of it, and it is sucked wetly onto the surface, before sinking into the depths. The fabric billows as it goes down, and it is as though my mother is there, turning, trapped beneath me.

There are seven dresses in all. The last dress is made of green silk. My father bought it for her at the coast, and she had worn it very occasionally, eliciting a look of hunger from him, an understanding passing between them that excluded me. I cannot bring myself to throw it into the water, and so I bundle it into a ball on my lap and row myself back to the bank.

When I turn, Michael is waiting at the edge of the water.

He wades out and pulls in the boat. Tears pour down my face. I step out into ankle-deep water. "It's all right," he says, and the patient softness of his voice loosens something in me. Without thinking I lean forward and rest my forehead on his shoulder. He puts a hand on the back of my neck, and I feel the warm, dry surface of his skin settle against mine, as it had in my dream. His hand is barely touching me, but it is there and I don't know how it became true or whether there is fault in it, but I know that he is the only person who

Jennifer McVeigh

can offer me comfort, the only person whose presence can make me feel as though everything might—after all—be all right.

IT IS STEVEN LOCKHART who brings the news. I see him step out of his jeep one morning, with Harold's rucksack in one hand. The one he left with a few months ago, carrying his small bundle of belongings. And I know what has happened before I stand at the door and hear Sara screaming. My father tries to hold her but she throws him off. Her cries come out of silence and fall back into silence, like the screams of an impala caught in the jaws of a lion. There is no crying in between.

She staggers to the table and sweeps her hand across it, knocking a yellow porcelain bowl to the floor; one of the set she had brought with her from Nairobi. It shatters on the boards. My father bends down to pick up the fragments, as though it might still be within his grasp to mend the situation.

Harold died out on patrol. An ambush. Two English boys killed and not a single Mick. They slipped away into the forest, Steven says, like bats into the night. Sara does not come to lunch. Steven says to my father, "We will make sure they pay. The whole disgusting, fucking tribe."

I knock on Sara's door. She is sitting on the far side of the bed, facing the window. She does not turn around. "I am so sorry," I say.

After a moment she turns her face to me. There are no tears. She looks at me, until I am uneasy, her eyes staring, her face blank and taut, full of grief, hate and accusation.

Harold is buried in Nakuru. My father and Sara go to the funeral, and I am left behind to watch the empty house. She does not want anyone with her but my father. They will be back before it is dark, my father says, and Kahiki is outside in case there is trouble. I walk down the corridor to Harold's darkroom and sit on the single bed, the springs creaking beneath my weight. We sat here, his head against my shoulder, his tears falling wet onto my nightdress. And where is he now? I lie down and close my eyes. It is not good to be in here like this, but I do not move, giving myself up to the darkness. My head spins, grief and fear turning a circle, one indistinguishable from the other, until I feel something dark and awful pressing down on me, and I open my eyes with a jolt and run from the room, down the corridor, along the track to the stables. There is no one there. The yard is silent. I open the stable door and sink into the straw beside Juno, her nose pushing into my hand, and her puppies tumbling over my legs, trying to shut out the fears that grip me.

My father and Sara come back in the late afternoon. Neither of them talk about the funeral, and Harold is not mentioned. When I say his name, my father shakes his head. Sara must have asked for it to be that way.

In the evening, I see my father on his own at the table, gluing the pieces of Sara's broken porcelain bowl; three fragments on a tray in front of him. He assembles them, holding them together, the delicate bowl perfect for a moment in his grasp; his hands shaking with the tension of keeping them steady. I realize suddenly that his jaw is clenched. He is pressing too hard. It will not hold. The pieces crush against each other, the bowl broken, but my father keeps pushing, his knuckles whitening, until the porcelain snaps into shards, squeezed into the palms of his hands. A drop of blood runs down one fist, into his shirtsleeve.

He hasn't seen that I am watching.

Sara retreats to her room and doesn't come out during the day. A few nights later she appears for dinner, fully dressed, but when I look at her I see that there is something changed in her—a looseness behind her eyes—as though the stitches have been picked out and she is unraveling.

XXI

✦

The Home Guard post needs volunteers to go out on patrol. All the farmers are on rota, offering their services. My father makes plans to leave. He says he has no choice; they need him to do his bit. He will be gone for three weeks.

"What are we to do without you?" Sara asks, her voice rising.

"You'll do fine without me," he says, putting a reassuring hand over hers, but she pulls her hand out from under his.

"Why can't they send one of the boys from the KAR?"

"They'd be lost before they started. I know the land like the back of my hand. It takes years for these boys from England to learn the terrain, how to track and how to hide. I can make a real difference—" He puts a hand on hers again and says softly, "I think you would like me to go. For Harold?"

Sara looks away, but there is consent in her posture.

"You'll both be fine," my father says to us. "Steven has said he will check in when he can."

I cannot imagine being in the house without him. What if there is an attack? I watched a Western once, two women alone on a farm, the Indians creeping up silently on the house, under the cover of night. The gunshots and the screaming. Mau Mau has the upper hand. Harold is dead. And if my father leaves, we will be more vulnerable than ever to attack.

When I find my father alone and tell him that I am afraid, he says, "They are not brave, and they are mostly poorly armed. They won't be able to get inside, unless you open the doors. So whatever you do, don't be fooled into letting anyone in. You are both armed, and Kahiki will be sleeping in the kitchen. If there is an attack there is every chance that you will be all right." He squeezes my hand. "I need you to be brave, Rachel. Sara has had a hard time of it, with Harold. It would be good if you could be strong for both of you." I want to tell him about Steven, that he scares me, but I can't see a way to get at it. It feels unimportant with everything that is going on. What did he actually do to me when I was twelve? What has he done to me since I have been here? Is it anything more than insinuation, and my own imagination?

My father insists that Juno is brought into the house, and even Sara agrees without a fuss. We need a guard dog. The puppies have stopped suckling—they are a few months old, and will live down at the stables.

We watch him drive off for his first patrol in the Land Rover. When we can no longer see the car through the dust, I go to my bedroom. I push against the bars on the windows—they are cold against my hands and immovable. We have been left alone in the house, with our guns, to ward off the evils of the night as best we are able.

I READ IN the newspaper the story of a Kikuyu laborer. When he refused to take the Mau Mau oath and kill the farmer for whom he worked, the Mau Mau gang tied him to a rope and put a panga in his hand. He was told—under the pain of death—to enter the farmhouse and kill the old farmer. He did as he was told. The judge suggested the courts should show him mercy, but the Governor disagreed. He will be hanged later this week.

MUNGAI IS ON his knees setting the fire. It is half past five and the sitting room is quiet. Sara is still in her room—I haven't seen her all day. I place my gun carefully on the table in front of me. It is different now, the feeling I have as night approaches. The menace is tangible; thick in the air. A slow drum starts beating somewhere in the hills. I prick my ears—I have not imagined it. A low vibration from far off that pulls my heart into its rhythm. A Mau Mau oathing ceremony? It is nearly dark. Curfew means no one should be allowed outside after dark. What does it mean? Are they mustering for an attack? Or just holding an *ngoma*?

Mungai looks as though he hasn't heard. He moves quietly around the room, putting out glasses, laying the table for dinner. He is only allowed in once at dusk to light the fire and lay out supper. We eat a lukewarm dinner every night, and the plates are cleared in the bright light of the morning.

Only when Mungai goes to draw the curtains do I see him stop and stare out into the dwindling light. The window is a dangerous place to stand—a precision rifle was stolen two nights ago from a farm not far away, but what should he fear? Night is gathering and the drums beat a little faster. His hand grips the yellow and white cotton print. I want to know what he is thinking. Have they been oathing in the *shamba*? Would our servants—under pressure—plot an attack against us? Everyone on the farm has been forced to take sides. Which side is Mungai on? Jim? Michael?

"They are louder tonight than I have heard them before," I say.

Mungai turns, as if he has forgotten me. *"Memsaab?"* The question is thrown back at me as if I am imagining what he has so clearly heard. As if hearing the drums might be admitting to guilt. I feel the confusion in him—compelled and repelled like the rest of us.

The low thudding of the drums continues as Sara and I eat dinner, lifting into the air with the rising moon—a theatrical score, heightening our anxiety. We eat with our revolvers on the table. The night outside feels vast and menacing, clamoring at our windows, seeping through the cracks of the house, the open seams, and dissolving our security into its blackness.

THE SOUND OF a leopard wakes me again that night and the nights which follow; the hoarse, rasping cough marking out the dark. Is it Mau Mau, come down from the forest to oath in the *shamba*? Do they know that my father is away? I struggle to sleep. At the edges of my waking mind I can hear the bleating of the goat as it waited, with its legs hobbled, for the inevitable, violent grasping of claws.

"HOW IS THAT bunting coming along?" Sara asks at breakfast, digging her spoon into the wet, pink flesh of a pawpaw.

"Do we still need it?" I ask, surprised. I had assumed, after Harold's death, that she would call off the celebration.

"Well, we can't have a Coronation party without bunting," she says, sliding the spoon into her mouth.

"I didn't think we would be going ahead with it."

"I think it's more important than ever," she says, looking at me. "To show them that we are resilient. All the fabric is in the barn, in boxes, and I have white cotton ribbon—enough to make at least thirty meters. That should keep you busy. And you'll have to go through the menu with Jim."

JIM IS IN the kitchen—his hands deep in a bowl, his face white with icing sugar.

He smiles when he sees me, but his eyes are lifeless. I have never seen him like this. He must miss Mukami, Njeri, his children. Or is it more than that? What happens in the *shamba* at night that we do not know about?

"Is everything all right, Jim?" I ask.

"*Sawa sawa.*" He pulls a damp handful of dough from the bowl, pats it into a ball and drops it onto the old slab of marble.

"Have you heard from Njeri? How is the baby?"

"Yes. They are fine," he says, but he does not look at me. He dusts the dough with icing sugar, his hands black against the white stone.

"What's that?" I ask.

"Shortbread," he says, in halting English. "I will cut a flag out of the top and paint jam, red and blue."

"She designed it?"

"No, Aleela. I did."

"It'll be wonderful," I say, but he does not meet my eye. I cannot reach him.

"She wants me to go through the menu with you," I say, eventually. He dusts off his hands and comes over to the table.

There is a lot for him to do. We will have cucumber sandwiches, Victoria sponge, coffee and walnut cake, Constance Spry's Coronation Chicken, raspberry jelly, Coronation Cup—a white wine and gin cocktail—sausages and pickles. Sara is buying sugared jelly sweets to decorate the Victoria sponge, so that it looks like a crown.

A booklet arrives with a note in it—addressed to my father. *Your Turn May Come.* It has been issued by the Department of Information in Nakuru. In the sitting room, by the light of the paraffin lamp, I read its warning.

Gangs of Kikuyu are entering the settled areas in increasing numbers in search of food, supplies, clothing, arms and ammunition . . . The probability of attacks being made against European lives and property in the coming months is therefore greatly enhanced.

I do not want to read it and yet I cannot stop myself. The situation in Kenya is overtaking us. Like the rising of a huge wave, I feel as though it will suck us under, and none of us—my father, Sara, Jim—will escape unharmed.

There follows a list of do's and don'ts.

Locking up: Do this yourself. Don't leave it to the servants.

Sara locks the house after Mungai has left each evening.

Windows: Have these protected with bars or expanded metal.
Ensure that opaque curtains cover the windows properly.

Servants: Do not employ Kikuyu servants. If you have an outside
kitchen, have a covered way to the house wired in with expanded
metal. If you cannot do this, then lock all servants out of the house
before dark. Do not admit servants to the house after dark unless
absolutely necessary. If they have to enter the house ensure that their
entrance is covered by a gun.

We have no choice but to employ Kikuyu servants, but none of
them are allowed in the house anymore, except for Mungai, and he
must be gone before it is dark. I think about Jim and all the Kikuyu
I knew growing up. It is impossible to imagine them acting with
violence, least of all against the family.

Chairs: Do not always have these in the same place. Move them
around from time to time. Never place a chair with its back to the door.

My father has already told us to always sit facing the door.
There is advice on labor lines, farm guards, securing cattle and
alarm systems.

Keep a good watchdog which barks and always keep it in the house
after dark.

I am thankful for Juno, lying sleeping at my feet.

Have a strong room, accessible from inside the house, for emergency rations, rockets and other supplies.

Sara and I have nothing but a few guns.

Have a plan ready against an attack on the house . . . Don't rely on
the telephone: the wires are invariably cut before an attack.

There is no telephone here. How will we call for help? Where
would we go? The Markhams are over an hour's drive away; our
only hope would be to wait until dawn forces the attackers to flee.
One point in particular scares me:

If your house is at all flammable, have buckets or containers of water
and earth always filled and ready.

I can't get the idea out of my head—waking up to a fire burning
the house, fumbling for the key to let ourselves out, running into
the dark night, into the arms of men waiting with pangas.

I daren't light the paraffin lamp at night in my room, in case
Mau Mau are beyond the window, and they should see where I am
sleeping.

A NOISE, a call in the dark, shattering my sleep. I am standing up,
halfway across the room, before I am fully awake—straining to
hear. Was it the cry of a bird? An animal? A man?

A thin light filters through the curtains. It is almost dawn. I
slide my gun off the table, press the safety. It is chill and heavy in
my hand. My arms feel leaden and weak, so that I wonder if I'll
have the power to lift the gun and fire should I need to.

The noise comes again, somewhere not so far from the house,

not far from my window. A low groaning. Something in pain. The sitting room is dark and full of shadows. I pad across the floorboards, my heart pounding. The gun is in my hand. I swallow heavily. Through the short hall to the door—still bolted. The silence is buzzing in my ears. Here is the door to Sara's room. I stop for a moment, collecting myself in the dark, my ears and eyes straining to pick up anything that might tell me what it is. I can't hear the noise from here. I consider calling Sara from her bed. But the light now is stronger behind the curtains and the night is receding as I watch. I slip the gun into my other hand. The lock turns easily, and I step outside.

It is that strange time of early morning when the air tastes wet and the sky lifts second by second from the darkness.

I walk around to the front of the house, onto the short grass that forms a clearing outside my bedroom window. I stand for a moment in the cloudless dawn. The noise again, and a dark shape lifting from the grass. For a moment I think it might be a man and I stop, breathless. The light illuminates a shadow, low and black against the sky. Two animals. Cattle. One is moving—lowing, deep from its lungs. I go closer, drawn despite myself, to see how it is.

The bull has been slashed across his thick hide, under his belly, so that his guts bulge out onto the grass. His ears have been sliced off. This is the one that is still alive. His breath heaves, coming from his open stomach, his nose sucking in air as though drowning. And the other has a stake driven into her, under her tail. Her two hind legs have been lopped off below her hocks so that all I see are the stumps. Her udders have been removed. There is blood, thick and wet on the grass, like afterbirth.

Sara appears beside me, and then there is Michael, running

toward us. Sara lifts her gun at him. She is in her nightdress and she has no shoes on.

"*Memsaab*," Michael says, holding his hands open. He is looking at her gun, at her face.

"Where is Kahiki?" Sara asks.

"He is at the *boma*," Michael says. "He sent me here."

"It's a warning," Sara says, lowering her gun. Her voice quavers. "They're showing us exactly what they're going to do to us."

The belly of the bull is heaving. His head is on the earth, too heavy to lift, his nose reeling in the air, as though he cannot suck what he needs from the grass.

"It should be killed, *Memsaab*," Michael says.

"I can't bear it. I can't bear it," she says, shaking her head, not listening. Her face is pale, and her voice is rising on hysteria. "Why did the men from the *shamba* not come? Why didn't they stop this?"

"They were scared. They wouldn't leave the *shamba*," Michael says.

"And the rest of the cattle?" I ask.

"We will find out," Michael says. "Kahiki is bringing them in."

Sara is backing up, walking toward the house, her hand held over her mouth.

"What should I do?" I call after her.

But she doesn't answer. She turns and runs to the door, her bare feet tripping on the grass.

The gun is small and heavy in my hand, surely too small for such a large animal. I know I haven't got it in me to pull the trigger, so close to this bull that heaves and pants his pain on the grass in front of me.

"Rachel—" Michael says, holding out his hand. I pass him the gun. His fingers are hot and dry against mine. A bird calls into the dawn, a flat three-tone whistle. *Three blind mice.*

He crouches down, puts the barrel to the bull's head and squeezes the trigger. A bolt of sound. My ears ring with it. Blood pulses. The breathing stops and the bull's head lies still in the grass. Michael turns the gun in his hand and passes it back to me. I wonder if he has ever killed a man so close. I look away; not wanting to see the bull that lies mutilated at his feet.

Light floods the twilight darkness. A coucal makes a cry like water being poured from a bottle; a wet, hollow glugging sound. Only then do I see the crimson rim of the sun rise throbbing from the horizon.

I look back at Michael. He is only two paces from me, but I cannot cross the distance. His gaze holds mine. I want him to put out his hand, to draw me into him as he did before, but he doesn't move, just holds my eyes with his. The silence screams loud in my ears.

When I see that I want something he will not give me, I run from him, into the house.

SARA DOESN'T TALK about the slaughtered cattle at breakfast. Instead she dictates a letter to my uncle. She asks him to bring a piglet from the factory to roast for the party. I wonder what he would think—what my father would think—if they were here, seeing us so alone. When Kahiki comes in to say that they have managed to recover most of the cattle she waves him away. Her powder is pasted thick and pale on her cheeks, and around her eyes it gathers in her wrinkles, stained black where her makeup has run. She has been drinking—I can smell the gin on her breath.

She wants me to go down to the stables to fetch fabric for the bunting. Says that I must do it or she will write to my father and tell him I am being uncooperative. She is going to make jam for the Coronation. I have never seen her cooking and this feels strange, for her to be doing this now. I do not want to go down to the stables—I am embarrassed by how openly I looked at Michael. I know he saw all my need and my fear, and I do not want him to see me so vulnerable again. But Sara is implacable and I agree.

Michael is not in the yard when I get there. In the barn I find a box of folded fabrics. Old tablecloths, extra runs of cotton, a patchwork bedspread my mother had stitched when I was very young. It smells musty in here, and dry, and there are droppings in the box. I shake out the bedspread. It is padded and heavy, and there are yellow patches—urine from the mice—and faded creases where it has been folded too long. I will wash it at home. I choose a few folded yards of different colored cottons. I find a pair of scissors in the barn and place them on top of the fabric. I am just about to gather up the pile and carry it back up to the house when I hear a car engine coming down the track. I look up and see Steven's jeep pulling into the yard. He turns off the engine and steps out.

"I gather you got a bit of a fright this morning," he says to me, lighting a cigarette and dropping the match to the ground. He holds out the packet, leaning back against the car. I have not had a cigarette yet today and the desire for one shifts and wakes inside me. But I don't come forward. I need to keep my distance. "We got rid of the cattle for you."

"Does it mean there'll be an attack?" I ask, my heart in my throat.

He inhales, licks tobacco off his lip. "Not necessarily. It's just a warning. They're trying to shake you up a bit."

"Did you find out anything in the *shamba*?"

He exhales and holds the packet out again. "Go on. You look like you could do with one."

The craving gets the better of me. I walk over to him and take one, blinking in the hot sun.

"There were no gangs at the *shamba* last night," he says, drawing on his cigarette. "A few Micks came down from the forest. They let the cattle out of the *bomas*, slashed a couple of them and left."

Michael walks into the yard. "Fill her up," Steven says, glancing at him. He strikes a match and holds it out to me. I am relieved that Michael is here; I do not think Steven will hurt me in front of another man. As I bend my head to the flame he swings his body round, drops his cigarette to the floor and jams my arms against the passenger door. I shout but the cigarette is in my mouth. Smoke curls up into my eyes.

I try to move away from him, but his hands are immovable—he has me pinned. The metal is hot against the backs of my arms. My eyes water. I can hear Michael in the garage.

"Stand still like a good girl," Steven says quietly, letting go of one of my arms and taking the cigarette from my mouth with one hand. He inhales.

"Do you know"—he strokes my cheek with the back of his fingers; I see the inside of his mouth, pink and wet, as he talks; I can smell the salt on his hand, can feel the sweat radiating hot and damp from his body—"I always had a feeling you would grow up to be rather attractive?" His body is very close to mine. I can feel my chest going in and out.

Michael comes round the back of the jeep and starts filling it up. He must see what Steven is doing to me. I cannot move my arm. His grip is tight against my skin. There is the clatter of metal against metal, the slow glugging of oil out of the can. There is no use calling out to him. I don't want to look to see if he is watching. I want to cry.

"I am going to give you a little kiss," Steven says, simply, looking me straight in the eye, still stroking my cheek with the back of his fingers.

"No," I say, through clenched teeth.

"Come, come," he says. "It's just a kiss. That's not a lot to ask."

"Leave me alone," I say, but I can't get out from under the bulk of him. He has me trapped. Michael is just beside us. Steven must know it too, but he doesn't care. He leans forward and I push my hand into his chest with all my force, but his flesh absorbs my strength. He is taller and stronger than I am and my spine is back against the car. His other hand is at my neck now, his fingers rigid on my throat so that I cannot breathe well. He puts his mouth on mine. It is wet and cold against my own, and I feel his tongue flickering like a fish against my lips. I want to bite him, but I won't open my mouth. I try to kick up with my knee, deep into his body, but it has no impact.

"The car is ready, *Bwana*." Michael's voice is close to us. I hear it but I cannot turn my head. Steven presses his body closer into me.

"*Bwana*." Michael's voice is louder this time, more urgent.

"What a lot of fuss you make," Steven says to me, drawing his head away and taking his hand off my neck. I can't escape yet—his body is still blocking mine. He wipes the palm of his hand across his mouth, slowly, his eyes on mine. Then he steps away from me and reaches out and cups his hand to Michael's cheek. "Oh, we liked men like you in the war," he says. "The blacker the face, the thicker the neck, the darker the skin, the better the soldier you made."

I stumble away from him and hear the car start behind me. When he is gone, I breathe out a ragged breath—a groan of anger and humiliation. My face is wet with tears. I can't bring myself to look at Michael—there is too much shame. Instead I see the red brown dust of the garage floor, the purple blooms of the jacaranda flowers scattered over it. The deep quiet, in the heat of the day.

"Rachel—" he says, in a low, soft voice, coming over to where I stand. "He has gone to Nakuru. He won't come back today."

I lift my eyes to his, no longer caring what he thinks of me or wants for himself, but knowing only what I need. His protection. His desire. I drop my head to his chest, wanting to feel his hands on me, giving in to what I am asking. His body is rigid and warm against mine. I thought he would put his hands on me, but he does not, and now I begin to doubt whether I have dreamed that he might want this.

"Please—" I say, through gritted teeth. I need him to take ownership of me. To obliterate Steven Lockhart. I will not feel safe until he has had me.

"Do you know what you are asking?" he says, softly. His hand has settled on my neck, more from instinct than affection, but it is all the touch I need; my spine contracts under his fingers.

"Yes," I say, though I do not. All I know is that I am giving myself to him. I do not dare to look at him. I might lose my nerve. He lifts the weight of me and carries me into the dark barn. I hold my head against his neck, my mouth tasting the tears that have fallen against his skin, salt under my lips, but I am not crying anymore. There are no shades of light in here, only the rub of his clothes against mine. His hands slide up under my shirt, but I want more than that. I wait—breathless—until I feel the shock of his hand between my legs. He has found the core of me. I hold myself against him, his body, his smell is strange. I move his hand away, pulling him closer, wanting all of him.

MICHAEL. A chink of light falling through the doors of the barn. His arms letting me go. I rest my head against the wall, watching him stand and dress, caught in this strange stillness. A closeness as though our bodies are still connected, even though he is no longer touching me. He crouches down and looks at me. I cannot meet his eyes. Instead I look at his chest, the layers of muscle, the ripples of brown skin, the nearness of him. I look up. There is no dialogue in his glance. No question. It is just a blank reading of what we have felt, the fierceness, and what we have done. I feel a current of fear that I can feel so close to someone who is so completely strange to me. His body already begins to feel separate from me, and I feel with regret the pulling away of myself from him.

He puts his hands to my face, palms cradling my chin, thumbs against my cheeks. I look into his eyes, breathing to steady myself. I feel as though I am falling. "Hey," he says, slowly. "Are you all right?"

I nod, smiling. I am not ready to show him the depths of my desire.

When I get up to the house, I check the kitchen for Sara. She isn't in there and there is no sign of Jim. The jam has boiled over the sides of the pot, and it has pooled wet and sticky on the floor like blood. I take the pot off the stove and go into the house. I lie on my bed and feel a strange emptiness inside me. As though Michael has carved himself in my flesh and left me unwhole. But there is also strength. I know there will be no fear when I am with him. No one can touch me. He will solder all my edges and absorb me into him.

XXII

-＞･＜-

The following day. I wait until Sara is having her midday sleep. I have an idea that I want to bring Michael something. I take the radio from my room. It is bulky and weighs more than I thought. I struggle to carry it down the track to the stables.

Michael watches me walk into the yard. I feel suddenly as though I am making a statement bringing it down here, and my face flushes red.

"I brought it from the house—" I say, when we are a few yards away from each other.

"I can see that," he says, wiping his hands on a cloth, but not coming any closer. I remember him touching me. The closeness of our bodies. His hold over me is like a wave, rising. I cannot breathe when I look at him.

He comes over to where I am standing, but doesn't look at the radio. I feel the full force of his presence—what it is to have him watch me, so close. I remember him carrying me inside, and it flows like liquid through me. I shift my feet. The radio is heavy, and I have carried it a long way. I want to put it down but he doesn't help me. I feel the current of his anger before he speaks.

"Why did you bring it?"

"My father hasn't seen it. He won't know—" It feels inadequate. I wanted to please him, but I see now that the risk is too great for him, with the Emergency. No Kikuyu—even Michael—are allowed to have access to the news. Trying to save myself, I say, "Anyway, why shouldn't I listen to the radio when I am down here?"

"When you are down here," he says, and I wonder if he wants me here at all.

Just when I think I will have to bend down and put the radio on the ground, he takes it from me, and I know that despite himself he is hungry for what it can deliver. He places it on his workbench and begins to stretch out the aerial. I watch his hands, their delicate movement, the same hands that held me yesterday and feel so distant now.

I move away, sitting in the dust with my back to the barn wall, my knees up, in the small strip of shade thrown out by the sun which has moved behind the corrugated roof.

The radio comes on with a burst of sound, and we both flinch. He turns the volume down. I hold my breath, listening for anyone who might be coming down the track, but no one is there.

He turns it up slowly and a voice filters out. The one o'clock news.

In Kenya, Jomo Kenyatta has been sentenced to seven years' hard labor for his part in the organization of the rebel Mau Mau movement. The leader of the Kenya African Union, who was found guilty on all charges, was also given three years' hard labor for being a member of the movement.

Michael is listening, with every inch of his body. I know what this means—the end of hope for an independent Kenya. *In passing sentence the judge, Ransley Thacker, told Kenyatta: "You have successfully plunged many Africans back into a state which shows little humanity. You have persuaded them in secret to murder, burn and commit atrocities which will take many years to forget." He added: "Make no mistake about it, Mau Mau will be defeated."*

Meanwhile settlers are being asked to exercise extreme caution . . . The clipped English accent permeates the yard with a strange, false security. Reporting from London, thousands of miles away, oblivious to me, to him, to this farm in the very heart of the conflict of which he speaks.

The news gives way to music, a slow song. Michael leans forward and switches the radio off. He doesn't look at me, and I don't say anything to break the silence. He is absorbed in thought, taut with anger.

Eventually he speaks. "Who are the British to talk about atrocities? The murders and burnings that will take so many years to forget?" He runs a hand over his face. "I was with the Fourteenth in Burma, the so-called Forgotten Army. For two years we clawed our way through the jungle, sweating with tropical disease. *Kabaw Valley*—Death Valley. It was a very hell on earth. At first we were terrified of the Japanese—we had all heard stories of what they did to African soldiers. But in the end I felt nothing but pity. They were rotting alive, down in holes, eating boiled grass, driven mad by starvation. I found a man whose teeth had fallen out. His hair had grown long beneath his helmet. And then the killing—"

He swallows heavily and stops talking. As though he has said too much. I can see the muscle ticking in his jaw. I stand up. I want to go to him and touch him, but I am not sure he wants me to. I am terrified by how little I know him; by how much courage I will need to cross the distance.

He does not look up, and I walk out of the yard, leaving the radio, and Michael standing there, his face tight with rage.

IN THE *STANDARD* there are two pages dedicated to Kenyatta's conviction. One line sticks in my mind: *When Kenyatta attempted to explain the nature of the grievances that lay behind Mau Mau, Judge Thacker expressed his exasperation, telling the court: "Grievances have nothing whatever to do with Mau Mau and Mau Mau has nothing whatever to do with grievances."*

Can the judge be right? I do not think so. Mau Mau must surely be born out of a sense of injustice. I remember the man killed by Steven Lockhart. The list of demands for the strike. The words he spoke before he died. *Kenya is a black man's country. You should go back to where you belong.* Nothing is as simple as I used to believe it was; the lines of right and wrong have blurred.

At the back of the paper is a short news piece. At dawn yesterday an army patrol operating in the outskirts of Nairobi stumbled upon a strangled, mutilated cat hanging from an archway of tree branches. A note fixed to the branches told the Kikuyu: *We are going to Mount Kenya but will be back like lightning.* It was signed: *The Mau Mau.*

I think of Michael traveling from Nairobi, here to the foothills of Mount Kenya. I do not believe that he has come to kill Europeans, to force us off our land, but the story nevertheless makes me uneasy.

XXIII

❯❯•❮❮

My father's Land Rover pulls up outside the house just after dawn. He will only stay a few hours. He tells us that they have caught three men from a gang living in the forest above Bowker's farm. He thinks they were responsible for raiding and mutilating our cattle. He says that he does not think they will come back.

"How large was the gang?" I ask. "What about the men you did not catch?"

"They fled—we don't expect them to continue operating in this area."

I struggle to be reassured. He looks exhausted. There are black rings under his eyes and his face is pale and drawn. He says they do not sleep more than a few hours on patrol, that it rains in the forest and they are never dry, and Mau Mau are always just ahead of them.

He leaves after breakfast. When we have said good-bye I sit against the wall of the house, in the sun, cutting fabric into triangles, with Juno and her puppies at my feet. Kahiki brought them up from the stables this morning to run on the lawn, along with my mother's sewing machine. I will take the cuttings later and hem each one, and sew them onto ribbon. The house is absolutely quiet. The heat is saturating. It warms my blood, my back, my skin so that every part of me submits to it.

I deliberately stay away from the stables. I do not know if he wants to see me.

When I have hemmed twenty triangles, I sew them to five meters of white cotton ribbon. Sara nods her approval, but says we need the same length again. As I sew I think about Michael. I worry that the things that passed between us in the barn might not be meaningful to him. That he might not need or want them from me again.

Michael comes up to the house the following day. I am sitting on the steps of the veranda, with the fabric in my lap, a needle in one hand, oversewing the corners of the bunting. His eyes settle on mine, for just a moment, and I feel—with a lurch—the power he has over me. The weaver birds chatter in their nest in the tree overhead. Juno leaps up and trots over to him, and he drops a hand to her head. Sara is sitting in a wicker chair. She slips her gun off the table when he approaches. It is midday, but she has not changed out of her nightdress. There are stains down the front. Michael bows his head to her. The gun flickers in her lap as she turns it in her hand.

Sara says she wants four trestle tables made up for the party. Michael tells her that they are short of labor. More men have left. They need him at the dairy. His face, when he talks to Sara, is calm, neutral.

"I don't want excuses," she says, waving him away. She is keyed up, breathless. My father leaving again has unhinged her.

He turns and goes, and I watch his back as he walks away, and feel the loss of it wrench at me, deep in my stomach.

Later that afternoon, I walk down to the stables. I cannot keep myself away. He is not there, and I try to quell the panic that starts up inside me. What if he does not come? I sit with my back to the wall, waiting. An hour later, he walks into the yard, his blue overalls peeled down around his waist. He stops when he sees me. I watch him. There is nothing I can say. He is both strange and familiar—I am not prepared for the shock of seeing him alone. The knowledge of what he might do to me.

"Rachel—" he says, "I am glad you are here." His words unravel something in me. I take a breath.

He walks over and squats down opposite me, his legs open. I want to stand up, to run away, but more than that I want to stay.

"I have been waiting for you," he says, softly.

My head brushes against the wall but his lips are on my mouth. I can taste him, all of him. We kiss for just a moment, then he leans back. I want him so completely, to be with him so absolutely, that the strength of it stuns me. I want him to put his hands on me, to close the distance between us. He is smiling at me, as he looks at me, and I know he will take me inside, where it is dark. My heart thuds in my chest. I cannot smile back. Desire is like pain. I feel as though the surface of my skin has been peeled off. Every part of me is raw to his touch. It hurts, and the anticipation of the hurt is almost greater than the touch. Everything has changed. I have moved over to the other side and there is no going back.

Afterward, when it is over, he pulls open the door of the barn a few feet. Light floods in. I see that I am lying on an old rug taken from one of the boxes. He pulls on his underwear, his vest, then crouches down. "You should get dressed," he says, placing a dry hand over my thigh. I can feel the skin on his fingertips.

I sit up slowly, struggling to move out of the strange world he has left me in. I pull on my shorts, do up the buttons of my shirt. I feel raw, exposed. I think I might cry. His hand comes away from my thigh.

"Look what's here," he says, pulling a book from an open box. I stand looking over his shoulder. It is an old textbook. Geography. He turns a few of the pages and laughs. I have scribbled down the margin; a childish scrawl.

"Boring class?" he asks, raising his eyebrows. I never liked geography.

He stops on a double page—a map of Africa, blocked out in primary colors, each one representing the country which had colonized it. He stops turning the pages—he is reading the text now, interested. "This is what they've started teaching in Kikuyu schools. Since the Emergency. In the old schools, Kenya was a black man's country. Now they are telling children that Kenya was virtually uninhabited before the Europeans discovered it."

I am conscious that he is trusting me, that it is dangerous for him to speak like this. Over his shoulder I read:

KEY MOMENTS IN KENYA'S HISTORY

1849—Mount Kenya—discovered by Dr. Johann Ludwig Krapf

1858—Lake Victoria—discovered by John Hanning Speke

"It's as though our people don't exist," he says. "How can something be 'discovered' when people have lived there for hundreds of years? Or at least how can you agree in good conscience to teach that to Kikuyu children whose grandparents lived on the slopes of Mount Kenya long before Europeans set foot in this country?"

And I feel the awful, comic absurdity of imperialism, but also the danger. That these children might grow up to disown and disrespect the parents, the grandparents, the culture from which they come.

SARA AND I sit in near darkness waiting for the news. Mungai has laid the fire and left out supper for us. We are lighting fewer lamps, by instinct, as though the house will attract less attention if the windows are dark. The doors are all locked and the curtains drawn. I think of Michael in his hut behind the stables, and wish I could be there with him, instead of here with Sara.

A night of waiting ahead of us, hoping that we will get through until morning without an attack. Big Ben chimes, ringing out the hour, and for a moment we are captivated by the idea of London, solid and immutable, so many thousands of miles away. But the news when it comes shatters the illusion that we might be safe.

We regret to announce, says the voice on the radio, *that a young farmer and his doctor-wife, together with their six-year-old son, were cruelly slashed to death with pangas near their farmstead sometime last evening. The Rucks recently opened up a free surgery for the Africans, and it is thought that they unlocked their door expecting to find a patient needing urgent treatment.*

"It's madness," Sara says, in a queer high-pitched voice. "Primitive, irrational madness. It's Africa laughing at us for trying to civilize her."

The room suddenly feels very small, as if it were a cell, and I am conscious that the doors are locked. We are aware of our backs, of the softness of our stomachs, of the sound of a gunshot when it ricochets through the silence.

I stand up and go to the window, lifting back the curtain to peer outside. The land beyond the house is black. I want to know what is out there, what it looks like and whether it will dare come for me.

"Perhaps we have driven them to it," I say.

"What do you mean?" she asks in a tight voice, going over to the drinks cabinet and pouring herself a gin.

"How else can they make us listen?"

"Rachel—I will not have it," she says, sitting down, her voice tremoring, her hands turning over and over on a tassel from the cushion in her lap. But I cannot stop myself.

"We have taken away their lands, crippled them with taxes, closed down their schools. Kenyatta—their only political voice— has been arrested. England has introduced a police state the likes of which we last saw under Hitler. But no—" I can feel my words coming faster than I can think them through, my face hot with anger. "We will never admit that Mau Mau might be political. That it might be rooted in a failure of British policy."

"There is nothing *rational* or *political* about terrorists who murder children in their beds, with knives. It's a sickness. We brought them down from the trees, we civilized them too fast and now they are reverting back to savages." She takes a gulp of her drink. "Killing a child—and with a panga. It's bestial. Unthinkable. They cannot be called human."

I do not disagree that it is a savage thing to do. But as I stare out into the dark, words come to my mouth. A passage we learned at school. "And it came to pass, that at midnight the Lord smote all the firstborn in the land of Egypt, from the firstborn of Pharaoh that sat on his throne unto the firstborn of the captive that was in the dungeon; and all the firstborn of cattle. And there was a great cry in Egypt; for there was not a house where there was not one dead."

"What on earth are you saying?" Sara says, looking at me with wide, staring eyes.

I do not reply. Her face is very white. She stands up, holding the cushion, her fingers still turning the tassel over and over. I remember Harold and too late I say, "I did not mean—"

But she is backing away from me. "I will tell your father that you are unwell. That you are possessed. No normal person could say such things. You might as well throw open our doors and invite them in to slaughter us all."

She leaves the room, her glass in one hand, and I hear the door to her bedroom click shut.

Later, in bed, I reach out to touch the gun on my bedside table, and I am only faintly reassured when I feel the metal, cold against my fingertips. I want to light a candle, but I do not dare. They might see the light in the dark. A hyena calls out, a lurid, human sound, like the whooping of a lunatic approaching the house, and I think of Harold, the first time I met him. *They mimic the call of wild animals.* How often had he lain in his room, alone and scared? And how scared had he been, just before the bullet hit him?

I WALK UP to my mother's eyrie. It is a rare overcast morning, and the air is full of humidity. I want to break free of the tight, claustrophobic fear that has descended on the farm. I want to get away from Sara. And I am wary of seeing Michael; I need to hold myself back. I am falling too fast.

The track—made by game—is not as overgrown as it might be—and I wonder if my father has ever come up here, and whether he thinks of the nights we used to spend camping, high on the hill, looking out over Kisima, the fire flickering under the moon. He will be home in a week. Sara is anxious that he gets back before the Coronation. There can be no party without him.

The bush seems to hold the heat, as though it is a living, breathing thing, and as I push up the steep hill I glance behind me, but all I can see is the patchwork of green and yellow branches.

There is a noise on the track up ahead. The tread of feet walking quickly toward me. I freeze. Someone is coming down. Terror grips me so that I almost do not move in time. At the last minute I dart into the bush and crouch down. An African emerges from the track ahead. At first all I see are his legs. Shorts. Sandals. His swift, loose gait. My fear quickens. I do not want to be caught here, alone with a Kikuyu. Then I see that it is Michael. The familiar jolt of pleasure, that it is him. I am about to stand up and call to him, when something stops me. He is walking fast and with purpose. His forehead is creased and his jaw is set. He is thinking about something, something that has just happened. There is no humor in his face. He is wearing thin black shorts, his chest bare. He looks less like the man I know and more of a stranger. I stay where I am, breathing softly in the trees, until he has passed.

I do not want to follow him down, in case he should see me, and I am almost at the top—so I keep pushing upward, cautiously, half-expecting to see someone ahead of me—until I see the track level off, emerging into a clearing, partly covered by a rush canopy. I am on top of the mountain, on a scree of rock. My heart is beating in my ears. It is all I can hear. The view is bright—too bright, after the dark of the trees. I feel giddy, as though I might fall.

Something is wrong. It smells of urine under the canopy, and there is an animal odor like the smell of unwashed men. There are peanut shells on the dirt floor, the tread of boots in the dust. I look around—expecting eyes in the bush, watching me. My blood quickens. I feel like I might not be alone. Terrified, I go backward, tripping on the roots of a tree, scrambling down the track, not stopping until I am at the bottom and emerge into the open by the dam.

AT HOME, the *Standard* has been delivered. The front page shows a picture of the Ruck family. There is more detail here than was given on the radio. They were in the middle of dinner when their groom—a Kikuyu—hammered on the door. The groom had been with them for ten years—he was teaching the boy to ride his pony. He was unarmed, and Roger Ruck followed him gun in hand to the workshop where a gang was waiting for him. They hacked him to death. His screams set off the cattle and the dogs barking. Esme ran out with her shotgun. They found her body a few yards from the house, as badly cut up as her husband. The boy was upstairs in his room. There is a photo of his bedroom. I have to steel myself to look at it. Amidst the toys and the patchwork blanket is the small bed pushed against the wall, the bedcovers thrown back, the white mattress scored across the middle by three long slashes, exposing the dark horsehair stuffing. Somewhere near the top of the mattress is a black puddle of blood. On the floor by the bed is a clockwork train set. The settlers, the white farmers, have marched in protest on Government House—they do not feel the Governor is doing enough to tackle Mau Mau.

I carry the newspaper down to the stables with me.

"Did you hear about the Ruck murder?"

He looks up at me. "Yes."

"On the radio?" I ask, uncomfortable with the idea of him using it, even though I was the one who brought it down here.

"Yes," he says, holding my gaze, "on the radio."

I imagine him turning it on in the dark, his fingers moving over the dials. I go closer to him, testing him, put the newspaper down on his workbench. I want to ask him what he was doing this morning, at the eyrie, and who the men are who have been using it, but something holds me back. Instead I say what is true, "Michael—I am scared."

"I know," he says, looking at me.

I swallow heavily, steel my courage. "Are you connected to the men fighting in the forest? To Mau Mau?"

He draws his long forearm across his face, wiping the sweat from his eyes. "We are all connected."

"Your brothers?"

"Samuel is in Yatta."

"But the others?"

He hesitates for only a second. "Kabutha—the youngest—is somewhere in the mountains. The other two went back to the reserves."

I want to ask him more, but I do not know how. Perhaps I do not want to hear what he might tell me.

He begins putting away his tools. "I'm going down to the dam to swim," he says, glancing at me. He steps out of his overalls.

Underneath, he is wearing the same black shorts that I saw him wearing on the track up to the eyrie. I am not sure if what he has said is an invitation or a dismissal, and I hover uncertainly. He picks up the broom which is leaning against the wall of the garage and sweeps the earth in steady, rhythmic strokes, and I watch, caught up in the movement, its constant, knowing pattern, the simplicity of it, the slowness. This is something he has done a thousand times, but there is no haste.

I turn to walk out of the yard, and he says softly, "You're not going to come?" There is no doubt in his voice. He knows I will come.

"Yes—if you want me to—" I say, stopping, the color rushing to my cheeks.

"Yes—I want you to," he says, still sweeping.

After a moment, he stops. A small pile of wood shavings, green leaves and jacaranda blossom, lies at his feet.

"The dustpan is under the bench," he says, looking at me, not moving.

I wonder for a moment what he means, but he says nothing. I go into the garage, bend down, see the metal tray, the wooden handle. I fish it out then kneel, close to his feet, and sweep up the small pile of shavings, steel nails, green leaves and blossom.

I stand up with it. For some reason I am coloring again and I am not sure why.

"Where does it go?" I ask, feeling awkward.

He is looking at me as though he has not heard me speak. We are standing very close. His jaw is set and I wonder what he is feeling. I cannot read him easily. I do not know if it is desire or anger.

"There is a bin in the corner," he says. I turn, and out of the corner of my eye I see him move, loosening whatever it was that gripped him for a moment. When I turn around, he has leaned the broom against the wall and he is smiling at me.

We walk down to the dam. It is humid and close, my shirt is sticky against my back, and—a rare thing in Kenya—there are no shadows. The clouds are darkening overhead and it feels almost as though night is drawing in.

When we cut off the main track down to the dam, he puts out a hand and lets it settle against the back of my neck. There is no conversation, but I feel now the current of his desire, and it slips like fire through my groin.

We cut around the dam, through the bush, to the place where the water curves out of sight. This is where I saw him swimming. His desire to be alone with me is still enough to set my blood beating in my ears. I feel very light, almost giddy, as though my whole self is gathered up into my fingertips, and I cannot feel the earth beneath my feet.

As we emerge from the trees onto the shoreline I see the surface of the water trembling under the pressure of the first scattering of raindrops. I turn my face up to the sky and feel the clean wetness against my skin, the cold taste of rain on my tongue.

Michael is stripping off his clothes. Wading out into the water. I watch him sink into the depths. He ducks his head under and is gone a long time, then emerges, drawing his hands over his face.

"Rachel," he calls softly, his voice traveling across the surface of the water. It is a beckoning, a tightening of the cord that binds me to him, and I shift uncomfortably on the shoreline. I know I cannot refuse it.

"I haven't anything with me," I say, opening up my arms, hoping it will be enough. The rain is falling more heavily now, and my shirt sticks wetly to my arms.

"The water is good," he says. His face—far off—is blurred by the falling rain.

I peel off my clothes, push down my trousers and wade out. My vest sticks wet and pink to my skin. It is cold but I am wet anyway. I duck underneath and feel the water seal itself against me like a second skin, covering every particle of my surface. When I open my eyes I see a thousand grains against a golden, dull, gleaming light, like insects caught in amber. I think for a moment that I can see something dark—a billowing fabric—turning beneath me.

When I come up for air Michael is there. A few feet from me. It is no longer just raining. Water is pouring in sheets from the sky, beating down on us. We are both laughing, suddenly, stunned by the power of it, the sky opening on us. The drumming of water on water is in my ears, and the screech of birds flying overhead, leaving the surface of the water for cover. And all around us is the thick, impenetrable bush, and we are just specks in the wide expanse of the dam, treading out the cold beneath us.

"Christ. I didn't think I would want you like this," he says, swimming close. "Not like this." His hands reach out for my body, bring it in under the power of him, and all my strength is gone.

As we emerge from the dam, shaking off water, the rain stops. The clouds move off and the sun settles its mantle of heat on the wet earth. The birds break the silence, tentatively at first, with their chattering. Michael pulls on his shorts and sits on a flat rock, and I spread out my clothes on the acacia bushes and lie naked, front down, on the warm, wet earth. Soon the sun's heat will have drained all the moisture from the ground so that nothing but rivulets will remain, and I will be able to dust the earth from my body.

He has a bit of wood in his hand, and he is cutting at it with a knife. The sun spreads its gradual warmth, heating my body, each moment deeper and warmer than the last, and I feel a deep, saturated contentment spreading through me, a softening of my limbs.

A line of black ants are sorting through the wet earth, wrestling small mounds and piling them in a heap.

"Have you always swum here?" I ask.

"No. I couldn't swim as a child."

"Where did you learn?"

"On the Red Sea. Two officers had a bet on whether an African could be taught to swim in an afternoon."

I prop myself on my elbows and look at him. "And you agreed?"

He is looking intently at his carving. "It took the whole afternoon. But I could swim at the end of it."

A small airplane drones in the distance. They must be searching for Mau Mau. They will not see us so close to the cover of the trees, not unless they fly low over the dam.

"What are you making?" I ask, but he does not reply.

I draw a stick through the earth in front of the ants, creating a canyon in their path. They flow over the surface of the walls, down into the canyon and up over the walls on the other side.

I give in to the heat and shut my eyes. When I wake Michael is standing over me. He has brought my clothes. They are so crisp and dry they would stand on the earth without support. My legs and chest are brown from the earth. I pull my shirt over my head, stand up, pull on my trousers. I feel a sadness suddenly, tugging at me. I don't want to leave. I think that this afternoon, with its rain and golden light, has been stolen from a place of darkness.

He walks ahead of me. He has pulled on his overalls but his back is bare. I reach out and touch the scar and he stops, but doesn't turn around.

"How did it happen?" I ask, feeling the ridged surface with my fingers. His back shudders and I pull my hand away.

"I was trapped in a fire. It was a tin hut. They pulled me out."

"It must have hurt."

He turns to look at me. He is breathing heavily. I see the quickening of his chest as it rises and falls. "I was lucky. Four men were killed." But he isn't talking to me. I feel the force of him, without him touching me. As though I have held a match to kindling. The same look he gave me in the garage when I stood in front of him with the dustpan full of leaves. And I know now that it is something close to desire. I feel the force of it, as steady and hot as anger, and it deafens me, my ears ring with it; I cannot breathe. We stare at each other. He doesn't touch me. He speaks, as if he is using all of his strength to control what is igniting inside him. "Careful, Rachel." He swallows, his throat sliding up and down. His tongue passes over his lips. "I cannot be responsible for you."

XXIV

→>·<←

A few days after the Ruck murder Steven Lockhart pulls up outside the house. Sara is in her room and I am sitting on the veranda alone, sewing.

I look up when I hear the jeep and wonder if I have time to escape, but his voice calls up soft and persistent, over the hum of the engine. "Rachel, I can see you. Don't run away." I stand, frozen to the spot.

"Sara is sleeping," I call down.

"It's not Sara I came to see." There is a pause. "Come down here. I have something I want to show you."

I watch the car, sun glinting off metal. The engine sputters and dies and there is silence. He pushes open the front door of the jeep—the one nearest me—and ducks his head so he can see me.

"What are you thinking about up there?" he calls out, and when I don't reply, "I've just been down to the garage. Had a chat with Michael. I thought you might want to know what we talked about."

Why has Steven been talking to Michael? I find myself drawn by a horrible curiosity, walking down the wooden steps in my bare feet, into the glare of the sun. He pats the seat beside him, and I slide obediently onto the hot green canvas.

There is a hessian sack at my feet. The air inside the jeep smells sickly sweet. A smell I recognize but cannot place. Steven is breathing heavily. Fear oozes thickly in my blood. I tell myself that Sara is in her room—that she will come if I scream, that there is nothing this man can do to me, but I am not sure either of these things is true. He reaches across me—his chest damp against my dress—and pulls the door shut with a click, and my heart races. He stays facing me slightly in his seat, beads of sweat clustered in between his blond eyebrows, dripping down the layer of dirt that covers his face. He is filthy, in the way that men only get when they have been out in the bush for days. His eyes are staring. He has been on patrol, I realize. He looks as though he hasn't slept in a long time.

His breath, his very body exhales and it mingles with the smell in the car. "There I am out in the bush, hunting down Micks, and all the time I was thinking I'd come back and you'd be wearing something pretty," he says, placing his hand just above my knee and sliding one finger up the inside of the hem on my shorts. I flinch, pulling my leg away, and he laughs, but doesn't put his hand back. "Don't mind me," he says softly.

I want to leave the car, but I also want to know what he was talking to Michael about.

"He's an interesting boy, Michael. Fixed up my jeep a treat." He smiles at me. "Said he enjoyed teaching you as a child. *You were an easy pupil*, he said. Those were his words. I thought that was rather nice coming from a nigger." His chest is going in and out, and he wipes the sweat from his forehead. The smell is more of a stench now. It is settling in the pit of my stomach, turning it to bile. "You two have been spending time together? Down in the yard?"

My chest constricts. What does he know about Michael and me? I don't answer.

"Open it up," he says, nodding at the sack which sits at my feet.

"I don't think I will," I say, finding the courage to look him straight in the face.

"Oh, I think you'll want to see this," he says. "It's right up your street. Go on. Open it." A piece of rough twine is tied around the neck of the sack, and with shaking fingers I manage to get it open. My heart is losing its rhythm and my tongue sticks in my mouth. I have a sense of what's inside before I actually see it. Perhaps it is the smell—a concentrated sweetness, turning into something putrid, like an animal rotting in the bush.

"Have a look," he says. And despite myself I glance inside. Two hands, knobs of flesh, sticky brown fingernails like slivers of half moons.

"What is it?" I ask in horror, pushing the bag away, panting for breath.

"I think you know what they are. We cut them off a Mick last night. Out on patrol. Fifteen shillings for every Mick the boys kill."

"Why his hands?" I cannot let the image go—the awfulness of it.

"It was too far to bring him in, and we needed to fingerprint him."

I put my hand on the door handle and wrench it open, but he reaches across me and holds it shut. The window is half open. I retch, swallowing down nausea, so as not to be sick here, in front of him.

"What do you want?" I ask, not looking at him. He doesn't let go of the door, and his weight rests hot and damp against me. He speaks quietly now, into my ear.

"I've been talking to the Mick we picked up in Nakuru."

"What Mick?"

"I think you know who I'm talking about."

I shake my head, but I do know. The sweep outside of town. Samuel. Michael's brother. My lie.

"You see he started talking yesterday, and he says he knew you. In fact, he says all sorts of things."

My heart beats rapidly in my chest.

"Michael's brother. I knew that you recognized him. So what I want to know is, why did you lie to me?"

I do not reply.

"Sara told me about the way you have been talking. About the Kikuyu. I wanted to have a little chat with you. I don't think you've come to terms with being here. There is a war going on. Everyone must be careful. Very careful. I want to make sure all your hotheaded talk is just talk. That you don't place your loyalties where they might get you into trouble."

"I'll tell my father," I say.

"About what?" he asks, then he lets go of the door handle and puts his hand on my breast. I lean back in the seat, turn my face away from him. A current runs through me like a sickness. "About this?" he asks. "Oh, but, you see, I don't think you will. Your father doesn't want to know about his daughter running around with a black boy. I'm sure you wouldn't want me to tell him. All I'm asking for is your cooperation." He runs his thumb lightly over my nipple and I feel a flood of hate and humiliation. Most of all hate. "Could you manage a little cooperation?"

"I want to go," I say, in as steady a voice as I can manage, speaking from a prison of despair.

"You need to start by asking permission to leave," he says, still cupping my breast. "You see, I'd like you to begin showing a little more respect."

There is silence in the jeep. I can hear the blood rushing in my head. I feel dizzy.

"The mechanic said you were an easy pupil. Perhaps he was wrong." His fingertips are under my arm, stroking at the hot, damp inside of my shirt. "I'm asking you to ask politely."

"Please may I leave?" I say, conscious that in saying those words I have committed myself to something awful.

"You may," he says, removing his hand, and with shaking fingers I pull on the door handle, get it open and run, tripping up the steps into the house.

A few minutes later, in my room, I hear the engine start up and the jeep drives away.

"You shouldn't come down here so often," Michael says when I walk into the yard.

"He spoke to you?" I ask, ignoring his words.

He nods. "But I would say the same thing anyway. It isn't safe."

"I hate him," I say. "I hate him."

"You need to be careful."

"Why?"

"You know why."

"Does it matter so much?"

"There is no room in either of our cultures for people who cross over."

I walk up to him and close my hand over his. "I don't want to be careful. I want this."

I take his hand, too large in mine, and lead him into the barn. He pushes the door shut and stands watching me. I get down on my knees and hold him, and begin on something, feeling my way toward his desire. I want to obliterate Steven Lockhart and everything he has done to me. I need something more potent than his power. Michael puts his hands in my hair, and I feel his weight slackening, his thighs tightening under my hands, and hear the slow, deep intake of his breath.

I GO DOWN to the stables with Juno and let her puppies out. I cannot see Michael in the garage. The puppies are six months old now, almost adult, but whip skinny, and they dart around my legs, excited, looking for the rub of my hands along their coats. Two will be tall like their mother, but not Pirate who has the short stubby legs of a Staffy; more like a *shenzi*. He is a rolling, tumbling, sharp-toothed bringer of joy and I crouch down and let him put his paws on me, his nose sniffing wetly at my face, laughing as he finds my ears, knowing that I cannot stand it.

Juno sniffs them nonchalantly, Pirate snapping at her whiskers, then they trot out of the yard as a pack, Pirate cantering his back legs to keep up. I see them disappear down the track. I call Juno just before she slips out of sight and she stops and looks at me, ears pricked. She does not want to come back to me, but she will if I ask her to. "Go on then," I say, and she turns and trots around the corner, and is gone.

I look for Michael but I cannot find him. The garage is empty. I walk in under the roof. A few tools are laid out on the floor, and one of my father's old jeeps is pulled in, over the long trench in the ground. I wait for half an hour, then curiosity gets the better of me. I walk around the back of the garage. Here are two huts, side by side. One round hut, unoccupied, the palm roof gray and shredded, the other belonging to Michael.

This is where he has always lived, ever since he first came back from the war—not in the *shambas*, but here, close to the house, as though it marked out his difference, his belonging to our family. His hut is not made of round earth walls, as are those in the *shamba*, to keep out the spirits who lurk in corners. It is rectangular with a corrugated roof. I have never been inside. Not even as a child. I hover outside the door. Apart from the birds, there is not a sound. I call his name, but there is no answer.

Eventually I push open the door. There is no handle. No lock. I am standing in a small room with raw concrete walls. Light falls through a small, high window. There is a wooden stool, a blue plastic chair, a narrow bookshelf and a map on the wall, *Sponsored by the British Overseas Airways Corporation*. I recognize the rug on the floor—it is something that used to be ours. There is a rip down the middle of it. My mother must have given it to him, and I see that this is all he can expect; that having anything material in Kenya, as an African, must be bound irrevocably with the humility of the grateful.

Beyond is an open doorway and what must be the bedroom. It is dark. This is different from a Kikuyu hut, but not yet a European house. I feel the intimacy of the space; the plastic chair, the small wooden shelf, the map stuck to the wall. How it defines him. The limitations on what he can achieve here, on this farm, despite his education, despite having traveled, despite the clarity of his political ambitions. There is no future beyond these four walls. I feel the crushing truth of it. I am an intruder standing here. It tells me too much about him, without his sanction, and I am ashamed and compelled, as though I am watching him when he does not know that I am there.

The shelf on the wall holds a row of books, English classics— Dickens, Thackeray, Conrad, Shakespeare, Defoe. Books from another world to this one, where the sun beats down and everything is returned to the earth. I see a small hardback lying on the floor beneath the blue chair. It must have fallen unexpectedly, because it lies turned over, and I have to reach down to pick it up. *A Christian Thesis*. I go to put it back, when I see on the reverse, in small writing, a row of initials. There is a still sickening in my stomach as the letters settle in my mind. *EJB*. I look back at the open door—there is no one there.

I have seen these initials before. On the handkerchief in Bowker's house. I remember the bath, the blood, the smears on the walls. The smell of men in the house. The same smell up in the eyrie, Michael coming down the path, and—a long time ago—him being at the strike at Uplands when he shouldn't have been. The look of hate and disappointment on his face. What had he to do with Bowker's murder?

I am in the bedroom now. It is dark in here. A rug has been tacked to the window and the little light that filters through casts a red glow on the mattress that lies on the floor. It is warm in here, and it smells of him. A blanket is folded on the end of the mattress. A stool stands in the corner. Everything is hostile. I am no longer curious—I am trespassing. There aren't many places for something incriminating to be hidden. I do not know what I am looking for. I slide a hand under the mattress and feel nothing but the slats on which it rests. Take the stool, stand on it, and feel along the flat edge of the concrete wall, beneath the roof.

My hand touches something smooth and solid. A quickening starts up inside me. I slide my fingers over it and pull it down. A long, curved section of wood, like a cricket bat. It takes me a moment to realize it is the body of a gun—no barrel, just the carved wooden form as though it has been made for a boy. My heart beats faster now. There are more that I can feel, and a bundle of long metal pipes that clank against each other in their cloth wrapping.

The room darkens, and I spin round, stepping off the stool. It falls against the floor with a thud. Michael is standing in the doorway watching me, his body blocking out the light. I am looking into the seams of daylight on either side of him—I cannot see the expression on his face, but I feel it in the cast of his shoulders. His anger. In my hand is the block of wood.

He walks a few paces toward me. The room without him was a thing that I might pity. It was static. I could feel out its possibilities and map out the man who lived here. Michael—now that he is here—is so much more than the room said he was. He is not bound by its limitations. I am—for the first time—afraid. My throat is dry, and I swallow heavily.

"Are you Mau Mau?" I ask, because I cannot bear the silence. Because I think by speaking, I might sound stronger than I feel.

"What do you think?"

"You said you weren't."

"And it was true."

"But not anymore?"

He walks forward, very close to me, and takes the wooden gun from my hands. I am backed up in a corner of the room.

"You're making guns," I say, my voice quiet.

"Yes." He is unashamed. And very cold. A stranger, outside of my grasp, in control of what he wants to happen here, and it scares me. I realize how little he has shown me of himself; how little I really know him.

"Guns to kill good Kikuyu? Guns to kill my family?"

"They are fighting for freedom. One day they will be Kenya's heroes."

"What about Bowker? Were you there?"

"No."

"But you have one of his books?"

For the first time he pauses. "It was given to me."

"And you accepted it."

"Why not? He is dead. And it is an interesting book." I feel the anger in the distance he is putting between us. He is goading me with it.

"Would you kill a man with a panga?"

I am aware of his closeness, his body his own, not mine. Tight with energy that he might use against me. "I have killed a man with a gun." He steps toward me, pulls out a knife from his pocket, slides it from its sheath. Wipes it against his trousers. "Is it so much more savage to kill with a knife?" He holds it up so I can see the steel blade with its smooth edge. I feel a moment of reeling, dizzying fear. He puts the blade of the knife flat against my neck. It is cold against my skin, sharp against my gullet. I remember my dream, the knife cutting me open. His other hand is at my neck, warm and dry, his thumb dragging the skin across my throat, feeling me swallow. "With the knife you look into your enemy's eyes, you feel the pressure of his skin, the warmth of his blood. How much worse to pretend his death is not on your hands."

He slowly pulls the knife away and drops his hand. I take in a deep, ragged breath. "It is time for you to leave," he says.

I stand there. I do not go. Fear drains away from me. I remember my dream. I think of the factory, the chute and the slaughter line, and the old Kikuyu woman I had once seen killing a chicken in the intimacy of her yard, the soft strength of her hands against its neck.

"Go," he says, and I remember that he said this to me once before, at Uplands. We all had to make our choice; Michael, my father, myself. And I realize now that I chose Michael. It was not conscious. But perhaps it was inevitable. I had nothing to gain from allying myself to an old Kenya, my father's Kenya, which had made no room for me. I was always going to be his.

I look at the shape of his body, facing away from me, the dark curve of his head, and I want to go to him, to put my hands on him, but I cannot cross the distance. And yet the space is all mine. The steps of betrayal now that I know what he is. I walk forward and reach out a hand to his shoulder, his skin warm and soft beneath my fingers. My heart is in my throat. I think he might turn me away. That he might not want anything that I can give him. But he turns and—leaning down—rests his forehead on mine. "I get nothing," he says in a hoarse whisper. "Nothing for myself. Not even this." His hands are on my arms, crushing them. I feel his anger and absorb it. It is the closest I have come to seeing him cry.

I STEP OUT of Michael's hut, into the bright sunlight, and walk through the yard up the track to the house. I hear a noise, and I turn and see a man walking up the path behind me. It is Steven.

His lips are wet and red.

"Been having a nice time?" he asks.

My legs feel weak, and my mouth is still full of the taste of Michael. I can feel his protection over me, but it is fading. I do not have my gun. Steven laughs, and I experience the familiar force of him—the futility of my own strength. He still stands some distance away from me. I see something in his face, some premonition of what he wants, and I turn and run, but he is too quick for me. His boots fall heavy on the track behind me. I push myself forward, but he grabs my shirt—it rips, and I fall. He stands over my legs, breathing heavily. I scramble away from him, but he says, "I always had my suspicions, and now I know."

I stare up at him, my eyes spitting hate. "What do you know?"

He walks over me. "I'm going to string up your black boy and have him skinned."

My heart is hammering. I cannot speak. "Of course," he says, squatting down over me, his legs astride my body. "Your father doesn't have to know."

I push backward, trying to get my knees up, but he sits down on my thighs, and his weight crushes my legs so that I cannot move. Panic flares inside me. "That's it," he says, rubbing the back of his hand under my chin. "You little bitch. Who would have thought."

"What do you want from me?" I say.

He laughs softly. "Did you know that seven is a lucky number in Kikuyu?"

I stare up at him.

"No? You can't guess why? There are seven orifices in the human body." He leans forward. "There are two here"—he touches my ears with his two forefingers, then he places his finger and thumb over my nostrils, closing them. "Two here." I am still out of breath. I have to open my mouth to breathe. "One here." His fingers touch my lips and rest there a second. I know where he will put his hand next. I push it away, but his hand is stronger than mine; it forces itself downward. I scream and he puts a hand over my mouth to smother it, and I suck in air through my nose, struggling to breathe. Then he leans down over me, so his chest is against mine. I cannot move from under him. He is dragging my trousers down. His hand is between my legs. I lean into him and bite—sinking my teeth into the pink flesh of his cheek and he shouts, pulling back and slapping me so hard around the face that I feel a blinding blackening pain and see nothing. When I open my eyes he is pulling the buttons on his fly.

"You can't get enough of it, can you?" he whispers over me, and I hate him. "Once I have fucked you, you'll take me down to the yard, and we'll find your black boy."

"I won't," I say, sobbing. He licks at my tears. His breath is hot against my face.

"I saw what you did," I say, suddenly. "At Uplands."

"What?" He cannot process what I have said. I can see his mind catching up.

"The strike. The man, in the room upstairs. You killed him."

He pulls his hand away from me. "What are you talking about?"

"I saw it happen."

"So what?" he says, laughing. "You were a girl. He was a political Kikuyu. No one gives a shit."

"My father will."

"That's what you think," he says, but the redness has drained out of his face. I have broken the moment. Then I see a man behind him: Michael. He has the knife in his hand. He crouches down behind Steven, and I feel Steven stiffen against me. He pulls the gun out of Steven's holster, cocks it. I wonder if he will shoot.

"You black bastard," Steven says, turning his head around. "I will make you sweat for this."

"There is a Kikuyu proverb," Michael says. "*Njita murume.* When you knock someone about—if you ask him to call you God, he will do so; but the truth is still that you are not God." Michael nudges the gun at him. "Get up."

Steven rises to his feet; his fly is undone. He turns and spits and it hits my cheek. "If you tell your father I will make your life a living hell."

Michael pushes him down toward the yard, the gun at the small of his back. I get up after a moment. My hands are shaking. There is a sickness in my stomach.

When I come into the yard Michael is pushing Steven into the barn. He has a thick metal bar in his hand. "I will be watching you. From the forest. From the trees. From the sky. If you touch her I will come for you."

He slides the bar through the steel brackets on the barn door, so that it cannot be opened.

"Are you all right?" he asks, turning and seeing me standing there. But he is moving away from me as he says it. Pulling down a blanket from a shelf in the garage, throwing tools from his work-bench inside.

"What are you doing?" I ask.

He doesn't answer. I follow him to the door of his hut.

"You don't have to go," I say, tears pouring down my face. The world I know is crumbling. "I'll tell my father about Steven. I can do it now."

"It will solve nothing," he says. He strips down his overalls, pulls on a shirt over his vest, an army jumper and over it a coat. It gets cold in the forests at night. They say water freezes on the mountain. He is moving fast, wrapping things into the blanket—a tin cup, a plate, a long knife. He wraps the guns in another blanket.

"What about me?"

"I can do more for you if I am not here. Go to the house. He will not touch you now, not in your father's house."

I can see that there is no saving him or me. We are both small in the world that is unraveling. I cannot ask for more than he is giving me.

He holds my face in his hands, kisses me once, on the lips, and he is gone.

In the yard Steven is shouting, "Let me out!" He throws his weight against the doors. The bar—a dull brown metal—shifts in its brackets. I wonder how long it will hold before it slips, and whether—if he sees me here—he will kill me. Time seems to slow down. I can no longer hear the tread of Michael's feet. A crow lands in the dirt in front of me, wings outspread, and hops over the ground. "I know you're there, you bitch." I should move, but I cannot. His voice is like treacle, softening my limbs. I shake myself and start running for the house.

Steven's jeep is parked outside, windows open, but there is no key in the ignition. Where would I go—even if I could get away? I don't see Sara anywhere. I go to my bedroom, lock the door and stand with my back pressed against it. Slowly I slide down the door until I am crouching, holding my knees.

The Markhams are thirty miles away across open bush, and it is growing dark. I would never make it. And he will find me if I run. Michael is right. Steven is less of a danger to me here, in this house. He likes the hunt.

This is not the first time I have sat like this. There was my uncle's house at Uplands. The day I heard that my mother was dead. Steven on the other side of the door; me waiting for him to leave.

My mouth opens in a silent scream. There is not room enough in my head for everything that has happened. Michael. The knife in his hand. Bowker's book. The guns. Steven. His weight pinning me down. Michael clutching me. *I get nothing for myself. Not even this.* My jaw hurts where Steven slapped me. My eyes sting but tears do not come. I cannot think. I am holding my breath. Waiting.

My father will be back tomorrow. If I tell him everything, will he understand?

At last I hear footsteps running up the track. Steven's voice shouting for Sara. Exclamations. Shouts for Kahiki. The voices of Africans gathering. He must have been let out of the barn. My jaw is clenched so tight that my teeth hurt and my face is shaking. I think he will knock down the door and pull me out of my room.

My heart pounds, waiting for it. I hear them in the sitting room but not what they are saying. There is urgency in his voice, not brute anger, and—after a moment—I realize he is not going to come. He is going after Michael, not me. I hear the engine starting, the car driving past my window. I breathe out, tears pouring down my face. It is over. He is gone.

"Open the door." Sara's voice, outside the room.

I scramble to my feet. My heart beats in a rapid, jerking movement. I have to face whatever she will say. This is what is demanded of my courage.

I unlock the door and open it. She walks past me into the room. I am not expecting it and I step back. She takes the key from the inside of the door, then she walks over to the corner of the room where the paraffin lamp hangs. She unhooks it.

"Is there word from my father?" I need him to come back. Only he can protect me from Steven. "Will he be back tomorrow, like he said?"

She does not reply. She takes the matches from the bedside table, slides the gun into her hand and picks up the candle.

"Wait—" I say, putting a hand on her arm.

She shivers and takes her arm back, as though I have spat on her.

"I want to explain. Why won't you talk to me—?"

She begins to pull the door shut. I try to force it open, but she has it closed before I can get a grip on it.

"You can't leave me without a candle." I plead with her, but she does not reply. The key turns in the lock.

"Don't lock me in!" I shout. I hammer on the door with my fists. "What if they come? What if you can't get to me in time?"

Her footsteps move off down the corridor. She is gone. I try the door—the handle turns, but it is locked. The window is barred. The room has become a prison and I am trapped.

I go to the window; a white square of light, crossed by wire mesh. I slip my fingers through the holes and hold on to the wire. Beyond the plains is the forest—a dark undulating blanket of green, cloaking the earth that rises over the mountains in the distance. Michael. He will be running still, through the bush and across open fields, trying to get to higher ground before Steven can track him down. I have walked up into the foothills of Mount Kenya. The forest is darker and colder than you can imagine. The undergrowth is dense and the sun scarcely penetrates onto the forest floor. Game tracks are broken by escarpments and fast-flowing rivers which must be waded, chest high, and the rain falls through the trees, soaking you to the skin. The nights—high up on the mountain— bring freezing chills, and the danger of leopard and hyena. It is hard to imagine that men have been living there for months, surviving on so little, hunted by the British, and hunting in return. What hope is there for Michael?

I hear Mungai moving around the house, lighting the fire. The room is darkening, dusk is approaching. I have not eaten since breakfast. I go to the door and knock softly. "Mungai," I say in Swahili. "Bring me some food." Sara says something to Mungai. She is in the sitting room. She has heard me. "The dogs—" I call out, remembering. "Make sure they are locked up safely tonight." No one answers; no one comes to the door. I do not knock again. Night falls and I have no light to break the darkness. I feel my way to the bathroom, wash my hands and face, and drink water from my cupped hands. It is cold and fresh, straight from the depths of the earth. I feel my way to the bed and lie down. The darkness is thick and heavy all around me. Dawn will not lighten the sky for over ten hours. Where is my father? Why has he left me here on my own, with a woman who does not like me? Why does he not come back for me? The sound of a leopard calling sifts hoarsely through the night.

I CANNOT SLEEP. In the morning the smell of cakes baking in the fire oven drifts in under the thatch. Jim must be preparing for the party. The Coronation is tomorrow. My father should be back today. Mungai knocks on the door and brings a bread roll and water, no butter. He avoids my eyes. Sara is standing at the door behind him. She looks at me but says nothing. It is disconcerting. I had expected her to attack me, to call me names. Her silence scares me. It keeps me pinned here.

"My father will blame you for this," I say, standing at the door, looking at her, but still she does not speak. When Mungai has put down the plate and the water, she motions for him to close the door, and the key rotates again in the lock. My whole mind is absorbed on my father coming home. His anger when he sees me imprisoned. I will explain to him what Sara will surely tell him—that Michael and I have been close. I can make him understand. And I will tell him about Steven—what he did to me yesterday, that Michael was protecting me. I will hold almost nothing back, but I will not tell him about the guns in Michael's hut. It is too late for that—he does not need to know.

In the afternoon I hear a car on the track. I rush to the window and see my father's Land Rover drive past. The engine cuts and I hear the rich, warm sound of his voice, greeting Sara. I let out a sob of relief and rush to the door. I hammer my hands against the wood.

"Papa! Papa!" I shout.

There is a small silence, then—with a dread beat, I hear Steven's voice. The soft, gravel undertone. And I freeze. I press my forehead against the door, my legs shudder and a cry of anguish spills out of me. I have waited for my father all through the long, dark night, and now I feel through my limbs a soft weakness. I have not slept and my eyes feel sharp and dry, and my stomach is clenched with hunger. I had not thought that Steven would come. He must have already told my father everything. He is not leaving anything to chance. But he is my father. I am his daughter. All that matters is that he is here—when he sees what they have done to me he will understand.

I stand at the door waiting for him, but it is Sara who unlocks it and I feel a leap of panic that my father has not come himself. He must have heard me cry out. He must know that I have been locked inside. Why has he not come? Has Steven already perverted his mind against me? It is two weeks since I have seen him. Despite all the tensions between us—I feel a longing for the sound of his voice. The sight of him. The feel of his hand on my shoulder.

I walk through to the sitting room. My father sits in a chair facing me. Sara is at my back. I have spoken scarcely a word to anyone since the previous afternoon, and my mouth feels dry. I lick at my lips to loosen them. Steven. He is there too, sitting to my right, opposite the cold fire, his feet outstretched, rubbing the arch of one socked foot over the other. I feel a sliding panic when our eyes meet, his jaw locked, his eyebrows raised in ironic appreciation, his gaze a deliberate, slow thirst for subordination.

My father's eyes are hollow and red. His head is down slightly like a bear, his face is creased with exhaustion and gray stubble grows over his grease-marked face. Who knows what he has been through in the forest. Sara hands me a glass of water and I notice as I take it that my fingernails are black with dirt, and my hand shakes as I hold the glass. The water tastes strange in my mouth.

"Rachel, sit down," my father says, gesturing to a chair in front of him. I want to ask him if we can be alone, but I don't know how. It might make my defense weaker if I cannot speak it in front of everyone. He runs a hand over the stubble on his chin, pushes his thumb and forefinger into his eyes, then looks at me, and I feel a moment of infinite sadness. Something inside me is breaking.

"Is it true you allowed Michael to be intimate with you?"

My face burns. I cannot answer. It is the wrong question. It leaves room for nothing but a hot, close shame. A truth that I cannot grapple with and articulate.

"How far did it go?" he asks, breathing into the back of his hand.

I do not answer. There is Michael lifting me. The barn. The things that pass between us.

"Rachel," Sara speaks for the first time. I look at her. Her voice is clipped and cold. "Your father is asking you a question. It is too late for embarrassment. He wants to know—did you have explicit sexual relations with the boy?"

"What if I did?" My voice sounds quiet and yet too loud.

"Goddamn it, Rachel!" he says.

My head is dizzy—I dig the knuckle of my thumb into my forehead to steady myself.

"Can we be alone?" I ask my father in the ghost of a whisper.

"It is too late for that," he says, waving a hand in dismissal. Too late. The words unroll themselves in my head. Why should it be too late?

"I warned you, Robert," Sara is saying.

"Did you know that he was Mau Mau?" my father says. I shake my head. Everything feels very light, as though I might lose gravity. My heart is beating rapidly. I blink and force myself to look at him. There were the things I wanted to say, that I had rehearsed, but they seem far away from me now.

"He stole the radio from the barn. He was listening to it in the garage."

"He didn't take it. I found it. I asked him to fix it for me."

"And you left it down there for him? Why?" my father asks, his mouth grimacing in disbelief.

"I told you something like this would happen if she wasn't better controlled," Sara says.

Where do I begin on what I want to say? How can I say it in front of Steven? He is there, at the corner of my vision. I feel his eyes on me, searching me out. The skin on my arms, the edges of my spine, prickle under his gaze. He has orchestrated this moment, and I am trapped within it.

"He had a right to listen to the news," I say, but my voice is not as strong as I want it to be.

"You may have to go to the Home Guard post with Steven," my father says, not listening to me. "To answer questions."

A tightness slips round my chest; panic stirring within me. I cannot be left alone with Steven.

Sara's mouth is moving, but I cannot hear her words. I try to concentrate but there is a buzzing in my head. I open my mouth to speak but nothing comes out.

"I don't think she is well." Steven's voice cuts through the dizziness that is engulfing me. I see out of the corner of my eye that he is beginning to move. I turn to look at him, horror rising like nausea in my chest. The crease on his trousers, the weight of his thighs, as he stands up. I'm on my feet, trying to get away, knocking the chair over backward. He is walking toward me. A shout spills out of me, from deep in my guts. I turn to get away, but he catches hold of my wrist, pulling it with a jerk, and I lose my footing, slipping down onto the rug. I scramble to get away, but he crouches down over me. I kick out at him with my bare feet but they make no impact. I try to slide out from under him but his hands are holding mine, pulling them apart, opening me up. My chest burns. I am screaming.

"I've got her. I've got her." His voice is like his hands, another form of control.

"Where is my father?" I cannot see him.

Steven is levering himself forward, down over my body. Just as he did before. "She's having a fit."

"Papa! Papa!" I am screaming.

His shins on my thighs, his knees digging into the soft part of my hips so that I cannot move, his hands still holding mine to the floor, as they strain against his. A nightmare repeating itself. My muscles are taut, but I cannot effect any movement. And this inability to move, to close my arms, to raise my hips off the floor, courses through me, a hot blind panic like my blood is made of molten lead. I smash my head against the floor, over and over. The pain is a relief. It blocks out my body, which is trapped under his.

Sara's face behind his; a small brown bottle; my chest still vibrating but I cannot hear the noise. His hand grasps my jaw, forcing my mouth to open. Sara tips a pill into my mouth, and another. Bitter on my tongue. One of his hands presses on my head so that I cannot move it, cannot strike it to the floor. I scream again, hearing it this time, cutting through the pain, and blackness rises up within me like a current, until I see no more.

XXV

→>•<←

W hen I open my eyes the bedroom is in near darkness. I feel groggy, unwell. I stagger to the bathroom, lift back my hair and I am sick. I sit for a while with my head against the cold enamel of the toilet bowl, then rise and suck water from the tap. There are voices from the sitting room. My father. Sara. But not the other man. The one I fear. I go to the door and turn the handle. It is locked. I sink to the floor, holding my knees, leaning my head against the wood. Sleep pulls at me.

"I foresaw this . . . incomprehensible . . . a danger to herself."

My father's voice is no more than a murmur. It sifts over me, soothing the sourness of my blood. For a moment I lose myself, and it is as though I am listening to my parents, their voices drifting through the house. "Ten cakes baked . . . Sandwiches to be made up fresh in the morning. Not a lunch exactly, more of a buffet. The wireless . . . The Markhams, Steven . . . around one o'clock. Eliot is coming from Uplands with the pig—first thing . . . seven o'clock. Plenty of time."

My mind drifts. Then there is Sara again. Clearer this time. "An

excellent doctor . . . very good results . . . a mental aberration . . .
awful . . . the mother's fault . . . too much isolation, too much con-
tact from an early age . . . suppose the servants have known all
along? What will they say in Nairobi? Tomorrow? After the party?
I don't see any other way."

The words wash over me. I try to make sense of them, but my
head is thick and heavy as though it is made of stone, and I need to
lie down. I crawl to the bed and slide in under the cold sheets, and
lay my head on the pillow.

When I wake again someone has lit a lamp in the corner of the
room. A thin light filters through the edges of the curtains. I go to
the window and pull back the fabric a fraction. The moon has
risen, and the land outside—the papyrus grass, the tangled arms of
the fever trees, are bathed in silver light. I have no idea what time
it is. There is bread and cheese on a plate by the bed. I try to eat but
it is difficult to break through the bread—my jaw hurts from where
Steven hit me; from clenching it so hard. I touch the muscles with
my fingertips, feeling out the swelling. I go to the bathroom. There
is a lamp in here also, turned down low. I look in the mirror. My
hair falls loose, long and unbrushed around my face; my eyes are
wide, my cheeks are pale, a bruise is darkening one side of my jaw.
It is my mother who looks back at me. A stranger in the mirror. I
shut my eyes. A long time seems to pass. When I open them again
nothing has changed.

In the cupboard hangs a single dress. The one I kept. The green
shot silk glows emerald in the lamplight, shifting softly under my
fingers. I pull off my vest so that I am naked. When I step into the
dress I see my legs white and thin, shaking. I slide my arms into the
sleeves. The fabric is cold against my breasts. I reach behind me for

the buttons, and manage—with unsteady fingers—to do up enough to hold me. It is the Coronation tomorrow. I will go to the party. My father will forgive me.

I go to the door and try the handle. To my surprise it yields when I turn it. They have not locked it. I step out into the corridor, the dress rustling as I walk. My ears are ringing. There is a soft, droning voice coming from the sitting room. The wireless. I listen, steadying my breathing. It is not clear to me what I should do.

Crowds are camped outside Buckingham Palace tonight as the world awaits the Coronation. The event will be broadcast in over forty-four different languages, in a service which descends directly from that of King Edgar at Bath in 973 . . .

My father sits in the chair facing me, his eyes half-closed. With relief I see he is alone. There is only one lamp on in the room, and the fire emits a crimson, shifting light, full of shadows. A shotgun is across his lap.

The Queen will be driven from Buckingham Palace to Westminster Abbey in the Gold State coach, pulled by eight gray geldings . . .

His face is creased into deep folds. I wonder if he is asleep, when he looks up suddenly and our eyes meet. His body does not move, but his eyes fix on me, as if I am a ghost. I stand in the near darkness. My legs feel brittle as though they might not hold me, and I put a hand to the doorframe. The dress shifts as I move.

"I thought you were your mother," he says in a hoarse voice, and I see the rise and fall of his throat as he swallows.

"Papa—" I cannot say anything more. My throat chokes.

"Rachel—" he says in a low voice, still staring at me. "What has happened to you?" I cannot read his face. Is it disappointment or shame he feels when he looks at me?

"Nothing, Papa. I am just the same." I want him to come to me, but he doesn't rise from his chair.

"I remember you when you were just born. You clenched your fists and cried, and I held you and I thought that I had known pain before but there was no pain like hearing you cry. It took my breath away." I am empty inside, but my face is wet, the tears spilling out of me so easily that I do not feel as though I am crying—like a bandage ripped from a wound, the emotion flows like blood, unfettered now. There is no stopping it.

"But you have forgotten me."

"I have not forgotten you." He leans his shotgun against the fireplace. He stands up and walks a few paces toward me; puts a hand to my cheek. His face is tight with emotion. "I tried to warn you in my letter. That you would not be happy here. That you should not come back. I knew that you would try and resurrect what cannot be resurrected."

"If you had brought me back with you from England. If you had not left me—"

"What kind of life could I have given you—out here, so far from other people?"

"It would have been enough to be here with you. It is enough now—" My voice rises. I do not want him to say what he is saying.

He takes my head in his hands and kisses my forehead, and the tears run down my face. He cannot put his arms around me. He will not draw me to him. "It is not your fault, Rachel," he says in a whisper. "It is my fault." It is not an apology; it is an admission of guilt, a plea for understanding; for what he cannot do; for what he cannot be. And I am sobbing now, for all the things that cannot be unwritten.

"Robert—"

We turn, and I see Sara in the open door. I feel my body freezing up under his hands, braced for what she will say. My father doesn't let go of me right away.

"Not now, Sara," he says softly.

She walks into the room. I am going to lose him.

"Surely you see that she isn't well?" she says.

"This isn't the time," he says. His voice is both a plea and a warning.

"But when is the time? After she has slept her way through the ranks of Mau Mau? After we have been murdered in our beds? After she has sold every shred of dignity associated with this family? She needs your help, Robert."

I see my father's face, frozen with anger, crippled with doubt. He wants to stop her but he cannot. He does not have the strength to extricate himself. We are ripping him to shreds, and despite all his weakness, I feel guilt. That I am causing this pain. I think of Solomon deciding which of the two women should keep the baby that they both claimed was theirs. The mother—the one who loved the child—would not see the baby cut in two. She would rather lose the child than cause him pain. I feel this way about my father.

Sara walks over to where we are standing. The back of her hand settles against my cheek. "This is all too much for you," she says, her voice full of a subtle manipulation. "You need to get some sleep."

"Steven—he put his hands on me," I say, looking at my father, trying to start on the truth of what happened. The violation. Before it is too late.

"He was trying to protect you from yourself," Sara says. "You are not yourself, Rachel. Don't you see?"

"Before. He put his hands on me before. Michael was protecting me from Steven." I need him to listen to me. I think I have caught his attention. When something happens that explodes the small room in which we are standing. A short, hard hammering on the door. And a shout. "*Bwana!*"

My father turns so sharply it is as though he has been struck with a whip. He lets go of me and is across the room in a moment, picking up his shotgun. I feel my heart expand with a thump in my chest. My hands are empty. I have nothing with which to defend myself.

We follow him into the hall. I listen, but all I can hear is the silence roaring in my ears.

Then—"*Bwana*, come quick." It is Kahiki's voice.

"What is it?" my father asks, taking the safety off his gun.

"There are strangers in the *shamba*. They are oathing the men."

My father crosses the hall into his room. Sara's voice: "Don't do it, Robert. It will be a trick."

"And if it's not? What should we do when the *watu* have turned? What about tomorrow night? And the night after? How will we sleep if we know the farm is overrun with Mau Mau?"

My father appears in the doorway with a second shotgun which he slips over his shoulder. His revolver is in his belt. He has a torch. He holds it in his teeth as he squats down to lace his boots.

There is a shout outside. We all start. Kahiki again. "Come quick, *Bwana*." And I strain my ears for some other sound. Another man breathing behind him. Setting this trap so they can burst through the door and cut at us with their pangas.

I am acutely aware of the door as our only protection. The soft parts of my body—my belly, my neck. The sharpness of their knives.

Sara is standing in the doorway behind him, in her dressing gown, a revolver in her hand. My father stands up. "Don't, Robert," she says, gripping his arm, as though she can squeeze a sense of reality into him. "For Christ's sake. It will be a trick. It always is."

"Not Kahiki. I know him. He would give me a warning."

I gulp down air. All the waiting has resolved into this—this moment.

My father gives her the other shotgun, and says, "Don't let anyone in. You hear me? Anyone."

"Robert—don't be an idiot. You don't know if he's telling the truth. You can't leave me here on my own."

"You're not on your own. Rachel is here."

"She can't help me."

"She won't have to. I will be back as soon as I can." He turns to me and kisses me quickly, on my forehead, then he slides back the steel bolt on the door, his revolver in his hand. I walk backward out of the hall. Ready to run—but where? Sara has her revolver raised, pointing past my father. I expect the door to fly open, brace myself for violence, but all I see is Kahiki's face, briefly illuminated by the wash of the torch; my father's back and the near darkness outside— visible for just a moment, before the door swings shut. Sara slides the bolt back across the door and we are thrown into a pool of silence.

She does not tell me where she is going. I watch her walk along the corridor to her room and hear her door click shut. She will drink in bed; I have smelled it on her breath in the mornings.

I go into the sitting room and put out the lamp. I do not want to draw attention. There is the light from the fire, but otherwise the room is in darkness. I have no gun to protect me. I sit down on the sofa, tucking my legs underneath me. The silence outside is overwhelming. Kahiki had said *men*. How many men? Had they come armed? With knives or guns? How would my father arrest them if the labor in the *shamba* had already been oathed? If they had already turned their loyalties against him?

I imagine them swarming up the hillside to the house. My heart is racing now, in my chest. What about Michael? Where is he now? Does he know about this?

I sit with my eyes fixed on the fire. Sleep drifts over me. When I wake the fire has dulled to a smoldering red and the room is in darkness. Did something wake me? A flash of light flickers across the window. I rise, startled. And another from the window behind me. Voices now, raised, talking quickly. Not English. Kikuyu. I swallow, standing fixed, strangely immovable. Anxiety scurries like insects, quickly, through my veins. I feel the urgency, the quickening, and it increases my sense of horror. My fingernails are digging into my palms, wet from fear. Time slows; my heart thuds out the seconds. There are voices now coming from behind the front door. They are all around the house.

"Sara," I call, knowing that it won't help. She is already standing in the doorway. Her revolver is in her hand. We both stare at the walls of the house. I see my own horror reflected in her face. Something is happening. We hear it before we see it. A crackling. Then the lick of a flame. Light at the windows. The truth of it terrifies me. They are setting fire to the thatch. I hear a crackling, a snapping, as the flames lick up the roof of the house.

Sara screams. I hear her panic and feel my own settle deep in my stomach. There are flames at both the windows in the sitting room, licking round the edges. And the sound of the thatch burning—like a wind blowing through the house. She runs to her bedroom and I follow her. There are no flames here, at this window. Not yet. She flings open the curtains. Her hands are on the wire. She is pulling at it, but it resists.

"Can we cut it?"

She is holding her weight on it. "A knife wouldn't be strong enough."

I put my hands on the wire, but I know before I feel the resistance that it won't come undone. We both pull with all our strength, but the wire doesn't move under our weight. I go into the sitting room. The thatch overhead is showing flames on its underside. Soon it will catch completely, and then it will burn in minutes, falling in on us. Roasting us alive.

I run down the length of the house, to my bedroom. It is cooler in here. The fire hasn't caught hold. I have no light. I do not want them to know I am here. The room feels cavernous in the dark. The crackling, the heat, is at my back. I stand close to the window. My head against the wall, trying to think. A thin breeze stirs the curtains. We had rats under the henhouse. Hundreds of them, black with thick hairless tails, hiding in holes, killing the chickens, eating their eggs. My father lit a fire. Smoked them out. I remember the shrieking of the rats, as they emerged from the earth like lava. My father and Kahiki picking them off with their rifles.

The air is getting thick. Smoke is pouring in under the door, and I am coughing.

"Rachel," a voice on the other side of the wall. A low shout. "Rachel."

"Michael?" The relief sends a new wave of terror through me— he is just on the other side, but I cannot get to him.

"Listen to me."

"Michael—it's hot in here," I cry. "The fire is getting stronger."

"Can you pull up the floorboards? Is there a way to do it?"

"I can't see anything."

"Open the curtains."

I don't move. My limbs have become thick and slow with fear.

"Rachel!" he calls. I don't reply. I am stunned by terror.

"Listen to me. I have only a moment. You can get yourself out of there. Your father has a hammer. You can use it to lever up the boards. Think where he keeps it."

I force myself to move. Draw the curtains open. Moonlight filters into the room. This end of the house is built on stilts. There is open space under the boards. I kneel down. Run my hands over them. He is right. If I can get them up I might be able to get out.

I open the door and step into a dense, thick cloud of smoke, billowing up from the floor. I run to the sitting room and pull open the door. Smoke envelops me. A wall of heat. I cover my mouth with my forearm and move into it, through it. A tangle of scarlet flames, more heard than seen, illuminates the smoke. I push myself through into the hall where the smoke is not so thick. There is a cupboard here. I am moving too slowly. There isn't enough time. I turn the small key. There is no window; no light by which I can see. My hands feel their way over the shelves. Trays of nails fall clattering to the ground under my fingers. The fire above me begins to take hold, crackling as though a living thing is scrambling over the roof, breathing hot flames down on me, sending fragments onto the floor. A clutter of metal. There is no hope of me finding it in the dark. Of getting up the floorboards. Of escaping. It is too late. Then my hands settle on something smooth and wooden. I feel a ridge of sharp metal. The hammer. I stagger back through the cavernous smoke, back to my room and shut the door behind me. Go over to the far corner where the floor is highest off the ground.

"Michael?" I shout, sobbing as I kneel on the floor. "Michael."

He does not reply. Has he gone? I let out another cry. Then try to lever the hammer under the boards, feeling for cracks with my fingers, where I might be able to wedge in the metal claw. Some of the rats died at the mouth of the hole. Asphyxiated. Not prepared to face the guns that were waiting for them, and my father dug them out later, hair scorched and skin blackened.

I want to live. I cannot get the hammer into the gap between the boards to lever them up. There is not enough room and the metal keeps slipping. I swear. It has to work. I need only to get a corner of the metal claw in and I'll have some leverage but it is too wide. Then I find a gap between two boards—broader under my fingers. I push in the claw and it holds. I lean my weight against it. The board moves. I lean again. It makes a cracking sound, and I throw down the hammer and pull on the board. It comes away, nails ripping from their sockets. I lean down and suck at the clean, cold air below.

The others come quicker. Four boards, and there is a hole large enough for me to squeeze my way through. I am sitting on the edge of the hole, about to lever myself down, when I remember Sara.

I run into the bathroom and turn the tap. I push water over my face, over my dress so that it runs down me, ice cold against my hot skin, breathe for a moment with my head below the floorboards, then plunge back into the house. The smoke is denser now, blacker, more hostile. It is like moving through something solid, and it holds the heat as though the air itself is burning. The sitting room is no longer smoke but fire. Great chunks of thatch are falling from the roof. The heat is scalding.

"Sara!" I shout to her at the door of her room. I can just make her out. She still has her hands wrapped in the wire. When I go closer I see that her hands are black and wet to touch. They are running with blood, but she keeps on pulling.

"I have made a hole in the floorboards. There is a way out."

She stares at me.

"Michael is there. He will help us escape."

"It's a trap," Sara says.

"It's that or burn alive in here." I pull at her arm, but she snatches it away. "Come. Quickly."

She does not move.

I stare at her for a moment, then run back across the sitting room. I can no longer see and I am not sure if my eyes have burned up or the smoke is too thick—it feels one and the same thing. They are no longer any use. My skin is on fire. I wonder if I will get through. I feel my breath failing. The heat. The sucking of the flames. My lungs are hotter than my body, or hot in a different way, layers of burning, as though I am breathing in fire. Then I am through to the corridor, shutting the door behind me. The smoke is thick in here but the heat is less. I am pushing at the door of my bedroom, struggling to get it open, thinking in the blackness that it might be beyond me, when it opens under me, and Michael is there pulling me through, kicking the door shut, pushing me toward the hole.

I fall toward the gap in the boards. For a moment I think there might not be enough room. I push my hips through and my feet touch the cool earth below. My dress snags on the boards. I yank at it until it rips, then lever the rest of my body through, pressing my face to the earth, taking great gulps of clean air. Michael drops down beside me. We are pressed low to the surface of the ground. There is about a foot of space above us, but more room at the corner of the house. The light outside is murky. Smoke clouding the glow from the fire. There are voices, but a long way off on the other side of the house—Africans shouting. They are waiting for us to burst out of the front door. The house is burning above us, there is smoke here too—we cannot stay here for long, but I do not think I will have the courage to leave.

"Go on now. Quickly. I'll be right behind you."

I rub my eyes. They feel hard as though the surface has been burned. I force them open again and realize I can see after all; the land beyond our hiding place is discernible.

"Rachel—you have to move. We cannot stay here." I do not want to listen. I cannot leave the safety of this place.

"Now. Rachel."

"They will kill me."

"They won't see you. Quickly."

He presses past me. His fingers close warm around my hand. He pulls me forward, and I scramble after him. And then I am out, in the open. He runs ahead and I follow. I don't look backward. I can feel the heat of the fire at my back. The flames licking into the sky. The sky glowing red like hell above us. The shouts of men. I am running, as fast as I have ever run in my life, across the lawn, my back arched, waiting for a gunshot. Or the pounding of feet and the stroke of a knife. I can see the cover of the bush ahead, looming dark against the sky. Then we are there, pushing through branches. My feet are scraped raw. They have been burned in the fire. I cannot keep up. I lose Michael ahead. Then he is back again, taking my hand.

"Quickly."

I stop, breathing hard. "What about my father?"

I can see his face in the moonlight. "Rachel—there is no time."

"I won't. Not until you tell me what happened."

"He broke up a meeting in the *shamba*. Men down from the forest, oathing the workers. Your father is trying to track them."

"You were one of them?"

"I got away. I knew they were planning on coming to the farm. It was a diversion. They wanted to get him out. Away from the house."

"So they can kill him."

He does not answer. "They will raid the barns. Take what they can from the house."

"How could you let it happen?"

"There was nothing I could do to stop it."

"But you are one of them." I slam my fists against him, into his chest. Using all my force against him. "You would have had me burned alive." I am nothing. I am all used up. Only this. He grasps my wrists and holds them, absorbing all my anger. I struggle against him, but he holds me still, and then he is pulling me into him. I strike my head against him but he has me held deep into him, so that there is no space for me to strike him, no room for conflict, and my anger flows into great racking sobs.

He holds me and for a long moment I give myself up to this— the warmth of his arms, the firmness of his chest against my head, the slow touch of his hands on my head, on my neck. Then he draws me away from him. He takes my hand.

We move on, slower now, pushing our way through the tight

undergrowth. We drop down into a valley, scrambling over rocks. Moonlight falls through the fever trees, dappling the ground where we tread. There is a small stone dam at the bottom. Three zebra—drinking from the water—scatter when we approach, their hooves clopping on the dry stones. We are in the midst of the ghostly shadows of the old *shambas*, empty, deserted, soundless. My feet are raw—the sharp stones feel as though they are cutting right through the skin, and I go slowly.

Ahead looms the dark shadow of thicker forest. I follow him blindly into the trees, where the moon cannot shine, and everything is dark. There must be Mau Mau here. And animals hunting in the dark. We begin to climb. It goes on for what seems like hours, until I stop.

"What is it?"

I put a hand to my feet. The soles are wet when I touch them, sticky against my fingers. It is blood. I curse myself for not putting on the plimsolls that lay beside my bed.

"Just a little farther," he says.

We climb down and up onto the other side of the mountain higher and higher, on and on until we emerge into a clearing. We are high up on the hill. I turn to look behind us, and there is the house lighting up the sky, orange and red, the smoke billowing black into the moonlight. Below us on the other side is the dam—a silver slip of water.

"We can stop here," he says, squatting down, and I sit, with my back against a tree, a little apart from him, wishing he was closer. My head is ringing. The land is a living, breathing thing—an amphitheater of sound, and we are tiny in its midst. From all sides comes the murmuring and chattering of a million living things.

"Sara wouldn't come," I say.

He says nothing, and I swallow down guilt.

"What do we do now?"

"We'll wait here for a few hours, then I will walk you back, close to the dam."

"Why here?"

"I am scouting for them tonight."

I watch him. The dark profile of his face as he looks out across the valley below. "They want to know how many police come. What direction they take."

"Why did you not tell me?" I ask, after a long moment.

He looks at me. His eyes shining white in the dark. "You already knew."

And he is right. I have always known, ever since I was a child, that his loyalties were divided.

I think about my father. Whether he will survive. About Sara—hands bleeding, trapped in the flames. A long time seems to pass, though it might be only a few minutes. It is hard to keep track in the darkness. Michael pulls a flask from his pocket and stretches out his hand to give it to me. The metal is cold against my hand.

"Stolen."

"But you will drink all the same."

I put it to my lips and remember Eric Bowker. Was it his? Had his lips touched the rim just as mine are touching it now? The water is cold in my mouth and tastes of metal.

Clouds drift across the sky, and darkness falls over us like a shroud. A clan of hyena move through the forest, calling to each other. A lone, lunatic wail, then the chattering and snapping of others, their voices echoing off the bowl of the land. Hyena are braver at night. A shiver grips me.

I know our time together is running out. Slipping through the hourglass faster than I can keep hold of it. The unspoken truth—that this might be the last time we shall see each other.

"I do not know my father," I say into the darkness. "I do not even know myself."

"And it scares you?"

"I have betrayed him." My eyes well up with tears.

He must sense it, because he reaches out his hand and takes hold of my wrist. He draws me toward him, pulling me down between his legs. His arms settle over mine, and I know that in the touch of his body there is something that I will not find again. And it is slipping away from me.

"There is always a betrayal," he says. "We all have to let something go—in order to be free."

I lean my head back against his shoulder and shut my eyes. *To be free.* Is that what I am? Free?

"Who have you betrayed?" I ask.

"I have betrayed so many people that for a long time I did not know myself."

"Tell me."

"I used to wash dishes in the kitchen, before you were born. I remember the brown ceramic sink, propped up on stilts. The tap leaked, a constant dripping of water. Over the years it had made a small dip in the ceramic, rough to touch. One day I came in and a small crack had spread itself across the sink. Eventually it would be two halves. That was how it was with me.

"Your mother was knitting in the garden, and I watched. A long ball of wool fell off her lap and rolled out across the lawn. It was scarlet. I had never seen anything like it. I ran across the grass, picked up the ball, rolled up the thread and gave it back to her. That was the first betrayal."

There is the touch of his skin against mine. And his voice, hypnotic, in the dark. "She set me to work in the kitchen. I had three shillings a month, and every Saturday she gave me sugar and salt to take home. I washed up the plates and saucepans, looked after the cats and dogs, fed the chickens, the ducks and the geese. I learned English in the kitchen. Your mother encouraged me. *Hello. Master. Wool. Water. Hot.* It singled me out at school. The teacher took special care over my education. When I was eight my father's lands in the reserve were struck by drought, and he pulled me out of school. The teacher spoke to my mother, and she raised money from the village to keep me in school. They knew the value of an education for the whole community. But my brothers were not so lucky. There was no one speaking on their behalf.

"Your mother gave me paraffin and a lamp, so that when our *shamba* fell dark at seven o'clock, I could read into the night. When I came home from secondary school, I was wearing shorts and shoes, and my brothers were in their old clothes that smelled of sweat and animals. I was fourteen, but they were older. They talked about the land we had lost, the lies of the Europeans, the inequality of work. I struggled to agree. Look how far I had come. Look how much they had given me. The white man was everything he said he was. I put my brothers' politics down to bitterness."

"But you changed your mind."

"Yes."

"Why?"

"The war. Belsen. Eleven million people killed by the Nazis. Sixty million people dead in five years of war. It taught me that the white man had no prerogative over the word of God. No prerogative over the idea of what it is to be civilized."

I had seen films showing the liberation of Belsen. Thousands of corpses, more bones than bodies, being thrown into vast trenches. Smoke, barbed wire and squalid huts where the living lay almost indistinguishable from the dead. Soldiers waist-deep in skeletal bodies. It was hard to believe that it was real.

"We had separate cinemas in the army, for whites and blacks. Our films were Westerns, gun-slinging, nice and simple. There was a British captain—we were friends. He smuggled me once into the back of his cinema. It was a film about a British family living in a city, strikes, hunger. There were white women cleaning the floors of the wealthy, begging in the streets. I was shocked. The British in Kenya had been careful not to let us see what life was like in England. In Kenya white women were always *memsaab*—they took tea and rarely dirtied their hands. Cleaning was something done by blacks. It occurred to me that this was why the British were in Kenya. Because in Kenya they didn't have to wash floors—there were blacks to do it for them. This was why they would try and hold on to power at all costs. Their position as rulers in Kenya relied on the fiction that they were here to civilize, but they had no intention of sharing what they had taken as theirs."

I do not speak, listening to him unravel himself in the dark.

"In Burma I saw a soldier crying, an English boy about my age. I had seen him before—he didn't want to be there, he was scared. He came up to me and said he wanted to write a letter home. 'OK,'

I said. 'Why don't you?' It took me a moment to realize that he was asking me to write it for him. It was difficult for me to believe then that a white man might not be able to write.

"The army showed me that there was not one type of white man, which was what we had been told by the British in Kenya, but many. There was a driving instructor who gave his demonstrations sitting on the backs of Africans; there were American privates who had less influence than black American officers; there were the Irish—fighting for freedom from the English. And there were other nations that had wrested their independence from the empire: Indians who were on the brink of winning their freedom under Gandhi."

His voice is soft and compelling in the night, slow and liquid. I hear the truth of what he says, in the richness of his voice. I do not want to hold it up against other truths, to test its veracity. I only want to listen.

"When we were in the trenches at the front, camped out in a bad position, the same boy—the one who was illiterate—said to me, 'What are you doing here anyway? All you Africans? At least if I die it will be for my country. But what will your country have got out of it?'"

He laughs, softly. "It seems ludicrous now, but I had always imagined that I was fighting for England. It was the first time I had thought of Kenya as a country, as my country."

He falls quiet. The house is a tiny, flickering ball of flame far below us. I can smell the bitterness of the smoke in the cool night air. My head rests in the dip between his shoulder and his neck. I hold his wrist with one hand, feeling out its surface with my fingers, the long smooth tendons on the underside, the hardness of the bone, the soft hollow where there is nothing but flesh, the steady throb of his pulse.

"And when you came back from the war?" I want to know everything; to store up this knowledge for the nights that will follow, when he will be far away from me.

"In the jungle the British soldiers painted their faces black, so they blended in as we did. Even the horses were given potassium permanganate to darken their coats. We sweated, fought, killed and ate together, one man indistinguishable from another. When we Africans—all seventy-five thousand of us—came back to Kenya, we hoped for recognition, that the same rewards given to European officers would be given to us—land and loans to stock the land. But instead we came home to discrimination, land loss, registration cards. So many of us had died for England in the war—where was the color bar then?

"We hoped our skills would help us press ahead with a new Kenya—that was what we had been promised. But Nairobi was a dirty, overcrowded place, sunk in poverty. There were eighty thousand Africans living in shanties in the east of the city. There were no opportunities, no jobs. We had no prospects. All our enthusiasm turned to bitterness. Burma market was run by soldiers who had fought in Asia—a black trade market. Anyone who has been there would have known why Mau Mau came about. I struggled to find work. My friends from the army were drinking, trading, stealing. I had a job selling charcoal for a while. Then I left to find work in the railway yards. Eventually I came back to Kisima."

"But you didn't stay," I say, thinking that all the time he had been teaching me he had been carrying this bitterness and frustration.

"I couldn't stay. My friends in Nairobi kept writing to me. I was in a strong position—with my education—there was so much I could do to help. I went to hear Kenyatta speak. He articulated for me everything I had experienced in Burma. He said that when the white man arrived, as strangers to our people, we had—in our hospitality—given them food and a place to stay. They were our guests; and now they claimed that our home belonged to them. It was time—he said—that they started behaving as our guests. I left Kisima—and was sucked into politics."

"Uplands."

"And everything that followed. It started to get dangerous. They began to make sweeping arrests in Nairobi. The movement became violent. I came back to Kisima."

"You told me before that you didn't come back to be political."

In the dark there comes the single note of an owl marking out time.

"It is true. I was hoping to get away from the violence. But the struggle followed me here. This was the very heart of Mau Mau. I couldn't avoid it. They wouldn't let me. My whole family were oathed. Even if I had wanted to I couldn't have resisted it. And—in the end—I didn't want to."

"What of my family?"

"That was another betrayal."

Quietness falls over us. The hyena move past us in the dark. I hear their chattering, their calls feeling out layer on layer of darkness, receding into the valley below. Time falls away faster than I can hold it.

Some time later Michael stiffens. Below us two tiny beams of light are making their way to the house. I feel a lurching in my stomach.

"Headlights?"

"Yes."

This is the beginning of the end. Of what will follow. Where is my father? I hope he is down there somewhere, alive. Would we have heard a gunshot from up here? And Sara—what of Sara?

Soon after there is another car. The house continues to burn—a beacon in the dark. We are too far off to hear voices, to see the light of torches.

The sky lightens, imperceptibly at first, until I can see my hands gray in the near darkness. The birds break the dominion of the night, puncturing the darkness, like pinpricks of light. A hollow, low dropping call rises softly from the dam, like the distant, wordless recalling of a dream. As the sky lightens again, the song lifts in volume. A birdcall like water slipping from a bottle. Frogs, squelching their throats in the water below. And the mist clinging to the valley, hanging like smoke over the mirrored surface of the dam. I sweep tears away from my eyes. There is a futility, a sense of human desperation, in the raising of this beauty over and over again, morning after morning.

Michael rises, the warmth of his body peeling away from me. I stand in the cold predawn light. The dress is ripped and blackened. My feet are covered in blood. My knees unlock stiffly as I push myself up.

"Why did it take us such a long time last night?"

"We walked around the mountain. It was safer. It will be fine now to go straight down," Michael says. "We should go quickly. I will walk you down to the dam."

"And then what?"

But he is moving already. The closeness of the night has fallen away with the darkness. He is no longer mine. I feel a tearing inside me. I follow him blindly down the track, limping across stones. We are down faster than I had imagined. When we are just above the dam he stops. He turns to me and I put out my hands, blackened from ash, to his dirt-stained shirt. I see now how ragged he is already, how filthy. The stubble that is beginning to cover his jaw is gray in the dawn, and shadows catch the angles of his face, making him appear suddenly as though he is an old man. I think—I may never see him when he is old.

"Is this a letting go?"

"Yes," he says softly. His eyes, hooded and black in the half-light, settle on mine.

"Why?"

"The ground is shifting—it leaves no room for us."

I lean my forehead for a moment against his chest and breathe deeply. There is nothing we can do to help each other, and our helplessness unravels me. I pull at his shirt. I want him to make things happen differently, to change the course that we are bound to follow. He stands and lets me, and all my defiance is meaning-less. We are insignificant in the path of the fate that is drawing us apart. Like ants swept away by the movement of elephants.

The tears fall down my cheeks. He kisses me on the forehead. I reach up and hold his face and kiss him on the mouth.

"You are stronger than you think, Rachel," he says. And he is gone.

I walk down to the dam and stand at the shoreline. The sun rises huge and heavy overhead, a burning, shimmering sphere that will pour its molten heat down on us later, but for now it is too low, and it holds in its breath only the premonition of what will come.

This was where we had swum. Where he had held me. Now I understand the anger in his face. The warning. *Be careful, Rachel.* He was telling me not to get too close, not to open him up because he would have to let go.

I walk up the track, skirting through the bush, so that I am above the farm. I pull myself into the branches of an old olive tree, balancing on my toes to avoid the raw soles of my feet on the rough bark, and look down on the house. It is a burned, blackened carcass. My eyes sharpen with tears. I suck air into my belly, as if it might steady the pain. Flames still lick at its edges, but the fire has burned itself out. I can see the innards of the house, poking out, walls burned away, floorboards crumbling. The house I grew up in, the house that holds the memories of my mother, like words in the pages of a book, crumbled to ashes. Something else turns heavily in my stomach. Guilt. I escaped when Sara did not—she must be dead, and her death is partly my fault.

A police truck is parked to the side of the house. Men are lying facedown on the earth, hands cuffed behind their backs. I recognize Mungai's short, slight build, but I'm not sure if one of the other men is Jim. There is no sign of my father. Then I see Kahiki—his hand is bandaged, but he is on his feet. He is talking to a white officer. It is Steven Lockhart. I stare, motionless. I cannot walk down there now. I do not know what he will do to me. They have not seen me and I slither down and sit at the edge of the track, in the shade of the tree, holding my legs to my chest. I stay there for what must be hours. I am hungry. It is a long time since I have eaten.

An engine starts up, and I climb the tree again. They are round- ing the men into the truck. Its edges catch the sun, bouncing back sparks of light. Steven Lockhart swings himself into the driver's seat. The engine revs, and the truck drives away, followed by the second car, churning up a cloud of dust in its wake that rises into the air like smoke. I breathe out relief, drop to the ground, and walk down the track.

Two white soldiers are sitting some way off from the blackened walls of the house. They are fiddling with the wireless, cigarettes hanging from their mouths, the smoke almost invisible in the heat of the day. It is the same two soldiers I saw at Bowker's house. One of them sees me and kicks the other with his boot. They straighten their backs and stare as I approach, and I glance down at myself— arms black with soot, my mother's green dress hanging in tatters from my body.

My legs are unsteady. Kahiki is dragging a table from the ashes of the house. He looks up as I approach and his eyes fix on mine, and I realize he had not expected to see me alive. He runs forward and puts a hand on my shoulder and I feel the strength of his fingers, locking onto me.

"We thought you were dead, *Memsaab*."

"Not dead," I say. Then—"Where is my father?"

"He has gone to hospital."

"He's hurt?"

"He was shot. Just before dawn." He puts a hand low on his stomach, just above his groin.

I swallow, my eyes fixed on his. "Will he be all right?"

"I do not know, *Memsaab*." His eyes are heavy with truth.

"Will he be all right?" I ask again, my voice rising.

"There is nothing you can do. The *memsaab* has gone with him. We will have news later."

"Sara? She is alive?" I take a breath in and feel relief flood through me.

"Yes, *Memsaab*. She was burned in the fire, but she is all right."

She escaped after all. But my father—what if he doesn't survive? What if I lose him?

"Did they raid the barns?"

"Yes." His eyes shift away from me.

"Juno—where is she?"

He shakes his head, and I see this is what he is hiding.

"The puppies. Were they in the stables last night?"

"You do not want to see," he says. But I want to see.

"Where?" I look back at the house. There is something hanging from the veranda. I hadn't noticed it before. Swinging. Three bodies on ropes.

"Can you cut them down? Why has no one cut them down?" I scream.

"The District Officer asked for them to be left as they are," one of the soldiers calls out, nonchalantly. "For photographs."

"Cut them down for me," I say to Kahiki, my eyes bleeding tears. He reaches up with a knife—wincing from the wall of heat—and cuts the ropes. The bodies are charred, blackened, but held together still by sinew. He lays them out on the ground. Were they dead before they were strung up here? Or were they strung up here alive? Three bodies. The one that is Juno, larger than the others. My heart catches. I did not think there would be more pain. I do not see Pirate's body, the short legs. "Where is the other puppy?"

"There is nothing at the barns. They have burned them down."

I walk down the track to the yard, to the blackened barns, the burned-out stables. I shout for Pirate, moving through layer on layer of heat. No sound comes back. Is it possible that he escaped? I do not think so. I fight back dizziness and walk back to the house. There are no cars here; there is no way of leaving the farm. There is nothing I can do but wait. I should have come down sooner. I should have had the courage to face Steven. But what might he have done to me here, in the ashes of the fire?

I walk over to the soldiers. "Can you radio out?"

They look at me with curiosity. I wonder what they have been told. "We have already radioed through to the Home Guard post. They know you have been found."

I stand under the glare of the sun, heat radiating from the walls, until Kahiki puts a hand on my arm and leads me away from the soldiers. Someone has dragged my father's armchair outside, where it blisters in the sun. Kahiki pulls it under the shade of an acacia. It is blackened on one side, but the floral pattern is still visible. I sink into it. He brings me a bowl of cold *posho*. A glass of water. I thank him and eat, pushing the meal into my mouth with my hand, forcing myself to swallow.

Ash falls like snow over the ground. The heat radiating from the walls is on one side of me, and the air in front of the house shimmers as if it is melting in the heat.

"We are pumping more water up from the dam," Kahiki says. "It will take time. We need men but we do not have them."

I nod, but cannot speak. There is nothing to say.

Then out of the stillness of the day, the clear chiming of church bells rings out. I look up in alarm. It takes me a moment to see that the soldiers have got the wireless working. It is the very sound of England, of empire, and my throat catches.

The bells fade, and a voice speaks in hushed tones; his words, each one still and slow. *This sceptered isle; this earth of majesty; this fortress built by nature against the hand of war; this happy breed of men; this little world; this realm; this England.*

Trumpets sound, setting off a troop of vervet monkeys, in the trees beyond the fire.

The Coronation ceremony, reported from London. I remember the party. It was to be today. That is why I am wearing my mother's dress. It all seems a long time ago. A different life. I see now the triangles of bunting which lie trodden into the earth. Three trestle tables stand naked in a clearing on the blackened stretch of lawn.

She comes to us in the sorrow of her father's passing . . . her sovereign lord King George the VI, who lived through dangerous years in the lives of his people.

And I think of the war, so recently ended; of Michael in Burma; of him hiding now in the forest. The guns, the killing.

Then "Jerusalem" is playing. The swelling of men's voices, resounding off the ancient walls of Westminster Abbey, feeling out the high stone arches, the marble tombstones, the hidden chapels. Summoning history. Year upon year of tradition. The idyll in the midst of horror. The beauty and the tragedy.

And did the countenance divine
Shine forth upon our clouded hills?
And was Jerusalem builded here
Among those dark satanic mills?

The whole abbey is singing. The choir, their voices rising in passion upon passion. What do the words mean? They are important in the way that a knife is important. I feel them cutting into me—I feel the pain they bring—but I do not know their purpose. And what does it mean that the music swells inside me, that I feel myself lifting with it, that I hate this England so many thousands of miles away? What do the tears mean that are running down my cheeks? How can I be one thing, and also another?

All the force of England, all its formality, all its contained emotion, its quest for conquest, is here.

Bring me my arrows of desire!
Bring me my spear: o clouds unfold!
Bring me my chariots of fire!
I will not cease from mental fight;
Nor shall my sword sleep in my hand
Till we have built Jerusalem
In England's green and pleasant land.

I am sobbing, mouth open, pain pouring out of me. The music fades. Throats are cleared, the sound echoing in the quiet of the abbey. Silence—the wireless crackling. Then Richard Dimbleby's voice again, its soft formal intonations, as familiar as a father, summoning England from four thousand miles away. *Here are the Banners of Chivalry, gold and crimson, green and blue . . . The Golden Lion of England . . . the black eagle with its wings outstretched . . .*

I stand up and begin to pick over the ruins of the house which have been dragged out from under the burning roof. *The Queen takes the five swords of state, the two swords of justice, and the sword of mercy with the blunted point.*

Soot drifts over the ground, mingling with the dust. Small

flames show white in the heat. Books are littered across the ground. A page sifts loose, carried across the earth by the heat of the fire. I kneel down. It is from the Swahili grammar book I found all those months ago on the boat to Mombasa: a paragraph of sentences to translate, for a settler to use with his houseboy. *Why is the cork lost? Clean my boots at once! You must fasten every button. A hippopotamus has destroyed our hut. My head is hurting me very much. Undo this lid with a knife, then bring the matches. Boy! I have lost my pipe. I see it, master, on the piano. If you listen hard you will be able to hear the rhinoceros making a noise. Clean these shoes again with black polish. That man is a witch doctor, see the frog in his pocket. The latrine is full of fleas.*

The phrases turn over and over in my head, senseless but compelling, until they are indistinguishable from the sound of the Coronation.

I find a photograph of my mother—from where? It lies blackening on the ground, its edges curled. I pick it up and dust off the soot. She is standing with Kahiki, smiling broadly, holding up a piece of broken pottery which she has dug from the earth; I can see the soil clinging to its edges. I do not remember this moment, and I choke back a cry; I scarcely knew her at all.

The Queen risen from prayer is disrobed of her crimson robe . . . It is the moment of the anointing, hallowing, a moment so old history can scarcely go deep enough to contain it . . . the Queen is clothed in white, and in cloth of gold with the golden girdle . . . she receives the jeweled sword and takes it and offers it at the altar . . .

So many articles of superstition. Such an elaborate swearing in. What of the oath Michael has taken? Is it any more primitive, any more drenched in superstition, than this one? *She puts on the imperial cloak. "The lord cloak you with the robe of righteousness."*

I turn over the photo. My father's writing, faded in the heat but still visible. *I do not stand at your grave and weep; you are not there, you do not sleep.* I feel the force of my father's desolation, left here without her. I picture her tombstone in the small graveyard on the outskirts of Hull, the stone marbled green with the mold which threatens each winter to overwhelm it.

Long live the Queen! Long live the Queen! Long live the Queen!

A car is driving toward the house. The soldiers switch off the wireless. We watch.

My uncle opens the door and steps out.

"Rachel. What the devil?" He comes toward me. "We thought you had run away."

I stand up. My head feels too heavy. "My father—is he all right?"

He walks closer, shakes his head. I think of the irony, that he was the one to tell me about my mother. "He lost a lot of blood. Sara is with him now."

"How did she escape?"

He looks at me, head slightly cocked, as though the question proves something. I am uneasy. "Lockhart walked in with some men. Jumped the Micks and they fled. Managed to pull her out in time."

He puts a hand on my arm. "Move away from the house. You'll get hurt. Christ, look at you. Your feet." I glance down. They are covered in blood. There is blood on my hand. I feel myself crumbling in exhaustion. I have held myself together for so long, and now someone is here to help me.

He leads me toward the car. I slide into the front seat. It has been baking in the sun, and the canvas is hot under my legs. There is a foul smell.

"The damn pig—" he says. He goes to the boot and drags out a piglet, pink skin. Its back legs bounce along the ground. He swings it into the bush on the side of the track. "It's been in there all morning." He gives me a quick, hard smile. I remember the telegram. The way he looked at me then. It is the same now. He is uneasy with too much emotion. I scare him.

"I've been out searching for hours. I promised Lockhart I would bring you back. Though God knows where I thought I'd find you. As far as I knew the boy might have thrown you into a ravine." He starts the engine. "How long have you been here?"

I lick my lips. My mouth is dry. It is strange to be sitting here. He is talking very fast.

"I came down this morning."

He reverses the car round and swings it in a circle, then we are driving away from the house. He glances at me. The curiosity of a man who has not had children. I look in the side mirror and see the blackened remains, the drifting trail of smoke, the soldiers eating their sandwiches.

"Where are we going?"

He gives me a quick sideways look. I see anxiety slide like liquid over his face, but perhaps I have imagined it. After a moment he says, "We'll stop at the surgery. Then we're going to Nairobi." It is open-ended.

"What is in Nairobi? Is my father being transferred there?"

"He might well be, at a later date. For the moment it is the safest place for you."

I ask what I have been too scared to ask. "How badly is she hurt?"

He doesn't answer for a while. Then looks at me again. "She will be all right."

The surgery is at the Home Guard post. Corrugation shimmers in the steady, breathy heat. I try to walk but my legs buckle. My uncle has to support me. Under the shade of a tarpaulin, a nurse washes and bandages my feet, peels back shredded skin. The water is pain. They look at me strangely, talking quietly when my back is turned, as if they know something that I do not. My dress is in tatters. I should change into new clothes, but no one offers them to me. They give me an elastic to tie up my hair. I am relieved that Steven is not here.

When we drive again, my uncle is quiet.

"I tried to get her out," I say. "She wouldn't come."

He glances across at me. There is no conversation in his look. It is all observation. Is he interested? Afraid? What has Sara told him? I shift in my seat. Something is not right. I cannot put my finger on it. I am exhausted. I lean my head against the window. Sleep comes at me like a dark wave, tangible and frightening. I resist it for a moment, then let it suck me under.

When I wake, my uncle is pulling off the main road. I see a sign: UPLANDS BACON FACTORY, EMPLOYEES ONLY.

My mouth is dry and my head throbs. I sit up and rub sleep from my eyes.

The white walls of the factory rise up in front of us.

"I'll be just a minute," he says, when he sees me stirring. "Stay here." He steps out of the car.

I see him go through the main factory gates. The car makes a ticking sound as it settles in the heat. I can hear the grinding of the factory machines, the clunking of the chains as they move along the chute. After a moment, I open my door and step out.

I walk through the pigpens. Animals behind bars. I breathe in the dense, meaty smell of them, so many crammed together. It is the same as it was all those years ago. Men in pinafores stained with blood are opening up the gates, siphoning each load into the factory like grain pouring through a funnel. They disappear faster than I can count them. I can hear the grunting, the squeals of panic, the clunking of the wheel and the terror—like the cries of the tortured—rising muffled, from behind the walls.

In front of me is the door, and beyond it the corridor I ran down so many years ago. The thing I witnessed. Michael pulling me off the floor.

"Rachel—"

I turn around—it is my uncle, standing in the middle of the pens, watching me. He looks alarmed. Perhaps it is the pigs in the pens around us, but it is as though for a minute he is the captor and I am the hunted. He holds one hand out slightly as if he can get a grip on me, even though I stand at some distance. "I told you to stay in the car."

"Was it an order?" I ask.

He doesn't reply.

"Do you remember the strike?" I call to him across the pens.

"What of it?" he asks, weaving his way closer.

"The man came with the telegram—"

"Don't think about it now, Rachel. You mustn't think about it now."

"Why shouldn't I think about it?" I step back a few paces, challenged. Something in his posture makes me want to run.

"Sara—" He shakes his head. "She said you would want to discuss it. She said you would get upset."

"Am I upset now?"

"You don't look yourself."

"Steven Lockhart killed the African."

"What African?"

"The leader of the strike. He killed him. I was hiding in the room on the first floor. I saw it happen." I remember him lining up his boots, the head snapping back. The silence in the room as I sat there watching him, blood seeping noiselessly from under his head. It is a relief to say it.

He puts a hand on my shoulder and I begin to cry. I am not going to run after all. "You have been through such a lot, Rachel. Now you need to stop. Give up fighting. It's time for you to rest."

"I want to show you," I say, turning to the door.

"Not now, Rachel." He is very close to me. "Perhaps another time."

"But it's important—don't you see? He killed a man—" He isn't registering what I am saying. As though it does not matter. I want to go back there. With an adult. To show what I have carried so long unshown. I want him to see it. Perhaps then I can forget. But he is steering me away, and I am following. I am not certain any longer that I know what is best for me. He puts me into the car, closes the passenger door with a click.

"Did you see the body?" I ask him, when he is sitting next to me.

"I did."

"He kicked him in the head. Didn't you see?"

"Rachel—" He has his hand on the car key, is about to start the engine. He turns to me, shaking his head. "He threw himself off the factory wall. They found him on the concrete, outside. There are men who saw it happen."

"But it's not true—" I look at him, desperate now. Will he not believe me? I have waited so long to tell someone. I feel unreal, as though I am disembodied. Like a dream when you hit out but make no impact, my words are unable to penetrate. "Steven Lockhart—I was hiding in the room—he kicked the man's head right back. It snapped. The man was dead."

If I can convince him of this, just this, then perhaps everything that has happened in the last few months will be understood. It is the key to unlocking everything. But he starts the engine, and I fall silent.

We turn out of the factory gates, onto the road to Nairobi. A few miles from Uplands, the road takes us through Lari. There are no signs of the massacre, until I see a wooden contraption behind trees.

"What is it?"

He doesn't say anything, and I look more closely. A structure. Then we are past it.

"The gallows," he says, after a moment. "The hangman came up from Nairobi yesterday."

"For Lari?"

"Yes. They're hanging a man every fifteen minutes. Mass trials. Mass executions."

I glimpse cages through the trees; high wire fences; barbed-wire compounds holding men. A truck with a closed wire top, crammed full of Africans, guarded by a white man with a gun. Most are facing away from the road, but one man holds the wire with both hands and gazes steadily out at me and my gaze locks onto his, until the truck pulls off the road and he is gone.

WE DRIVE THROUGH the outskirts of Nairobi, over a high bridge. A man far below bends down and dips a yellow drum into the brown river, collecting water. Men dig trenches shoulder-deep in the rich red earth. Fires burn in the distance, smoke spiraling into the hazy heat of the afternoon. A girl runs barefoot alongside us, in a dress edged with frills, which might once have been pink but is now soaked in dirt. The car sweeps past her, drenching her in dust.

The sun has slipped down the sky behind us, and the low corrugated buildings sit deep in shadow. I do not recognize this part of town, and I am suddenly and unaccountably anxious. "Where are we going?"

He glances at me again. That quick look of curiosity, shot through with guilt. As though he doesn't know how this thing will play out.

Then I see the golf course. I have been here after all, with Nate Logan. This is where the Muthaiga Club is, on the outskirts of town.

We pass a row of light blue railings. I glimpse a dirt courtyard beyond, buildings edged with low shrubs and hedges. The trappings of an institutional world. My uncle is slowing the car. This is not the turning for the Muthaiga Club. I crane my head to read the sign. MATHARI. I grip my uncle's arm. I have heard of it—but I can't remember where. Something Nate Logan said. A thread of panic is needling its way into my skin, stitching a pattern out of half-remembered words. *An excellent doctor. Very good results.*

"Why are you turning in? What is this place?"

He doesn't answer. The security guard at the gate waves us through.

My uncle drives the car up the short driveway to a series of low, single-story concrete buildings, with tin roves and walls painted half height in blue—a municipal space. A hospital. Time slows down. I see in the rearview mirror the blue gates closing behind us.

He turns to look at me. The engine is still running. "They are waiting for you inside. You have to try to understand that this is for your benefit."

"What is? What do you mean?" I take in a gulp of air. Try to hear myself through the panic that is surging up inside me. I need to listen to what he says. I need to understand what is happening so I can try to stop it.

"They will look after you here. Assess you. Treat you if necessary. They specialize in cases like yours."

"Cases like mine—how do you mean?" I take another deep breath. I need to see and speak as clearly as I can.

"Your mother, Rachel. It affected you more than you realize. You are not yourself."

Mathari Mental Hospital. I remember it now. Nate Logan had said it was where they sent Kenya Colony's insane. "Does my father know?"

He turns off the engine. Opens the car door. I glance through the windscreen—a white woman in a nurse's uniform and a black man in a white shirt and khaki shorts are walking in our direction. Her eyes settle on mine, and I realize with a quickening in my stomach, that they are walking toward us.

"Does my father know?" I scream at him.

He doesn't reply. Instead, he steps out of the car and nods slightly to the woman. She speaks through the open window to me.

"Miss Fullsmith? Would you like to step out of the car?"

I don't answer. I am looking around the car; my eyes see but they can't make sense of anything. I need to act. How to get away?

I push the door lock down. Wind the window up. My uncle is outside of the car now. I scramble into the driver's seat but my uncle has the keys, and he has his hand on the door. They come around the car, force open the door against my grasp and reach in. Put their hands on me.

"Let me go!" I scream, but they are implacable. Like cats fishing a goldfish out of a bowl. I try to slip away, but they have their claws on me. Slow and precise, they pull me out.

"Why are you doing this?" I say to my uncle, turning my head, though they have my body fixed in their grasp. "Tell me why?"

"They are going to help you, Rachel."

"Why do I need help? What have I done?" I am shouting. Rage spills out of me. Desperation.

"Come with us, Miss Fullsmith," the nurse says, needling my arm with her fingers. "Come along now." And in her voice I hear the years of boarding school, so recently escaped, the complacent power of institution, the crushing weight of an inescapable authority.

I turn one last time. My uncle has lit a cigarette, and the smoke is caught in the evening light. He looks haggard, pale, drawn.

"Tell me why."

"Look at yourself—" he says, gesturing at me with his cigarette. I see the ripped silk dress, the bandaged feet, the mud beneath my fingernails; a picture of madness.

"This is not me—" I say, shaking my head, exhaustion clouding my speech.

He takes a step backward. "You are a danger to yourself, Rachel. You are a danger to your family."

"What I said at Uplands—" The words are wrenched out of me. "It is true. It is not a lie. Steven Lockhart killed the man. I saw him do it."

LEOPARD AT THE DOOR 353

He looks at me directly. His hand holding the cigarette hovers in midair. And I realize—suddenly—that he already knows. That this has something to do with why I am here. I stare at him—his face impassive as he registers what I have seen—swallowing down the cold taste of panic. The nurse jabs her fingers again, and I am dragged away from him, down the path into one of the buildings.

We walk into a long hall, with a black-and-white linoleum floor that smells of bleach. She steps into the first room on the right and I follow, the man closing the door behind us. It smells of something sharp and acrid in here that sticks in the back of my throat. Voices echo from the corridor. The room is small, with a white tiled shower cubicle in one corner. There is a chair and I begin to sit, but the nurse asks me to stand. She comes round behind me and unbuttons my dress. The green fabric falls, muddied and torn, around my feet.

"Now you can sit."

I step out of the fabric and lower myself onto the chair.

The metal is cold and hard against my thighs. She takes a pair of scissors and walks around behind me.

"What are you doing?" I ask, craning my head to see. She places a hand on my head and straightens it. She unties my hair. It falls soft against my shoulders, and she begins to cut at it, the scissors cold against my neck, sawing under her fingers, struggling to sever so much at once. I feel the weight of it falling to the floor. Then the metal is close to my scalp. She is shearing my head. And I am crying, warm tears running cold down the inside of my bare legs.

She sits down in a chair next to me and takes my hands, and one by one cuts my nails, right down to the quick so my fingers feel blunt and raw.

"Go stand over there." There is a cubicle that looks like a shower. She picks up a long tubular contraption from the wall and comes toward me. It has a nozzle on the end of it.

"What is it?" I ask, backing away from her.

"For the lice."

"I have no lice."

But she is spraying me already, in great spurts, a thick white powder drenching my hair, under my arms, and once between my legs.

Then she hands me a white smock. "Put it on." And I do, because I am cold and naked and I want to cover myself. She gives me a pair of leather sandals.

She opens the door and we walk across a courtyard, past buildings with wired-in yards, where Africans hang their arms through the wire and stare.

We come to a building with its own garden plot, smarter than the rest.

"What is this?" I ask.

"The European blocks." There is a sign on the gate which says in capitals WARD 9—WOMEN. She unlocks the padlock on the gate and we walk inside. It is three-sided with blue-painted steel doors at intervals down each side. A few women sit on the step that raises the block from the dusty earth below. Two play checkers. They stare at me. Another woman is lying stretched out on the ground, rolling back and forth. The nurse goes to a door in the middle and unlocks it. Inside the room is small, with an iron bed against each wall. The floor is boarded. I step inside, ahead of her. A woman is lying on the bed on the left, facing the wall. The nurse nods at the bed on the right.

"You cannot leave me here." I turn to the nurse. My voice sounds very loud in the room. "I want to explain."

"The doctor will see you in the morning."

She leaves the room, and the door remains open. I have no belongings. Nothing to claim the bed as my own except the weight of my own body. It has grown dark and the blue-painted window has wire on the outside. I remember the fire and it sets my skin prickling. I do not want to be locked in again.

I cannot face the other women, outside, in the near darkness, so I climb beneath the cold sheet. The springs stretch beneath my weight. I put my head on the thin pillow. Outside a bird chatters in the dusk, and then there is the low call of an owl. I try to remember the words I heard between my father and Sara, but I cannot recall them clearly. I was in a half dream. Had he agreed to sending me here? I feel him kissing my forehead; unable to put his arms around me, crippled in a prison of his own making. Why did my uncle not want to admit to the death of the African at Uplands? Was he involved? Has Steven told him that I am a threat? Steven. Crouched over me. *She is having a fit.* Holding me down. Sara putting a hand to my cheek. *He was trying to protect you from yourself—you are not yourself, Rachel. Don't you see?*

Later the door is shut and bolted. The woman in the bed next to me still doesn't move. The moon has risen and the room is full of shadows. I stand up and go to the peephole. I can see a small patch of the yard, and the wire beyond. Laughter rises from one of the rooms, unearthly, like a hyena, spilling through the night.

I see Michael as he was at the dam, when we said good-bye, the feel of his body beneath my hands. *You are stronger than you think,*

Rachel. I want to believe him but I feel nothing but fear. I draw in air to steady myself. Where is he now?

I sleep fitfully. I dream that I am consumed by fire. That I am hanging by my feet, blackened, from a rope. I can hear it creaking. There is Steven in the skin of a leopard bending down to look into my eyes. *Not quite dead,* he says. *Give her another half an hour.* And my father is there, but I cannot see him, and I shout but he does not hear me, and there is only the fire, and the rope spinning me round and round.

XXVI

In the morning I wake. There is no mirror. I have nothing that shows me to myself. I run a hand over my head and feel the short hair flicking between my fingers. I am a stranger to myself.

I am led out of the compound to a separate building. A European doctor sits at a desk. A window. Curtains. He looks up benevolently, over the top of his glasses, when I come in. His glasses are pointed, turned up at the corners, giving him an eccentric look.

"Miss Fullsmith. I am Dr. Measden. Take a seat."

He puts down his pen, crosses his hands and looks at me. I am aware of my nakedness under my smock. I feel stripped of any defense. Silence stretches out between us. The way he is watching me makes me uncomfortable. His lack of shame gives him authority over me. He does not care what I think of him. I am here to be inspected.

"What is this place?" I ask.

"Mathari Mental Hospital."

"Why am I here?"

"Why do you think you are here?"

"I do not know." I lick my lips to moisten them. Yesterday I might have told him there was nothing wrong with me, but I cannot say it now. I am scared. I do not feel myself.

"Do you remember having a fit?"

I shake my head. My voice is very quiet. "It wasn't a fit."

"The District Officer has told me that you had to be restrained. Your limbs went rigid. You foamed at the mouth."

The weight of Steven's body on top of me, riding me; my father not visible; Sara's voice. I try to push the images away—I cannot bear the power of them; the panic, the physical weakness, the violation. I look away from the doctor.

"Can you tell me when you first heard that your mother had died?"

"My mother?" I am not expecting it. The question strikes me in a soft place, where I am least protected.

"Yes. Your mother."

"It was almost seven years ago. I was staying with my uncle. There was a telegram from England."

"Where was your father?"

"He was in England."

"How did you feel when you heard?"

A long silence draws out between us. I begin crying. I cannot stop myself. The tears run down my cheeks. My mouth is wet. "I'm sorry," I say, wiping at my eyes with the sleeves of my gown, embarrassed by so much emotion, but I cannot stop them coming.

"That's quite all right. You don't need to apologize."

I take a deep breath and try to pull myself together.

"Miss Fullsmith?" His eyes are searching out mine. "Do you remember putting on your mother's dress?"

I remember the green fabric in my hands. My father's face when he saw me wearing it.

"She gave me two pills. She made me swallow them. I don't remember everything clearly—"

"She did the right thing. You might have been a danger to yourself." Then—"Do you remember why you put it on?"

"There was a party the next day. For the Coronation. I wanted to see if it would fit."

"But why that particular dress?"

I wonder what he is getting at. He is losing me, though I feel the shadow of significance in the accumulation of his words, in the soft surety of his voice.

He looks at me again, and I am unsettled. It is as though he is undressing my soul. There is shame there. I want to keep parts hidden, but he won't let me. He wants to see all of me. More than that—he is using the undressing to his advantage. For the first time I feel afraid, but I am also drawn to him. He can save me from this place. I cannot escape.

"I do not know."

"Do you feel anger toward your father?"

"Yes."

"Why?"

I do not know how to answer. No one has asked me this question. I have not had to articulate it even to myself.

"Is he living with another woman?"

"Yes."

"And you feel he has betrayed your mother?"

"Yes." I nod. I cannot deny it.

"Perhaps you hold him accountable for your mother's death?"

I say nothing. I feel the pain swelling inside me.

"Is it hard to watch this new woman with your father? Do you wish it was your mother and not her who was with him?"

I shake my head. "It isn't that."

"What is it then?"

"I don't know."

Then his voice comes, with such deft confidence that I think he must have meant to say it all along. "Do you feel he has betrayed you?"

The truth of what he has said brings a sob from me, like he has hooked a dirty rag inside me and is drawing it up my throat from my belly.

"Why? Why do you want to know all this?" The tears are streaming down my cheeks. He has me pinned. It hurts.

He is speaking faster now, and his questions do not follow in sense, one from another. "There is an African at your farm that you felt particularly close to?"

"Yes."

"What was his name?"

I do not want to say his name, here, in front of this man.

"What was his name?"

"Michael."

"Were you physically close to him?"

I don't answer.

He asks it again, more intimately this time. "Did you have sexual relations with the boy?"

"What does that have to do with any of this?"

He ignores me. "Was he intimate with you?"

"Yes." I cannot deny it, but I begin to hate him. He has dragged Michael into this place of horror.

"And you did it to get attention from your father? So that he would notice you?"

"No—" I say, taken aback.

He looks at me, over the top of his glasses. "There are many ways to harm yourself, Miss Fullsmith."

"It was nothing to do with my father."

He gives me a small, indulgent smile.

"Did you know that he was Mau Mau?"

"No."

"But you knew that he was planning to attack the house?"

"No." I stand up. "That's not how it was. It was not him."

He glances up at me, standing, and makes a note in his pad.

"And you arranged an escape plan with him?"

"No."

"But he assisted your escape?"

"Yes." I feel awkward now, hovering above my chair. "He helped me to get out."

"But not your father's mistress? She was left inside?"

"I tried to get her to follow me. She thought it was a trap."

"Was it not a trap? Do you think he would have let her go—as he let you go?"

"Yes."

There is a pause.

"So you believe, Miss Fullsmith, that he was trying to help you?"

"Yes."

"To what end?"

I do not answer immediately. Why did Michael help me? "Because he loves me."

"And your father does not."

I say nothing. It was a statement not a question.

"There is nothing wrong with me." I say it now, but my voice is not quite steady.

He closes his book and smiles at me again. "Please, Miss Fullsmith, do not upset yourself. You have been through a great deal." I feel exposed, weak. He has taken my life apart in this little whitewashed room, noted it down in his book and will pick over the contents, piecing it back together like a jigsaw puzzle as he sees fit. I am utterly in his hands and it frightens me. Whatever version of me that he decides is the right one will become the one I will be forced to read back to myself.

"How long do I have to stay here?"

"There is a ten-day period of observation. After that I will make a formal diagnosis."

"Am I allowed visitors?"

"We have advised against it for the moment. What you need is complete rest. We will keep you under observation. I am going to prescribe a course of ECT and some pills to help you."

"What is ECT?" I do not like the sound of it. I don't want them to do anything to me.

"Electric therapy. It is quite safe and has wonderful results in restoring a brain to equilibrium."

"What if I don't want it?"

"You haven't tried it, Miss Fullsmith. But ultimately, it isn't for you to decide. The first treatment will be tomorrow."

He stands up, goes to the door and opens it. The same nurse is waiting for me outside.

WHEN I RETURN to my cell, there is an envelope on my bed.

Dear Rachel,

I hope this letter finds you well. You are in good hands with Dr. Measden. He was recommended to Steven as being the very best psychiatric doctor in East Africa. He has advised against visiting or discussing with you what has unfolded in the months since you returned to Kisima, but he has reassured Steven that with the right treatment, he expects, over a period of time, a full recovery. That it is not unusual for a girl of your age, exposed to the trauma that you have been exposed to, to break down as you did. I want you to know that I am here for you and will look forward to hearing of your progress.

Your father is not yet out of danger, but yesterday he said a few words, and the doctors are hopeful that he will make a good recovery. I have—for reasons you will understand—avoided talking about what passed that night. In good time, when his condition improves, I will explain everything.

With hopes for his recovery, and yours,
Sara

What has Sara told my father? Does he even know that I am here? I can guess the lies that Steven has spoken to them, to serve his own self-interest; to have me stowed away here; to keep me quiet. I remember his warning in the yard: *If you tell your father I will make your life a living hell.* Mathari is both his protection and his revenge. I tell the nurse that I want to write a letter, and she returns with a pen and some paper. I am surprised—I hadn't thought it would be so easy. I sit down and begin writing to the only person who can help me.

Papa—

Are you reading this? If you are it means you are recovering and I am overwhelmingly happy if it is true.

I need to know—did you agree to have me sent here? I do not think you would have done. Not if you had known what really happened at Kisima.

I put down my pen. What did happen? I think of Steven Lockhart chasing me, straddling me. His hands beneath my trousers. His words whispered in my ear. *You bitch.* I cannot write these things.

Dr. Measden has been told that I conspired with Michael. That I knew about the attack before it happened. You need to know that this is not true. I had no knowledge that there would be an attack or that he was involved with Mau Mau, until the very end. Even then Michael helped me at great personal risk to escape the fire. I tried to get Sara out, but she would not come.

Will he believe my word over Sara's? I decide that I will send the letter to Lillian Markham and ask her to give him the letter directly, so that Sara cannot intercept it. The idea is a good one. I feel a glimmer of hope.

I want to see you, Papa. Please do not leave me here. Dr. Measden is going to give me something they call electric therapy. I am scared. Please send for me. I will not cause trouble with Sara. Send for me and bring me home.

"You are writing a letter?"

A face at the door. An older woman with shorn gray hair. My eyes are drawn to her hands—they are moving. Her forefingers sliding against her thumbs as though she is rolling something between them.

"Yes."

"And what are you saying?" Her chin jerks up, every few seconds, so that she looks as though she is at the whim of a careless puppeteer.

"I want my father to take me away from here."

"He won't receive the letter."

I put down my pen. "Why not?"

"Because they read all the letters before they are sent and decide which ones should go."

"So what can I do?" Desperation is tugging at the edges of me. I am struggling to breathe.

She sits on the step just outside the door of my room, her pale legs poking like bones out of her white smock.

"There is nothing you can do."

"The doctor said he is going to give me electric therapy." I breathe in heavily. "What is it?"

"Electric therapy." Her fingers go over and over against her thumbs in a motion that seems in time with the beating of my heart. "There is a cloud afterward. It is difficult to remember everything. But it comes back, eventually. If they don't administer it too often."

The restless movement of her hands works on my anxiety, sharpens it.

"How long have you been here?"

"Five years. Longer than some. Shorter than others."

I hear other patients talking about shock therapy. That they restrain you. That it breaks bones. That you cannot eat afterward. Or remember your own name. That it was invented by a doctor who visited a slaughterhouse which used electric shocks on pigs to stun them before they were killed. He saw that if you use enough electricity to bring the pig to the very brink of death—then you could induce a fit. I am filled with dread.

The woman next to me wakes in the night and begins to scream. I go to her bedside, but she throws me off. After a long while a nurse comes and injects her and she is quiet.

I RECEIVE another letter. There is no post stamp. It has been hand-delivered. I look straight at the signature: Nate Logan. It is like sucking in a breath full of cold, fresh air. Is he in Nairobi?

Rachel—

Keep your chin up. We are working on a solution. Your father is increasingly well.

Nate Logan

There is a world outside of this nightmare. Someone has found me. A solution.

MORNING the following day. The nurse leads me into a small tiled room. There is a bed in the middle on wheels, a trolley full of electrical equipment, wires snaking out of a machine. Dr. Measden is writing notes in the corner. I begin to moan. I will not lie down there. I try to step backward, but they propel me forward. I shout. Tell them to stop. To take their hands off me. Dr. Measden doesn't look up from his writing. His posture is one of complete indifference. Is he deliberately ignoring me? I am like a ghost; my protests are not heard; my voice is merely gabbling. It increases my anxiety, my sense of futility.

And yet my body is here. I can feel the tiles cold beneath my feet. They force me down onto the bed. Straps are slipped over me. They winch them tight, so that I cannot lift my chest off the bed. There is one over my forehead.

Dr. Measden looms over me. His face is impenetrable, his voice jolly. "How are you feeling today, Miss Fullsmith?"

"Please, don't do this to me. Please." But he is giving instructions to the nurse.

She puts dabs of Vaseline on my scalp, cold and sticky against my skin. I cannot lift my hands. I shout. My body tightens in panic.

"Just a small electric current." Dr. Measden's voice is unaffected by my shouting, as though he has seen my fear so many times and it is meaningless. I am nothing more than a child having a tantrum. My defiance is irrelevant. I scream louder, but he appears not to hear me. "It will be over very shortly."

He fiddles with the equipment. I crane my head. See a steel wire. It is curved to the shape of my head. I cannot move away.

"What is your name?" he asks me.

The clarity of the question means I answer it. As I open my mouth the nurse slips something large and rubber into it and holds it there, so that I cannot speak.

"Bite down on it," she says.

I feel my eyes widen. I press myself into the bed, but I cannot get away. And the metal is over my head. The current comes. A searing pain, a tightening of my body and a blackness.

I am in a tunnel. I am weightless. There is no emotional substance to me. My mind is empty. A sickening, lurching vertigo. Nothing to hold on to. A being made up of nothing. Panic brings it back; pieces of me; difficult to assemble. Words that carry a weight but mean nothing. When I open my eyes the room is too bright. I will be weak after this. I will not be able to tell myself who I am. He will know better than me. My grip on myself is slipping. What exactly am I?

The nurse is over my bed. I am back in my cell. I grasp at her. "Will they give it to me again? When? When?"

She smiles at me and does not answer. There are two pills in her hand. I let her slide them into my mouth. I swallow and I sleep.

"You're not helping yourself." The patient with the gray hair and the moving hands is leaning over me. I am in my cell. In my bed. Relief floods through me. "The quieter you are, the more effective the treatment. The happier the doctors, the quicker they will discharge you."

And I think they must know that I screamed, and screamed and screamed.

———

HOW LONG WILL they keep me here? What does my father know of my treatment? Has he been told? Another day passes. The doctor had said a course of ECT. The old woman with the moving hands tells me that is once every three days, though the nurse will not tell me anything. I dread it. Will I be the same after another? And another after that? What of Nate Logan's letter? I keep it in the Bible by my bedside.

"AH, MISS FULLSMITH." Dr. Measden folds his hands and smiles at me. "How are you feeling today?"

I sit down opposite him. It is two days later. My head buzzes. It is hard for me to hold my thoughts.

"The nurse. She gives me pills."

"Y-e-s," he draws out the word, as though he knows my question before I ask it. My dissent is to be expected. I feel the withdrawal of his approval and it is unpleasant—I want him to like me, to protect me, to assess me and tell me that I am normal. Yet—I do not trust him, and something in me insists on fighting him. I do not know if this thing that fights him is a symptom of the sickness of which he accuses me.

"What are they?"

"Largactil."

"I think they make me dizzy. I don't feel myself."

"That can be a common side effect." He smiles at me. I feel my certainty drain away. I sense that I am boring him, and this is somehow a failure, yet I persist.

"What are they?"

"They are an antipsychotic."

I look at him, summoning up the vestige of authority and self-respect that remains within me. "I do not think I am psychotic."

He sighs. "Miss Fullsmith, if I had a penny for every patient who told me that, I would be a very wealthy man."

"When will you release me?"

"When I believe you have made a full recovery."

"Does my father know that I am here?"

"Ah—your father." He lights a cigarette, leans back in his chair and studies me. "That's good." He licks tobacco off his teeth. I feel him settling in. "What difference do you feel it would make if he did?"

"I need to know . . . whether he approves of the decision—"

"And if he does?"

I watch the smoke spiral to the ceiling. I do not know what to say. I sense that he has trapped me, but I do not quite know how he will get at me.

"It is not unusual for a girl to have feelings for her father, Miss Fullsmith. To want more from him than he ought to give." He inhales again. The smoke is making me feel nauseous. "Have you heard of Freud?"

I nod slightly. I have heard of the name, but cannot remember in what context I have heard it.

"He is perhaps the greatest thinker of the twentieth century. He believes"—Dr. Measden inhales his cigarette, knocks off the ash and exhales slowly—"that girls suffer from penis envy. Do you know what a penis is, Miss Fullsmith?"

I nod, feeling my face redden underneath the steadiness of his gaze.

"He believes that when girls discover, as infants, that they do not have a penis, they sublimate their desire for a penis into a desire for their father." He breaths out a cloud of smoke. "Did you feel guilt when you heard that your mother was dead?"

"No," I say quietly. His question disturbs me. It carries with it an accusation. And in his hands an accusation can be all-consuming, like a viral contamination. It might take hold of me.

He looks at me steadily. "The death of the mother is very often associated with guilt in girls, since it is the fulfillment of a wish— the desire to have the mother removed so that they can be closer to the father."

"There was no guilt." I shake my head. "I was—" but there are no words to describe what I felt that day.

"Of course. It was very upsetting. But I am talking about what you felt deep down—what was taking place in your *unconscious* mind."

I swallow heavily. There is one thing I can tell him which might vindicate me. Which might get his attention. I have resisted talking about Steven Lockhart. There is shame in it, and I do not want him to use it against me. But I cannot hold it back anymore. "The day my mother died, I saw the District Officer, Steven Lockhart, kill a man."

"And what is it that you think he did afterward?" I realize he already knows the accusation. That Steven has told him everything.

"He forced me onto his lap." I am crying again now. "He touched me."

"Did you solicit it?"

"No." I remember his grip on my arm, the terror, his hand sliding my own down my chest.

"Do you not think it a coincidence that on the day your mother dies, you imagine your first sexual experience? Consider the possibility that your desire for your father—both suddenly available to you and yet not present—was transferred onto Steven Lockhart?"

I shake my head, but his logic inexorably continues.

"You witnessed Steven Lockhart roughing up an African. And you later believed, stricken by guilt for the feelings you had on your mother's death, that you had a sexual encounter with this man. That this man—not your father, but in place of your father—had committed the crime which you had so desired; eliciting in you a fantasy of sexual fulfillment. That you and Steven Lockhart, your father substitute, had colluded in the symbolic murder of your mother."

"No—" I shout, standing up and shaking my head. "He has done things to me at the farm."

"But you didn't tell your father?"

I stare at him.

"Why not? Because you felt ashamed? Because you were complicit in what took place between you?"

Why could I not tell my father about the subtle sliding of hands? The things Steven said to me when he had me on my own? He is right—I feel tainted, humiliated.

"There is no shame in it, Miss Fullsmith. It is possible that you solicited his attention. In the same way that you solicited the African's attention. Because you were unable to have the attentions of your father. Your father who was so obviously engaged with another woman." He sits back in his chair, looking up at me.

A nurse opens the door and stands looking at the doctor. "It's all right," he says. "Miss Fullsmith will be fine." He closes his book and stands up. "I think that's enough talking for today. I can see how difficult it is for you. We'll have to go more slowly in future." I feel the awful implacable pull of his power, setting out my timetable, my meals, my pills. Telling me when I have behaved well and when I have not. The terrible battle between falling under his approval and wanting to hold on to my old self.

I turn toward the door.

"Miss Fullsmith?"

I glance back at him.

He gestures to the bed. "We haven't finished yet. Would you lie down?"

I stare at him.

"Come along now. Or I'll ask the nurse in to help."

I get up onto the bed. I have no choice. He has turned over the hidden places of my soul. Now he will feel out the hidden places of my body.

He smiles down at me. "We've had the results in of your tests." He slides his hand under my smock, and I feel his fingers on my lower belly, cold against my skin. I shudder, but he does not show that he has noticed. He feels along my abdomen. "They show that you are pregnant."

I stare up at him. My heart is thudding in my chest. His hands press against me.

"Pregnant?"

"Yes, Miss Fullsmith. Pregnant."

I do not know what to say. I lie there looking up at him. There is no room for me to hide. I feel shock. And a terrible sadness. And beneath these things a glimmer of something else. Something worth protecting.

"When will you give me ECT?"

"I don't want you to worry yourself about that."

"But you will give it to me again?"

He smiles at me—a man condescending to a child.

"Will it hurt the baby?"

"There is no reason to think that ECT interferes with the fetus. There is a slight increased risk of gastric regurgitation, so we will use a tube to keep your airways clear."

He withdraws his hand and pulls down my smock.

"Does my father know?" I ask, and he smiles patiently, but does not answer, and I know I should not have mentioned my father.

"You're free to go, Miss Fullsmith. I will see you again shortly."

I sit at the edge of the bed, my hands over my smock, palms against my womb. My face is wet with tears—gratitude and the horror of helplessness. I carry something—something of Michael's—that is already more valuable to me than myself. I must protect it—and yet I cannot. My body is not my own.

XXVII

->-•-<-

Rachel Fullsmith?"
The nurse is standing in the center of the compound. She is looking for me. I feel a tremor of terror. I do not want to be noticed, but when she sees me watching she nods. I look around. Others are staring also. The patients for ECT have already been taken this morning. What does she want with me?

I walk toward the gates.

"You are to be discharged," she says, when we are outside the compound.

I stare at her in disbelief. "I can leave? Today?"

"Yes. You are free to go."

I follow her across the yard, past the African compounds where men stand leaning, with their arms hanging through the wire, into the administration building that first received me, and along the black-and-white lino floor.

"Rachel?"

I stop and turn. The voice is familiar, but the sun shines too starkly through the blue, latticed window and it is difficult for me to see. A face that I recognize. Lillian Markham. She is walking alongside me, on the other side of the wall. The nurse walks ahead of me and opens the blue metal door at the end of the corridor. I stop for just a moment and press my hands into my eyes. The fire, Sara tearing at the window, Steven's lies, the horror of this prison. I have held so much together and now I feel it all unraveling. I take a deep breath. She is silhouetted just outside of the open door. Only a few paces from where I stand. I run forward, into the light, and she is pulling me over the threshold. She has her arms around me. Her tears fall wet against my neck. She smells of jasmine and tea. Behind me the door to the hospital clangs shut.

It has only been five days, but I feel as though I might have lost myself forever.

THE MUTHAIGA CLUB. The tweed jackets, collared shirts and tea dresses of the men and women who know nothing of where I have been. We stand in a corner of the car park—Lillian has brought clothes—she pulls a jumper over my head, and I slip on a pair of her slacks. An African opens the doors, and I follow her into the paneled hallway that smells of cigar smoke and beeswax. My legs feel unsteady, and I put a hand to a pillar, thinking I might fall down. Lillian sees, and she puts my arm over her shoulder and helps me down the corridor. A stuffed lion's head gazes out at us from a glass box. There is a dark paneled room. Africans in white robes and crimson fezzes pour tea into delicate china cups. Trolleys squeak by with a tiny turning of wheels. I drop into an armchair in the corner. She orders me a whiskey and as I drink my hand begins to steady.

"Can you talk?" she asks.

"I think so."

"I want you to tell me everything."

I think I might not be able to begin, that the images that whirl around my head, that haunt me day and night, might not conform to the simple pattern of words. But once my voice begins to feel its way over what has happened, the events slip into place. I tell her about being twelve years old. The strike at Uplands. The room upstairs in the factory. About what I saw Steven Lockhart do to the man. I tell her about what happened afterward in my uncle's house; him pinning me in his lap; his hands touching me. I tell her about what he has done to me since I have been back, and what he has tried to do. I tell her about Michael, about my fear that he is dead, about our closeness, his politics, how he helped me escape the fire. I tell her that I tried to get Sara out of the house, but that she would not come. I tell her that I am carrying Michael's baby. There can be no secrets. I am beyond the judgment of others.

She listens, and when it is over she reaches forward and takes my hand and holds it, and I know that it is all right. I can let go now; of all the horror, the shame and the fear. I lean back in the chair and shut my eyes, and feel myself drown in a sea of colors. Nausea pulls at me. I open my eyes again and focus on Lillian.

"How did you find me?"

"Nate Logan. Sara told him that you had been admitted to Mathari. He tried to get you out, but Dr. Measden wouldn't discharge you unless you were under the care of a European woman."

I take a breath and ask the question I have wanted to ask since I saw her. "Did my father know?"

"He had a conversation with Steven, after you fainted—the evening of the attack. But he did not sign you in. He was scarcely conscious when it happened. Steven Lockhart organized your admission with Sara's help. Nate Logan went to your father with your discharge papers and he signed them immediately." He released me, but is it enough? Had he agreed that night—before he saw me in my mother's dress—to send me to Mathari? I wonder where he is right at this minute. In Nairobi Hospital?

"How is he?"

"He lost a lot of blood, and there was some internal damage, but he has managed to avoid infection. The doctors say he will make a good recovery. There will always be an inherent weakness—but he will be able to return home."

Home. The blackened buildings. Sara.

"What happened that night? At the farm?"

"A gang came down from the forest to the new *shamba*. They stirred up trouble—a distraction to draw your father away."

"Was Jim involved?"

"He was killed, Rachel. The gang had been attempting to oath in the new *shamba* for months. Jim refused to be a part of it. They tried to get Kahiki as well—but he managed to escape to the house."

I swallow heavily, remembering the tortured look in Jim's eyes over the last few months, remembering Njeri, on the day she left; their baby scarcely a few weeks old; remembering his broad hands on my waist, as a child, lifting me up to set me on the kitchen counter. My eyes are wet with tears. He is dead. And what kind of life will Njeri have now?

Lillian is looking at the table, and I know there is something else that she has not told me yet. Something she has held back. She gives me a quick, reassuring look. "You were released, Rachel, on one condition."

"What is it?"

She takes my hand again. "That you are repatriated."

"What does that mean?"

"It means you will have to go back to England. Dr. Measden insisted."

"Why?" I don't understand what she is saying.

"You know Kenya Colony. They like to uphold appearances. It's their way of tidying the whole thing up." She squeezes my hand. "I'm going to come with you, on the ship. I'm repatriating myself—" She smiles at me. "I've had enough of it here. We're getting older, the two of us, and Gerald struggles with the farm, and there were never any children." She is smiling still, but I see the tears welling in her own eyes. This is her good-bye. "Gerald will sell up and come back in a few months." She squeezes my hand again and looks at me. "I thought you might live with us—that is, if you wanted to." She falters for a moment. "Just at the beginning, until you get settled."

"Even with the baby coming?" I struggle to grasp what she is saying.

"Especially with the baby."

I do not hear what she has said, so much as feel it. A warmth that spreads through my body, melting the pain. I smile. "So you're not going to leave me?"

She holds my hand and smiles back at me. "I'm not going to leave you." I think of leaving Kenya. Leaving Michael. England— wet and cold. I know I can face the future if I am with her.

I close my eyes. I am not sure how long. Time slips past me.

"What about my father?" I ask, when I open my eyes. Though I know the answer already.

"He will stay, Rachel."

After a moment she says, "Our ship doesn't leave for two days. There is still time."

Time for what? I do not ask. Instead I close my eyes, and let the world within cover me in darkness.

I DO NOT sleep well at night. I wake, sweating from nightmares. Lillian is in a room next door and I do not wake her. When morning comes, filtering through the glass, it brings relief. She said that he would come today, just after sunrise.

My room has a veranda that leads—past a spread of lawn—to a shallow, colonnaded terrace. It is rarely used by guests. I step out just after dawn. Everything is quiet except for the chattering of the crows in the half-light. I sit in a wicker chair in my nightdress, my feet cool on the stone, my hands in my lap just below the thickening in my belly. Waiting. Coconut palms grow at the edge of the veranda, shielding me from the eyes of strangers. An African is sweeping the red earth, the rhythmic sound of my childhood. *Sweep, sweep, sweep, scrape.* I think of Michael in the yard, his eyes lifting to mine, the current that passed between us, and I feel again the vital, crushing want to have him here, and the helplessness. We are leaving for Mombasa in a few hours. I will not see him again. I have no way of knowing whether he is dead or alive; of telling him that I am carrying his child; that I am leaving Kenya.

A frail old lady crosses the lawn, pushing a hand over her white hair, and a man of about sixty-five, perhaps her son, an officer, pulled-up socks, chino shorts and a collared shirt stretched tight over a slight paunch, helps her to the other side. A gun hangs in a holster around his waist. He represents the colonial enterprise— cricket pitches, the army, Sunday lunches and the Queen's Coronation. No doubt they are leaving to go up-country. I feel uneasy as I watch them, no longer comfortable here in Kenya, among these people. They disappear into the club, and for a long while the gardens sit in a tranquil half-light.

Time passes. The swing door pushes open. I know before I can make out his face that it is him. His injury has crumpled him— he is hunched over the walking stick that he holds in one hand— but there is the familiar bulk of his shoulders, the large hands that picked me up as a child, the eyes that loved me and did not. He glances around the gardens. He is searching for me. I do not move. A bird calls above us. The African has stopped his sweeping. My father crosses the lawn to the terrace. He sits in a chair under the stone colonnades. He has not seen me and I do not call out to him. My cheeks, my mouth, are wet with tears. Something inside me is tearing. I see a young girl running in her nightdress across the lawn. She throws herself in his lap, and he pulls her, laughing, into his arms. This is my childhood. This is our good-bye.

There is a knock at my door. "*Memsaab*, your father is waiting for you."

"*Sawa sawa*," I call out softly, my voice catching, but I do not rise. It is too late. I am no longer the girl I was.

My father's face glistens. It might be a trick of the light, but for a moment I think that there are tears falling from his eyes. A waiter brings him a glass of water. His glass sits untouched for a long time. When he brings it to his lips I see that his hand shakes. I do not call out to him. I do not go to him. He is my father. I am his daughter. There is nothing greater between us than this.

EPILOGUE

→>•<←

I sit on the brown carpet in a small patch of winter sunlight. The electric heater glows hot and red, giving out the faint smell of dust singeing. The boy next door is kicking a ball against the wall and I hear the scuff of his heels, and then the bounce as it thumps off the brick. I take the large brown envelope, stamped from Kenya, turn it over and slide my finger into the crease to open it.

Inside is a folded newspaper: the *East African Standard*, dated 17 October 1955. I scan down the page until I see the article circled in red.

DISTRICT OFFICER CONVICTED
OF MANSLAUGHTER

Colonel Steven Lockhart, a District Officer of the Nakuru District, has been convicted of the manslaughter of Kikuyu political activist Jomo Kimoi, in a strike at Uplands Bacon Factory in 1946. Mr. Eliot Fullsmith, owner and manager of Uplands, and present on the day of the strike, testified against Lockhart. Fullsmith was the first person to see the body of the deceased. There was a written testimony from

his niece, Rachel Fullsmith, twelve years old at the time of
the strike, who was a witness to the events. Jomo Kimoi—
the deceased—was a prominent figure in the Kenya African
Union. Lockhart has been sentenced to five years in prison.

It is barely enough. And yet it is something. There is no men-
tion of what he tried to do to me, on the track, under the sun, at
Kisima; the pressure he put on my father to have me committed to
Mathari. The violence against the Kikuyu which I had seen in
Harold's photographs. It is manslaughter not murder, but it is a
conviction.

I open the newspaper and a note slips out:

Rachel—

>   *At last, something of what you deserve.*
>   *I saw your father last week. Pirate is well. Your father says*
> *he is the worst kind of shenzi, but I think he means it as a*
> *compliment.*
>   *How are your studies?*
>   *Write to me.*

Nate

I smile at the thought of Pirate. He was found in the bushes by
the stables, after the fire, and my father took him in. They are
living in Nairobi. Sara is still with him, though they are not yet
married.

I turn the note over. There is no mention of Michael and I try
to swallow my disappointment. What news should I hope for? Nate

has promised to keep an ear to the ground, but I have read the liberal papers in England. They report on the forced labor camps in Kenya, the abuse and death of hundreds of prisoners, and the men still living in the forest, fighting British troops. The war carries on. How will I ever know if he is alive or dead?

At the university, where I am specializing in African politics, I do not tell them what I have been through, but I soak up the political dialogue. All the articulate rage, and store it away. It is the start of something for me. I do not know where it will take me, but I think my journey is just beginning.

"Mama?" The voice carries downstairs, and my heart gives a leap of joy. Michael—he is awake. I run up the stairs. Lillian will be home later, and Gerald at the weekend. But for now the house— the boy—is all mine.

"Mama?"

I open the door, smiling, eager for the feel of his warm, brown skin against mine, eager for the sheer miracle of him, proof against all odds of where I have been. Proof against all odds that love is greater than separation.

POSTSCRIPT

→>•<←

In his book *Histories of the Hanged: Britain's Dirty War in Kenya and the End of Empire*, David Anderson notes, "Contrary to public perception, only thirty-two European settlers died in the [Mau Mau] rebellion, and there were fewer than two hundred casualties among the British regiments and police who served in Kenya over these years. Yet more than 1,800 African civilians are known to have been murdered by Mau Mau, and many hundreds more to have disappeared, their bodies never found. Rebel losses were far greater than those suffered by the British security forces. The official figures set the total number of Mau Mau rebels killed in combat at 12,000, but the real figure is likely to have been more than 20,000. . . .

"In the final tally, the British hanged 1,090 Kikuyu men for Mau Mau offences.

"Convicted murderers among this total numbered [only] 346. All the other executed men had been convicted of offences specially defined as capital charges under the Emergency Powers Regulations. . . .

"In no other place, and at no other time in the history of British imperialism, was state execution used on such a scale as this."

A GLOSSARY OF KITCHEN SWAHILI

➤➤•⤙⤙

asante—thank you

askari—soldier

ayah—nursemaid

boma—livestock enclosure

bwana—master

effendi—sir

gakunia—colonial agent dressed in a sack hood with eye holes

jambo—hello

jambo sana—welcome

kali—severe

kikoy—a garment made of striped cloth

kipande—identity card

leleshwa—a small shrub, also known as African wild sage or camphor bush

lunghi—a sarong-like garment

maganga—curse of witchcraft

mchawi—witch doctor

memsaab—madam

mtoto—a child

mzuri—good

ndiyo—yes

ngoma—a dance

panga—a sword, a large chopping knife

posho—maize meal porridge

sawa sawa—OK

shamba—cultivated plot of land

shauri—dispute

shenzi—mongrel, mixed breed

watu—people (African)

Acknowledgments

→>•<←

I owe a huge debt of gratitude to a number of people without whose help and encouragement the book could not have been written. Araminta Whitley, Venetia Butterfield and Sara Minnich, for their insight, critique and enthusiasm. Richard Britten-Long, whose battered red suitcase—handed down from his grandmother—contained the rich wealth of documents, photographs and police pamphlets that inspired the novel. David M. Anderson, Professor of African History at the University of Warwick and author of the seminal *Histories of the Hanged*, for so generously answering my questions on the period; Dr. Sloan Mahone, who talked to me about Mathari in the 1950s; and Dr. Will Jackson, for his informative writing on the white, marginalized underclass in colonial Kenya. The novel is also indebted to the memoirs of the men and women, on both sides, caught up in the Mau Mau struggle, in particular Ngugi wa Thiong'o's memoir *Dreams in a Time of War*, Josiah Mwangi Kariuki's *Mau Mau Detainee* and *The Gate Hangs Well* by James W. Stapleton, which was the source for the radio broadcasts on pages 217 and 218.

My thanks and love go to my father and Jenny, who first took me to Kenya on that wild and extraordinary journey—the one which lit the fire and so nearly ended in disaster. And to Sveva—who had Dave and I to stay and who looked after us so well. I am grateful to my late father-in-law, Lee Harragin, who described so clearly life in Kenya in the 1950s and his work defending Mau Mau detainees; to Ron Stanfield, for his description and photographs of the Uplands Bacon Factory; to Nick and Vinnie Day, who offered valuable insight; to Jenny McPhee and Alba Arikha, who gave me confidence when I needed it most; and to Kirsty Gordon, who unfailingly helps me to see my writing more clearly.

Most importantly, thank you to Dave, Alice, Daisy and Tommy Lee. You are the best.

LEOPARD

AT THE

DOOR

JENNIFER McVEIGH

———

Discussion Guide

———

Excerpt from THE FEVER TREE

———

BOOK
ENDS

PUTNAM

Discussion Guide

1. Over the course of the novel, Rachel—though always one of the more progressive characters—develops a more nuanced, less naive view of the impact of imperialism and racism in Kenya. How does this happen? Which characters and events are most influential in this transformation?

2. Were you surprised by the romance between Rachel and Michael? Why, or why not? What does each see in the other? How does their relationship develop and grow?

3. Discuss the role of memory in the novel. How does the past come to bear on Rachel's aspirations, values, fears, and triumphs? How might Michael's perception of the past differ from Rachel's?

4. How does the legacy of World War II figure into the story?

5. Consider the reference to the fairy tale "Hansel and Gretel" in the novel. How is Rachel's story similar? How is it different? Do you feel any sympathy for Robert, Rachel's father, and Sara, his mistress?

6. Rachel's home, Kisima, is located in rural northern Kenya and is so isolated that the closest neighboring farmhouse is an hour away. What impact does this setting have on the story? Why

was it important for this story to be set there, rather than in a metropolitan area like Nairobi?

7. Much of the novel is concerned with imbalances of power and the fight for control and dominance. What relationships and institutions illustrate this theme? How do various characters try to exert control over Rachel? How do the European settlers try to control the African natives?

8. Discuss the importance of some of the smaller characters, such as Harold, Jim the cook, Kahiki, Nate Logan, and Lillian Markham. What does each add to the story?

9. The novel is not only a love story and bildungsroman but also a gripping and tense depiction of a turbulent moment in history. How did the author build the suspense in the story? Which were the most heart-pounding moments, and why?

10. Near the end of the story, Rachel is involuntarily committed to a mental institution because of her affair with Michael. What do these scenes convey about the function of asylums in British colonies in the 1950s?

11. In the postscript, Jennifer McVeigh quotes a historian who notes that only thirty-two European settlers were actually killed by the Mau Mau, yet the European characters in the novel treat the Mau Mau as a mighty threat to their own safety. What accounts for this discrepancy? Do you see any parallels to how rebellious and subversive groups, especially those whose members are mostly not white, are perceived today?

Excerpt from THE FEVER TREE

One

The first indication that her father was unwell had come in June.

Frances woke in the night and stared into the dark, listening. The house held its silence for a moment, then exhaled in a murmur of low voices which drifted up from the landing below. She drew a shawl from her bed and pushed open the door.

"Lotta?" she called down. Quiet for a second, then the creaking seesaw of Lotta's weight on the stairs, and the bobbing light of a candle. A billow of white nightgown, and the maid's broad, placid face swam into view.

"It's your father, Miss. He's back but he's not been himself." She pressed past Frances into the bedroom.

"How do you mean?"

Lotta bent to light the candle by the bed, her chest expanding and contracting like bellows, the flame flickering as she breathed.

"What's wrong with him?" Frances demanded, grabbing at her wrist.

Hot wax spilt over their hands and Lotta drew back, wincing in pain. "I don't know exactly. A coachman brought him in. Said he'd had a collapse."

Frances struggled for a moment to imagine this. Her father, the sheer bulk and power of him, didn't seem capable of collapse. He was, in every way, a man of strength. The errand boy, so they said, who had conjured his furniture empire out of shillings like a magician pulling banknotes from the pockets of paupers.

She took the candle from Lotta and went down to the ground floor, her feet sticking on the checkered stone tiles in the hall. Her father was in his study, sitting in an armchair to one side of the cold fireplace. His shirt was unbuttoned and a grizzled beard was beginning to cover the deep grooves that lined his cheeks. He looked pale against the green walls and glossy rosewood furniture, but when he saw her his face broke into an affectionate smile. He was exhausted, she decided with relief, but otherwise fine. A glass of brandy hung casually from one hand. If it tipped any further it would pour out onto the carpet. The breadth of his chest was exposed, and she saw that his body was tighter and more compact than she remembered, as though it had withdrawn into itself with age. She had admired his brute force as a child, the strength of his hands as he drew her wriggling onto his lap.

"Ah, Frances. I asked Lotta not to wake you," he said, holding one hand out to her in apology for not standing up. She took it and smiled, bending to kiss him. He had been away on business, and it was a relief to have him home.

"When did you get back? Are you ill?"

"Not at all, just a little tired."

Then, because it occurred to her that it might all be his fault, "Have you been drinking?"

Her father laughed, a rich, deep sound that soothed the edges of her fear and made her, involuntarily, smile. He glanced at the armchair which sat opposite him. "You see, Matthews, how sharp she is, my daughter?"

Frances turned. She hadn't noticed the man sitting in the chair behind her, on the other side of the fireplace. He had a neat, angular face with a narrow forehead and greased brown hair cut close around his ears. It took her a moment to recognize him, but when he stood up and stepped towards her she remembered. "Mr. Matthews."

"You must call him Dr. Matthews now," her father said.

"Of course." He was a cousin on her father's side who had stayed with them for a few months when he was a boy. He had the same serious expression she remembered as a child. "Where is Dr. Firth?"

"Dr. Firth is out of town," Edwin Matthews said with careful articulation. Even at sixteen he had sounded as if he were a master giving the lesson at school.

Frances was standing on the floorboards by her father's chair, her back to the empty grate and her feet nudging against the edge of the carpet. The dark, polished oak was coarse on the soles of her feet, and she rubbed her big toe across the smooth butt of a nail. She was dressed inappropriately and she shivered, too cold to be standing in the study in her nightdress. She had the feeling that she had interrupted a private conversation, and the silence of both men seemed to be an invitation for her to leave. Perhaps she ought to have been grateful to Edwin Matthews for coming out to see her father in the middle of the night, but she felt only frustration. It had been a long time since she had seen her father, and she wanted to talk to him properly, which meant alone.

"Well, now you're back," she said to her father, "we will make sure you are well looked after."

"Frances, I am fine." He waved his hand, suddenly impatient. "And you must go to bed. I am overworked, that is all, and I called for the doctor to give me something to help me sleep."

She looked at him for a moment longer. He raised his glass as if to say—that's enough concern, leave me—but his hand tremored as he brought it to his lips. He hadn't mentioned a collapse. Perhaps Lotta was exaggerating. Either way, she wouldn't push him on the subject, not now. She bent down, kissed him again, and went upstairs.

She paused on the landing outside her father's room. Lotta was turning down the bedcovers. "I would like a few words with the doctor once my father has gone to bed. Would you ask him to wait?"

THE WINDOW in her bedroom gleamed pale and cold behind the curtains. She drew her shawl from the back of the chair, stepped behind the red damask folds, and stood looking into the street below. The rain had stopped. It was perfectly quiet. Too early yet for the butcher boys in their blue aprons. The lamp at the end of the street throbbed a dull yellow through the milky fog, and she watched a lamplighter appear out of the shining gloom, lean his ladder against the crosspiece, and turn off the dial. The flame shrank to an orange ball, guttered, and went out. He paused, one hand on the post, and gazed along the street behind him as if waiting for the city to stir itself and shake off sleep.

The candle wax had sealed itself in a smooth, hard film over the back of her hand. When she flexed her palm it cracked in shards onto the carpet. She trailed her fingers across the burnt skin, to the soft inside of her wrist. Her pulse came in a quick, restless beat, echoing the dull thud which knocked against her stomach. What if he was seriously ill? This was the terror that had kept her awake as a child, when his booming voice and unruffled calm had been the only thing to puncture the gloom and silence of the house after her mother had died.

After a moment she stepped out from behind the curtain and lit the lamp at the dressing table, illuminating an assortment of brushes and combs, bottles of perfume, scented oils, and china powder boxes. She brushed out her hair until it became a crackling, fiery mass of copper curls, then dampened it with lavender water and wove it into a long plait. Her reflection looked back at her from the small mirror on the table. At nineteen years old she had the sense that her life ought to be full of opportunity, but instead she felt as if she were suffocating. She shook her head slightly, running her hand over her plait, and saw, in the reflection, the two porcelain dolls her father had given her as a child sitting on a chair by the bed. They stared back at her with glassy eyes, silence breathing from between their half-opened lips.

There was a knock at the door. "The doctor is waiting for you, Miss."

HE HAD BEEN SHOWN into the morning room on the ground floor, and she found him standing at the window with his hat already in his hands, ready to leave.

"How is my father?"

"Sleeping." Then, walking a little way towards her: "I have looked forward to seeing you again, Miss Irvine, though I might have hoped it would be under better circumstances." His warmth disconcerted her, and though she couldn't have said why, she found it threatening. His eyes, she noticed, were very pale, almost gray in the half-light that warmed the green glass at the garden window. They were intent and watchful, and very bright: without them his face would have been a mask. She didn't think he was a handsome man—perhaps he looked too serious to be handsome—but he had a certain intensity which demanded your attention.

"Should I be concerned?" she asked, and when he didn't reply: "Dr. Matthews, tell me—is something wrong with him?"

The doctor stood perfectly still, almost a silhouette against the window, with the fingertips of one cupped hand resting on the corner of her desk. There was something cold-blooded about him. Where the light caught the edge of his face, she could see his skin was sallow and drawn. He must have been up all night. He licked at his lips to moisten them. "I think he is suffering from nervous exhaustion."

"Nervous exhaustion?" She gave a small laugh. "You're sure it's nothing else?"

He didn't reply.

"I don't think you know my father, Dr. Matthews. He isn't the nervous type."

"They often aren't."

"And what, in your professional opinion, has brought this exhaustion on?"

"Miss Irvine, you should get some sleep." He touched her lightly on her upper arm. "There is no use in worrying."

She shivered, shrugging off his hand, which might have been there out of professional concern but seemed to assume an intimacy between them. She regretted not having dressed before coming down. "Thank you, but I'm all right."

Then after a moment, she said, "Dr. Matthews, what concerns my father concerns me also."

"I suspect I couldn't tell you anything about him that you don't already know."

Whatever Edwin Matthews might think, this wasn't necessarily true. There was very little she knew about her father's life outside the house.

"I should like to know if he said something to you."

"Your father and I talked—yes—but for the most part about mining in Kimberley."

"He has investments in coal?"

"No!" He gave a thin, dry laugh. "Diamond mining, and he didn't mention investments. Kimberley is in South Africa. I live at the Cape."

She flushed. Of course, Kimberley was the famous diamond-mining town.

"Who painted these?" Edwin had picked up the watercolors of her father's roses which were laid out on the desk.

"I did." The weather had kept her indoors, and she had spent most of the past two weeks at her easel in the morning room. There had been few visitors, and the time had been marked out by the tapping of her paintbrush as she cleaned it in the jar and the muffled voices of the tradesmen which drifted up from the kitchen below.

"They're very good." He was looking at her closely, as if adjusting some calculation in her favor, and she felt an old annoyance. This was the same arrogance he had had as a child, always judging the world according to his own criteria.

"Were you taught to paint?" he asked.

"A little." She shrugged. "But always portraits. I prefer to paint plants." Frances enjoyed the meticulous task of committing every detail—the veins, hairs, and shifts in color which most eyes failed to notice—to the page. The painting was always a compromise. It looked so little like the thing you painted, but its difference—the struggle for representation—was also its beauty. She pointed to the cut blooms in a jar on the table. "My father's roses. They're lovely, don't you think?"

"Perhaps, but I have never liked domesticated plants. There is something excessive in their prettiness." He paused. "They seem decorative to a fault."

"But splendid nonetheless."

"I can't admire splendor if the cost is sterility." He gestured to her watercolors. "These roses are either grown from cuttings because they can't propagate themselves, or they are grafted onto the stronger roots of other plants to help them survive. They have to be nurtured by the careful gardener in a perfectly controlled environment. Monstrosities, Darwin has called them. Deviations from their true form in nature."

"And if they were left to grow in the wild?" she asked, curious.

"They would either die or revert back to their aboriginal stock." He put the pictures down and said, "I should leave you to rest." As he walked past her towards the door, she stopped him, not wanting him to go without some kind of explanation.

"I don't see what could have brought it on," she said, insisting. "I have never seen my father under pressure. He isn't afraid of any-thing."

"We are all afraid of something, Miss Irvine," he said in a quiet voice, his cool gaze flickering over her. "Some of us are just better at hiding it than others."

His words unlocked a kernel of fear. When he was gone she felt it growing inside her, winding cold tendrils round her ribs, and let-ting an agony of sadness seep into the edges of her exhaustion.